# ACT OF TREASON

# ACT

## – OF –

# TREASON

# VINCE FLYNN

**SIMON &
SCHUSTER**

London · New York · Sydney · Toronto

A CBS COMPANY

First published in Great Britain by Simon & Schuster UK Ltd, 2007
A CBS COMPANY

5 7 9 10 8 6 4

Simon & Schuster UK Ltd
Africa House
64–78 Kingsway
London WC2B 6AH

Simon & Schuster Australia
Sydney

www.simonsays.co.uk

A CIP catalogue record for this book is available from the British Library

ISBN-13: 978-0-7432-6875-2
ISBN-10: 0-7432-6875-X

This book is a work of fiction. Names, characters, places and incidents are either a product of the author's imagination or are used fictitiously. Any resemblance to actual people living or dead, events or locales is entirely coincidental.

Printed and bound in Great Britain by
CPI Bath

*Dane, Ingrid, and Ana*

# ACKNOWLEDGMENTS

With the exception of researching and touring, the life of a writer tends to be very solitary—never more so than when under deadline. Every year my wife, Lysa, puts up with the long hours and the fact that even when I'm home, I'm often mentally elsewhere—usually trying to figure out how Mitch Rapp is going to wring someone's neck. I am a lucky man to be married to such an awesome woman.

To my editor, Emily Bestler, and my agent Sloan Harris, thank you yet again for your patience and sage advice. To Alan Rautbort of ICM for pushing me to write my first script. To David Brown, who in addition to being a great guy, is one fantastic publicist. To Jamie Kimmes, my new assistant—you've been a huge help this year. Thank you for all of your hard work. To everyone at the Simon & Schuster family, especially Jack Romanos, Carolyn Reidy, Judith Curr, Louise Burke, Sarah Branham, Jodi Lipper, and Alyson Mazzarelli. And a special thanks to production for yet again putting up with my frantic writing schedule.

To Dr. Jodi Bakkegard, the best chiropractor in the Twin Cities, thank you for keeping me fit all the way to the finish line. To Dave Woodfill and the entire crew at the Apple Store in Edina, thank you for solving all things technical. To Dan Marso for his humor and patience while designing my new website, and to Chad Harris for his input and the great job he did on that website, thethirdoption.net. To Tom Aslesen for his friendship and helping me out with a few technical aspects of the book. To Al Horner, retired Navy SEAL, and firearms instructor extraordinaire.

To Blake Gottesman, thank you for your commitment to the big guy. I'm sure you are missed. To Rob Richer, a good friend and an even bigger smartass. To Mary Matalin for your honesty, class, and wit. To Paul Evancoe and FNH—the new 5.7 is awesome. To Colonel Kevin M. McDonnell, Command Sergeant Major Parry L. Baer and the Combined Joint Special Operations Task Force—Arabian Peninsula, you have given me a great honor that I will never forget. And to all the men and women who serve, your commitment and sacrifice is something that I think of every day.

# ACT OF TREASON

# PRELUDE

The motorcade rumbled down the cobblestone street. Three motorcycles led the way, followed by a DC police squad, two Secret Service sedans, and then two identical limousines. After the limousines came the Suburbans and more sedans. It was an impressive sight, especially when one considered that the two men being protected had yet to win the White House. However, earlier in the week a fringe terrorist group had announced their intent to disrupt the upcoming election, and the Secret Service had no choice but to take the threat seriously.

Mark Ross sat in the back seat of the second limousine and massaged his forehead. A monster headache was building from the base of his brain and slowly spreading to the front. He tried to block out the incessant chatter of the man sitting next to him, while at the same time wondering just how in the hell he had gotten himself into this mess. He would have been better off staying in the Senate where he had real power. It was power, though, that had gotten him here. Or at least the promise of it.

The relationship was cracking. There was no doubt about it. It had always been an arranged marriage of sorts. They each had their strengths and weaknesses, and for the most part they didn't overlap. It was explained to them by the power brokers and gatekeepers that they would complement each other perfectly. On paper it all looked perfect. A real marriage made in heaven. If they had bothered to read any of the classic Greek tragedies, though, they would have known that the gods could be very cruel. Especially when it came to the hubris of men.

Ross had naturally been aware of Josh Alexander all along. Alexander, the up-and-coming star of the Democratic Party, was governor of Georgia. The old white men who ran the party had finally got it through their heads that a Northeast liberal was simply unelectable. Their only real chance of winning was to draft a Southern governor who believed in Jesus Christ. This way they could split the Bible Belt vote and steal enough red states to win it all. Alexander was the obvious choice. He was handsome, smart, and polished, and his wife's family had more money than most third-world countries. His only drawback was his relative youth. At forty-five he was deemed a touch green, and definitely weak on foreign affairs. His early polling numbers suggested that people weren't sure he would be a strong enough leader in the war on terror. That was where Mark Ross came in. A three-term senator from Connecticut, Ross was the new director of National Intelligence. He had a reputation as one of the more hawkish Democrats in Washington.

In a normal national election, the two men would have never ended up as running mates. This election, however, had been turned on its ear when the current president announced that he had

Parkinson's disease and would not be seeking a second term. With only a year to go before the general election, the party was caught flat-footed. The primary season was upon them and the only real candidate they had was Vice President Sherman Baxter III. Everybody, including the president, agreed that Baxter would be a disaster. He was perhaps the most marginalized vice president in the history of the republic, and that was saying a lot. The man's approval rating in his home state of California was below thirty percent. A lot of things could have been ignored, but not that number. The party elders pulled him aside and told him it was the end of the road. Having been confronted with his limits and deficiencies for the last three years, the man did not put up a fight.

Ross, in the meantime, worked feverishly behind the scenes. He was well connected on Wall Street; regarded highly by his old club, the U.S. Senate; and savvy enough to know not to throw his hat in the ring too early. He waited until New Hampshire, when Alexander walked away as the clear front-runner. Then he began networking, pushing the idea that the young governor needed a running mate who had some gravitas in the national security arena. He sent his surrogates to lobby on his behalf. He personally wined and dined the party's big money people and he carefully began to court the handsome, young governor from Georgia.

Everything fell into place exactly as Ross had wished. When he took the stage at the national convention, the place erupted. They hit the ground with a bounce and an eight-point lead. That had been three months ago. The pinnacle. The apogee of the campaign. Since then they'd been bleeding like a stuck pig. With two weeks until Election Day they trailed their opponents by three points, and Ross was feeling the pressure. Their pollsters kept coming back with the same problem. Voters perceived the pair as weaker than their opponents on national security. This was where Ross was sup-

4 / VINCE FLYNN

posed to step in and fill the breach, but how could he have known the president would leave them high and dry?

The man had abandoned them in their hour of need. Yes, he had endorsed them, but what in the hell else was he going to do? Endorse the Republican ticket? Campaigning on their behalf was assumed. It was all part of the battle plan. He would help them raise the millions of dollars it would take to win the TV ad race. He would step in and use that bully pulpit to announce his confidence in the young candidate and his seasoned running mate. But all they got was silence and a cold shoulder.

The press was told that the president's disease was taking a toll on him, and he simply didn't have the energy to campaign. His obligation was to his office and the American people. Ross believed the excuse for a few days, and then reality set in. Word had gotten back to him through two solid sources that the president had a real problem with the ticket. He was offended that no one had bothered to consult him as to who Alexander should pick as a running mate. Beyond that, the president made it clear that he considered Ross the wrong choice.

The words had stung Ross to the core, but he had since written them off as the musings of a bitter old man at the end of his journey. True to his never-quit attitude, Ross redoubled his efforts and stayed positive. This morning, however, he was feeling a sense of dread. There were only two weeks left, and the polls could move only so far in such a short period of time. They needed a real October surprise to put them over the top, and then Ross would take great pride in sticking it in the president's face on Inauguration Day.

As the motorcade slowed, the lead vehicles began peeling off. Ross looked through the tinted bulletproof window at the media who had gathered in front of the mansion. The heavy black iron gate opened and the two limousines pulled into the narrow circular

drive. Dumbarton Oaks was a twenty-two-acre estate in Georgetown that was noteworthy for hosting a conference in 1944 that led
to the formation of the United Nations. It was Ross's idea that they
host a national security conference at the estate and bring in the
greatest minds to discuss the issues that threatened the country. A
former chairman of the Joint Chiefs was on hand, as well as two former secretaries of state, a former secretary of defense, several retired
CIA directors, a few lesser-known generals, and a smattering of
Middle Eastern experts and Muslim clerics from around the world.

After the three-hour event they were to head to the vice president's house at the Naval Observatory. The vice president was set to
host a diplomatic reception on their behalf. All of the important
ambassadors would be there, and both Ross and Alexander would
present them with their vision for security, peace, and prosperity in
the twenty-first century. The event should have been held at the
White House, but they had been denied. The entire election—
hell—his entire political career was going to come down to this one
afternoon. If he believed in God he would have said a prayer, but he
didn't, so he cursed the president instead.

The limo came to a stop and Ross looked his yammering campaign manager in the eye for the first time in five minutes. "Stu,"
Ross checked to make sure his tie was straight, "shut up. You're giving me a headache."

With that, Ross stepped from the back of the limo. He buttoned
his suit coat with one hand and waved to the reporters and photographers with the other. He was about to comment on how beautiful a day it was when the whole gaggle swung their lenses and
microphones away from him. Ross turned to see the tanned and
slender legs of Jillian Rautbort Alexander emerge from the other
limousine.

The press loved her. They called her America's Diana. Her like-bility number was in the seventies. Far higher than either of the candidates. She was a stunning beauty in every conceivable way. She was five foot nine with shoulder-length blond hair and a body to die for. She'd been raised among the super elite. Schooled in Switzerland and then Brown, where her father had gone. The family's fortune was in real estate and lots of it. New York and Florida was where they had made their killing. There were homes in Paris, Manhattan, and Palm Springs. At thirty-six Jillian was one of those rare women who got better with age. She drew men into her orbit without having to bat an eye or flash a smile. She was gorgeous, classy, and hot all at the same time. Ross had thought about taking a run at her on more than one occasion. She was no vestal virgin, that was for sure, but a real opportunity never presented itself.

Josh Alexander joined his wife, and the flashes erupted once again. He was six-one with black hair and the tanned skin of a low-handicap golfer. He was polished in that southern televangelist sort of way. His suits were always a bit shinier than everyone else's, his hair a bit longish and perfectly styled, and his teeth a few shades too white. This appearance, of course, fit the master plan to split the southern Christian vote, and the polling numbers told them it had worked. A little too well in fact. Their real problem now lay with the base. They felt betrayed, and were threatening to stay home on Election Day.

Ross watched the presidential candidate and his wife pose for the cameras. They stood there smiling, those same forced smiles that Ross had grown to hate. Even so, he kept his own fake smile going and acted like he was admiring the sheer beauty of the super couple. Ross's wife was back in Connecticut at the bedside of their daughter who was about to give birth to their first grandchild at any moment. It was just as well. She had grown sick of the campaign. It was no joy being outshined at every stop by a woman twenty years her junior.

Alexander finally left his wife's side and came over to Ross. He stuck out his right hand and clapped Ross on the shoulder with his left.

"How you feeling today, Mr. Vice President?"

"Good, Mr. President." Ross strained to keep the smile on his face.

Calling each other president and vice president had been Alexander's idea. The week after the convention, when they'd had their eight point lead, it had been fun. Now it just seemed delusional and childish. Ross still thought they had a chance. He just didn't think the power of positive thinking was what was going to put them over the top. Five key states were up for grabs. The negative ads were in the can and if they didn't shrink the gap in the polls by Monday morning, things were going to get real ugly. Ross knew they'd be using those ads against their opponents. It was just a question of whether they started this week or the following. This was going to be a street fight right to the bitter end.

FOUR BLOCKS AWAY Gavrilo Gazich paid for his espresso with cash and was careful to keep the brim of his red Washington Nationals baseball hat tilted down so that the security camera mounted above the teller couldn't get a good shot of him. He was also wearing sunglasses to help conceal his features. It was a sunny, fall morning in Georgetown, and the killer fit in perfectly.

Gazich preferred to operate in Africa. That was where he had made a name for himself after years of training in his war-torn homeland of Bosnia. The corrupt politicians and generals of the subcontinent made it an extremely target-rich environment. The billions in aid that were simply thrown at the impoverished region by foreign governments and international relief organizations provided an extra incentive for them to slaughter each other. The prevalence of graft from the national level all the way down to the smallest village was astounding. Of every dollar in aid, it was estimated that only ten cents actually made it to the people who really needed it.

The men at the top—warring heads of political parties, tribal leaders, gangsters, military commanders, and thugs—all fought for their piece of the action, and little value, if any, was placed on civilian life. A half a million people dead one year, a million the next. The level of carnage was mind-boggling. Respect for human life nonexistent. The lawlessness staggering. It made the civil war in Yugoslavia look like a skirmish. A simple dustup between a couple of neighborhood gangs.

During the siege of Sarajevo, Gazich had witnessed some horrible things, but nothing that compared to the sheer scope of suffering that existed in the war-torn areas of Africa. He used it to his advantage, though. The mix of chaos, corruption, brutality, and lawlessness created the perfect working environment for him. The warlords of Africa were constantly looking to expand their hold and increase their plunder. They operated under the principle of market share. If you weren't growing, you were on your way out. The most difficult part for Gazich was keeping all the players and their shifting alliances straight.

He had a simple rule in this regard. Work only for the most ruthless, and never meet them face-to-face in their own backyard. If they wanted to hire him they had to send someone to Athens or Istanbul. Occasionally, he would travel to Cairo, but since the towers had fallen in New York, he no longer felt safe in the Egyptian capital. Their president was too close to the United States, and his security service was far too efficient and brutal to toy with.

Cyprus had been his home now for more than a decade. It was where he went to find the solitude that he needed between jobs. To get in and out of these war-torn countries he'd posed as a reporter, an oil company engineer, even a mercenary from time to time. More often than not, though, he was acting on behalf of international relief organizations. He had a small business in Limassol, Cyprus, called Aid Logistics Inc that specialized in cutting through the red tape in the war-torn areas of Africa. He'd even been recognized by the International Committee of the Red Cross for his services. The business turned a tidy little profit on the side, but more importantly it gave him legitimacy. It helped him build up his contacts and keep track of the ever-changing players in the subcontinent's continuing saga.

Now, here in America he was simply a tourist. A Greek tourist at that. Somewhere in his family's history there had to be a few drops of Greek blood, or at a bare minimum, a healthy portion of Macedonian. He'd traveled Greece extensively and knew the language well enough, since it was also the national language of Cyprus. The customs officer at JFK had waved him through with a smile, which seemed to confirm Gazich's belief that the Greeks were well liked by mostly everyone with the exception of the Turks.

As with pretty much any job, Gazich had his reservations, but with this one there were more than usual, in part because he was operating in America, a country that was on high alert for terrorist attacks. Their border controls and linked computer systems made traveling under false identities very difficult. In Africa he rarely had to worry about being picked up by a surveillance camera. Here in Washington, though, they were everywhere.

This was a rush job, which was never good on the nerves. He had been given one hour to accept or decline the job without even knowing what it was. All he was told was that he would have to travel to America, the hit would take place this coming Saturday and he would be paid two million dollars. This was double the most lucrative contract he'd ever landed. His initial thought was that it was a trap, but after he analyzed it for a moment he dismissed that possibility. He had done nothing to offend the Americans. There would be no reason for them to go to this effort to capture a man who'd made a living in the killing fields of Africa.

Pretty much without exception Gazich dispatched his targets in one of two ways. He either shot them in the head from a safe distance or blew them up with high-powered explosives. Simplicity was at all times his primary objective. Having grown up on a farm outside Sarajevo, Gazich and his older brothers had been raised to hunt. They were all expert marksmen by the age of ten. When he was sixteen, his father sent him and his three older brothers off to fight with the Bosnian Serb forces who had laid siege to Sarajevo. That was when Gazich turned his crosshairs from wild game to man for the first time. In certain ways, he found hunting man less of a challenge. In other ways he found it far more exhilarating.

Today would be one of the most thrilling kills of his career. His only regret was that he hadn't been given more time to plan the hit. Killing a man with a single shot from up to a mile away was the biggest rush he had ever felt. Killing the target by remote detonating a bomb was a distant second, but a thrill nonetheless. That's what it would be today. There simply wasn't enough time to prepare for a head shot.

On Monday he was given the target and the motorcade's route. That same day he gave them the list of what he would need. He never spoke with his employers directly. He in fact had no idea who they were, although he had a good idea. They were Muslims to be sure. Terrorists who had promised to upset the American election.

Gazich did not care for Muslims, but the money and the thought of screwing with the Americans was exhilarating. They had meddled in the affairs of his country. It would be poetic justice to return the favor.

These terrorists were getting smart. Sneaking their own devoted followers into America had become extremely difficult. Hiring a freelancer was much easier, and even with the two-million-dollar fee, it was probably cheaper than training, equipping, and transporting a team to handle the operation. The most difficult part for them had to be getting the explosives and detonators he'd asked for. It had all been waiting for him in a storage garage in Rockville. Sneaking five hundred pounds of high explosives into America was not easily done. And this was good stuff. High-grade Russian military plastic explosives. Not the decaying unstable crap he was forced to use from time to time when he operated in Africa. The blasting caps, the prime chord, and the remote detonator were also the best the Russians had to offer.

Gazich tried not to think too much about the fallout that would take place after the van exploded. In Africa he rarely had to think about such things. They all wanted to kill each other. One more body on the pile meant nothing. This was different, though. Washington was the grand stage of espionage and diplomacy, not some backwater, mosquito infested Third World hellhole. This was elephant hunting, and Gazich had tracked the real beast. To kill the giant with a rifle shot from a safe distance was not difficult. The real sport of it was getting close, belly crawling for hundreds of meters, and sneaking in among the herd. That took skill, fortitude, and a bit of insanity. Still, the shot itself was relatively easy. The real danger lay in getting trampled by one of the massive gray beasts after the herd was spooked.

Gazich left the Starbucks with his espresso in one hand and a newspaper under his arm. So far the most difficult part had been finding a parking spot. Two million dollars for finding a parking spot. Gazich laughed to himself and started up the street. Screwing with the American political system was sure to bring about a backlash. He told himself he would worry about that later. Now it was time to sneak up on the herd and hope he didn't get trampled.

SPECIAL AGENT RIVERA stood near the door and looked into the large conference room. At thirty-five she'd managed to keep her figure by beating up her fellow agents on a weekly basis. Karate burned a lot of calories and Rivera worked on her moves as if it was a religion. The campaign had cut into her classes, and the other agents on the detail had grown wise to the fact that she was a second-degree black belt. They were done sparing with her and she was getting bored. Although she'd avoided weighing herself, she could feel the extra pounds. Two more weeks, she kept telling herself. Then she would decompress back in Arizona. She'd sleep, eat, and work out. Kick some ass at the gym. Pay her old dojo a visit and show him who was the boss now. Maybe she'd even bump into a real man. Someone unattached, and not looking for anything serious. *Boy, would that be nice,* she thought to herself. She didn't even want to try and figure out how long it had been.

Her boys were seated at the head of the U-shaped table. The cameras had been allowed in for the first fifteen minutes of the meeting and then they were asked to leave. Alexander's campaign manager had decided they would look more legitimate that way. At some point, if you were going to get serious about national security, you had to exclude the press and at least look like you were talking about important secrets of state.

Rivera was as tough as they came, but even she was exhausted. It had been a hellish campaign. Each day brought a new city, and with each city came an entirely forgettable hotel room, bland hotel food, and a cramped hotel fitness center. Every morning she received a wake-up call from one of her fellow agents that, in addition to telling her what time it was, also reminded her where she was and where she was headed. Sometimes there were as many as four states in a day. The events were one after another from sunup to midnight, and she and her people had to be sharp every step of the way.

These presidential elections were a logistical nightmare. As hard as they were on the politicians and their staffers, though, they were worse on the sentinels who were tasked with protecting them. Rivera was the special agent in charge, or SAC, of presidential candidate Josh Alexander's Secret Service detail. She'd been with the Secret Service for thirteen years. During that time she'd worked in the Los Angeles, Miami, and New York field offices. She'd also done two presidential details and had risen through the ranks quicker than any other agent in her class. Along the way she'd had one brief marriage, and a thankfully quick divorce to go along with it. That was almost ten years ago. It had been a pretty easy decision for Rivera. Her husband was a federal prosecutor working out of the Manhattan District. They'd met on an organized crime task force, and he'd swept her off her feet. Looking back on it now, she should have known marrying an attorney was a mistake. Four months into the marriage she stopped by her husband's office one day to surprise him and busted him instead. Right there in the middle of the afternoon he was screwing a female NYPD detective on his couch. Rivera knocked him out cold and filed for divorce that very afternoon.

Maria Rivera was second-generation American, but she spoke Spanish fluently thanks to her grandmother, who still prayed every day for her marriage to be resurrected. Grandma Rivera had been crushed when she parted ways with the Harvard hotshot attorney.

He was a good Catholic boy and quite the charmer. Rivera didn't have the heart to tell grandma that the Ivy League attorney was a whore.

Free of her matrimonial bonds, Rivera took every tough assignment the Service threw at her. She'd worked major counterfeit and credit card fraud cases for years and in-between managed to do stints on presidential details. A year ago she'd been promoted to assistant special agent in charge of President Hayes's detail, or ASAC. When Alexander took the lead after New Hampshire, her bosses called her into headquarters and told her to pack her bags. They put her in charge of Alexander's detail and told her not to screw up. That she was on the short list to run the next presidential detail.

To run a presidential detail was every agent's dream. It was also a position within the Service where the glass ceiling was still intact. If Rivera could keep it together she had a legitimate shot at being the first female agent to run a presidential detail. She had thought of little else for the last nine months. The pace of the campaign had been tolerable for most of that time. Early on Alexander didn't have to work too hard. He was ahead in the polls. He was a fresh face and the new political darling of the moment. He had ridden that wave all the way to the Democratic Party's convention in August where he walked away with a landslide of the delegates and a new running mate.

Then everything went to hell. Rivera had been expecting the pace to pick up as they hit the home stretch for the November election, but the demands of the campaign had surprised even her. Alexander's opponents launched a blistering ad campaign that made hay out of the young governor's penchant for embellishing stories and sometimes simply making things up. His youth and relative inexperience were brought into doubt, as well as his integrity.

By the time Labor Day rolled around, a five-point lead in the polls had evaporated.

The answer from the Alexander camp was to fire their campaign manager and redouble their efforts. The first two weeks of September were spent on trains and the second two on buses. They crisscrossed the country, hitting every state that was deemed winnable. Events were scheduled, canceled, and then rescheduled. Advance teams were left stranded in cities as the campaign changed directions on an almost hourly basis. It was an absolute logistical disaster, but through it all Rivera had stayed at the helm and rolled with the schizophrenic scheduling of the campaign. Now, with just two weeks to go, she could finally see light at the end of the tunnel.

"Rivera," a voice whispered urgently.

Maria Rivera backed out of the doorway and came face to face with Stuart Garret. Like most people in law enforcement, Rivera was a quick study when it came to people. When she was assigned to protect someone she was careful to not let her personal feelings or opinions affect her work. Josh Alexander, for instance, was a pretty nice guy. Well-mannered, sometimes aloof, but for the most part appreciative and respectful of the job she and her people performed. Mark Ross, on the other hand, was arrogant and condescending. Rivera didn't like the man, but she kept it to herself. Garret, however, pushed her professional demeanor to the limits. He was quite possibly the biggest asshole she had ever met.

She was now face to face with the abrasive Californian who was running the show.

"Yes, Stu."

"We're fifteen minutes behind schedule."

Rivera nodded. The campaign was behind schedule, not the Secret Service. Rivera and her people were not conductors on a train.

They were not in charge of keeping people on time. They were in charge of keeping the candidates and their families alive.

"As soon as they're done in there," Garret continued, "I want everybody in the cars. I'm going to need some one-on-one time with Josh and Mark, so put Jillian in the second limo. She's going to the vice president's only for the receiving line, and then she wants to go back to her hotel for some *fucking* spa treatment or something."

"Fine," Rivera answered, ignoring Garret's foul mouth.

Rivera had spent the last nine months of her life with the presidential candidate and his wife, and she still hadn't had more than a two-sentence conversation with Jillian. She was very reserved, very attractive, and very aloof. It had been Garret's idea to bring her along today. "Eye candy," was what he called her. Her likability number was higher than her husband's and his running mate's combined. Jillian was currently in the second floor salon meeting with a group of Muslim women and discussing their role in combating Islamic extremism.

"She wants that big agent of yours to go with her," Garret snarled.

"Special Agent Cash?"

"I don't know his *fucking* name. He's the big guy."

A lot of Rivera's agents were big guys. She thought she knew which one he was referring to, though, so she said, "I'll take care of it."

"Good. Be ready to roll in five minutes." Garret turned and rushed off down the long hallway.

Rivera watched him leave. On more than one occasion she'd visualized delivering a roundhouse kick to the man's head. The scuttlebutt among the campaign staffers was that, win or lose, Garret wasn't sticking around. He'd been chief of staff for a brief period under a previous administration and openly complained that it was the worst six months of his life. He was a hired gun who had accepted a rumored seven-figure fee to come in and bail out the campaign. Rivera had heard him say on more than one occasion that anyone willing to work for a government salary was a chump. This, of course, further endeared him to the agents who were assigned to protect his candidates.

Rivera started for the front door. She was dressed in a dark blue pantsuit with a light blue blouse. She never wore skirts or dresses, at least not when she was on duty. They simply weren't practical. Every agent on the detail carried the new FN 5.7 pistol and two extra clips of ammunition. The FN 5.7 was the finest pistol she'd ever fired. It carried twenty armor-piercing rounds in the grip plus one in the chamber and had half the recoil of the old Sig. In addition to her weapon she carried her secure Motorola digital radio, a mobile phone, and a BlackBerry. All of that gear had to be stowed someplace and a dress just wasn't going to cut it.

Rivera opened the large, front door and stepped out onto the stone terrace of the Dumbarton Mansion. She was a walking contradiction—understated yet beautiful, graceful yet athletic. Her shiny black hair was almost always pulled back in a simple ponytail. Thanks to her ancestors she was blessed with a wrinkle-free complexion. She wore very little makeup while on duty and made every effort to downplay her looks. The Secret Service was still very much a men's club. A men's club with an extremely difficult job. Part of that job was to be seen. To let people know they were there at all times monitoring the situation. At no point, though, were they to outshine the people they were protecting.

Donning a pair of sunglasses, she surveyed the scene from the elevated terrace and checked her watch. It was almost a quarter past noon. She couldn't wait to get Alexander and Ross safely tucked away at the Naval Observatory. Then the vice president's detail could take over, and she and her team could get a few hours of much needed down time before they had to fly to St. Louis.

Rivera spotted the man she wanted to talk to at the far end of the veranda. She started in his direction. It was drilled into agents to look presentable at all times. Clothes were to be cleaned and pressed. No ties with ketchup stains or dirty shirt collars. Footwear was stressed to the point where one would think they were training for the Olympics. Agents had to stand post for long hours. They needed to be comfortable. It was function over form. Rivera remembered an instructor she'd had at the training center in Beltsville, Maryland, who used to tell female agents if they couldn't sprint two blocks in their shoes, then they shouldn't be wearing them. This was the same instructor who used to admonish female agents for wearing skirts. He'd tell them, "Do you want to be remembered as the agent who saved the president's life by wrestling a gunman to the ground, or do you want to be remembered as the agent who showed the world her panties while tackling an assassin?"

Rivera took all these lessons seriously. That was why she was wearing a pair of black, lace-up loafers with two-inch heels and rubber soles. They were made of patent leather because she hated shining shoes. The rubber sole made them comfortable and quiet. Rivera was reminded of this second attribute as she neared the agent at the far end of the veranda. He had no idea someone was coming up from behind him. This was a bad sign, rubber soles or not. Her people were running on fumes.

A few feet away she decided to have some fun. She stuck out her finger and jabbed it into the small of the large man's back. Matt Cash, a nine-year veteran of the Secret Service, jumped as if he'd just been startled from a nap.

"One wrong move and you're dead," Rivera laughed.

Cash wheeled around and it was obvious from the expression on his face that he was not amused. "What in the hell is wrong with you?"

Rivera grinned, showing her perfect white teeth.

"The press is right there on the other side of the fence," Cash whispered.

She looked at the TV vans parked on the street and the photographers perched on ladders so they could shoot over the brick wall. She stepped in front of the agent and looked down at his groin. "You didn't piss yourself, did you?"

"Yeah," he said angrily. "Hurry up and give me one of those super jumbo maxi-pads you carry around. Maybe I can soak it up before it seeps through my boxers."

"Wow . . . aren't we in a good mood today?"

"Don't start with me." Cash grabbed the lapels of his suit coat and gave them a yank. "I'm sick of this shit."

Such an open admission caught Rivera off guard. As the special agent in charge of the detail she wasn't just their boss. She was also their den mother.

"By *shit* . . . are you referring to me, your job, or both?"

"Not you," he snarled. "The job. I've been on the road for three straight months. My kids miss me, my wife hates me, and here I am back in DC for the day and I can't even stop by my own house and say hello."

Rivera smiled. "Well, I've got some good news for you. HQ is going to let us stand down for a few hours while the vice president's detail babysits our boys."

Cash's jaw went slack. "You're serious."

"Yep. Take a few hours . . . go surprise the family. Just don't miss the plane or I'll shove one of my maxi-pads up your ass and transfer you to Fargo."

"So once we get to the Observatory I can take off?" he asked with a smile.

"Not right away. You have to hang around for thirty minutes and then take the princess to her hotel. After that you're free until five." The princess Rivera was referring to was Alexander's wife.

"Why me?" Cash complained.

"Because you're her favorite, and she asked for you personally."

"Send someone else."

"You think this is fuckin' democracy?" she shot back and waited to see if he would be stupid enough to disagree with her. "I didn't think so. Take her to the hotel, put her to bed, and then go see your family."

"What in the hell is that supposed to mean?"

"What in the hell is what supposed to mean?" asked a genuinely confused Rivera.

*"Put her to bed,"* he said in a falsetto. "You trying to say something's going on?"

Rivera frowned and said, "It's a figure of speech, Einstein."

"Well, I don't appreciate the connotation."

"I think you mean implication, and there is none." Rivera straightened up and took on a decidedly more businesslike tone. "You're in the second limo with her. I'm in the lead limo with the principals. We get to the observatory and she shakes hands for thirty minutes. Then you take her to the hotel, make sure she's secure in her room, and then turn things over to whomever HQ sends. Do you have any questions, Special Agent Cash?"

"No."

"Good."

GAZICH CROSSED THE STREET and started up the east side of Wisconsin Avenue. He had seen the itinerary. The thing was actually posted on the Internet. They were supposed to be on the move at noon, but it was likely they would be running late. Rarely were these types of things ever on time. This next part of his plan was a bit risky. Gazich could have set up a camera and done this from a safe distance, but the window for success was too small to risk it. He needed to be precise. The shaped charge in the cargo area was more than capable of defeating the protective shell of the armored limousine as long as it was detonated at the right moment. Gazich figured he had a twenty-foot window. Not all that much longer than the limo itself. If the motorcade was moving at a good clip, the timing would be difficult. That was why he had parked the minivan as close to the corner of Wisconsin and S Street as possible. The motorcade would have traveled only one block by the time it reached Wisconsin. The vehicles would then be forced to slow for the ninety-degree turn onto Wisconsin Avenue where the minivan was perfectly positioned for a broadside blast.

If it were the president's motorcade things would be quite a bit more difficult. In addition to the armored limousines and Suburbans, the ambulance, and a myriad of other vehicles, the presidential motorcade also contained a special vehicle that was designed to jam all signals except those used by the Secret Service. This made the remote detonation of a device impossible. Gazich had checked and discovered that the detail assigned to the candidates had no such equipment. Even so, he would still need to get close enough to make sure he could see when the limo came even with the minivan.

Gazich passed a young couple sitting on a bench eating bagels. Two blocks ahead he could see the orange stepladder he'd strapped to the roof of the van. It had been a last-minute idea when he'd noticed that white minivans were more common than he would have thought. The color of the ladder would also make it easier for him to time the detonation. Not wanting to get too close to the van, he stopped and looked at the listings posted in the window of a real estate office.

He felt the vibration of the Treo phone in his pocket and grabbed it.

"Hello?"

"Two o'clock works for me. Does it work for you?"

"Two o'clock works." Gazich pressed the end button, breathed a sigh of relief, and put the phone away.

He kept meandering his way up the street, taking his time, window-shopping as he went. A few minutes later he heard the quick blast of a police siren being flicked on and then off. He looked up the street and watched as one of the DC Metro Police motorcycles eased out into traffic and blocked the northbound lane on Wisconsin Avenue. Gazich flexed his hands several times and asked himself how much closer he dared get. The motorcade would be along shortly. There was a good-sized tree of some sort a little less than a block away. It was about four feet across. Even though the full force of the blast would be directed away from him, there would still be flying debris and a concussion wave that could kill him if he didn't get cover.

Gazich reached the tree and pulled out the Treo phone. He fished out the small stylus and used it to tap the web browser icon on the screen. A few seconds later he was logged onto the site. He punched in the password and looked up at the motorcycle cop standing in the middle of the street. All that was left to do was hit the send button and the blast would be nearly instantaneous. The cop would be dead for certain, and quite possibly the people in the first several cars he had stopped. There were also shops and apartments directly across the street. There was a chance the limo would block the brunt of the blast, but it was unlikely. A five-hundred-pound shaped charge of Semtex was just as likely to hurl the limousine across the street and send the vehicle directly through the building.

Gazich tried to remember the phrase the American generals used when one of their two-thousand-pound bombs missed its mark and flattened the home of one of his countrymen. The first police car reached the corner and turned toward Gazich, its lights and sirens going. Pedestrians stopped to watch the impressive sight as the motorcade moved from the side street onto Wisconsin Avenue.

The phrase came to him and as the first limousine reached the corner, he smiled and said . . . "Collateral damage."

THE TRUTH WAS, her people could do this in their sleep. That was how well trained they were. The candidates stepped out onto the veranda of the mansion and waited for the former Cabinet officials, intel gurus, and generals to join them for one last photo op. Rivera stayed close, but out of the picture. Her entire detail was shifting now. They were a protective bubble that floated with the candidates as they moved. There was one counter sniper team on the top floor. They'd been up there since before sunrise, scanning the windows of the houses across the street, getting the general lay of the land, noting the range of certain targets and identifying the most likely spots for a shooter to set up.

Rivera's head was on a swivel, her dark sunglasses concealing her dark eyes. She was like a radar sweeping the sky for an incoming raider, except her job was much more difficult. The press was penned in behind some ropes, snapping away, recording tape, and shouting questions. Rivera paid almost no attention to what they were asking. On a subliminal level she was listening to their tone as her eyes scanned everything. Never hovering on any one person for more than a second or two. Most agents did this naturally. A few had to be taught. The ones who didn't catch on were weeded out. The job was nothing if not instinctual.

Their concern was the nut bag. Their fear was the professional. The nut bag they could detect. They were the ones with the wild eyes, dirty fingernails, and unkempt hair. Occasionally they were women, but mostly they were men. Fidgety, nervous men who paced back and forth. They were for the most part mentally ill, which made them sympathetic, but no less lethal. The professional was an entirely different matter. The lone man who was cool enough to act completely normal right up until the moment he pulled out a gun and blew her candidate's brains all over the side-walk. That was why she stayed close.

Today was no big deal. She knew all the faces in the press gallery. They were the only people close enough to do anything, and she had two agents watching them, ready to pounce at the first sign of trouble. The only other possibility was a shooter from one of the houses across the street, but the odds of them getting an accu-rate shot off before the counter sniper boys drilled them in the head was negligible. All she had to do was get them down the steps and into the limo and she could relax. The Naval Observatory was only a few blocks away. This was a gravy run compared to the rest of the campaign. No rope lines with hundreds of unscreened people touching the candidates. No banquet hall where she had to escort them through a kitchen with knives everywhere and temperamen-tal chefs sulking over ruined meals. Everything today was con-trolled.

Rivera saw Garret gesture to the campaign's press secretary. The woman stepped in front of the cameras and thanked them for com-ing. Alexander and Ross had done this so many times they no longer needed to be given direction. Both men started down the stairs for the waiting limo. The rear passenger side door was already opened and an agent was standing next to it. Rivera fell in behind the two men and stayed close as they went down the steps. Alexander got in first, followed by Ross and then Garret. Rivera closed the door and looked to her left to check the status of Alexander's wife. She was sliding into the backseat. Special Agent Cash turned to look at Rivera. It was impossible to tell what his eyes were doing behind his sunglasses, but from the tension in his jaw line it was apparent that he was still in a foul mood. Cash shook his head and then disappeared into the backseat. Rivera didn't give it a second thought. Egos, feelings, and friendships needed to be put on hold for two more weeks and then they could all get drunk and tell each other off.

Rivera climbed in the front seat, closed the heavy door, and looked at the driver. "Let's roll, Tim."

The driver pulled the gearshift into drive and took his foot off the brake. The heavy limousine began to roll along the narrow cobblestone drive. Both vehicles pulled up to the open gate and they turned the emergency lights in the grilles on. The other vehicles were waiting on the street. The limousines eased into the open slots and then Rivera gave the word to pull out. Her eyes kept scanning as they moved. They were as safe as babies in this rolling tank, but habits were hard to break. The old cobblestone street was rough and they were jostled around as they accelerated. They reached Wisconsin Avenue, where traffic was stopped in both directions for five blocks. The limo slowed for the right-hand turn and then accelerated, the twelve-piston 500-hp Detroit engine roaring as they gained speed.

Rivera was looking at the faces of the pedestrians who had stopped to watch the motorcade. All of this was very normal. They referred to it as stopping and gawking. Up ahead, barely half a block down a man caught her eye. He was partially shielded by a tree and holding something. Even though the man was wearing a red baseball hat and sunglasses, she could sense intensity in the way he was watching the motorcade. Suddenly, almost as if he was trying to hide from someone, he disappeared behind the tree. Before Rivera could give it another thought, there was a thunderous explosion, the limousine started to rise in the air, and then everything went black.

# 1

Irene Kennedy looked out at the white landscape from her seventh-floor office. Three fresh inches of snow had fallen overnight. The capital had a majestic winter wonderland feel to it when it snowed. It tended to be the kind of wet, heavy snow that coated every branch, statue, and park bench. The city looked frozen in time, and in a sense it was. A lame-duck president occupied 1600 Pennsylvania Avenue, and the president–elect was one week away from taking his oath of office. Traditionally, the only business that got done the week before the inauguration was the business of pardons. Lawyers, lobbyists, and big-money players lined up to ask the president to forgive someone for a crime they had committed, or been accused of committing. Politics had gotten so rough that sometimes just being a friend of the president could bring about the unwanted attention of a special prosecutor. With that attention also came a mountain of legal bills. It was quickly becoming a tradition for outgoing presidents to wave a magic wand and make these legal problems go away. Pardons could also be about bricks and mortar. A new presidential library needed to be built, and they were not cheap. With this president, however, it was mostly about setting things right.

This should have been on Kennedy's mind, but it wasn't. As director of the Central Intelligence Agency she should have been lobbying for a blanket pardon herself, but her mind was occupied with the here and now. This transition period between presidential administrations was always stressful, but even more so this time. The nation was without decisive and focused leadership until the new administration took over, and that left them vulnerable. To make matters worse, the word was out that the new administration was going to clean house. This was no surprise to Kennedy. She knew the minute the election results came in that she was out of a job. Actually, she knew several weeks earlier when the CIA's Global Ops Center called to alert her of the attack on that Saturday in late October.

The motorcade of presidential candidate Josh Alexander had been hit by a car bomb. Alexander and his running mate had narrowly escaped. Their limousine had been flipped by the blast of the bomb, but the structural integrity of the outer shell held. Alexander walked away unharmed while his running mate, Mark Ross, suffered a separated shoulder and a cut above his left eye. The second limousine did not fare as well. The front third of the vehicle collapsed under the blast and exposed Alexander's wife and three Secret Service agents to the superheated gases of the explosion. All four people were virtually incinerated. Fifteen other individuals were also killed, and another thirty-four were wounded, seven of them critically.

An al-Qaeda splinter group had released a statement the week before the attack that they were going to disrupt the American elections. In the immediate aftermath of the explosion, Kennedy had a pretty good idea how the American people would react to such foreign intervention in the democratic process. Two weeks later they proved her right. They turned out in record numbers on election day, and Josh Alexander and Mark Ross were swept into office by a landslide. Shortly after the election Ross began making statements to the press that he was going to do a top-down review of the CIA. That was code for cleaning house.

Despite twenty-three years of service, Kennedy took none of this personally. It simply wasn't worth it. The people had spoken, and in one week there would be the peaceful transfer of power from one administration to another. Her chief focus for this last week would be to purge every possible piece of information that could come back and bite her, or any of her people, in the ass. Part of her unpleasant history with Ross was that he was a vindictive prick. Simply running her out of the job after two brief years as the first female director of the Agency might not be enough for him. Kennedy felt there was a real chance he would want to burn her at the stake, tie her up in investigations for the next decade. She made a mental note to ask President Hayes for that blanket pardon. After all she'd done it would not be out of line to do so.

Kennedy took her eyes off the frozen landscape and checked her watch. They were late. *It must be the snow,* she thought to herself. It was a Saturday morning, and Kennedy worked most Saturday mornings. At least for another week. For all she knew, they'd take away her pass and cardkey when she showed up for work a week from Monday. That would be Ross's style. He'd make it as painful and embarrassing as possible.

There was an upside to all of this. At least, that was what she kept telling herself. At forty-five, she'd given twenty-three years of

her life to the CIA. She had a beautiful ten-year-old son whom she
didn't get to spend enough time with. Soon he would enter that
stage where he would want nothing to do with her. This premature
departure from the Agency would give her a chance to spend more
time with him. It was no secret in Washington that she was on her
way out. She'd already received two offers from local universities to
teach, three from think tanks, and another from a private security
firm. That was without lifting a finger. She tried to stay positive.
Tried to tell herself they were great options, but in the end nothing
else would match the mission and the people she worked with. That
was what bothered her most.

There was a knock on the door and then it opened. Kennedy
smiled when she saw it was Skip McMahon.

"Sorry I'm late," said the hulking six-foot-four FBI special
agent. "People in this town lose their minds when it snows."

"It's a good thing it's a Saturday."

McMahon was holding a large briefcase. He crossed the room
and kissed Kennedy on the cheek.

"So what's this all about? Have you finally decided to announce
your intention to marry me and make me an honest man?"

Kennedy smiled and gestured toward the sitting area. "Coffee
or tea?"

"Since when do I drink tea?"

She poured him a cup of coffee while McMahon sat on the
couch. He kept the briefcase close. Kennedy handed him the cup
and sat in one of the wing chairs.

The FBI man gestured with his hands and said, "I half expected
you to have all of your stuff boxed up and ready to go."

Kennedy sipped her tea. "Do you know something I don't?"

"Funny." McMahon looked around the wood paneled office
ignoring her feigned naiveté. The walls were covered with photos

of people and places. Some of the photos were self-explanatory: former CIA directors, the Twin Towers, the Berlin Wall. Others were more obscure: a baby's hand wrapped around a father's finger, a demolished building with a man standing in the foreground sobbing, and a group of Arab women covered in black from head to toe walking down a dusty street. McMahon had been to the office many times. A naturally inquisitive person, he had asked Kennedy about some of the photos before. Her response was always the same. She simply smiled and changed the subject. It occured to him that this might be his last chance to glean the importance of the more cryptic shots.

"The photo of the Arab women in black. Is that Saudi Arabia?"

"No. Yemen."

"Why do you have it in a frame?"

"It's a reminder of the subjugation of women in the Arab culture."

McMahon nodded. "That's what I thought."

Kennedy began laughing.

"What?" asked McMahon.

"It's not a reminder of the subjugation of Arab women. It's actually a team of Delta Force commandos who were on their way to say hello to an individual who, let's just say, wasn't playing by the rules."

"You're shitting me?" McMahon stood up so he could examine the photo more closely. "Who were they going after?"

"That's classified."

"Did they get him?"

Kennedy nodded.

"Good." McMahon settled back into his spot on the couch. "So what's the deal with the meeting this morning?"

"Do you know Cap Baker?"

"The Republican strategist."

"Yes."

"He's the mystery person you dragged me out here to see?"

"He assured me it was in your best interest."

A scowl of irritation fell across McMahon's leathered face. "Why in the hell would I want to spend two minutes with a political whore, especially a Republican one?"

Kennedy looked at her watch and ignored the question.

"Why the hell didn't he just come see me at the Hoover Building?"

Before Kennedy could answer, there was a knock on the door. A second later it opened and Cap Baker entered. If it weren't for his signature shock of gray hair they might not have recognized him. They were used to seeing him on TV wearing suits, expensive shirts, and fancy ties. He was rumored to charge eight hundred dollars an hour for his advice and lobbying skills. This morning he was dressed in boots, khakis, and a plaid flannel shirt. A puffy winter jacket was held under his right arm. A second man, wearing a suit, followed him into the room.

"Sorry we're late," announced Baker in his deep baritone voice. "The roads are horrible."

Kennedy stood to meet the visitors. "That's all right." She extended her hand. "Cap."

Baker took it. "Thank you for seeing me. I know this is a bit unusual."

McMahon stood but stayed silent. Baker turned to the FBI man. "I promise you, Special Agent McMahon, this will not be a waste of your time." As if he could sense McMahon's disdain, Baker didn't bother to offer his hand. Instead, he gestured to the man who had followed him into the office. "This is my attorney, Charles Wright. He won't be staying long. Sit." He motioned with his hands. "Sit."

McMahon and Kennedy took their seats, and Baker and his attorney grabbed two smaller chairs opposite McMahon. Kennedy gestured to the tea and coffee service on the table, but before she could speak, Baker declined.

"No, thank you. I have a plane waiting to take me to Vail. I need to get the hell out of this town before all the crazies start showing up for the inauguration."

"Vail," McMahon said with feigned excitement, "I would have taken you for an Aspen man."

Baker smiled. "Aspen is a Democratic ski town, Agent McMahon. Vail is where us Republicans go."

"Life must be rough," replied McMahon.

Baker stared at the FBI man for a moment. The smile on his face was one of amusement. "I like you. You're an open book. You don't know me, but you don't like me, and that's fine because in about five minutes I'm going to walk out that door and we're never going to see each other again."

"Is that right?" asked an amused McMahon.

"Yep . . . and you're never going to forget this meeting."

"Why's that?"

"Because what I'm about to give you is going to change your life."

"Is that right?" McMahon didn't sound too convinced.

"Yep, but before we get started, there's one piece of business we need to take care of."

Baker looked to his attorney and nodded. The attorney opened his large briefcase and extracted a file. He handed the file to Baker, who opened it and grabbed three contracts. He kept one for himself and handed the other two to Kennedy and McMahon.

"What's this?" asked McMahon.

"Confidentiality agreement," answered Baker. "I'd tell you to read it, but I don't have that much time. Just turn it to the last page and sign and date. Charles will notarize each signature and then we can get this over with."

"This is bullshit." McMahon tossed the contract on the table. "I'm not signing anything."

Baker looked to Kennedy, who was speed-reading through the document. "Irene?"

Without looking up, she asked, "Cap, tell me why it would be in my interest to sign this."

"It's not in your interest. It's in mine. But if you want to see what I have inside that briefcase, you're going to have to sign this contract."

"Why us?" asked McMahon.

"Good question." Baker placed his hands on his knees and thought about it for a second. "Three reasons where you're concerned, Special Agent McMahon. The first, as far as feds are concerned, you're someone who is known for his discretion. The second, what I'm about to show you will have a direct impact on your current investigation."

"And your third point?"

"You're a son of a bitch, you hate politicians, and you can't be bought."

"That's five points," McMahon said flatly.

"Yeah," Baker grinned, "but the last three kind of go together, so we'll just count them as one."

"He's hard to argue with," smiled Kennedy. She then turned to Baker and asked, "Why me?"

"That's easy. I lived in awe of Thomas Stansfield and so did you. He was a good friend . . . a mentor. This town has never had anyone who worked so effectively behind the scenes. Before he died he told me to keep an eye on you. He also told me that you were someone I could trust."

Kennedy pulled off her reading glasses and looked at Baker. Thomas Stansfield had occupied this very office until cancer took his life two years earlier. He had also been a mentor to Kennedy. He was the greatest man she had ever known and he had told her the same thing about Baker. Without further thought, Kennedy flipped the contract to the last page and signed above her printed name.

"What are you doing?" asked McMahon.

Kennedy slid the contract in front of Baker so he could sign. "Skip, just sign it so we can get this over with. I don't think Cap would have gone to this effort if it wasn't something serious."

"But I need to run this by Justice. I can't just go around signing confidentiality agreements while I'm on the government dime."

Kennedy glanced at him sideways. "Since when do you care about what Justice thinks? Just let go of your control issues and sign it."

Kennedy handed him her pen. McMahon hesitated for a second and then took it and signed his name.

"If this comes back and bites me in the ass, I'm going to make someone's life miserable."

Baker laughed as he took the contract from McMahon. "Don't worry, in about two minutes this contract is going to be the least of your worries."

The attorney finished notarizing the contracts and placed them back in the briefcase. Baker stuck out his hand and Wright gave him a legal-size manila envelope.

"Thank you, Charles. Why don't you wait for me down in the car."

The attorney left without saying a word, and when the door closed behind him McMahon said, "This better be pretty fucking good."

"That's going to depend on how you look at it." Baker stared at the mysterious envelope in his hands. "Let me ask you something, Agent McMahon. How is your investigation going?"

"That's confidential."

"I hear it's pretty one-dimensional."

"What's that supposed to mean?"

Baker shrugged. "You guys are only looking at this one way."

"When all the evidence points in one direction, that's pretty much the way it works."

"All the evidence? From what I've heard there is very little evidence."

"You know what? I didn't come here to talk about my investigation with you. This meeting was your idea, and I think it's time you put your cards on the table."

"Fine." Baker nodded. He opened the sealed envelope and extracted a series of 8x10 black-and-white photographs. He turned the first one over and placed it on the coffee table so both McMahon and Kennedy could view it. It was a close-up of a woman. The photograph had the slightly grainy quality of a surveillance photo taken from a distance and then blown up.

"That, if you didn't know it already, is Jillian Rautbort. President–elect Alexander's deceased wife."

Baker grabbed a second photo and set it down next to the first. This one was not blown up. It showed Jillian Rautbort and a man. It was evening and they were standing on a terrace. Jillian was in a halter dress and the man was in a suit. Baker put down the next photo. This one was of just Jillian from the waist up. She had a very mischievous look on her face and she was reaching behind her neck with her hands.

Baker glanced at Kennedy. "This is where it gets interesting, and I apologize in advance, but you need to see this."

He laid down the next photo. Jillian Rautbort was now standing with her dress around her waist; her tanned and perfectly sized breasts exposed. Baker put the next photo down. Now Jillian and the man were kissing. The photo after that captured Jillian on her knees, her face buried in the mystery man's groin. Baker began lying the photos down like a blackjack dealer would cards. They showed Rautbort and her lover in an escalation of sexual acts culminating with him on his back on a lounge chair and her completely naked on top of him.

Baker placed the empty envelope on the table next to the photos and said, "That's pretty much it."

"Are you sure," asked Kennedy, "that the woman in these photos is Jillian Rautbort?"

"Yes."

"When were they taken, and how the hell did you get your hands on them?" McMahon asked.

"I think they were taken over Labor Day at the Rautbort estate in Palm Beach, and no, I didn't hire someone to do this."

"Then how in the hell did you get your hands on them?"

"I was contacted by the man who took them," replied Baker.

McMahon scoffed. "So you didn't hire him, but in the end you paid him."

"There is a distinction, Agent McMahon. I'm not going to sit here and tell you I'm an angel. Politics is a rough business. Since you were willing to sign my confidentiality agreement, I'll give you the straight facts. I paid for these photos. I paid a lot of money for these photos, and it was all legal. My only regret now is that I didn't destroy them the moment I received them."

"Why is that?" asked Kennedy.

"Because I allowed my ego to get in the way, and in the end it cost my candidate the White House."

"How could these photos have cost your candidate the White House?" asked a skeptical McMahon.

"There are very few people in the world who I truly despise. Mark Ross and Stu Garret are two of them."

Kennedy and McMahon shared a look, and McMahon said, "You'll get no argument from us."

"Well, with a month to go in the race, my guys had an eight-point lead, which, if you know how polls are conducted—who answers their phone, who doesn't, who says they vote, and who actually votes, and all these national polls have a built-in bias for the Democrats—with four weeks to go is huge, especially if you're on the Republican ticket. I never really wanted to buy these photos, and I certainly never wanted to use them. At least, not in terms of releasing them to the press."

"Then why did you buy them?" asked McMahon.

"To take them out of play," Kennedy answered.

"That's right. Elections are about controlling as many factors as possible, and I'll be damned if I was going to allow these things to float around and do God only knows what. The conventional wisdom would be that they would hurt the Alexander camp, but one never knows for sure. The smart thing is to leave nothing to chance. We were flush with cash, so I paid the guy."

"That was the only reason why you bought them?" Kennedy asked in a slightly skeptical tone.

Baker grinned. "There was one other small reason." He shifted in his chair and crossed his right leg over his left. "I wanted to make Garret and Ross sweat."

"You sent them these?" McMahon asked with his mouth agape.

"Only a few. I had them personally delivered to Garret's hotel room during a campaign stop in Dallas."

"Did he know you sent them?"

"No."

"Are you sure?"

"He may have guessed, but I made sure the delivery couldn't be traced back to me. I did, however, send a message along."

"What kind of message?"

"I only sent three photos. I wrote one word with a black Sharpie on each photo."

"What word?"

"Three words. You'll never win."

"You and Garret have a history?" asked Kennedy.

"You could say that. We've been on the opposite sides of some pretty big battles."

"And let me guess," said McMahon, "one of your favorite sayings with him was, You'll never win."

"Actually, he was the one who was fond of the saying."

"So you thought you'd rub his nose in it."

Baker nodded. "And if I'd just left it alone, I'd be the one getting ready for an inauguration, and they," Baker pointed at the photos on the table, "would still be alive."

"What do you mean, they?" asked McMahon.

"Jillian and the man she had the rendezvous with."

McMahon picked up one of the photos and pointed to the person underneath Jillian Rautbort. "This man is dead?"

"That man is Special Agent Matt Cash of the United States Secret Service."

# 2

McMahon couldn't sit any longer. He'd been down this road before, just never on such a high-profile case. Instinctively, it was a nightmare. Law enforcement was in great part about maintaining order in society. There were rules, and they needed to be enforced. The people who enforced them tended to be very organized individuals who approached their jobs in a methodical manner. Never more so than when they were investigating a crime. And with a sensational crime such as this one, you investigated the case with one eye on the crime, and one eye on the eventual prosecution of the perpetrators. Usually prosecutors were brought in later, but on this one they'd been looking over his shoulder every step of the way.

This steaming pile of crap that this Republican shark had just dropped in his lap was now forcing him to rethink all of the suppositions and evidence that he and hundreds of agents had spent months running down and collecting. He wanted to dismiss it as inconsequential bullshit. Tell him to take his envelope and his confidentiality agreement and take a flying leap off a cliff. But, as much as he hated to admit it, his gut told him that there was something here.

McMahon wished Kennedy would break the ice and speak, but she wasn't going to. That wasn't her style. She was too smart. For all he knew, this was a setup. She could have known about this for weeks. McMahon didn't like any of this. He stopped his pacing and looked down at Kennedy.

"How long have you known about this?"

She looked at her watch. "For about six minutes."

McMahon studied her placid face and fought to conceal his own rage. He loved Kennedy and he trusted her, but at the end of the day she was still a spy. A professional perpetrator of deceit and lies. As much as he wanted to believe her, he could never really be sure. He turned his attention back to Baker.

"Why should I believe any of this, and why in the hell did you wait two months to tell anybody about this?"

"I'm no saint, Agent McMahon. I'm not afraid to bend the rules here and there. Especially when it comes to stuff like these moronic campaign finance laws, but this . . ." Baker gestured to the photos. "If someone on the other side decided to make this go away and do it in such a way as to make it advantageous to their cause . . . then they stepped way over the line."

"That's a big if, and you still didn't answer my question. Why did you wait until now? Why didn't you come forward the day after the explosion?"

"Are you kidding me? The opposing candidate's wife gets incinerated by a car bomb, and you think I should have gone public with a bunch of pornographic photos of her screwing her bodyguard, who, by the way, also got killed in the explosion? I would have been branded the biggest bastard in the history of politics."

"I didn't say go public. Why didn't you bring it to me?"

Baker stood and waved his hand in frustration at McMahon. "You're where I was in the weeks after the attack, except I still had a campaign to manage. A campaign that we almost won, which is amazing, when you think about it." He grabbed his jacket off the back of the chair. "I didn't want to believe any of this. Things were happening so fast those final two weeks. There were the funerals, and then Alexander decided to go on with the debates, after we'd been informed that he was pulling out. We were in a street fight with our hands cuffed behind our backs. We couldn't fight back. We had to just sit there and take it."

"So again," McMahon said forcefully, "why now? Why sit on this for two months?"

"Because I didn't want to believe it. This is going to sound really corny to you, but I believe in this country. I believe in the two-party system. I believe in the peaceful transfer of power, and from everything I've seen, Josh Alexander is a decent man. I'm not about destroying institutions and ruining the people's faith in their government, but . . ." Baker fell silent.

"But what?" prodded McMahon.

"Mark Ross and Stu Garret are motherfuckers! And I mean motherfuckers!"

The severity of the comment caught even McMahon off guard.

"Pathological liars, the both of them," Baker continued. "The more I sat and thought about this, the more I realized they are absolutely capable of orchestrating some fucking coup like this."

"That's great," McMahon said sarcastically, "your personal opinion and all, but do you have a shred of evidence that the vice president–elect of the United States plotted to have his own motorcade attacked?"

"Evidence . . . no." Baker shook his head. "But motive, yes. And trust me, Agent McMahon, I've been following your investigation. In fact, I've already read the draft you're going to deliver to the president on Monday. It's heavy on supposition and light on the facts. Yeah, you have all your standard lab analysis on the bomb. You guys are great at that, but beyond the lab report, it's all fluff. You guys don't know where that van came from or how the explosives got into the country. Most importantly, though, you don't have a sui-cide bomber, and we all know how the Islamic radical fundamen-talists love to martyr themselves."

"That's not always the case."

"Fine. Then where's the guy in the red Nationals baseball hat?"

McMahon's eyes widened. "What are you talking about?"

"Who, not a what, and don't act so surprised. I told you, I've been following your investigation."

McMahon looked anxiously at Kennedy and then back to Baker. "Who have you been talking to?"

"You know that is something that has always driven me nuts about this town. Everybody gets hung up on who said what to who, and they ignore the fact that the truth is staring them right in the face. You have a thirteen-year veteran of the Secret Service who has an impeccable record, and she reports that just before the blast, she saw a man in a red Nationals baseball hat and sunglasses stand-ing behind a tree and acting suspicious. The man was, and I will quote from your original draft, not the one that you are going to give to the president on Monday. In your first draft you wrote Agent Rivera saw a man holding a device and right before the explosion he suddenly ducked behind the tree."

"Agent Rivera was under a lot of stress at the time."

"Don't start acting like one of those attorneys over at Justice. I can see from your face that you believe that BS about as much as I do."

"And you're sounding like one of those crazy conspiracy theorists."

Baker laughed loudly. "Better than some shill for the government who'd rather bury evidence than face the facts."

McMahon was up off the couch with surprising quickness for his size. "I'd be careful about questioning people's motives, Mr. Blackmailer."

"I did no such thing, and you know it, but I'm glad to see you're angry. You're going to need it if you're going to get to the bottom of this."

"You're out of your mind."

"And you're in denial. You've accounted for every person at the scene of the crime that day except the man in the red hat."

"The man in the red hat doesn't exist."

Baker stepped back and smiled. "Oh, really? If he doesn't exist, then why does the Starbucks on Wisconsin have him on digital surveillance buying a cup of coffee roughly thirty minutes before the explosion?"

"What in the hell are you talking about?"

"Black-and-white surveillance tape. Red doesn't look red. Your people had it right in front of them and they missed it. Go back and check. You'll see."

McMahon was at a complete loss for words. This shark knew more about his own investigation than he did.

"Watch your back, Agent McMahon. These guys don't play by the rules, and neither should you, if you want to find the truth." Baker turned to Kennedy. "One last thing. You know that Ross will move to get rid of you right after the inauguration."

"Yes."

"And anyone else he deems a threat."

"Are you thinking of anyone in particular?"

"Mitch."

"Mitch Rapp," said McMahon. "What in the hell does Ross have against Rapp?"

"It's a long story," said Kennedy, not wanting to answer the question. "Cap, I know you have a plane to catch, so cut to the chase."

"I think it would be a good idea to bring in a fresh set of eyes on this."

"Are you sure you don't mean you'd like to let the bull into the china shop and see what he breaks?"

"Oh, that's a tempting visual, but it's not what I had in mind. I was thinking more along the lines of an assassin's assassin. Someone who knows the ins and outs of this world."

"It's not a bad idea."

What Baker and McMahon didn't know, and what Kennedy was not about to tell them, was that she already had Mitch Rapp on the case. She had known about the mystery man in the red hat for almost a month, and Rapp and his team had been working quietly to find out who he was, and more importantly, who had hired him.

# 3

H e was six inches taller than her and ten years older. "I think you should kiss me," she said softly.

Mitch Rapp ignored her and watched the door to the café across the street.

"If we were really lovers you wouldn't be able to take your hands off me." She slid her chair closer to his and placed a hand on his thigh. She ran her hand through his long black hair. Streaks of gray were coming in on the sides. For three straight weeks she'd studied him. She knew every wrinkle and scar and there were quite a few of the latter. Some visible. Some buried in his psyche. She had no proof the mental scars were there, but they had to be. No body lived the type of hard life he'd lived and came out unscathed.

She lifted her sunglasses off her nose just enough to reveal her hazel eyes. They were more green than brown, which she thought might be part of the problem. His ex-wife—no, that wasn't right, his deceased wife—had the most stunning green eyes. Cindy Brooks made the mistake of calling her the ex one night and he'd made her sleep on the floor. Brooks had been with the Agency for only five years, and she considered it a huge honor to work side by side with a living legend like Mitch Rapp. At least she had when she was first given the assignment.

"Listen, hard-ass." Her words were harsh but hushed. The expression on her face was pure feigned adoration. "You handpicked me for this. I'm supposed to be your wife. We're on our honeymoon. When people are on their honeymoon they kiss a lot, they talk, they hold hands . . . they act like they love each other."

"Your point." Rapp turned toward her, but kept his eyes on the café. He was wearing a pair of black Persol sunglasses that allowed him to see out, but no one else to see in.

"No one is going to believe our cover because you keep acting like I don't exist."

"People fight on their honeymoon all the time."

"We fought yesterday."

"We were in Istanbul yesterday. None of these people know we were fighting."

"I'm sick of dealing with your foul mood." She took her hand off his leg and leaned back. After a moment the smile on her face disappeared. "Fighting it is then."

Brooks stood with such quickness that it surprised even Rapp. Her chair tumbled over and she put her hands on her hips. "My mother," she yelled, "told me I shouldn't marry you!" She reached out and grabbed her glass of wine from the table.

Rapp looked up at her from behind his sunglasses. His jaw tight with tension, he whispered, "Sit down! You're making a scene."

"I know I'm making a scene!" she yelled. "I want to make a scene! You're an ass." Then with a great flourish she took her wine, doused Rapp's blue polo shirt and khaki pants, and stormed off down the street.

Rapp sat there motionless. The people at the surrounding tables all looked on in amusement. It had been a bad year. The worst year of his life. He went to bed every night blaming himself for her death, and woke up every morning hoping it had all been a nightmare. But it wasn't. The unborn baby she was carrying, the other children they would have undoubtedly had—a lifetime of dreams and memories gone in an instant and he never saw it coming. That was the other problem. The thing that ate away at him from the inside out. He had let his guard down. He had allowed her to change him, to give him hope that he could be something different. Something other than a killer.

He supposed there was a chance she would have succeeded in changing him, but it was small. His was a vocation that was very difficult to walk away from. Especially with so much on the line. He was unwilling to let go of his past. There was always one more job, one more operation to handle. She'd told him to let someone else man the ramparts for a while. He'd seen the younger guys, though. He'd even helped train a few of them and they had a lot to learn before they were anywhere near as good as he was. At thirty-nine he was at his peak. His knees and back were not what they once were, but he still had no problem keeping up with the rookies, who in some cases were nearly half his age. The years of experience were what really made the difference.

If he could do it all over again, the decision would have been easy. He would have given it all up for one more day with her. The hunt for her killers was the only thing that got him through the first nine months. After that, he'd tried pills for a while. At first they worked. At least they helped him sleep. But after a month they started to make him crazy, so he threw them all away. That was when he dropped out. He flew to Paris, made a stop in Switzerland, and then disappeared for two months. He drank profuse amounts of alcohol and went on an opium binge in Bangkok that lasted for a week. He even slept with a couple of women along the way, but the brief flings only worsened his guilt. Finally, in late October, he woke up one early evening in his hotel room in Calcutta and turned on Sky News. That was how he heard about the attack on the motorcade. He looked at his puffy red face and bloodshot eyes in the mirror and knew he had reached the tipping point. He either went back to the States and got back to work, or he would drink himself to death. Rapp was a lot of things, but nothing more so than a survivor.

Kennedy was happy to see him, but there were questions, and Rapp wasn't good at answering questions. The CIA got a little skittish when their operatives disappeared. The FBI also took notice. Kennedy covered for him as best she could, and told the inquisitors that Rapp had taken a leave of absence. Most understood. The death of his wife was a very public affair. Rapp had his enemies in the government, however, and they wanted answers. Rapp, in his typical manner, told them to go fuck themselves, which only served to make the situation worse. In the end it was the president who intervened on his behalf. The commander in chief came down extremely hard on those who questioned Rapp's loyalty. This was not the Cold War. No longer did agents get turned by the enemy. This new war was about terrorism, and the thought of Rapp going over to the other side was simply preposterous.

This all came down the week before the election, and it was Ross's people at National Intelligence who made the biggest stink. When Alexander and Ross pulled off their come-from-behind victory, both Rapp and Kennedy knew their days were numbered. Almost two years earlier, he had warned Kennedy that he thought al-Qaeda, or one of its offshoots, might try to hire outside help to run some of their operations. They had the cash to do it, and they also had a practical motive. The U.S. and her allies had done a tremendous job of rolling up terrorist cells, which operationally left al-Qaeda ineffective when it came to striking at the heart of America. The motorcade incident changed all of that. Somehow they had managed to stage a spectacular attack inside, and they had left surprisingly few clues. In Rapp's experience, lack of evidence meant a professional was involved.

Nowhere in any of the early reports did Rapp read a thing about the mystery man in the red hat. He learned that when he sat down to talk to Special Agent Rivera. At first Rapp was shocked that there was no mention of him in the reports, but then it began to make sense. Rivera was the only one to notice the man. He didn't show up on any surveillance monitors from the surrounding businesses. Paramedics did not treat him after the explosion. He simply disappeared, or as several doctors tried to tell Rivera, he never existed except in her mind. She'd suffered a serious concussion. It was a given that she might be confused about when and where things had occurred. The long and short of it was that the lawyers at the Justice Department didn't like loose ends. Especially loose ends that would fan the flames of conspiracy theorists for decades to come.

Rapp went back to the scene of the crime with a map that listed where every pedestrian and vehicle was on that afternoon in October when history was changed. Two of the apartment buildings across the street were now holes in the ground. The adjacent buildings on either side were under construction. Other than that everything looked normal. The huge crater in the road had been filled and repaved, and fresh trees had been planted. Rapp found the tree where Rivera said the man had been standing right before everything faded to black. The large oak was still there, but damaged.

Some of the bark that faced the explosion was gone and there were several scars left by debris that had imbedded itself into the trunk.

For Rapp, it came down to the tree and one other thing. If the attack had really been carried out by jihadists, there would have been a body, or more accurately, tiny parts of a body. A true believer willing to martyr himself for the cause. No body parts meant remote detonation. And if Rapp had been the trigger man that day, he would have stood right where Rivera said she saw the man in the red hat. The FBI and the rest of the government could scour the planet for the terrorists who claimed responsibility, but Rapp was going to look elsewhere. The shadowy world of contract killers.

It was a world Rapp knew well. The covert ops business required rubbing shoulders with people who were on par with Swiss bankers when it came to secrecy. In essence it was a loose network of former intelligence, law enforcement, and military types. Many of these people worked for real security firms. The firms handled legitimate work and subcontracted out the black bag stuff on the side. Rapp ruled these companies out from the start of his investigation. Targeting a presidential candidate and setting off car bombs in Washington, DC, was way off the reservation. No big security firm or foreign intelligence service would touch a contract like this. The downside was simply too great. The job would have been taken by someone out of the mainstream. Someone small. A one-, two-, or three-man shop at the most. It would also have to be someone who didn't mind taking money from terrorists, and that made the list of potential suspects pretty thin.

All of this was going through Rapp's head when they got the first big break—the Starbucks tape. There had literally been hundreds of tapes to review from local Georgetown businesses. A computer genius at Langley named Marcus Dumond had caught the oversight. Dumond had written a computer program that piggy-

backed the recognition software they already used. The thousands
of hours of surveillance footage was scanned with the new program
looking for baseball hats. It came back with over a hundred hits, but
it was the Starbucks one that fit the time frame and Rivera's de-
scription of the man she'd seen. It did not provide them with a clear
photo of the suspect, but it was a start. The brim of his hat blocked
most of his face from the camera, but they knew what his mouth
and chin looked like, and they also got a brief glimpse of his nose
and the lower portion of his eyes. They also knew his height and ap-
proximate weight.

Most important for Rapp, though, was that he now knew how
the man moved. How he carried himself. They had him on tape for
twenty-seven seconds while he waited in line to order his drink.
Thanks to the time stamp on the surveillance footage they were
also able to go back and find out exactly what the assassin had ordered—a double espresso. Definitely more European or Middle
Eastern than American, and that was where the hunt had led
them—to the countries that bordered the Mediterranean.

Rapp started with the CIA's database and then contacted his
colleagues in Britain, France, and Italy. For close to four weeks
Rapp and a small team had been hopping all over the Mediterranean running down leads. They'd been in Tunisia, Italy, Greece,
Turkey, and now Cyprus. They had narrowed the search down to
three names. Whether those three names represented three separate
individuals or one, they couldn't be sure. The business was funny
that way. It was very easy for an operator to take on multiple identities and use different pseudonyms depending on the target, the type
of hit, or the region. With each passing day, though, Rapp was beginning to believe it was one man. There were too many similari-
ties. Too many intersecting paths.

Rapp's contact in Istanbul was dependable: a deputy undersecretary in the Turkish National Intelligence Organization who had been on the CIA payroll for almost three decades. He told Rapp there was a good chance the man he was looking for lived in Cyprus. He did business in Istanbul from time to time, but Limassol, Cyprus, was his home. The Turkish spy gave Rapp an address, an e-mail account, and a low-quality surveillance photograph. Dumond pulled all the information together in less than a day and was still trying to connect the dots. They had real estate records, tax returns, past and present e-mail accounts, and banking records. The guy he was looking for operated a front company out of an office above the café he'd been sitting across from for the past two hours. The owner of the café was his landlord. The tenant went by the name of Alexander Deckas. Rapp thought it a strange irony that the suspected assassin went by the same first name as the last name of the man he had tried to kill.

Rapp stood and dabbed the wine from his pants. A sympathetic waiter handed him a second napkin. He cleaned the wine as best he could while trying to come up with the worst possible overseas posting for Brooks. The waiter gave him a third napkin, and Rapp gave him the two soiled ones. He glanced around the area to see how much attention he had garnered. The café was on a one-way street in front of the hotel so all the parked cars were pointed east. Halfway down the block to his left, something caught his eye. Casually, he threw some cash down on the table and thanked the waiter in Italian. He didn't know Greek and figured it was the next best option. Rapp then started down the street. He pulled at his wet shirt and continued to act concerned over his soiled clothes. He glanced to his right and confirmed what he had seen. Two men were sitting in a car. One of them was holding a camera with a tele- photo lens and it was pointed at the same café Rapp had been watching.

Rapp looked away and grabbed his phone. After several rings a man answered.

"What's up?"

"Where are you?" asked Rapp.

"Athens."

"Get your ass to Cyprus, and I mean yesterday."

"What's wrong?"

"I don't think we're the only people looking for this guy."

"I'm at the airport right now. I'll see what's available and get back to you."

Rapp hit the end button and kept walking. He was trying to figure out his next move when it presented itself in the form of a mannequin perched in a storefront window near the end of the block. New clothes and a view of the two men across the street were exactly what he needed.

# 4

The partygoers in the Alex Hotel were all in a good mood, and they should have been since not a single one of them had paid for a thing all weekend. This particular environmental conference was one of the hottest tickets on the annual circuit. One day of workshops and panels, and two days of skiing and debauchery at one of Europe's finest ski resorts. A Grateful Dead cover band was on a tiny stage playing "Cumberland Blues" as the crowd of rhythmically challenged, Birkenstock wearing, patchouli oil–smelling, prematurely gray, Mother Earth lovers danced a herky-jerky dance that would have made any lover of the Motown Sound either cry or double over in laughter.

Mark Ross stood near the back of the room with a permanent smile on his face. He had attended the event five previous times as a U.S. senator and the attendees had always been nice to him, but now they treated him like royalty. He had been smart to embrace this issue years ago. If one was to rise to the top of the Democratic Party it was very important to have the proper credentials. No résumé builder was more vital than the role of compassionate environmentalist. These were the foot soldiers. The people who got out the vote. Who organized things from the grass roots with their e-mail blasts and blogs. He appreciated everything they'd done for him, and would hopefully do for him in the future. He was already thinking about his turn. Eight years wasn't so long. There were limits though. He was now at the top of the political heap. One place from the pinnacle. He'd put in enough time with the unwashed. Now it was time to head off to Mount Olympus and bask in the adoration of the truly powerful.

The toughest invite of the entire weekend was for Joseph Speyer's party at his mountainside villa. The Deadheads were not welcome. Speyer's party was for the heavy hitters—European royalty; fashion icons from Paris, London, New York, and Milan; international financiers; media moguls; the occasional movie or rock star; hip politicians; and ultra-wealthy trust funders. In other words, the beautiful people who flew in on their private planes, partied hard, wrote big checks, and then flew on to the next big party, or one of several mansions they owned. Conservation to these people meant having their staff recycle their diet pop cans and designer plastic water bottles. Some of them went so far as to buy a small hybrid car, but the purchase was simply to drive to a friend's house on the weekend. They still kept their limos, SUVs, luxury sedans, and sports cars.

For Ross, Speyer's party was a must. It allowed him to tap into people with obscene money. People who could write million dollar soft-money checks, because that was how much money their bond portfolio had earned the previous week. Ross had been welcomed into this crowd from the get-go. He was tall, relatively handsome, and fit. But equally important was the fact that he'd built himself a small fortune on Wall Street, which endeared him to his fellow multimillionaires. The ultra wealthy had a much easier time writing checks to people who were already in the club. On some level they thought a fellow millionaire was less likely to abscond with the funds.

Ross shook a few more hands and turned for the door. The smell of cannabis was pungent. Michael Brown, the Secret Service agent in charge of his detail, stood a few steps away with a frown on his face. He fell into step with Ross as they left the room.

"What's the matter, Michael?" Ross asked with a smile. "You've never been stoned?"

"I don't do drugs, sir. Never have."

"You don't have to lie to me," Ross said casually. "I'm not going to tell anyone."

Five more agents fell in around them. The shortest was six feet one and the tallest was six feet six. They looked more like a basketball team than a security detail.

"I don't lie, sir." Brown's eyes scanned the crowd in the lobby. "Just so you know, I'm going to have to put this in my report."

"What, in your report?"

"The presence of marijuana."

Ross looked at him sideways. "You can't be serious?"

"It was pretty thick in there, sir, and we take drug tests. I have to write it up."

Ross frowned. He could just see the press getting a hold of something like this.

"Don't worry, sir. It'll be internal. We're good at keeping secrets."

The Secret Service agents and the vice president–elect stepped through the front door and onto the sidewalk. Two more six-plus-foot agents were waiting for them. They were traveling light, which was the other reason for Agent Brown's foul mood. Motorized vehicles were banned in the town of Zermatt. Brown wanted to get an exemption from the Swiss, but Ross wouldn't let him. It was after all an environmental conference. Ross would ride the electric city busses just like everyone else.

This was both a logistical and security nightmare for the Secret Service. There was no bombproofing, let alone bulletproofing, electric vehicles. They simply didn't have the horsepower to handle the extra weight, especially with some of the steep inclines they had to deal with. That meant Ross would be exposed to and from every venue all weekend long. In light of the attack on the motorcade, no one at the Secret Service liked this idea, but Ross held his ground.

The other problem was that Ross had sprung this trip on them at the last minute. That meant the advance team had arrived barely a day before the rest of the detail. A city bus was commandeered for the weekend, and two agents set about learning how to drive the large, low-powered vehicles. Brown arrived the next day to discover that his boys had crashed the bus. The narrow village streets were simply too difficult for amateurs to navigate. So now they had a civilian driving them, and no backup bus available as a decoy, nor a replacement should this one fail. The entire trip had degenerated into everything he'd been taught not to do. With Ross refusing to allow him to bring in one of the limos or Suburbans on standby in Milan, they were forced to adapt and settle for a less than ideal situation.

A perimeter had been formed around the yellow and green village bus. Black paper had been taped over the large windows along the back half. Brown escorted Ross onto the bus and walked him to the rear, where he sat him down between two black clad and heavily armed members of the Counter Assault Team. More agents piled on the bus and they started to roll. A light fluffy snow was falling as the bus hummed through the narrow streets. They didn't have far to go. That was one good thing about Zermatt. The village was small. Speyer's house was barely a mile away, most of it uphill. Two agents had been deployed in advance. Brown had wanted to send a team of six to sweep the house and wand the other guests as they arrived, but when Ross got wind of it he hit the roof. Ross chewed his ass out and Brown had to stand there and take it. He kept headquarters appraised of his every move and left a significant e-mail trail explaining that Ross had overruled him every step of the way. If something happened Brown wasn't going to take the blame for it. He'd watched what they'd done to Rivera after the attack on the motorcade. She'd been put on administrative leave pending the completion of the investigation. Now she'd been cooling her heels for two and a half months. Even if they cleared her, there was no way she would get anywhere near the president's detail.

With barely a hundred meters to the house the bus rounded a hairpin turn and stalled. The driver turned to Brown and in clear English said, "Too heavy. Too much weight."

"Wonderful." Brown scowled and then mumbled to himself, "What a chicken shit operation." He looked around at his fellow agents and said, "Everybody off accept Kendal and Fitz." Brown was referring to the two men sandwiching Ross.

One by one eight agents piled off the bus and then slowly but steadily, the vehicle climbed the last steep incline. The agents who had disembarked dogged it up the hill double time without having to be ordered. The bus couldn't go very fast so they kept pace, but when they got to the top they were all panting due to the thin mountain air. One of the two advance agents was waiting for them with a smile on his face. It vanished as soon as Brown stepped off the bus.

"What in the hell do you think is so funny?"

"Nothing, boss," the man said sheepishly.

"What's the situation in there?" Brown jerked his head toward the house.

"Eighty-three guests plus sixteen people from the caterer. No whack jobs."

"Exits?"

"We're piggybacking his security system. Everything is wired and covered."

Brown stepped back onto the bus and said, "Sir, we're ready."

Ross stood and buttoned his tweed sport coat. He was wearing a gray and blue Nordic sweater underneath and some jeans. He exited the bus and proceeded to the front door, where it was opened for him by one of the host's servants. The heavy wooden door swung in, and Ross was met by Speyer, who was waiting for him.

The banker was dressed in a red velvet smoking jacket, black pants, and a pair of black suede house slippers. He was every bit the stylish host, even here in the mountains.

"Mr. Vice President." Speyer made a rolling motion with his right hand and then bowed at the waist. "It is an honor to have you as a guest at my humble abode."

Ross laughed. "I'm still just Mark to you, Joseph. I won't be sworn in for another week."

"Oh . . . do not deprive me the joy of using such an exalted title." The banker looked up at Ross and smiled.

"Stand up you imbecile, before I have you flogged."

Speyer winked and said, "Promises, promises."

"You look well."

"And so do you. What can we get you to drink?"

"I would love a martini."

"We will get you one, and then I would like to show you my new wine cellar. I think you will be most impressed."

Ross started to follow the host and after a few steps could feel that someone was following him. He looked over his shoulder at Agent Brown and gave him a look that clearly told him to back off. "Wait by the front door. If I need you, I'll scream."

A bar was set up between the stone fireplace and the massive picture window that looked down on the village and out onto the most recognizable peak in the world. The Matterhorn. With the light snow falling the sheer face was all but obscured, but Ross knew it was there. He'd stood at this window just three months before and coveted the view.

The guests all gravitated toward him, extending their sincere congratulations. Many of them had helped finance the campaign. He was their horse, and they had backed him. Ross was well into his martini and Speyer was well into his second hilarious story, when Ross noticed a familiar face watching him from across the room. Ross became uncomfortable before he even knew it. His hands got sweaty and his throat tightened a bit. He avoided looking at the man directly. He expected him to be here, but not out in the open. Ross suddenly felt the need to dull his nerves a bit. He turned to the bartender and motioned for another martini. A little liquid courage was what he would need to get through the evening.

# 5

Rather than fly into Limassol's International Airport, Gazich took a more circuitous route. He flew first from Bucharest to Athens and then took the ferry to Rhodes, where he stopped for a few days before jumping another ferry to Cyprus. Immigration and passport control at the ports was virtually nonexistent. It had been more than ten weeks since he'd set foot on the island he called home. He had spent much of that time hopping from one country to the next and trying to remain as inconspicuous as possible. Before the bomb had exploded, he'd already decided to lay low and hide out in America for a week or two. That was his style. Where others rushed to get out of a country after a hit, he remained calm and waited for things to blow over.

Every step of the way he had been relaxed and deliberate. Run away from the scene of a crime and you attract attention. Stand and watch, lurk and loiter for a while and nobody notices. You blend in with all of the other gawkers who congregate to stand in awe of the carnage. Carnage was plentiful that Saturday afternoon in late October. At first Gazich had been unable to take in his handy work. The dust and debris cloud was massive. Fortunately, he had remembered to put in earplugs before the bomb went off. It had been more powerful than he'd expected and surely would have blown both his eardrums.

He had stayed pressed against the tree for ten seconds, his eyes closed and his T-shirt over his mouth and nose, holding his breath. When he opened his eyes a crack, day had been turned into night. With a cautious step Gazich left the protection of the tree, and started down the sidewalk. Even though he could barely see, he wanted to make it to the perimeter before the dust settled. He wanted to be standing amid the first group of onlookers. Slowly, the air cleared and the sky began to brighten. Debris was everywhere; broken glass, hunks of metal, bricks, and wood were strewn about the sidewalk. With the earplugs pulled out, he began to hear cries for help. He walked past those cries and made it to the bottom of the hill across the street from the Starbucks where he had been before the attack.

A man stopped him and asked if he was all right. Gazich still had his T-shirt over his mouth and nose. He nodded, coughed, and kept walking. A half a block later he reached the Safeway parking lot and stopped. This was his first chance to turn around and take in the destruction. The size of the crater surprised even him. It crossed both lanes of traffic and looked to be at least six feet deep. It was as if a meteor had come in at a shallow angle, slamming into the middle of Georgetown. It was hard to tell, due to the smoke and fire, but it looked like the apartment buildings across the street were no longer there. Most importantly, Gazich counted only one limousine. It was turned over on its back like some helpless turtle. Gazich guessed that the other limo had been close to incinerated.

As the crowd of onlookers grew, Gazich fell farther and farther back. With each move he was careful to shake more dust from his clothes. Emergency vehicles began to arrive within minutes and they just added to the chaos. When the pandemonium reached its peak, he simply crossed Wisconsin Avenue and walked four blocks to his parked car on T Street. Twenty minutes later he was merging onto Interstate 95 and on his way north.

He changed out of his clothes as he drove, not daring to pull into a rest stop. Too many cops patrolled those places. With the windows down and the cruise control set at the legal limit, he shook the dust from his hair and put on a new T-shirt and a pair of jeans. When he crossed the state line into Delaware, he finally relaxed a bit. The reports on the radio kept repeating the same information over and over, so he turned off the radio and drove in silence. A couple of hours later he ditched the car in Newark and took the train into Manhattan. He'd already booked a room at the Sheraton Hotel and Towers near Times Square—1,750 rooms, lots of tourists, and near complete anonymity. He'd arranged for two tickets to a show that night and he picked them up from the concierge before he headed up to his room. He didn't want to go to the show. He would much rather go to one of the high end strip clubs and blow through a wad of cash, but he reasoned that if he was playing himself off as a tourist he should act like one.

When he got up to his room, he turned on the TV and any thought of going to the show, a strip club, or anywhere else for that fact, completely vanished. He could barely believe how quickly everything had gone from perfect to disastrous. He'd missed the target. The candidates were alive, and the wife and a whole lot of other people were dead. Gazich knew it had not been his fault. The man on the phone had told him they would be in the second limo. The limo that he incinerated. Would the person who hired him believe it when he told him he'd hit the car he'd been told to hit? Would they want him to try again? Gazich already knew what the answer to that would be. You only got one shot at something like this. Anything after that was a death wish.

Gazich barely slept that night, despite the fact that he'd put a serious dent in the minibar. As soon as the stores were open he found a T-Mobile kiosk and purchased a PDA with web browsing capabilities. He'd been paid a million dollars in advance and promised a million more upon completion of the assignment. In Gazich's mind, the second million was still his. His employer had assured him that they had an impeccable source. Everything on his end had been done to perfection. This screwup was the source's fault, and he was not about to take the blame for it.

Gazich logged onto the e-mail account using the password he'd been given and opened the draft menu where a message was waiting for him. It was pretty much what he had expected. They were blaming him for screwing up. As quick as his two hands could type, the assassin punched in his terse reply, placing the blame where it belonged. He finished by demanding the rest of his fee and then logged off. Over the next forty-eight hours they went back and forth, with things getting worse before they got remotely better. Both sides made threats and both were presumably in a position to follow through even though they had never met face-to-face. One side had the money and presumably could find the assets to retaliate while the other side had the talent and determination. In the end it was a standoff. This was a war that neither side wanted to fight.

The demands for a second attempt on the candidates' lives was dropped and they eventually admitted that their inside source had relayed bad information. Since the job was not completed, they asked if he would accept a reduction in his fee. He told them he would take his full fee and kill the inside source free of charge. They went back and forth several more times and eventually settled on

$750,000. When the money showed up in his Swiss account Gazich breathed a sigh of relief, but only for a second. The next day he called his banker and gave him instructions on how he wanted the money relocated. He then left New York and headed west by train to begin his ten-week journey home. Throughout his travels, Gazich couldn't shake the feeling that this entire affair was going to come back and bite him in the ass.

When he finally stepped off the boat in Limassol he couldn't help but smile. He'd traveled two thirds of the way around the planet and had done so without raising the suspicion of a single law enforcement or intelligence agency. Maybe his worries had been exaggerated. It wouldn't be the first time. Gazich threw his bag over his shoulder and threaded his way through the terminal toward the taxi line. He was suddenly eager to see a few familiar faces. To find out how things had been on the island, and most importantly, if anyone had been looking for him.

He powered up his cell phone and then punched in a local number. After a few rings a woman answered and Gazich said, "Andreas." He waited for the woman to get his landlord and joined the line of people waiting for a taxi. Gazich had talked to the landlord two days ago and had asked him if anyone had been looking for him. It was not an unusual question. Gazich often left on short notice and was sometimes gone for a month at a time. This trip was longer than usual, though, and Andreas had expressed some concern when he'd first checked in almost a month ago. Gazich answered by telling him he'd been detained in Darfur by some overzealous government soldiers. The main thing where Andreas was concerned was that he paid his rent on time and stay away from his daughters. Five of them worked in his café and they were all drop-dead gorgeous. Gazich's office was on the third floor above the café. When he was on the island he took his meals in the café almost every day.

"Hello," the voice said in Greek.

"My friend, how are you?"

"Ah . . . Gavrilo, are you finally home?"

"Yes."

"Good. Will I see you for dinner tonight?"

"Yes."

"What time?"

"Around nine. I have a few things to take care of first."

"I will save a table for you, and put aside your favorite bottle of retsina."

Before Gazich could respond, the old man hung up. He stared blankly at the phone for a second and then climbed in the waiting cab.

# 6

Ross was holding court in the corner of the vaulted living room, his back to the giant picture window. He looked like he was standing on the altar of one of those New Age churches that focused more on entertainment than theology. A six-foot-one, wafer-thin model hung on his every word as Ross spoke about environmentalism being the key to bringing the Middle East and the rest of the world together. A common ground that everyone could agree upon. The others all nodded in earnest and threw in an occasional comment of their own, but this was Ross's show. He was the new man of the hour.

"How is your president?" asked the model. She had a Dutch accent.

"The current one or the new one?"

"The new one."

Ross consciously hesitated before answering. "He's . . . he's hanging in there. He's a pretty tough guy."

"I can't imagine the pain," a slender older woman added. She tried to convey a sense of sadness, but her new face-lift prevented her from showing anything other than a look of permanent alertness.

"They seemed like they really loved each other," the model added.

"Yes, they did. Very much so."

"Enough melancholy," Speyer announced as he wedged his way into the semicircle. With a flippant wave of his wrist he said, "This is a party, and more importantly it is my party. I demand that you all start having fun."

The group relaxed a bit and cracked a few smiles. Several of the men laughed and begged Speyer for his forgiveness.

"I will consider it, but I will not tolerate boring or depressing conversation at my parties. Start having fun or I will not invite you next year." He said this with great theatrical flair and the group dispersed with the exception of Ross and the model.

"I have something I would like to show you, Mr. Vice President."

"And what would that be, Joseph?"

"My new wine cellar."

"May I join you, as well?" the model asked hopefully.

"I'm afraid not, my darling. Boys only." Speyer grabbed Ross by the arm and led him through the living room. A few people tried to stop them, but Speyer simply smiled and kept moving. They reached the entrance hall where Special Agent Brown and two other agents were standing watch by the front door. The agents watched their protectee and his host walk across the stone floor. Speyer opened a wooden door to what looked like a closet, but was actually an elevator.

Agent Brown turned to the man on his left. "You didn't tell me there was an elevator."

"I didn't *know* there was an elevator," the agent responded in an embarrassed tone. "I was told it was a closet."

Brown moved quickly, crossing the entrance hall in six long strides. "Mr. Speyer, where does this elevator go?"

"To my wine cellar."

"I'm fine, Michael."

Brown ignored the vice president–elect. "Is there another way to get to the wine cellar?"

"There is also a back staircase from the carport."

The wood paneled elevator door slid open. Before the two men could get in, Agent Brown stuck out his arm to block their path. "I'll need to clear the room first." Brown turned to the other two agents, but before he could motion them over, Ross stopped him.

"You'll do no such thing," Ross said firmly. "I have known Joseph for years. This place has a better security system than the White House. Go wait by the door and I'll call for you if I need you."

"But, sir, you know I can't allow you to enter a room without protection unless it has been checked."

"You can and you will. Now go stand by the door."

Brown hesitated briefly and then relented. He stepped out of the way and watched as the person he was charged with guarding stepped into a steel cage with a man Brown barely knew. The door slid shut, and somewhere behind the thick walls Brown could hear the electric motor of the elevator kick in. This entire trip was quickly becoming a textbook example of how not to run a security detail. Brown returned to the other two agents and began venting.

"I want you both to write this up before your heads hit the pillow tonight. Make it very clear that he has prevented us from doing our jobs." Brown looked back at the elevator and added, "Now go find that staircase and secure it."

• • • •

THIRTY FEET BENEATH the house the elevator came to a stop. The door retracted to reveal a huge underground cavern. They stepped onto a hewn stone slab that had been polished to a reflective sheen. In front of them was a vault with row upon row of wine racks. The dimension of the room, and the lack of any support columns shocked Ross more than the size of the wine collection.

"Joseph," was all he managed to say.

"I know. It took me three years, and it had to be done with the utmost secrecy."

"But why?"

"This is Zermatt, the heart of the environmentalist movement. This wine cellar is carved right into the mountain. The town would have never granted me permission for such a project. It was difficult enough to get my house built. I had to bribe and cajole every official and inspector in the valley."

Ross stepped forward and looked into the cavernous room. Expensive crystal chandeliers hung from the barrel vaulted ceiling every fifteen feet or so. Racks of wine jutted out from the wall on both sides like pews in a grand church. To his immediate left was a door, to his right, a wine tasting table and four leather chairs.

"How big is it?"

"One hundred feet deep by thirty feet wide."

"Amazing. How did you do it?"

"I brought in a family of Albanian miners. A father and four sons."

"How many bottles?"

From the shadows a voice answered, "Thirty thousand, give or take a few."

Midway down the cavern a man stepped from between the racks. He was wearing a blue blazer with gold buttons and an open-collar white shirt. His hair was brown and slicked back, which made it appear darker than it actually was. He was of average height, tan, and overweight in a way that could be attributed more to indulgence than neglect. His nose was by far the most prominent feature on an otherwise forgettable face.

"What are you holding there?" Speyer asked with uncharacteristic concern creeping into his voice.

"Oh . . . this?" The man flipped the bottle up in the air. It turned end over end twice and he caught it.

Speyer gasped, his entire body going rigid. "Please tell me that is not one of my forty-two Rothschild Château Moutons."

"No. It's one of your forty-one Château Moutons." The man spoke with a slight New York accent. "Isn't that the same year your father's friends rolled into France?"

"They were not my father's friends, and the year was nineteen forty." Speyer marched forward and took the extremely expensive bottle from the man's hands.

"I thought it was well documented that the Nazis carted off the Rothschilds' private collection during the war. It just seems a bit of a coincidence that the son of a Swiss banker would be in possession of so many rare bottles of wine."

"I can assure you," said a slightly more calm Speyer, "that I paid for every bottle of wine in this cellar. Most of it with the fees I earn by hiding your vast fortune from the U.S. government."

The man with the New York accent smiled broadly showing a set of freshly capped white teeth. "You are worth every penny, Joseph. Now how about we open one of these rare bottles in celebration of our victory?"

The banker hesitated for a second and then said, "I think that is a wonderful idea. An absolutely wonderful idea." Speyer was now nodding with enthusiasm. "I will decant it, and in the meantime I will find something significantly less expensive and infinitely more suitable to your boorish American palate." Speyer sauntered off, leaving the two Americans alone.

"Cy, you look well."

Cy Green was born in New York in 1950 to Jewish immigrants who had fled Hungary as the communists consolidated their power over the country in the wake of WWII. He'd made his first million by the age of twenty-five and his first billion by the age of thirty-five.

"Thank you," replied Green. "I've been on vacation for a long time now."

Ross grinned, but didn't dare laugh.

"Congratulations on winning the election," Green said with a raised brow.

"Thank you."

"How is my pardon coming?"

"We're working on it," Ross said.

"Working on it? That doesn't sound very convincing."

"Cy, I can't guarantee that I'm going to be able to pull this off."

"You were willing to give me guarantees three months ago when you were desperate."

"This is a delicate situation. If we push too hard it might backfire."

"If you don't push hard enough it might backfire," Green said with an edge. "And I mean really backfire."

"There's no need for threats."

"I have over one billion dollars in assets that have been frozen by the U.S. government, my companies in the States are paying fifty thousand dollars a day in contempt of court charges, and I have not set foot in the country I love in more than four years. My estate in Palm Beach, my penthouse in New York, my mansion in Beverly

Hills . . . all of them have been seized by the feds. My own children aren't even allowed to step foot in my homes."

The mix of vodka and recent success made Ross a bit braver than he normally would have been. "Maybe you should have thought of some of this before you started trading with the enemy. Not to mention committing fraud and tax evasion."

"Don't lecture me on the intricacies of multinational corporations," Green snapped. "I am the victim of an overzealous prosecutor."

"If that's the case, you should meet him in court with an army of high-priced lawyers and show him for the hack that you claim him to be."

Green was not used to anyone speaking to him in such a way. Especially someone who was so indebted to him. He was about to blow his lid when Speyer returned with two glasses of wine.

"One of your countrymen sent me a case of this. Caymus Vineyards nineteen ninety-four Special Selection Cabernet. A perfectly fine table wine to be served at one of your backyard barbecues. But not at one of my parties."

Green took his glass and said, "Joseph, I think you will need to leave us alone for a few more minutes."

"Certainly. I will go put on some music."

When the host was far enough away, Green's face twisted into a questioning frown and he said, "You are either drunk or you have grown awfully proud of yourself."

"It's probably a bit of both." Ross smiled. "I am after all the vice president—elect of the United States of America." He held up his glass in a toast to himself.

Green ignored the glass. "And how did you get there? Do you think for a minute that Josh would have picked you for a running mate if his father-in-law hadn't told him to do so? His father-in-law . . . my real estate partner."

"Cy, let's not make a big deal out of this. We're . . ."

Green cut him off. "I told him if we put you on the ticket, you could make our problems go away, and guess what? I got you on the ticket and then I had to save your ass a second time. Now it's your turn to deliver."

Suddenly Ross wished he had been sober for this meeting. He could use a clear head right about now. "I'm sure your partner would find it interesting to know that you had his daughter killed."

Green clenched his jaw and took a half step back. "I suppose you've deluded yourself into thinking that you played no part in that entire affair."

"I most certainly did. I almost died."

"You're unbelievable. You're more self-absorbed than I am."

Ross took a sip of his wine. "I think we were beginning to close in the polls. I think we could have . . ."

"I think you're an idiot!" snapped Green. "You were not closing in the polls, and even if you had been, they would have released the photos of Jillian, that little slut, giving a blowjob to a damn Secret Service agent. Now the American people might have loosened their morals a bit over the years, but they sure as hell aren't about to accept a whore as their First Lady."

"Those photos could have just as easily backfired, if they had re-leased them."

"You really are delusional." Green laughed. "Need I remind you of the frantic phone call I received from you with one month to go in the campaign? Your pit bull of a campaign manager had received the photo of Jillian having the sword put to her by the hired help."

"He was a Secret Service agent."

"Exactly . . . and on the back of that photo someone had writ-ten the words, *You'll never win.* Do you remember the phone call you made? Do you remember that you were practically in tears? Do you remember saying we should have the bitch killed?"

Green was five inches shorter and he got right up in Ross's face. "Go right ahead and convince yourself that you had nothing to do with this. It's probably a good place to be when you're dealing with other people, but when you're with me, drop the attitude. You're a motherfucker just like I am. The only difference between the two of us is that I'm under no illusion to the contrary."

"I have devoted the last twelve years of my life to public service, and I most certainly . . ."

"You've devoted your entire life to yourself. You didn't run for the Senate because you wanted to help people. You ran for the Senate to feed your ego. So don't stand here and try and sell me a load of crap. I know exactly who you are even if you don't."

"You know, Cy, a little gratitude might go a long way."

"Gratitude for what? For being allowed to stand in your presence? Are you fucking kidding me? The only person who should be showing any gratitude right now is you. I'm the one who got you elected. You haven't done shit. I'll show you my gratitude when you get my pardon signed a week from today."

Ross nodded. "I'm working on it, but we might need more time."

"You don't get more time. You assured me you could get President Hayes to sign the pardon, so get him to sign it next Saturday with all the others."

"I'll make it happen," Ross said because he knew it was the only answer Green would accept. Wanting to change the direction of the conversation he asked, "The man you hired . . . have you taken care of him yet?"

"I'm working on it. Why?"

"The FBI knows he exists."

"Do they know he was the trigger man?"

"No, but it's not worth leaving it up to chance. He needs to be taken care of."

"Don't worry about him." Green pointed a finger at Ross. "Just worry about getting me my pardon."

Ross took a big gulp of wine and smiled. He had no guarantees that he could get Green his pardon. In fact, if he had to guess, it was more likely that President Hayes would turn them down flat, which would mean that Josh Alexander would have to start out his term with an extremely controversial pardon. Either way, this would not be easy. There was one other option that occurred to Ross. He looked into Green's eyes and held up his glass.

"To your pardon."

"To my pardon." Green clanged his glass against Ross's. "I'll drink to that."

Ross smiled and thought to himself, *and may you die of some tragic accident before next Saturday.*

# 7

Rapp was careful to stand back from the window. He looked through the telephoto lens and adjusted the focus. A second man entered the frame. Rapp's right index finger pressed the trigger halfway down, and the digital camera automatically adjusted the focus. He pressed the button all the way down and snapped off two quick images. With a deep exhale he lowered the camera, but kept his eyes on the street.

A frown creased his brow and he said, "Who the fuck are these guys?"

He'd been asking himself that question since mid-afternoon, and he wasn't any closer to an answer. The photos had been sent back to Marcus Dumond at Langley so he could run them through the facial recognition system, but so far they'd come up with nothing. The system worked well when you could narrow the parameters a bit, but Rapp didn't have a clue where these guys came from or for whom they worked. Rapp told Dumond to start with the assumption that they were local cops, so the cyber tech hacked into the Limassol Police Department database. Dumond ran through the personnel files and came up with nothing. Then it was on to the national police, and after that the Hellenic National Intelligence Service. Again they came up with nothing.

Rapp had spent time in Cyprus before. Most of it in Nicosia, the capital of the Greek side of the island. The Northeastern side was controlled by the Turks. Geographically, Cyprus had occupied a position of great strategic importance throughout history. It dominated the eastern end of the Mediterranean. For thousands of years the island had been fought over due to its value in controlling the sea-lanes between Europe, the Middle East, and North Africa. The Phoenicians, Assyrians, Greeks, Persians, Egyptians, Romans, Arabs, the Frankish Lusignan dynasty, Venetians, Ottoman Turks, and many lesser-known countries had all controlled the island at one point or another throughout recorded history. Because of its significance to the trade routes, the island had also long been favored by outlaws. Real pirates and slave traders and their modern day cousins; narco traffickers, mafiosi, and now terrorists. After 9/11 it was discovered that Cyprus was one of Osama bin Laden's favored banking venues. The island was famous for its seedy underbelly, which only deepened the mystery of who these guys might be.

The only thing Rapp did know for sure was that he had spotted three of them. To do really good surveillance you needed bodies and gadgets. Rapp was in short supply of both at the moment. He'd sent Brooks to pick up Coleman and his men from the airport. He could have asked Kennedy to send some bodies from the embassy in Nicosia, but there was a real downside to going that route. It was likely the ambassador would end up catching wind that the CIA was running an operation in his backyard, which would lead to him throwing a shit fit and calling the State Department, and then the whole thing was likely to spin out of control. The key with these operations was to move slow and stay off everyone's radar screen if at all possible.

On the gadget front, Rapp wished he'd at least brought along a parabolic mike so he could hear what these guys were saying to each other. Since they were flying commercial, Rapp had made the decision not to load himself and Brooks down with surveillance kits. It was hard enough to sneak a gun, a silencer, and two extra clips of ammunition into a country. The electronic listening devices, scopes, cameras, scanners, and parabolic mikes took up a lot of room and raised a lot of eyebrows. It simply wasn't the type of stuff newlyweds brought on their honeymoon. Coleman and his boys were in charge of transferring that stuff and they were doing it under the guise of a director doing location scouts for a film. They had business cards with the name of a development company, an address in Beverly Hills, and a phone number with a 310 area code that was answered by a woman in Langley, Virginia.

The sun was setting over the Eastern Mediterranean. There was maybe another ten minutes of sunlight at best. In this part of old town the streets were narrow and winding, so the shadows were already falling across large areas of the street and sidewalk cafés below. The hotel was four stories high and Rapp was on the top floor. The contact in Istanbul had said the man they were looking for used a front company called Aid Logistics Inc, the office of which was located on the third story of the stone building directly across the street. The first floor was the café and the second floor was a real estate company. There was no alley behind the building so the only way in was through the front door of the café and then up the stairs to the right. Rapp knew this because he'd visited the real estate office earlier in the afternoon and walked to the landing between the second and third floors before coming back down.

Rapp watched an old man come out of the café located below Aid Logistics Inc and the real estate office. As best Rapp could figure, this guy was the owner. He wore a white apron and doled out a lot of orders to the wait staff. The man walked down the sidewalk to where the sedan was parked and began talking with the two occupants. This was the first time Rapp had seen the old man converse with these guys.

Stakeouts all had their own vibe. Their own rhythm. Most of them were literally as boring as watching paint dry. Sometimes the subject knew he was being watched and he tried to lull you to sleep so he could make his move. That's what the real pros did. You could watch them all day and have no idea that they'd done two dead drops and a pickup. It was like they had eyes in the back of their heads. Which was partially true. Like Wayne Gretzky, gifted hockey players had a bird's-eye image in their mind of where everyone was on the ice at all times. The great spies had the same ability, but in an infinitely more complex and dangerous game. They remembered faces and shoes and pants. Things that were hard to change. They ignored hats, glasses, jackets, and facial hair. Things that were easy to change. They cataloged each face that passed them and anticipated not just the actions of those in front of them, but those behind them. Even people they couldn't see.

Very few criminals were actually that good. Most had no idea they were being watched, but more importantly, they knew on some level they were doing something illegal. And in many of these countries they were doing something that could result in having their head separated from the rest of their body. Under this type of pressure, it was next to impossible to stay relaxed and normal as you prepared to do whatever it was that might get you killed. Whether it was making a dead drop, meeting a contact, or preparing to grab someone, it didn't matter. People's body language changed. Their pace quickened and their moves became more rushed and sporadic.

Rapp had noticed the pace of things below begin to pick up over the last hour or so. He was watching the body language of the café owner and the other man standing next to the car. He was trying to read their lips, but he couldn't make out what they were saying. It did look like they were speaking English, though, which Rapp found interesting.

Rapp's mobile phone started ringing. It was lying on the bed, but he didn't bother to leave the window. He had a tiny Motorola wireless earpiece stuck in his right ear. With his longer hair it was nearly impossible to detect the device, which picked up his voice through vibration in the ear canal. Rapp tapped the end of the device and asked, "What's up?"

"We just landed."

It was Scott Coleman. Rapp wanted to ask him what in the hell had taken so long, but he didn't bother. "Brooks rented a blue mini-van. She's waiting at the curb."

"We're stuck on the tarmac."

"What do you mean stuck?"

"There's another plane at our gate. We can't pull up to the gate until it leaves, and then we have to wait for our luggage."

Rapp watched the big man standing next to the car put his arm around the older man in the apron. As the big guy moved to put something in the shirt pocket of the old guy, Rapp pressed the trigger on the camera and held it all the way down. The camera clicked off six photos in quick succession. The big man then patted the café owner on the cheek several times before releasing him.

Rapp frowned as he watched the older man walk back into the café. He looked down at the viewing screen on the back of the camera and toggled back a few frames. He then increased the zoom until he could see what the man had placed in the owner's pocket. It was cash. Cops, for the most part, didn't go around stuffing cash in people's pockets. Especially in this part of the world, where they could throw someone in jail for a week by simply making up a reason.

"Did you hear me?" asked Coleman.

"Yeah." Rapp looked at the horizon. Nightfall was fast approaching and when the darkness came something was going to happen. "Have one of your guys wait for the luggage. I need you to get your ass here ASAP."

# 8

Retsina is a Greek wine that is preserved with pine resin. To some deluded Greek nationalists it is the wine of the gods. To anyone who has ever tasted a decent bottle of French Bordeaux, retsina is about as enjoyable as drinking turpentine. Gazich hated retsina, and so did Andreas. The old man's promise that he would set aside his best bottle of retsina could have been taken as an attempt at humor. One friend ribbing another, but Andreas did not stay on the line to listen to his tenant's response. He didn't even laugh. He hung up right after taking his shot. That was not Andreas's style. He liked to goad and tease.

Something was wrong. Gazich could feel it. His house was in the hills on the outskirts of Limassol. He was tempted to go there first, but he resisted the urge. He had the cab drive him by his office nice and slow, but not too slow. He saw the man sitting behind the wheel of the parked car and the other man on the sidewalk. Gazich then asked the driver to take him to the Amathus Beach Hotel where he checked into a room, cleaned up, and plotted his next move.

Gazich was not someone who was quick to anger. He was more apt to stew over things and let them come to a boil. That was what happened while he ate his dinner on the private balcony of his hotel room. In his mind it was already a foregone conclusion that these assholes who had hired him had decided to go back on their word. There was a chance that the law had come looking for him, but it was slim. Gazich had followed the FBI's investigation in the press and their was no mention of them looking for a lone trigger man. Everything coming out of Washington suggested that they were going after several terrorist groups. Gazich did not have a complete sense of the FBI's capabilities, but he did know it was next to impossible for them to run an investigation without leaking to the press.

Running would be the smart thing to do. He had over three million stashed in various banks around Europe and the Mediterranean. Invested properly, he could live in relative luxury in any third world country of his choosing for the rest of his days. He had grown attached to Cyprus, though. His house, his office, the lax banking laws. It was the perfect fit. An island nation unto itself. The more Gazich thought about it, the angrier he became, and not just at his double-crossing employer, but at himself. Why had he been in such a rush to take their money? The answer was obvious. The money. He should have followed that old axiom—if it sounds too good to be true, it probably is.

There was the issue of Andreas and his family to consider. Gazich could only guess what kind of pressure was being put on him. They were good people trying to make an honest living, and now they were sucked into this lethal drama. The easy thing for

Gazich would have been to leave the island. Hop on the first ferry in the morning and forget about Cyprus, his assets, and the friendships he'd forged there, but he was tired of running. For over ten weeks he'd been packing and unpacking every few days. Running may have been the smart thing to do, but it was also the cowardly thing to do.

Gazich was no coward. Never had been. Never would be. He knew he was a thrill seeker. Someone who needed action. Someone who often liked to choose the path of most resistance. He did it to test his skills. He did it to prove that he was better than all the others. He needed to prove he was king of the jungle. In DC he had gone elephant hunting. Here on Cyprus he was going to turn the tables on the hunters.

The objective was survival. The side game would be to kill these men without getting caught or even raising the attention of the local authorities. One more body dumped in the Mediterranean was nothing. Although a couple of men killed on the sidewalk in front of Andreas's café might actually be good for business. Either way, the end game was to find the man, or men, who had hired him, and kill them. That was the only way to finish it. The tricky part would be keeping one of these guys alive long enough to get something useful out of him.

Gazich checked his watch. It was a Saturday night, which in Limassol meant the dance clubs and bars would get hopping soon. He would have to make one stop and then by the time he arrived at the café things would be nice and busy. These men would never know what hit them.

# 9

As darkness fell on the old part of town, things seemed to come to life. Music floated up from the cafés below. People were heading in every direction, darting across the street, dodging the scooters, taxis, and cars. Laughter and lively conversation could be heard as couples and groups lined up at the various establishments to wait for a table. Rapp kept the lights off in his room. The window was actually a skinny French door that opened inward. A black ornamental railing ran from waist height to the floor, providing the illusion of a balcony.

To help fight boredom and keep himself alert, Rapp dropped to the floor every fifteen minutes and did either push-ups or sit-ups. The alternative was drinking profuse amounts of coffee, but that also meant frequent trips to the bathroom. He still had five pounds to lose from his six-month binge, so he opted for the exercise. His eyes casually swept the scene from one end of the block to the

other. Every vehicle and pedestrian was noted. He paid special attention to those heading in to the café across the street, and of
course the man sitting in the car near the café. Earlier in the day he
spotted the other two men getting off the elevator in the hotel
lobby. Until reinforcements arrived, all Rapp could really do was sit
and wait. He'd spoken to Coleman twice since he and his men
had landed. He was finally in the van with Brooks and on his way
here.

Rapp checked his watch. It was eight minutes past nine.
They should be arriving any minute. A car horn sounded at the
far end of the street. Rapp shifted from one side of the open window to the other and scanned the scene. A man and a woman were
standing in the middle of the one-way street. The man was flipping
off the driver of the car and screaming in Greek. From Rapp's angle,
he spotted a lone man enter the picture on the far sidewalk. Something about this guy made Rapp give him a second look. He was
dressed in the hip nightclub style of the younger generation, with
faded and ripped designer jeans, retro track shoes, a blue warm-up
jacket, and a John Deere baseball hat. The baseball hat was pulled
down low, the collar on his jacket was turned up, and he had his
hands stuffed in the pockets. His head was slowly, almost impercep-
tibly, sweeping from left to right. Rapp's mind thought back to
those twenty-seven seconds of surveillance footage from the Starbucks in Georgetown. The average person could glean very little
from that tape, but for Rapp it was a treasure trove of information—
a virtual admission of guilt by the mystery man captured buying an
espresso.

At first glance, the man on the tape seemed very casual. Rapp
looked at things a little differently, though. Like a magician watching another magician, Rapp knew what to look for because he had
been there before. In a foreign land, on an operation, trying to bide

time until the hit took place. He had acted in almost the same manner: baseball hat pulled down low to block surveillance cameras, physical demeanor relaxed, yet alert. Eyes always scanning and on guard.

"Is that you, Alexander?" Rapp whispered to himself, while he leaned back slightly.

Without taking his eyes off the man, Rapp brought the camera to his eye and snapped a few photos as the man approached. The moment of truth was fast approaching. Would he turn into the café and go to his office or would he circle the block and check things out? Rapp knew what he would do and was slightly disappointed when the man stopped in front of the café. He started talking to the old man who was standing at the hostess stand. Rapp had a sudden pang of anxiety. He needed this guy alive. With his back to him Rapp could now see the man's warm-up jacket had a white Adidas logo across the back. Rapp's eyes slid to the man sitting no more than forty feet away in the parked car. He hadn't moved a muscle.

The guy in the Adidas jacket lit a cigarette and continued talking to the old man, then kissed him on both cheeks and walked away. Everything about the guy matched the surveillance footage, except the cigarette. But then again, he wouldn't have been able to smoke a cigarette while waiting in line at a Starbucks in the United States. The man in the John Deere hat threaded his way through a few pedestrians who were waiting to get into the café. Rapp relaxed a bit, but kept an eye on him. He lowered the camera and wondered if this was actually the guy he was after, or if he was reading too far into things. He rubbed his eyes and checked his watch again.

When he looked back down at the street he saw something totally unexpected. The man in the Adidas jacket suddenly veered toward the parked car with the guy sitting in the front seat. Rapp hastily brought the camera up and hit the auto focus button. The image of the pedestrian and the car came into focus. The glow of the street lamps threw off enough light that he could see what was going on, but Rapp worried that there might not be enough light for the camera to capture any clear images. Suddenly, the pedestrian began waving to the guy sitting in the parked car. As he got closer to the vehicle he casually bent over so he could see through the open driver's side window. It was a one-way street and the car was parked facing the café on the same side of the street. The man in the car was sitting in the front passenger seat, probably so he had more legroom.

Rapp realized what was going on only a second or two before it happened. He twisted the lens as far as it would go and held the trigger down. The high-speed digital camera began clicking away at the rate of six frames per second. In the faint light, he glimpsed the man in the hat reaching into the car and then there was an ever-so-brief flash. Not the white flash of a camera, but the yellow flash of a muzzle. Rapp took his finger off the camera's trigger and stood completely still. He didn't want to miss what would happen next. Three seconds went by and then five. Rapp counted to ten and the man in the hat was still at the car window chatting away, moving his hands like he was telling an involved story.

Rapp lowered the camera and said, "You're talking to a dead man, aren't you?" He shook his head and said, "You're going to stand there and act like nothing happened, and then you'll slowly put your gun back in your pants and walk away."

Rapp watched all of this unfold with sincere professional admiration. This guy had a set of balls on him. What he had just witnessed verified his suspicions. The terrorists who paid to have Alexander and Ross killed were not happy with the services

Alexander Deckas had provided them and now they wanted him dead. It was not unusual in this line of work. In a sense, the business arrangement was a bit like a man leaving his wife for the woman he's been having an affair with. The fact that the same man decides to then cheat on the woman he originally cheated with should surprise no one, least of all the woman herself.

Rapp watched as the assassin stood up and stepped away from the car. He then waved at the dead man sitting in it and started back down the street. Rapp quickly glanced back toward the café to see if anyone was following him. The big guy he'd spotted earlier in the day was nowhere to be seen. Only the old man appeared to notice what had just happened. Rapp's eyes glided back to the man in the John Deere hat. He expected him to turn the corner and vanish, maybe lose the jacket and hat and come back around for a shot at the other two should they appear. The urge to follow was strong, but with so many unknowns it was not wise. This was Deckas's neighborhood. He would know every crack and crevice, and there was no telling who he might have working for him.

The assassin surprised Rapp by entering the last building on the street. It looked like it was probably an apartment building.

"What the fuck?" Rapp muttered to himself.

He scanned the apartment building and noted the windows where lights were on. After thirty seconds not a single light had been turned on or off. Something told Rapp it would be a good idea to move further away from the window. He took two steps back. If this guy had a night vision scope, he could be sitting in one of the dark apartments scanning the hotel to see who was watching. If Rapp were in his shoes, that was exactly what he would be doing. Rapp took another step to the side and looked at the screen on the back of the camera. Using his right thumb he spun the wheel and scrolled through the photos. When he got to the right sequence he tightened the frame. The quality wasn't great, but he could make out what looked like an arm coming through the window of the car and extending across the front seat. He went back one more photo and the screen went bright with a muzzle flash. Suddenly, everything was much clearer. Rapp could now make out a gun with a silencer attached to the end.

This had to be Alexander Deckas, and if he knew about the guy in the car it was likely he knew about the other two men who were looking for him. That was where his focus would be—either trying to avoid them or coming to kill them. Based on what he had just witnessed, Rapp felt it was the latter. But why the apartment building? Rapp thought back to the big guy who earlier in the day he had spied stuffing money in the shirt pocket of the old man who ran the café. The old man did not appear overjoyed to be talking to the goon. It was likely that they had leaned on him. Probably threatened him in some way. The old guy had several choices at that point: play along, go to the authorities, or tip off his tenant. And if the tenant was in fact Alexander Deckas, or whatever his real name was, and the old man knew what he did for a living, why wouldn't he go to him? Rapp had just watched him dispatch a hired gun in the middle of a busy commercial district without raising even the slightest suspicion.

Rapp's thoughts were interrupted by the ringing of his phone. He assumed it was Coleman or Brooks so he pressed the button on the earpiece and said, "Where are you guys?"

"It's Marcus, Mitch."

Marcus Dumond was a computer expert who worked Counterterrorism for Langley.

"What's up?" asked Rapp.

"I just spoke to a buddy at the DGSE." Dumond was referring

to the Direction Generale de la Securité Exterieure, France's top external intelligence organization. "They have a line on this Alexander Deckas. They say his real name is Gavrilo Gazich. He's a Bosnian who cut his teeth during that nasty little thing they had over there."

Rapp stepped away from the wall and looked out the window. "Lovely. What else did they tell you?"

"He's wanted in The Hague."

"For war crimes?" Rapp asked somewhat surprised. "How old is he?"

"Thirty-five."

"Well he couldn't have been more than a grunt when they were killing each other back in the mid-nineties." Rapp checked the windows on the apartment building across the street. "Why in the hell would they mess with someone so far down the chain of command?"

"He was a sniper. I guess he shot over fifty civilians when they laid siege to Sarajevo."

Rapp's entire body went rigid for a split second and then he casually walked away from the window. It took him a few seconds before he even took a breath, and then he swore out loud.

"What's wrong?" asked Dumond.

"Next time you might want to get to that part first."

"What part?"

"Never mind," Rapp growled. "What else do you have on him?"

"He's rumored to have operated in Africa, mostly the east side . . . Sudan, Ethiopia, Uganda, but they don't have anything concrete on him."

"How about a photo?"

"Yeah, but it's not very good."

"Good enough to give us a match on the surveillance tape?"

"Not a definite, but it doesn't exclude him either."

"All right. Send this stuff over to the Africa Division and see what they have on him."

"Will do."

"And see if you can get the evidence The Hague has on him. I want to know how good of a shot he is."

"I'll get on it."

"Good work, Marcus."

Rapp pressed the button on the earpiece and disconnected the call. Very few things rattled him, but snipers were one of them. Sneaky little bastards. The good ones could kill you from nearly a mile away. That was hardly a fair fight. Rapp sat motionless in the dark hotel room and tried to process the new information. Would this guy have any idea Rapp was looking for him? The answer was probably not. Rapp had been very careful, and other than Coleman's team and a few select people in Washington, no one knew he was on the case.

Rapp wondered if there was a chance these other guys had worked with Gazich in the past. Maybe, but for some reason Rapp doubted it. These assassins were usually loners out of necessity. They couldn't afford to trust anyone else. Rapp had met the type before: former soldiers and paramilitary types, who always performed better on their own than they did within a unit. Rapp knew because he was one of them. Then there were also what the CIA euphemistically called thugs, drugs, and outlaws. Guys who came out of the ranks of organized crime and the drug cartels. These guys typically didn't operate alone. They traveled in packs like hyenas.

It was the old man. He was the key. These goons, whoever they were, had leaned on him, and like a good Greek, the old man played along all the while plotting their demise. He alerted his tenant, who just happened to be an assassin, that these guys were looking for him and now the problem was in the process of going away in a very permanent manner. What would Gazich's next move be? If he was in fact a trained sniper, his options were plentiful. The specter of this guy sitting on the rooftop of the apartment building with a high-powered rifle and night scope made the hair on the back of Rapp's neck stand up.

It occurred to Rapp that the other two guys probably were not as disciplined as he was. It was likely that they were sitting around, with the lights on, watching TV and waiting for their guy on the street to let them know the target had showed up. Rapp moved to the edge of the window and looked down at the car. He could barely make out the silhouette of the dead man sitting in the front seat. Nothing had changed. No one had gone down to investigate. With only his left eye peering out from the edge of the curtain, Rapp scanned the roofline of the apartment building that Gazich had entered a few minutes ago. Everything looked normal. At least as far as he could tell, but a good sniper would have no problem concealing his position. The possibility occurred to Rapp that the other two guys might already be dead. If the angle was right, and they had their window opened like Rapp did, it would be an easy shot.

Rapp was scanning the rooftop again when a flash of movement caught his eye. Someone was on the roof next to the apartment building. Rapp's room was on the fourth floor of the hotel. All of the buildings across the street were three stories high and their flat roofs pretty much matched up to within a few feet of each other. Rapp saw the movement again. Someone was moving from Rapp's left to right, toward the café. Rapp leaned out to get a better look and saw a shadowy figure make the short hop from the building onto the roof where Gazich's business was located.

Rapp smiled as he realized his instincts had been correct. When he'd checked out the building earlier in the day he questioned why their guy would set up shop on the third floor of a building that had no side or back alley. The only way out was through the front door. Not exactly code back in the States, but over here where the streets had been laid out thousands of years ago, they had to make do. It was almost unthinkable for a guy like Gazich to back himself into a corner with no avenue of escape. The answer was that he hadn't. Gazich's escape route was the roof. From there his options were plentiful.

Rapp's eyes searched the darkness for more movement, but there was none. The roof was dotted with air-conditioning units as well as some ventilation pipes and a few other things. He assumed Gazich was hiding behind one of them, or that he had crawled over to the edge where there was a lip. Suddenly, the front left window on the third floor lit up. A few seconds later the silhouette of a man appeared on the cream colored shade. Rapp realized the access hatch must be located behind one of the air-conditioning units.

"Why the hell would you turn on that light?" Rapp asked himself.

The silhouette moved about, disappearing and then coming back into view. It looked like he was gathering something. Even so, Gazich had to know these guys were watching him. This made no sense. He could have easily snuck in, used a small penlight to get what he needed, and go back out through the roof without anyone ever knowing he'd been there.

Rapp was stuck on the stupidity of this when he suddenly realized what was going on. There was almost no time to react. Grabbing his phone off the bed, he stuffed his arms into his jacket and rushed for the door.

# 10

―――――

"Russians," Gazich growled to himself. "Goddamn Russians."

He stood, bent at the waist, his forearms draped across the open window-frame of the car, his gun dangling out of site in his right hand.

Gazich hated Russians almost as much as he hated Muslims. The two groups had ruined his ethnic homeland: the Muslims with their all-or-nothing, backward religion and the Russians with their arrogant, clumsy, bullying, pagan ways. Bosnia could have been so much more if only they'd left her alone. But of course they hadn't. The Muslims had encroached from the southeast and the Russians from the northeast. The Muslims did so slowly over centuries, while the Russians swept in after WWII and took everything by force. While Western Europe flourished, communist Yugoslavia suffered.

The Russians were now gone and the Muslims had either been killed or turned into refugees.

Gazich looked at the dead man and resisted the urge to spit on him. Leaving DNA at the scene of a crime was not a wise move. He had shot the man once in the heart and then a second time because he was so pissed. He'd wanted to shoot him in the head, but given the relatively public environment he was in it was ill-advised. The man even smelled Russian. He reeked of cheap cologne and unfiltered cigarettes.

"What are you . . . KGB or Russian mob? Not that there's a big difference anymore. I should shoot you again," Gazich muttered.

He honestly didn't know what upset him more; the man's nationality or that the people who had hired him to do the job in the States thought so little of him that they had sent a Russian to kill him. Gazich casually took a drag of his cigarette and slipped the tip of the silencer into the waistband of his pants. With his right hand he pulled the bottom of his jacket over the gun. He spotted a small two-way radio on the seat and decided it might come in handy. After stuffing it in his pocket, he stood and took a step back. As he waved good-bye to the dead man, he pushed the gun further into his pants and looked up at the hotel across the street and to his left. About half the rooms were lit up.

Gazich had surreptitiously stopped by the café owner's house earlier in the day. He had come in through the garden even though he doubted the Russians had enough men to watch both his office and the old man's house. Gazich told Andreas that he was sorry he'd been caught up in the middle of this. Andreas accepted the apology and then eagerly agreed to do whatever he could to rid himself of these Russians. He told Gazich everything he knew about them including the fact that they had two rooms on the third floor of the hotel directly across the street.

A quick survey of the windows told Gazich they were every bit as lazy as he expected them to be. No one was keeping an eye on the street. Who knew with Russians, there was a very good chance they were already drunk. The Bosnian stuffed his hands in his pockets and started down the street with renewed anger. Part of him wanted to march over to the hotel, kick in their door, and shoot them in the head, but as tempted as he was, he needed to talk to them. He needed to find out who had sent them.

Two doors down, Gazich entered an apartment building and proceeded to the top floor. At the back of the building, in a maintenance closet, there was a metal ladder screwed into the wall. Gazich climbed it and popped the hatch that led to the roof. He pulled himself up, lowered the hatch, and started working his way toward his building. He stayed in a crouch, not because he was worried that someone would see him, but because he was afraid he'd walk into a clothesline. A minute later he knelt next to the hatch that accessed his building. Gazich lifted it up and descended into the darkness, closing the hatch behind him. He was now in the center hall at the rear of the building. He walked toward the front and pulled out his cell phone. He punched in the number for the café and after a few rings one of the daughters answered. A half a minute after that the patriarch was on the phone.

"Hello?" the old man answered.

Andreas had told him the phones were tapped, but at this point Gazich didn't care. "Andreas, it is me, Alexander. How are you?" Gazich slid his key into his office door and turned the lock.

"Fine, my friend. Are you coming to see me?"

"Yes. In fact I'm up in my office." Gazich hit the light switch. "I have a little work to do and then I'll be down for a drink."

"Good. I'll see you when I see you."

Gazich put his phone away and looked around his office. Everything was not as he had left it. They had tried to put things back, but they were too sloppy to do it right. In addition to the slight disorder he could smell their cigarettes. They had been so arrogant they actually smoked while pilfering his stuff. Gazich continued surveying the room. There was a large wood desk with the usual stuff on top: a lamp, an old Rolodex, computer monitor, keyboard, mouse, and phone. The walls were lined with bookcases. Gazich turned to look back at the door. That was when he noticed something. It was a motion sensor placed just above the trim board by the floor.

"Good," he said aloud. "We can get this over with sooner rather than later."

Gazich grabbed the two-way radio and clipped it to his belt. Next, he moved the coat rack next to the desk and draped his jacket around the top pegs. To finish it off he set his baseball hat on top and turned on the desk lamp. The radio on his hip crackled to life and a male voice began speaking in Russian. Gazich didn't know Russian, but he didn't need to. He knew what they were asking. Two similar radios sat in a charger on the bookcase across from the desk. Gazich grabbed one, turned it on, and set it to the same channel as the one he'd take from the dead Russian. Next, he held them within inches of each other and pressed the transmit buttons. High-pitched feedback squawked from each box, creating an extremely irritating noise.

Gazich released the transmit buttons and walked back out into the hallway. He closed the frosted glass door and inspected his work. The silhouette of the jacket and hat on the coat rack wasn't perfect, but it would be enough to confuse them. The two-way erupted again, with an angry Russian voice yelling what Gazich guessed were curses. The Bosnian held the devices next to each other one more time and let loose a blast of feedback. As he walked to the window, he pressed the button one more time and then turned his attention to the entrance of the hotel across the street. Five seconds later two large men came tearing out the front door shoving a pedestrian out of their way. One of them was still struggling with his jacket, a shoulder holstered pistol clearly visible against his off-white shirt.

With pure professional disdain, Gazich shook his head and positioned himself for the ambush.

# 11

Rapp turned the phone to vibrate mode, dialed Coleman's number, and stuffed the phone in the breast pocket of his coat. As he grabbed the door handle with his right hand his left hand slid around to the small of his back and gripped the handle of his Glock 19 pistol. Rapp drew the weapon and looked through the peephole to make sure no one was waiting outside his door. With the gun at the ready, he flipped the dead bolt and opened the door. A stubby suppressor added another three inches to the gun. He did a quick check of the hallway, slid the gun into a specially designed pocket on the inside right side of his jacket, and moved out. Rapp bypassed the elevator and went straight for the staircase. As he opened the fire door, Coleman's voice came over his wireless earpiece.

"Brooks says we're five to ten minutes out. Traffic's pretty bad."

"This whole damn thing might be over by the time you get here."

Rapp had just reached the first step when he heard a commotion from below.

"What do you mean it might be over?" Coleman asked.

Rapp couldn't answer right away. Two men burst into the stairwell one floor beneath. One of them was speaking loudly in Russian. He recognized one of them as the man who had shoved money in the old man's shirt earlier in the evening. It was exactly as Rapp had feared. Gazich had already killed one of them, and now he was drawing these two into a trap.

"What's going on?" Coleman asked.

Rapp waited for the two men to get to the second landing before he whispered his reply. "I think we've got an unsatisfied customer."

"What in the hell are you talking about?"

"I'll explain it when you get here." Rapp started down the stairs. "That is, if I'm still alive."

"Slow down, Mitch. You're not making any sense."

"Tell Brooks to call Marcus so he can bring her up to speed on who this Deckas guy really is, and tell him the guys in the surveillance photos are Russian." Rapp hit the next flight.

"Where are you?"

Rapp glanced over the railing as the two men hit the first floor landing. "I'm in the hotel following two Russian idiots who are about to get killed."

"Just wait until we get there."

The men hit the fire door hard and burst into the lobby.

"You don't think I can take care of myself?" Rapp bounded down the steps two at a time, now that he was the only one in the stairwell.

"That's not what I said. You're going into this blind with no backup. That is not what I would call a prudent tactical decision."

Rapp laughed. "You SEALs are all such pussies."

"Don't make this about some macho bullshit. Just hang tight for a few more minutes."

As Rapp hit the first floor landing he could hear Coleman yelling at Brooks to step on it. He pushed the fire door open and entered the lobby.

"Two minutes okay?" Coleman pleaded.

"Sorry buddy, the train is leaving the station. I need to make sure these idiots don't all kill each other." Rapp walked casually through the lobby so as to not raise any unwanted attention. This was not difficult due to the fact that everyone was staring at the two bulls squeezing through the turnstile door. "Just stay on the line," Rapp said, "and I'll keep you appraised as best I can."

Rapp calmly smiled at the bellman as he reached the door. Out in front of the hotel one of the Russians was stopped in the middle of the street trying to get the attention of his friend sitting in the parked car. The other Russian was already across the street and yelling at the man to follow him. Rapp continued to give Coleman the tactical update as he waited for a car to pass. He watched as the Russians bullied their way through the crowd of people waiting to get into the café. Rapp moved to the left and crossed between a row of parked scooters. He avoided the dozen-plus people standing by the hostess stand. While all of the patrons were focused on the commotion caused by the two rude men shoving their way through the crowd, Rapp stepped over the sagging, faded, velvet rope that formed the perimeter of the patio. He discretely threaded his way through the tight tables and bobbed his head to avoid the corners of table umbrellas.

Rapp checked the patio to see if the old man was about, but he was nowhere to be found. This thing was going to go one of two ways. Either bad or good. Rapp was not exactly sure how he was going to proceed, but he had a rough idea what his rules of engagement were going to be. The Russians were now pressing through the front door of the restaurant. Through the large plate glass window Rapp watched them start up the stairs to the right. With a dose of caution he slid through the front door and resisted the urge to follow them. Going up a set of stairs blind like this was a good way to get shot, which Rapp presumed was exactly what was about to happen to them.

Straight ahead the old man was conversing with a table of customers, but it was obvious his concern was elsewhere. He kept looking up at the stairs. Rapp turned to his left. There were two tables between the bar and the front window. The bar ran a good thirty feet, taking up the front third of the restaurant. In the back and to his right there were more tables. The customers were stacked three deep at the bar and virtually every single person had a drink in one hand and a cigarette in the other. The place was loud. Plaster walls, with a tin ceiling and tile floor. Wood tables and wood trim. Lots of hard surfaces.

As Rapp smiled, excused, and nudged his way through the crowd he kept an eye on the mirror behind the bar. Two shelves of liquor bracketed the top and bottom of the mirror, and in its reflection he could watch both the old man and the staircase. Rapp did not hear the noise, but he did catch the mirror and the bottles shake ever so briefly. No more than a second later the liquid in the bottles danced yet again. Rapp sighed and cracked his neck from one side to the other. As he thought about what had just happened upstairs he flexed his fingers, extended them and then scrunched them into the palm of his hands. One dead for sure, probably two dead.

His left hand slid over to his right wrist and without looking, he pressed the stopwatch function on his digital watch. Next came his breathing. It automatically settled into a steady, almost hypnotic rhythm. He was about ninety-nine percent sure the tremors were a result of the Russians hitting the ground one after the other as they'd been shot by Gazich. Was there a chance Gazich was already climbing onto the roof? Rapp doubted it. The way he'd stood next to the car after he'd killed the first man suggested he was too cool to turn and run. There were also the police to consider. Simply leaving the bodies lying around would mean the police would show up at some point. And they would have a lot of questions. Rapp's bet was that he would stay and clean up his mess.

Someone was still alive upstairs. In truth, any of the three would do, but Rapp wanted it to be Gazich. He was the man who had been standing on the street that day in Georgetown. Someone had hired him to do the job and now they wanted him dead. Rapp wanted that information, and playing it safe wasn't going to get it. In life there's the phrase, the calm after the storm. In war there is the letdown after the battle. Some people call it an adrenalin hangover. Elite soldiers train methodically in an effort to reprogram their biology to fight off this letdown. It is drilled into them to replenish spent magazines, clean weapons, and make sure they are battle ready before they so much as relieve themselves in a roadside ditch. Gazich was not an elite soldier. He was a sniper and an assassin. He would be focused on other things right now.

Rapp was going upstairs. That much he'd already decided. There'd been too much watching and waiting lately. The only real question was how long should he wait? At least a minute. That would allow for the post adrenalin hangover to kick in.

The old man started to move. Rapp watched him in the mirror. He came toward the front of the restaurant. One of the waitresses tried to ask him a question, but he ignored her and went straight for the staircase. Rapp checked his watch and casually pivoted away from the bar. He brought his right hand up, squinted his eyes, and covered his mouth and nose as if he was about to sneeze.

Instead of sneezing he said, "I'm going up to his office."

The steps were worn, checkered, linoleum tiles turned on their side so as to give the squares a diamondlike appearance. Black and white with a black rubber cap on the edge of each riser. To the left and right the tiles and cap were in good shape, but in the middle they were so worn the tan backing of the linoleum was beginning to show through. Rapp smiled at two women who were standing at the bottom of the steps. He placed his hand on the shoulders of one and slid around behind her. Rapp stayed to the right. Less noise and almost no chance of being seen until he made the turn at each landing. He moved quickly to the first landing.

Assumptions—more often than not that's what it came down to. Educated guesses based on real-life experiences were what gave you the edge in these situations. Rapp pictured what was going on upstairs as he placed each foot carefully on the treads. The old man was about five foot eight and weighed close to two hundred pounds. On top of that, he favored his right side when he walked. His hips and knees were probably shit from working on his feet all day and carrying an extra forty pounds around. He'd make it up one flight all right, but the second would really get his heart and lungs going. Add to that the stress of the situation and there was probably a pretty good chance that by the time he got to the third floor he'd be on the verge of cardiac arrest.

The first landing was no trouble. Rapp hugged the outside wall and kept moving, taking the turn and heading up the next flight to the second floor. The last thing he wanted was for one of the waitresses or bartenders to notice him and start yelling for him to come down. Back pressed flat against the wall, he stood completely still and listened. Below there was light music and loud conversation. Above there was darkness and silence. Rapp slid the pistol from its pocket. Three tiny green dots marked the tritium sights. Two in back and one in front. Rapp brought the pistol up and held it next to his face, the stubby suppressor pointing at the ceiling. The aroma of metal and oil mixed together to create a unique comforting smell.

There was one more choice to make. Rapp's pistol was currently chambered with a Federal Hydra-Shok 9mm hollow-point cartridge. The ammunition was subsonic, and near silent. It was perfect for taking care of business in a discreet way, but it had one significant drawback. The subsonic round had eighty percent less velocity than its supersonic cousin. Forget body armor; the bullet could be stopped by a thick leather jacket at about thirty feet. It was not the type of round you wanted to use in a gunfight. The problem with the supersonic rounds, though, was that they were not silent. They made a fairly loud snapping noise as they broke the sound barrier. Rapp glanced down the staircase and remembered how loud it was in the bar area. The scale in his mind weighed velocity and stopping power against stealth. Velocity won.

Rapp switched the pistol from his left hand to his right and hit the magazine release. The black magazine dropped into his left hand, and he stowed it in his right front pocket. Rapp turned the weapon on its side, placing the butt of the grip against his chest. He cupped his left hand over the ejection port and moved his right thumb up under the slide release. Using his fingertips and the meaty part of his palm, he gripped the slide and pushed back until he felt the cold brass of the chambered round fall into his cupped hand. At the same time his right thumb pushed up on the slide release and locked the slide in the open position. He dropped the loose round into the same pocket as the magazine and fished out a different magazine from his left pocket. Rapp took the first supersonic round off the top of the magazine and placed it between his front teeth. He then quietly slid the magazine into the grip using the palm of his hand to make sure it was locked into place. The gun was switched again to the left hand. Rapp carefully took the single round from his teeth, and while pointing the muzzle at the ground he dropped the round into the chamber. It was a bit like loading a torpedo into a launch tube. Grabbing the top of the slide with his right hand, he pulled back just enough for the slide release to drop and then slowly let the slide come forward until the breach was closed.

This wasn't Hollywood. Real shooters carried their weapons hot. That meant a round in the chamber. None of this racking the slide macho bullshit. All that did was slow you down and make a bunch of noise. Rapp's only alternative to this complicated process would have been a soft rack, which basically meant putting a fresh magazine in the grip and then carefully letting the slide come forward in a slow, controlled motion. The problem with a soft rack was that you risked an improperly chambered round, which was the last thing you wanted. Especially when you planned on getting off the first shot.

Rapp gripped the weapon with both hands and extended it, pressing both hands away from his body. His arms formed a triangle. He moved to his right, his weight perfectly distributed, his footfalls as light as a featherweight boxer's. He started up the stairs slowly, two steps at a time. When he reached the landing between the second and third floors he could hear voices. A swath of dim light shone on the wall up above. Rapp guessed it came from Gazich's office. He stared at the wall for a few seconds to see if he could make out any shadows. There were none. That meant no one was standing in the doorway to the office. Rapp listened. The voices were faint. Barely audible. He thought it was Greek.

Suddenly, the silence of the third floor was shattered by an unsettling scream. Rapp instinctively took a step back. His whole body coiled, his muscles tensed as he prepared to strike out. The scream was followed by a harsh but controlled voice. The language was definitely Greek. The Greek was followed by heavy breathing and Russian. Rapp immediately knew what was going on. He crouched low and moved forward two steps to get a view of the landing above. The first thing he noticed was that the office door was closed. The second thing he noticed was a dead man lying on the floor.

# 12

Rapp moved halfway up the next flight until he was eye to eye with the dead body lying across the top landing. In the poor light, Rapp couldn't be sure, but he thought it was one of the Russians. The way the guy was positioned, Rapp figured he'd been shot in the right side of his head, spun ninety degrees, and then crumpled to the floor. Literally dead before his mass settled against the worn, dirty linoleum. His eyes were wide open, his left hand pinned under his body, one leg bent and the other straight. Rapp doubted the guy even had the time to register the pain of a piece of lead slamming into the side of his head. Not a bad way to go, all things considered.

Rapp paused to take a closer look at the body. It was definitely the second Russian, the one who had stopped in the middle of the street to yell at his friend. Gazich would have been hiding in the hallway to the right. He would have let the first guy pass. Let him open the door and then he would have shot them one two. Subsonic rounds from ten, maybe twenty feet max. First shot to the head of the second guy, second shot probably right into the first guy's right hip or maybe the knee if he was an exceptionally good marksman. The big Russian would have gone down hard. Gazich would have been moving after the first shot. He would have closed the distance for the most difficult shot of all. He wanted at least one of these guys alive, which meant he might have to shoot the gun out of the first Russian's hand if he didn't drop it after he'd been winged.

Rapp was practically lying on the steps now. His right hand was out in front of him, flat on the tread. His left hand held his gun. It was angles and inches now. He'd maximized his position of cover. Three quarters of the frosted glass office door lay in plain view. Shadows floated back and forth and at least two distinct voices could be heard, one much louder than the other. Rapp figured that had to be Gazich. He would be the one asking the questions. Staying on the stairs was not a good option. The position offered minimal cover, and left him vulnerable should someone wander up from the café. Tactically, that left two choices. Either rush the office, or move to the relative cover of the hallway.

Rapp made a mental picture of what the office was probably like on the inside. They were all pretty much the same. A desk, a few chairs, maybe a couch and some bookcases or a credenza. A guy like Gazich would never sit with his back to the door. That was for sure. It was also likely that his main work area would put him in a spot where he could not be seen directly from either window. Snipers were like that. They were always thinking angles and trajectory. Not just their own, but that of their most feared enemy—another sniper. With two windows facing the street that left pretty much one place for the desk. There was still the old man to consider, though. There was no way of telling where he might be when the door flew open. If he was directly between Rapp and Gazich he might have to be put down. The thought of having to kill a potentially innocent bystander pushed Rapp away from one tactic and toward another.

Hovering in no-man's-land was untenable, so Rapp made his decision. He moved to the top step staying as low as possible, and stepped over the dead Russian. Hugging the wall he moved down the corridor a few steps and settled against the outside wall of Gazich's office. The hallway was like a sewer culvert. The farther he went the darker it became. Rapp looked to the end. He could barely make out the dark wood frame of a door against the yellowed plaster walls. If the third floor was set up the same as the second floor, that was where the bathroom would be and maybe the access to the roof. There was one more door directly across the hall from him. That was the other office suite. Rapp had no idea who it belonged to. All he cared about was that the place was empty.

He was thinking of Coleman and was about to ask for an ETA when Gazich's office door opened, throwing a splash of light into the dark corridor. Rapp's pistol was up and aimed in the flash of a half second. He took three silent steps back, retreating farther into the darkness, both hands gripping the weapon. A solid immovable base. Three neon green dots lined up in a perfect row, the pad of his left forefinger resting gently on the trigger.

The old man appeared. He stepped into the hallway, closing the door behind him. He stood there for a five count, his left hand still holding the doorknob, his chin slowly sinking until it rested on his chest. It was a posture of contemplation. He was a man trying to gather his thoughts before he decided what to do. He held the pose for just a second longer and then with a shake of his head, he bent over and grabbed the feet of the dead Russian. The first tug did nothing. The second tug moved the body maybe a few inches. The third tug was more of an all-out yank. The old man really leaned into it and the body started sliding across the worn linoleum floor.

Rapp matched him step for step, with little worry that he would be detected. The old man was preoccupied in thought and deed and probably mostly deaf from working an espresso machine his entire life. They retreated almost to the end of the hallway, where the old man gave up and dropped the Russian's lifeless feet. They thudded against the floor, one of the shoes falling partially off. The old man swore and bent over, placing his hands on his knees. He made no effort to put the shoe back on. He was too exhausted. He stayed where he was breathing heavily and cursing to himself.

Rapp silently slid the pistol into the inside pocket of his jacket and extracted a folding knife from his belt. With one hand, he opened the knife and took a step forward. He hovered for a second, waiting for the old man to make his next predictable move. When he finally stood, Rapp lunged forward, clamping his right hand around the man's mouth while pulling him up and nearly off his feet. The knife hand came around and Rapp pressed the flat edge of the blade against the man's throat.

"Don't make a sound," Rapp whispered, his mouth only inches from the man's left ear, "or I'll slit your throat."

# 13

Rapp had no idea how involved the old man was in all of this. He'd had ample time to think about it over the last day. He had obviously tipped off Gazich about the Russians and now he was helping him again, but this was not necessarily proof that he had been involved in what had happened in America back in October. Not by a long shot. Helping get rid of the bodies was in his own self-interest, regardless of any involvement with Gazich. He had to run a business, and in a resort town like Limassol, a few dead Russians found on your property could spell real trouble.

Then again, he could be Gazich's business partner. Complicit in every action. Maybe he was the one who negotiated the contracts. Almost anything was possible, and until Rapp had proof, one way or the other, the old man would live. In no way, shape, or form was Mitch Rapp the picture of mental health, but through it all—the killings, the torturing, violence piled upon cruelty—he'd managed to stay relatively sane. The answer lay in the fact that he was different from the men, and yes, the occasional woman he hunted.

Many of them killed for an idea. Often, the idea was a perversion of Islam. These were all men. No women were allowed to join their crusade of intolerance. Yes, occasionally the Palestinians had used female suicide bombers, and so had the Chechens, but they were few. Others killed for a paycheck, like Gazich. Some of them, the ones who did their job with precision and avoided harming innocents, Rapp was indifferent toward. Gazich was not one of them. What he had done crossed the line by leaps and bounds. He was a terrorist not an assassin. He proved that when he set off the car bomb in Georgetown killing nineteen people, seriously wounding another thirty-four, and ruining the lives of who knew how many more. And who was the target in this case? Was it a corrupt arms dealer, a narco trafficker, a sponsor of terrorism? No, the target was two political candidates. And what was their crime? Did they preach death to Islam and the Arab world? Did they advocate the wholesale murder of every Palestinian? No. They did no such thing.

That was what the mullahs and clerics preached in places like Iran and Saudi Arabia. Death to America, the Great Satan. Death to Israel. Nuke the entire Zionist state and push the infidels into the ocean. These two liberal politicians, on the other hand, preached tolerance and acceptance every chance they got. They advocated real statehood for Palestine and sincere respect for religious diversity. And what did they get for it? They got some crazy Islamic fascist like Osama and his ilk putting a price tag on their heads.

Rapp still recalled the anger he'd felt while sitting in his hotel room in Calcutta months before. Sky News showed footage of the crater left by the car bomb. Rapp had been up and down that street at least a thousand times. From the size of the hole alone he knew it had been a powerful bomb. The death count was sure to be high. The next set of images provided by Sky News came from Muslim cities across the Middle East and beyond. They were all a slight variation on the same theme. Young men clogged the streets. Again, no women. American flags burned, Molotov cocktails were thrown at U.S. embassies, cars were torched, and men chanted, cheered, and danced. All in celebration that the Great Satan had been dealt a grievous blow.

The fact that so many could so brazenly celebrate such a barbarous act snapped Rapp back to reality. This clash of cultures trivialized his pain and anguish. The images on the TV that evening in Calcutta crystallized for him what was at stake. The only time you ever saw anything like this in America was when Detroit won an NBA title. And they were merely celebrating their home team's victory. Not the indiscriminate destruction of human life.

The old man would live. That was how Rapp was different from Gazich. He didn't simply eliminate innocent people because they were in the way of his objective. Yes, Rapp was capable of restraint when the situation called for it, but he was equally capable of committing acts of sheer, ruthless violence. Gazich would die. But before he drew his last breath he would talk.

"Down on your knees," Rapp whispered.

He kept his right hand on the man's mouth and the knife at his throat as the man got down on one knee and then the other.

"I'm going to take my hand off your mouth," Rapp whispered, "but the knife is going to stay at your throat." Rapp took the point of the knife and jabbed the tip into the fleshy skin just beneath the old man's Adam's apple. The steel point slid through the first two layers of skin, drawing a drop of blood.

"That's your voice box. Keep your mouth shut until I tell you to open it. If I see your lips begin to move, the knife goes all the way in, and I promise you whatever it was that you were going to say is going to die right there in your throat. Nod if you understand."

The old man did and Rapp decreased the pressure on the tip of the knife.

Rapp could feel the man breathing heavily through his nose. "Listen, I'm not going to kill you unless you give me a reason to. Just relax and take a few deep breaths."

Keeping the knife at his throat, Rapp used his right hand to reach down and grab a towel that was stuffed into one of the pockets at the front of the old man's apron. Rapp looked at it before bunching one end into a ball with his fist.

"Open your mouth wide," Rapp whispered.

The old man did as he was told and Rapp stuffed a third of the towel into his mouth. He then made the man lay down flat on his stomach and put his hands behind his back. Rapp cut the long ties off the apron and used them to hog-tie the man's ankles and wrists together. When he was secured, Rapp stowed the knife and drew the pistol.

Rapp showed the gun to the old man and whispered, "Any noise at all and I'll shoot you. Don't try to bang your feet against the wall or roll over. Otherwise you're a dead man. Do you understand?"

The old man nodded.

"How many people are in the office? Blink your answer."

The old man's eyelids opened and closed twice.

"Deckas and the big Russian?"

The old man nodded his head up and down.

"Is Deckas interrogating the Russian?"

Again he nodded.

"All right, sit tight." Rapp patted the old man's head. "This whole thing will be over in a minute."

Rapp sprang to his feet and started down the hallway, gliding along the right edge. Gazich would have used a silenced weapon. Most likely subsonic rounds, probably nine millimeter. The walls were old. Probably lattice covered with plaster. They would definitely stop a nine-millimeter round, subsonic or not. Maybe even a forty-five. Rapp again tried to visualize the layout of the office. Desk in the middle on the left and a couple of chairs or a couch on the right. Gazich would be standing and that meant he would have minimal cover. The Russian would not be a problem. He was either immobile from gunshot wounds or tied up. If Gazich was interrogating him he had probably switched to a knife. Options increased and techniques varied with a knife.

Rapp stopped one step short of the door. His mind was made up on a plan of action. It would be lightning fast. One, two, three, four. He listened for a moment. It sounded like Gazich was asking a question. The Russian pleaded with him in broken English, his voice much louder and more fearful than that of his inquisitor. Rapp took all of this as a good sign.

Reaching out, he placed his right hand on the doorknob and waited a second. As soon as he heard Gazich begin to speak, he twisted the old brass knob and flung the door inward with a good push. He was ninety percent sure Gazich was on the right, but he had to make sure he wasn't on the left first. Rapp hugged the door frame as his left hand and gun filled the void of the open doorway. The door sailed past ninety degrees, revealing the edge of the desk exactly where Rapp thought it would be. The gun came straight up and locked in a level position. The door continued its arc, swinging inward on its hinges, revealing an empty desk. Rapp started swinging the gun back to his right. At the same time he shifted his weight to his left while hugging the door frame and leaned just enough into the open doorway so his left eye could take in nearly the entire right side of the room while exposing only a fraction of his body.

Gazich came into view first. He was standing sideways, the Russian was in a chair directly in front of him, but Rapp wasn't worried about the Russian. Rapp's eye was locked on Gazich. A literal tunnel. His gun not quite there yet. Ninety-nine percent of his focus on the threat. He heard the door bang hard against something as his eye searched Gazich's hands. The Bosnian was turning toward him, his hands still at his side. He was expecting the old man. Some recess of Rapp's brain registered that the door had not opened 180 degrees against the wall so it had probably hit a bookcase or some other piece of furniture. The black finish of a gun and its long silencer against the faded denim of Gazich's pants caught Rapp's eye. The elevation of Rapp's left arm dropped immediately. Gun seeking out gun. A tenth of a second later Rapp squeezed the trigger, letting loose the first shot.

Gazich stood a mere fourteen feet away. The round caught him square in the back of his right hand, plowing its way through flesh, crucial tendons, and then bone. His hand clenched for a millisecond and then opened like a clamp with a broken spring. The brain made none of these decisions. It was simply mechanical failure. The gun dropped free-falling to the floor, but before it hit, a second round caught Gazich in the right knee and then a third in the left knee.

For two seconds time stood still. Nothing moved. Rapp waited, still concealed by the door frame, and watched the same way you would watch the demolition of a building. That strange moment of disbelief in the immediate aftermath. When the explosive charges have just blown out all the support columns, yet the building still hangs there for a second or two defying gravity. And then physics takes over and everything comes crashing to the ground.

Gazich's legs wobbled. His arms began to move away from his body in an effort to provide balance, but balance wasn't the problem. The problem was two shattered kneecaps. It was structural. He picked up his right leg to widen his stance and when he put it back down the limb folded like a cheap rental chair at a backyard wedding. Gazich went down hard, somehow managing to get his left hand out in front of him to prevent a face plant. He ended up on his side, his left hand stretched out a mere four inches from the pistol he had dropped.

Rapp stayed right where he was, completely aware of the proximity of Gazich's hand to the weapon. He watched as Gazich's eyes moved from the pistol to the stranger in the doorway. Rapp knew what was going through his mind, so he stepped partially into the doorway and started to lower his weapon. His eyes were locked on Gazich's. Rapp's pistol almost got to a point where it was perpendicular with the floor, but he saw the fingers on Gazich's hand open and reach for the weapon. Rapp's pistol came up and a fourth shot spat from the end of the silencer. It bored a hole through the center of the assassin's palm before it ever reached the gun. One, two, three, four. Just like Rapp thought it would be.

Rapp stepped into the room and kept his gun trained on Gazich's head. He walked over, placed his right foot on the gun and slid it back toward the doorway. Gazich started to move.

"Keep your hands away from your body, or I'll put a bullet in your head."

The Russian took all of this as a sign of his salvation, and exclaimed, "Thank god you are here."

Rapp looked at him with a furrowed brow. The guy's left ear had been partially carved away from his head and the tip of his nose looked like a filleted lobster tail. Blood cascaded down his face and onto his white shirt.

"Untie me, my friend."

Rapp didn't move.

"Untie me right now," the Russian demanded.

Rapp leveled the pistol at the Russian's groin. All three green dots in a row. "Shut the fuck up, or I'll blow your balls off."

# 14

Groin injuries could be really messy. Lots of blood, and lots of pain. Since the Russian could barely keep his mouth shut as it was, Rapp assumed the lout would scream like a stuck pig if he pierced one of his testicles with a ball of lead. Rapp was not one to make empty threats, and the Russian's inability to keep his mouth shut and follow a simple order was pushing him to the brink. He was one of these irritants who liked to think out loud. The type who gives a running narrative of the obvious. He alternated between muttering to himself and attempting to bribe Rapp with riches, his volume increasing with each passing moment.

Rapp was on the phone with Coleman, giving him a quick situation report. They were less than a minute out. Rapp told him to have Brooks drop him off in front. If anyone tried to stop him from going upstairs, he should tell them he was going to meet Alexander

Deckas from Aid Logistics Inc. The Russian jabbered during the entire conversation.

Rapp had already frisked Gazich, and now he was rifling through the assassin's desk as he finished giving Coleman instructions. Everything was going fairly well except the Russian. The man simply wouldn't shut up. Finally, Coleman asked Rapp who was making the racket. Rapp reached his boiling point. He raised his pistol and squeezed the trigger. A round spat from the thick suppressor and imbedded itself in the wood seat of the chair a mere two inches in front of the Russian's crotch.

The Russian's eyes opened wide with fear and his mouth hung slack with shock.

Rapp muted the phone, walked over, stuck the smoking barrel into the Russian's groin, and growled, "Shut the fuck up!"

The Russian closed his eyes, whimpered for a second, and then slammed his mouth shut.

Rapp took the phone off mute and said, "Hurry up. I need some help up here." With that he jabbed the red end button on the phone and considered his next move. He walked over to the door and leaned out into the hallway to check on the old man. All he could see was a dark mass on the floor at the far end. Rapp paused for a second while he did the time conversion. Ten o'clock in Cyprus meant it was four in the afternoon in DC. Kennedy could be anywhere. Rapp decided to call her secure mobile. He punched in the country code, area code, and then the number. It started ringing almost immediately.

The Science and Technology people at Langley provided the top echelon of employees with the most secure phones available, and then installed special encryption software. They issued new phones at least once a year if not every six months. Rapp's phones never left the box. He didn't trust them, and it wasn't because he feared the Russians or the Chinese. It was his own agency and the National Security Agency that he feared most. The full capabilities of the NSA and what they could do with their satellites, listening stations, and eight Cray supercomputers that they kept deep underground in a vast cooled chamber, was known to only a select few. What Rapp did know was that they collected an unbelievable number of foreign calls made into the U.S. every day. Those calls emanating from the Middle East received special attention. The NSA acted like a big fishing trawler. They threw out their nets, reeled them in, and then decided what fish to keep. Except with them it was phone calls, e-mails, and other electronic transmissions. These were prioritized by criteria. Like fishermen who throw the worthless fish back into the sea, the NSA was getting more efficient at maximizing its resources.

At the heart of their mission was code breaking. It always had been and always would be. These billions of intercepts were worthless if they couldn't decipher them. Rapp knew there were elite teams of brainiacs within the NSA whose sole job was to defeat encryption software. As good as the folks at Langley's S&T were, the truth was they were no match for the talent that the NSA employed. From a patriot's perspective, one would think none of this should matter. After all they were all on the same team—the CIA, the NSA, the Pentagon, the Department of Justice, the FBI—all Americans working to defeat global terrorism.

The reality was far more complicated. Just because one administration advocated a certain policy, it didn't mean the next one would, or that some opportunistic politician on the Hill wouldn't seize the chance to grab the limelight by calling for an investigation into any one of a dozen things Rapp had done in the last year. What a veteran of the Clandestine Service deemed appropriate action was often very different from what a lawyer at the DOJ might think.

And then there were budgets and interagency turf wars. In many ways the domestic side of the business was more dangerous than the operating abroad. At least when he was in the field Rapp knew who his enemies were. At home, politics and personalities were thrown into the mix and any sense of a unified mission was lost.

The climate had gotten so bad that Rapp couldn't trust his own people at Langley. The CIA's own Inspector General's office had gotten into the game of leaking things to reporters. Senior officers were contributing to politicians' campaigns, spouses were serving on advisory committees for candidates, and admin types were regularly dining and rubbing shoulders with journalists, lobbyists, and political strategists. Add to that Amnesty International and a dozen other human rights groups and you had a climate that was about as unfriendly to someone in Rapp's position as you could imagine. He couldn't even trust his own employer to hand him a secure phone, for at the end of the day, the Inspector General's Office could be recording everything he said. In Rapp's mind, there was no such thing as a secure line, so he went with the odds. Practically every month he bought a new phone from a major carrier and got a new number. And every time he went on a mission like this, he picked up a phone that rarely lasted the length of the mission. Even with all of the precautions he took, he was still very careful about what he said. He gave only the vaguest information and spoke in generalities.

When Kennedy finally answered, Rapp did not bother with greetings. He simply said, "I need a plane."

There was a brief pause. "What kind of plane?"

"The plane."

Almost as if on cue, the Russian started his running narrative again. Rapp looked at him, the gun in one hand and the phone in the other, his palms up and his arms out from his body a couple feet.

The expression on his face seemed to say, *You have got to be kidding me.*

The Russian said, "I work for the KGB."

Through his earpiece, Rapp heard Kennedy ask, "Who is that?"

Rapp said, "Give me a second." He pressed the mute button on the phone and moved around to the side of the Russian. "I told you to keep your mouth shut, you stupid fucker."

"I am Russian Intelligence. Former KGB. We are on the same side now. America and Russia."

Gazich was immobile on the floor and no doubt in a great deal of pain as the adrenaline wore off and he was left with the searing pain of four gun shot wounds to extremely sensitive areas of his body. Despite his less than humorous situation, he started to laugh and said, "You work for the Russian mob."

"I do not!" the Russian shouted.

Gazich laughed harder. "You are a bitch for the oligarchs and nothing else."

Rapp was standing midway between the Russian and Gazich. If he didn't need to talk to these two morons, he would gladly shoot them both in the head, just to shut them up. The Russian was craning his neck looking up at Rapp, babbling on about his distinguished career with the KGB. Rapp took another step, putting himself off to the Russian's left side about three feet away. Rapp pointed across the room and asked, "You see that computer over there?"

The Russian looked away from Rapp and fixed his attention on the large off-white monitor sitting on the desk.

Rapp turned to the side and shifted all of his weight onto his left foot. His right leg came up and his torso leaned away from the Russian. Rapp's leg hung in the air for a second; his hands were pulled in tight gripping the phone and the gun, his forearms and fists providing a shield for his upper torso and face. He did it out of habit, not out of fear of being hit. It was years of training. A simple side kick. Done properly it could be delivered with more force than any other blow. Done poorly it still provided quite a punch. Rapp hadn't delivered a poor side kick in more than fifteen years. The toe of Rapp's heavy soled shoes was drawn up toward his shin. His eyes were locked on the Russian's chin like the three green dots on the sights of his Glock.

In a flash, Rapp's leg straightened—his one-inch, layered, leather heel striking the large chin of the Russian. The directed force of the blow broke the Russian's jaw. The speed of the kick caused the Russian's head to move laterally so quickly that his equilibrium was thrown completely out of whack. The effect was the physiological equivalent of turning off a light switch. The Russian's entire body went limp, and he slumped forward in the chair, unconscious, his bound hands the only thing keeping him from falling to the floor.

Satisfied with the results, Rapp took the phone off mute and said, "Sorry about that."

"What is going on?" Kennedy asked a bit irritated.

"Nothing you need to worry about." Rapp looked at Gazich and said, "Just get me the plane."

There was a long pause and then Kennedy asked, "You found him?"

"Yes."

"You're sure?"

"One hundred percent. Go see Marcus. Tell him he was right about the Bosnian. He'll fill you in on the rest."

"Where are you?"

"Limassol, Cyprus."

"I think the plane is in Eastern Europe. Let me make sure, and I'll get back to you with an itinerary."

"Make it quick. I need to get off this rock fast."

"What have you done?" asked a worried Kennedy.

"I haven't done anything, but there's a third party involved and some of their boys got hurt."

"How bad?"

"Body bag bad."

"I see." This was followed by more silence and then Kennedy skeptically asked, "And you had nothing to do with this?"

Rapp never liked to be second-guessed by people who spent their days sitting in comfortable leather chairs behind large, important desks while he risked life and limb. "Watch your step," he snarled. "I don't need this shit. I'm over here with a fucking rookie, and Blondie and his boys have been stuck in airports all day. What I need is some serious support right now. I need the plane, and I need it ASAP, and then I'm going to need a follow-up team to come in here and do a little cleaning."

Kennedy should have known by his tone that it was a mistake to question him while he was still in the field. They'd been down this road dozens of times and it never ended well. She relented by saying, "I'll get back to you with an answer in ten minutes or less."

"One more thing. Our friends on the other side of the pond . . . they have a base close by. That would be best. No customs. Freight delivery to the back gate. Make the transfer in a hangar. Real private. No do-gooders shooting video."

"Absolutely. I'll arrange it. Anything else?"

"For now that should be enough."

"Good. Great work! Give me a few minutes to get the pieces moving, and I'll get right back to you."

"Thanks." Rapp disconnected the call and looked down at Gazich. He'd lost a bit of his color and he was starting to shake a bit. Rapp knew he hadn't hit any major arteries, both by his aim and the lack of blood on the wood floor. Nonetheless, shock was fast approaching. Gazich's body would be trying to shut certain things down to stave off the excruciating pain. Rapp had no fear of losing him. Gazich was young and fit. He could take it, and he honestly deserved this and a whole lot more.

Rapp squatted down on his haunches and looked Gazich in the eye. "I don't suppose you'd like to tell me who hired you?"

# 15

The plane was big. Bigger than they needed, but Rapp wasn't complaining. It was a Lockheed Martin TriStar. She was designed to carry up to 400 passengers, or 88,000 pounds of cargo. This one, with its wide body and three big engines, was configured for cargo. She was a sister ship to the venerable DC-10. As far as aviation went, she was a little long in the tooth. From the outside the plane looked like any other international freight carrier. There were no windows other than the ones in the cockpit. The skin was painted a generic white, and the name *Worldwide Freight* ran along the back half of the fuselage in large blue letters. The CIA had more planes than some small air forces, but thanks to a politically motivated hack in the CIA's Inspector General's Office Rapp couldn't go near them. At least not for something like this.

A little over a year ago, this same bureaucrat took it upon herself to tell a reporter that the CIA was ferrying terrorists around Eastern Europe in a Gulfstream 5 and a Boeing 737. Many of these terrorists were high ranking al-Qaeda operatives. They were taken to undisclosed locations and put in uncomfortable situations until they decided to talk, which all of them eventually did. The information they provided proved invaluable in picking apart al-Qaeda's operational and financial infrastructure. That single leak had crippled one of Langley's most important operations in the war on terror. Yet again, Rapp was forced to stay one step ahead of his own government.

The strategy with the planes was not very different than the one Rapp used with his mobile phones. The worldwide aviation market was a vast and intricate association of sellers, resellers, leasers, and lessees. Carriers were constantly updating their fleets, replacing older models with newer, more fuel efficient ones. That left a surplus of unused aircrafts. These planes were often kicked down the line, leased and subleased a half dozen times until they either broke down or crashed flying in and out of some war-torn country in Africa. The big Lockheed TriStar was still in good shape. She had been leased for one month through a company in Seattle. The company specialized in subleasing planes on a short-term basis. Their business model was simple. As power companies sold excess power to other utilities, these guys leased planes that weren't being used during slow times of the year. They had no idea the CIA was their client. Everything was done through an attorney's office in Frankfurt. The pilots were a couple of old U.S. Air Force colonels who liked cash and knew how to keep their mouths shut.

Rapp stood on the tarmac next to a battered gray Royal Air Force hangar. The big TriStar was inside. The sky in the east was showing the first signs of morning. The humid, salty Mediterranean air rolled in across the flat expanse of the base. There was nothing but asphalt, concrete, dirt, and scrub brush for miles in every direction. About fifty feet away Scott Coleman was talking with a British officer who had met them at the back gate fifteen minutes earlier. Coleman handed the officer something and the man took it. Then they shook hands and the RAF officer jumped in a Land Rover and sped off. Coleman walked over slowly shaking his head. A grin on his face.

The retired Navy SEAL said, "God, I love the Brits."

Rapp nodded. "They know how to keep their mouths shut."

"He gets off in a couple hours. He said he'd leave the van in the airport garage with the keys under the mat. All we have to do is call the rental company."

"Good. And the plane?"

"Refueled and cleared for takeoff."

"Good. Let's get out of here before the sun comes up."

The two men turned and walked into the shadowy hangar. Where Rapp was dark-haired and olive-skinned, Coleman was fair-haired and fair-skinned. Rapp fit in pretty much anywhere in the Middle East. Coleman, with his blue eyes and blond hair, would have looked more at home in Sweden or Norway. Probably Iceland as well. He had the high cheekbones and the stoic demeanor of the Northern Tribes. The stoic part worked well with Rapp. Less was almost always more, especially when it came to conversation. Coleman, like Rapp, was not one for idle chatter.

After Coleman had arrived at Gazich's office, he and Rapp had taken a moment to figure out a plan of action. Neither liked the idea of staying put. If the police showed up, they would have to explain two dead Russians, another Russian who looked like some African tribe had gotten hold of him, and a Bosnian with four bullet holes in him. Marching everyone out of the café in the middle of a busy Saturday night would also not work. Sitting tight until the place closed was the best option. In order to do that, though, they would need the old man to cooperate. Sooner or later someone was sure to come looking for him.

They untied the old man and sat him down for a talk. The big Russian was still unconscious and Gazich remained silent on the floor despite the obvious pain of his wounds. The man's name was Andreas Papadakos, and he was the owner of the building. He had met Alexander Deckas five years ago. The man paid his rent in advance every six months. He traveled frequently and had never been a problem. That was until the Russians showed up a few days earlier looking for him. They told Papadakos that Deckas was a hired gun. An assassin. They told him they worked for the Russian State Police and they were there to arrest Deckas and bring him back to Russia for trial.

The old man asked the Russians for identification. They told him not to worry, so he said he would call the local cops. That was when things got ugly. Papadakos had five daughters who worked for him. He had grandchildren coming and going all day. Sixteen of them. The Russians had already cased the place and told him if he called the authorities, or warned Deckas, they would dismember his grandchildren one by one.

Up until this point, the only real opinion Rapp had formed of the big Russian was that he was an irritant. He even felt a little sorry for the guy now that his face looked like one of those latex masks costume shops sell around Halloween. After hearing that he had threatened to cut up little children, all of Rapp's sympathy vanished.

Over the years Rapp had done a lot of interrogations. They ranged from the mundane, like talking to a street vendor in Damascus about something he may have seen, to threatening to blow a man's head off. All those years of experience had led to an ability to pretty much tell from the start when someone was being either forthright or deceptive in their answers. Papadakos denied any knowledge or involvement with Deckas. Furthermore, there were the five daughters and the sixteen grandchildren. Why would he endanger them by getting into business with a guy like Gazich?

In the end, the situation dictated what they needed to do. Involved or not involved, Papadakos did not want the cops snooping around. If Rapp found out later that the man and Gazich were full business partners he would come back and get him. Papadakos had spent his whole life in Limassol. He was not going to simply disappear and leave his business and grandchildren behind. So a deal was struck. Once the café was closed, Rapp would get rid of the bodies and the old man and his family could go on living their lives as if nothing had ever happened.

Rapp followed Papadakos downstairs and kept an eye on him. The rest of Coleman's men showed up a few minutes past 11:00. All three were former SEALs who had served under Coleman. Wicker and Hacket casually walked up to the sedan with the dead Russian in the front seat. Wicker climbed behind the wheel and Hacket got in back. Wicker started the car, put it into drive, and slid out of the space. Fifteen minutes later they found a nice dark alley a little more than a mile away. Hacket got out and walked it from one end to the other, just to make sure it was deserted. Wicker circled back around, drove halfway down the dark canyon, and turned off the car. The dome light was extinguished and the trunk popped.

Hacket was waiting at the rear bumper snapping on a pair of disposable latex gloves. When the trunk lid came up, he reached in and yanked the clear plastic cover off the light casing. He flicked the cover into the recesses of the trunk and pulled the small bulb out of its slot. With darkness restored, Hacket walked around to the front passenger door and opened it a few feet. The body began to fall out of the car. Hacket placed his left hand on the head of the dead man, opened the door the rest of the way and then grabbed the limp body under both armpits. He dragged him out of the car and back to the trunk. Wicker stood on the other side of the car, his head slowly turning from one end of the alley and then back. The Russian was at least 200 pounds, but Hacket was a solid 225. He hefted the torso into the trunk face down and then picked up the legs, and twisted and bent the body the rest of the way in. Hacket softly closed the lid and they drove away.

By the time they got back to the café, the place was nearly empty. Parking was not a problem. Brooks was across the street packing and sanitizing the hotel room. Coleman and Stroble were treating wounds, securing the prisoners, and going through Gazich's stuff looking for information. Both the big Russian and Gazich were given morphine. Rapp sat at the bar, drank a glass of wine, and kept an eye on Papadakos. As business slowed and the place began to empty, the old man joined Rapp at the bar and ordered a bottle of red. He drank three glasses in under thirty minutes and ordered another bottle. He was clearly anxious to be done with the entire drama.

At 1:00 in the morning the last two patrons were shown the door. They stumbled off, weaving their way down the sidewalk in search of the nightclubs a few blocks over. By 2:00 a.m. the street was pretty still. Brooks stood watch at one end of the block and Wicker the other. The big Russian was marched down the stairs under his own power. The dead Russian and Gazich needed to be carried. They debated wrapping them up in tablecloths, but decided the better route was to make it look like they were drunk. Hacket and Stroble carried Gazich out first, the two former SEALs bookending the Bosnian, one under each arm, like three drunk sailors on shore leave. They stuffed him in the back of the van and then went back for the dead Russian. He was carried down in the same fashion and placed in the backseat of the car that Wicker had driven earlier.

Wicker came back from his post at the end of the block and climbed behind the wheel of the car with one dead Russian in the backseat and another one in the trunk. He pulled away from the curb with Hacket following him in the rental car they had picked up while they waited for their luggage at the airport. They were headed back to the same alley. The dead Russian in the backseat would join the dead Russian in the trunk, and then Wicker would abandon the car in a nice shady spot, where with any luck the stench would go unnoticed for a few days. After that they were to head up to Gazich's house in the hills where they would search it from top to bottom.

Rapp said good-bye to Papadakos and thanked him for his co-operation. The old man asked Rapp what would happen to Deckas. Rapp lied and told him he wasn't sure, even though he knew exactly what he was going to do with him. He was going to squeeze every last bit of information from him and then he was going to give him a death befitting a man who set off car bombs in the middle of an urban neighborhood. He needed to be made an example of. Rapp could tell the old man was worried so he told him that people way above his pay grade would be sorting the whole mess out. If Rapp had only known how accurate that statement was he probably would have finished off Gazich right there on Cyprus.

# 16

The phone rang at 6:01 a.m. Kennedy noticed the time before she answered the phone. She was lying on her left side, and the glowing green numbers of her alarm clock were staring her straight in the face when she opened her eyes. She reached out with her right hand and grabbed the handset. Attempting to view the small caller ID screen without her glasses would be futile. The cord got caught on something, so she tugged. A magazine and the TV remote fell to the floor. For security reasons she did not own a cordless phone. She kept her head on the pillow and brought the sturdy beige handset to her right ear.

"Hello."

"Director Kennedy?"

"Speaking."

"Major Hansen . . . duty officer White House Situation Room."

"Yes, Major."

"POTUS has called a meeting for zero seven hundred." POTUS was the military's acronym for President of the United States.

"In the Situation Room?"

"No, the Oval, Ma'am."

"I'll be there."

Kennedy placed the handset back in its cradle and thought, *So much for sleeping in on Sundays.* She threw back the covers and laughed to herself. She was going to be out of a job pretty soon. Or at least this job, and whatever job came after this one would be undoubtedly less demanding. She could sleep in all the Sundays she wanted.

The tile on the bathroom floor felt cold on her bare feet. January in DC. Kennedy turned on the bathroom light and studied her face in the mirror. At forty-five she looked pretty good for her age, but at six in the morning with no makeup and bed lines on her face, she was frightening. Being a woman in this town wasn't easy. She turned on the shower to give it a chance to warm up and started brushing her teeth. With toothbrush in mouth she walked out to the kitchen and put on some hot water for her tea. On the way back she poked her head in her son's room to check on him. He was safe and warm beneath the covers.

Kennedy did not like being cold. She put her hair up and stepped into the hot shower. For five minutes she stood under the water, increasing the temperature until her skin turned pink. It took her five minutes to dry off and get dressed and another five to put on her face. By 6:33 she'd alerted her security detail of the meeting and was in the kitchen taking her first sip of tea and dialing the Global Ops Center at Langley on a secure line. The duty officer answered on the first ring. Kennedy asked him if there was anything worth reporting. He said it had been a pretty slow night. She was surprised by the answer and asked him if he was sure. He told her he was. The director thanked him and hung up.

Kennedy grabbed the warm mug with both hands, leaned against the kitchen counter and asked herself why the president was calling a 7:00 a.m. meeting on a Sunday morning. If the Global Ops Center was in the dark, the odds were the crisis had emanated at the Pentagon, or maybe Justice. With one week to go until the ax fell, Kennedy found herself strangely ambivalent about the whole thing. She took another sip of tea and wondered if this was good or bad. She'd been the consummate professional her entire adult life. She spent more than twenty years at Langley and she had given it her all. The job had even cost her a marriage. She thought about that for a moment and realized it wasn't fair to blame the failed marriage on Langley. It would have failed if she'd been a stay-at-home mom. Her ex was too selfish. He proved that yet again when his second marriage fell apart after nine short months. He was a decent man, but a mama's boy, which made him extremely high maintenance and Kennedy had neither the time nor the desire to give his ego the attention he desired. Plus, one-way relationships were never a good idea.

Kennedy climbed into the back of her Town Car and picked up the Sunday edition of the *Post*. Maybe withdrawing from the job was her subconscious protecting herself from the inevitable disappointment of being shown the door. Anything was possible, she supposed. She did not want to leave Langley, especially after such a brief stint as director. She'd been there over twenty years. Practically her entire adult life. She would miss the people and the action that went along with running the world's most unfairly maligned spy agency. She wouldn't miss the hours, and she most definitely wouldn't miss the politics. She'd miss the place though. There was no doubt about it.

When they pulled up to the first checkpoint, it was already 7:00 a.m. By the time she cleared security she was five minutes late. When she entered the Oval Office she found four men standing in a loose circle around the president's desk. They were the president himself, Attorney General Stokes, FBI Director Roach, and President–Elect Alexander. Roach was in a gray suit and striped tie. The other three were wearing blazers, dress slacks, and open-collar shirts. At first glance she was surprised by the absence of several key players, the Secretaries of Defense and State, the president's national security advisor and his chief of staff. Then she remembered it was a Sunday morning with just six days left until the peaceful, democratic transfer of power. Very little got done this week. The career bureaucrats and professionals were busy running the government while the political appointees had either moved onto new jobs or were busy looking for one.

President Hayes stopped talking when he saw Kennedy and said, "There she is. The woman of the hour."

All four sets of eyes focused on Kennedy. She blushed slightly and asked, "And why would that be, Mr. President?"

"Always modest, this one," Hayes said to President–Elect Alexander. "You'll figure that out soon enough. No offense to these two over here," Hayes gestured to Stokes and Roach, "They have done admirable jobs, but this one here . . . she's done an amazing job and she gets almost no credit for it. All of her victories and successes are locked up in a vault out at Langley. A hundred years from now they'll be writing about her in the history books."

Kennedy blushed. She stood motionless midway between the door and where they were standing. She was not used to such attention and looked uncomfortable.

Hayes smiled, gestured toward the furniture opposite his desk, and said, "Let's sit."

Two lengthy couches, big enough to comfortably seat four adults each, faced one another with a glass-topped coffee table in between. In front of the fireplace sat two blue and gold striped silk armchairs. President Hayes gestured for Alexander to sit next to him in front of the fireplace. The place of honor.

"Would anyone care for coffee or tea?" Hayes was hovering in between the two couches. He bent down and dropped a bag of Green Tea in a china cup and added hot water. His hand shook ever so slightly. "Irene." He placed the cup on a saucer and handed it to Kennedy.

Kennedy had not missed the president's unsteady hand. Even with the medicine he'd been taking for his Parkinson's, the tremors had grown in frequency and severity over the last few months. He'd lost nothing mentally, but she understood why he'd decided to not seek reelection. In this new media age the scrutiny would have been horrible. The other side would have attacked him as selfish for not stepping aside. Elements of his own party would have undoubtedly done the same, and with an approval rating in the low forties, his chances for victory were a crapshoot at best. With his decision not to run he had secured his reputation in the history books. He would be looked on as a wise, unselfish man. Kennedy agreed with that assessment. Robert Hayes had never lost sight of the fact that the office was bigger than the man.

The other three men took coffee and then Hayes settled in next to Alexander in front of the fireplace. He looked over at his replacement and asked, "Where are you staying this week?"

"The Willard."

"Ah," the president nodded. "A grand old hotel."

"Yes."

"They have you in a good room, I hope," Hayes grinned.

"The top floor."

"My offer still stands."

"Blair House," Alexander said in a dead voice.

"It's close, and very secure."

"Thank you, Mr. President, but there are simply too many people coming and going this week. The party has me booked from sun up till sun down."

"Thanking all the fat cats." Hayes nodded, having gone through the same thing four years earlier.

Hayes was turned sideways in his chair half facing his replacement. He barely knew the governor from Georgia, but it was obvious that he had changed since the attack on his motorcade. He seemed more distant. His eyes were not as full of promise as they'd been during the early months of the campaign. Hayes wondered if this would help him when he took over the reins of power. Make him more thoughtful and reflective. Or if he'd become jaded from his experience. The president felt sorry for him. This should be a week full of hope and promise. A renewal of sorts. Maybe the news he had for him would help bring about some closure.

Hayes smiled. "Well . . . if you change your mind and decide you need to get away from it all, just let me know."

"I will, Mr. President. Thank you." The president–elect took a sip of coffee and then asked, "Is there anything I can do for you, Mr. President?"

"For me?" Hayes grinned and shook his head. "I'm looking forward to retirement. Although my dreams of becoming a master model plane builder have been dashed," Hayes held up an unsteady hand, "there's still a lot of other things I can do. My doctor, who happens to be my old college roommate, tells me the Parkinson's shouldn't affect my golf game at all, which really surprised me. His explanation was very interesting. He said I've never been able to putt and since it was impossible for my putting to get any worse, there was actually a chance it might improve."

Hayes laughed at his own humor and the others smiled.

"Can you believe that? One of my oldest friends. And I actually have to pay him to hear crap like that."

Everyone laughed. Alexander smiled briefly and then stared at the man whose job he was about to take. "Mr. President, your attitude amazes me."

Hayes shrugged and said, "What are you going to do? You've been dealt a bad hand. If you don't laugh about it, it'll eat you up."

"I don't think I've laughed . . . I mean really laughed in over two months."

Hayes cringed slightly. "You're situation is a little different from mine. I have a disease. A manageable disease," he added in a hopeful tone. "It's no joy, but I still have some good years ahead of me. Your situation is a little different. You were blindsided, and someone very important to you was taken away. Forever," he added with a force that surprised everyone. "It's hard to find any humor in that."

"No, just anger, shock, and sadness."

"Well . . . this might help." Hayes uncrossed his legs and leaned forward. "As you know, after the attack on your motorcade, the FBI launched one of the biggest investigations in the history of the organization. Homeland Security, Defense, State, NSA, CIA . . . everyone got on board to help, but the FBI was the lead agency. This is where they excel . . . the forensics, the thousands of man-hours it takes to run down every lead. Director Roach tells me he has kept you fully briefed on the investigation."

"Yes."

"Good. Now here's the part you don't know." Hayes pointed to Stokes and Roach. "They don't know about it either. Homeland Security, National Intelligence, tearing down walls between the FBI and the CIA . . . that's all fine in theory, and in the wake of 9/11 it actually looked like it might happen for a brief period, but it's a pipe dream. It'll never really work. Not in this town. Not with all the gotcha politics, and the journalists who care first and foremost about making a name for themselves. The FBI must follow the law and tread very carefully everywhere it goes. Lots of rules. Now the CIA on the other hand . . . they deal with a different crowd. And when it comes to international things . . . they can move much faster and in circles where the FBI would find themselves in over their heads. Agree or disagree with some of their methods, the CIA is much more suited to go up against an enemy that does not play by the rules. An enemy that's willing to set off car bombs in Georgetown on a Saturday afternoon."

Alexander looked down at the floor and slowly nodded.

Hayes continued. "After the attack on your motorcade, I sat down in private with Director Kennedy and told her to pull out all the stops. To put her best people on this . . . and once again she did not disappoint me."

Alexander looked up, his eyes wide with hope. "Did you find out who was behind the attack?"

Hayes looked to his spy chief. "Irene."

Kennedy set her cup back on its saucer. She'd only realized a minute before what the president was up to. She covered her mouth with her fist, cleared her throat, and got down to business. "Do you recall hearing about the man in the red hat during any of your briefings with the FBI?"

"No." Alexander looked to Roach and Stokes to make sure he was remembering things accurately.

"The man in the red hat," Attorney General Stokes said, "is something that has never been proven. As with any chaotic event, like the attack on your motorcade, there was conflicting testimony among the eyewitnesses. Several recall seeing this man on the street just prior to the explosion, but most do not. We culled surveillance tapes from all the local businesses and nowhere does this individual show up. We believe that he is . . ."

Kennedy's gaze moved from Stokes to Roach. She was sure

McMahon would have informed his boss of the meeting he'd had in Kennedy's office less than twenty-four hours ago. The one where Baker had dropped the bomb on them. The two FBI men had worked together for a long time. McMahon would have called him immediately. She doubted, though, that the FBI director would have bothered his boss on a Saturday afternoon. It was a potentially crucial, but small piece of the investigation. He would have figured telling the attorney general could wait until Monday morning.

Stokes was sitting closer to Alexander. Roach on the other side. Kennedy watched as Roach's face twisted into a frown and he leaned forward. Sticking his arm out to get his bosses' attention.

"In an investigation like this," Stokes was saying, "we have to be very careful . . ."

"Marty," Roach said, "I have to interject something. Yesterday afternoon I was informed by the special agent in charge of the investigation that the man in the red hat does in fact exist. I was planning on telling you about it in our staff meeting on Monday morning. I had no idea the CIA was already pursuing this matter." Roach's basset hound eyes settled on Kennedy and his expression seemed to say, *thanks for blindsiding me.*

"As the president said," Kennedy reasserted herself, "we operate under a different set of rules than the FBI. A special team headed up by Mitch Rapp has been pursuing this individual for almost a month. Last night their hard work paid off, and they found him."

"Where?" Alexander asked eagerly.

"Cyprus. A town on the western end of the island called Limassol."

"Have we arrested him?"

Kennedy pursed her lips as she considered the word *arrested*. Rapp had not briefed her on the specifics of the operation, but she doubted he had asked permission from the local authorities. "Let's just say we have him in our possession."

"What is that supposed to mean?" asked Stokes.

The president laughed. "It means Mitch probably whacked him over the head and hog-tied him."

"Are we sure he's the right guy?" Stokes asked with great concern.

"Irene?" the president asked.

"Mitch says he's one hundred percent sure this is our guy."

"That's good enough for me." The president slapped his knee with finality.

"Are they still on the island?" Roach asked.

Kennedy shook her head. "No. They're in transit."

"Where?"

"They had a layover in Germany . . ." Kennedy glanced at her watch. "They're probably somewhere over the North Atlantic right now."

"I want this man put on trial," Alexander said with absolute conviction. "I want these terrorists to see that no matter how well they plan, no matter how far they run, we'll hunt them down and they will be brought to justice."

# 17

Rapp's eyes fluttered and then opened. He checked out his surroundings, not sure where he was for a moment, and then things fell into place. He rubbed his face and then stretched his arms over his head. Behind the cockpit was a small cabin with seating for twelve. Old, gray, worn leather first class seats had been installed in two rows. Four seats on the port side, four in the middle, and four on the starboard side. No personal DVD players or entertainment of any kind. It was a bare-bones operation. What it lacked in ambiance it made up for in space. Plenty of legroom and the seats reclined to a comfortable napping position.

Rapp sat in the back row on the port side. He checked his watch and for a second couldn't remember if he'd changed it before they'd left Germany. He must have. As was his custom, the arrow on the red and black dial on the outside of the submariner was pointed at 11:00. That was the time they were due to arrive in DC. A little more than two hours from now. The layover in Germany had lasted a little longer than intended. They'd stopped to take on a load of cargo so as to cover their tracks, and then the warning light for the portside cargo door wouldn't shut off even though a visual inspection showed the door to be seated properly. They sat on the tarmac for almost three hours while they waited for the faulty warning light to be switched out.

That was when the big Russian woke up. The only thing they'd gotten out of him so far was a fake name. Rapp knew it was fake, because Dumond had run it through Langley's database and come up with a dossier for Aleksandr Zukof. Everything was wrong. Age, height, weight, eye color. Everything except the black hair, and the fact that Zukof was a former employee of the KGB.

Rapp's instinct was to pummel the big idiot for lying to him, but caution got the best of him, and he decided he should at least wait until they were back in the air. Even with the broken jaw, the Russian tried to speak. Rapp was running out of energy and patience. Brooks sensed this so she shot the Russian up with another dose of Thorazine and sent him back to la-la land. By the time they were wheels up, and pointed west toward home, Rapp was too tired to do anything other than sleep. That was over three hours ago.

Rapp unbuckled his seat belt and stepped into the aisle. The years of pushing his body to the limit were catching up to him. His lower back, his knees, his hips; everything ached. He was hit with a flash of vertigo and grabbed the leather seatback in front of him to steady himself.

Brooks was sitting in the seat, working on a laptop. She felt her seat move and looked up. "May I help you?" she said with a bit of attitude.

Rapp knew he'd been unduly hard on her, but he hadn't decided yet if he was going to apologize. This was a hard business. The

CIA in general was one thing. It was more like IBM than most people realized. But the Clandestine Service was a different thing all together. It was more like Wall Street. Timid artists and wilting flowers need not apply. If you needed a lot of positive reinforcement to motivate you to do your job, you were at the wrong place.

"Would you like some coffee?"

She stared at him for a long moment before she answered. "Sure."

There was a small galley at the front of the cabin. Next to it were two sleeping berths. Stroble was sleeping in one, Coleman the other. Blue privacy curtains were drawn across each. Rapp quietly opened one of the metal cupboards and grabbed a packet of coffee. He dropped it in the top of the machine and pressed the green button. Rapp stretched and cracked his neck while he waited for the coffee to finish brewing. When it was done he poured two cups and brought one back to Brooks.

Brooks set her laptop on the seat next to her and took the white mug. "Thanks."

"You're welcome." Rapp sat on the armrest of the seat directly across the aisle.

"You see, that wasn't so hard, was it?"

"What?" Rapp frowned.

"Manners . . . I say thank you . . . You say you're welcome."

He rolled his eyes and said, "You know, you didn't do a bad job over the last month."

"Whoa . . . slow down there, partner." She arched her brows in a show of mock surprise. "That's a hell of an endorsement. Is that how you're going to write it up in my file. 'Didn't do a bad job.'"

"Listen, you need to understand this is not an easy job. I don't . . ."

"Stop!" Brooks put her hand up cutting him off. "This isn't about me. That's what I finally realized. When I threw the wine in your face I was still thinking about me. I was frustrated with the way you had treated me. The way you ordered me around like a little kid. Like I was some brainless rookie."

"I did . . ."

"Let me finish. You're Mitch Rapp. The living legend . . . bla . . . bla . . . bla. I was really impressed for the first month. Intimidated beyond belief, and then something clicked when we were on Cyprus. It wasn't me. It was you."

"You're going to have to get a little more specific."

"I didn't do anything wrong other than the fact that I didn't stand up to you earlier."

"Listen . . . you have a lot to learn."

"I wouldn't disagree with you for a moment, but you need help."

"What?" Rapp didn't know if he should laugh or be offended.

"My dad was a little bit like you . . . well, no one is really quite like you, but he was similar in the sense that he was a horrible communicator. He was a fixer. He had to do everything himself. Never thought anyone could do as good of a job as he could."

"Sounds like my kind of guy."

"Yeah." Brooks stared off into space for a second. "You would have liked him."

"He's not around anymore?"

"No. We lost him five years ago. Massive heart attack."

"Sorry to hear that."

"Thanks. He was a good man. Very faithful to my mother and us kids. Just couldn't communicate for shit. What about your dad?"

"Died when I was little."

"Was he in the business?"

"No." Rapp shook his head. "He was a suit. Good man, though."

"You see, this is good."

"What?"

"Talking."

"Talking is overrated."

Brooks smiled and her eyes lit up. "You've got some issues, and you're not going to solve them by keeping things bottled up."

"We all have issues."

"You really have issues. Your wife died over a year ago, and I'll bet you haven't talked to a single counselor about it."

Rapp's face turned hard. "Watch your step. You never met my wife, and you don't know me well enough to talk about this."

"Fuck you."

Rapp cocked his head to the side as if he couldn't believe what he'd just heard.

"Excuse me?"

"You heard me. I learned it from you. No bullshit, speak the truth, and get the job done. That's you. You don't respect people who are incompetent, you don't respect people who waste your time, and you really don't respect people who are intimidated by you."

"And?"

"I'm speaking the truth and you know it. You just don't want to admit it. Big tough Mitch Rapp can't go see a shrink and talk about his problems because that would be a sign of weakness and the one thing you despise more than anything in others is weakness. So your solution is to repress. To bury the pain and all you're doing is making it worse."

Rapp dropped his head into his right hand and mumbled, "Oh . . . fuck. My head hurts." He'd had virtually the same conversation with Kennedy on Christmas Eve. "Why do you women always have to psychoanalyze me?"

"Because we all secretly want to be your mother or your lover."

Rapp lifted his face out of his hand. "Huh."

"I'm teasing . . . kind of. But let's not get off the subject. You need to talk to someone about what happened to your wife."

"You need to watch your step."

Brooks defiantly shook her head. "No. What are you going to do? Hit me? Throw me out off the plane? I don't think so. You need help. You're just too scared to admit it."

"I don't need any help." Rapp stood.

"Keep telling yourself that. You might actually believe it someday."

# 18

Rapp opened the door at the rear of the cabin and stepped into the forward pressurized cargo area. He closed the door behind him and leaned against it. The metal floor was streaked with dirt and grease where cargo had been pushed in and dragged out. A series of three overhead lights lit the space. It was empty except for one half-moon cargo container that was secured flush against the far bulkhead. Rapp looked at the shiny, dented aluminum container with a complete lack of enthusiasm. Subconsciously, he'd been hoping to put this off. Let someone else deal with it. Someone who was properly motivated. He was sure they could find plenty of Secret Service agents who would give up their badge for five minutes alone with Gazich. Maybe even the president-elect himself would like a private audience with the Bosnian.

Rapp tried to focus on his next step, but couldn't get his mind off what Brooks had said. He'd allowed a twenty-something rookie to get under his skin to the point where he'd actually thought of hitting her just to get her to shut up. She'd driven him out of the windowless cabin and back into the cargo hold, simply because he didn't want to hear another word. He was not well. He knew it. He just didn't want to hear it. Especially from someone he barely knew.

With two hours left in the flight he could think of only one excuse to get away from her. The unofficial manual on interrogation was pretty straightforward when it came to a situation where time was not critical. You softened up the detainee by stripping them of all sense of time and place, while at the same time building up a dossier on their history. Then you carefully crafted your plan of attack in the same way a prosecutor prepares to question a defendant at trial. Except in this situation there is no defense attorney to object and no judge to sustain the objection.

You start by asking only questions that you already know the answer to. That way if the detainee lies, you have grounds to make him uncomfortable until he tells you the truth. When he finally does, you move on to the next question. If he is honest, you move on again. If he lies, the pain/pleasure principle is put in to play. This continues until a pattern of honesty is developed and then you begin with the important stuff.

Usually twenty-four hours was the minimum time needed to properly disorient a subject. Gazich had been in the container going on thirteen hours. Not ideal, but then again the man had four gunshot wounds to very sensitive areas of the body. His last morphine shot had been delivered on the tarmac in Germany. Right about now, the drug would be wearing off and the pain would be hitting him in waves—increasing in frequency and strength.

Rapp approached the aluminum box and grabbed the handle. The front wall was basically two interlocking doors. Rapp was not worried that Gazich would be able to make any attempt at escape.

He twisted the handle, spun it ninety degrees, and then swung the right door open. The inside of the door, as well as the rest of the container, was lined with gray acoustic foam. The box was five feet deep by eight feet wide. Rapp grabbed the other door and opened it as well.

Light spilled into the dark chamber throwing Rapp's shadow onto Gazich's body. The Bosnian was lying on a nylon field stretcher that sat only a few inches off the ground. His pants had been cut away so Stroble could clean and dress the gunshot wounds to his knees. Rapp looked at the bandages. They were clean and white. No sign of blood. Four wide straps secured Gazich to the stretcher as well as two wrist cuffs. Even if he were healthy he would have a hard time breaking free. With the wounds to his knees and hands it was hopeless.

Gazich squinted and turned his head just enough to look at the shadowy figure before him. "Is it time for my in-flight meal?"

Rapp laughed. "Yeah . . . filet mignon accompanied with a first-class Cabernet."

"I prefer Bordeaux."

"Great. So in addition to being a terrorist you're also a wine snob."

"No. I just hate America." Gazich smiled showing off a slight gap between his top two teeth.

The fact that Gazich might harbor ill will toward the United States was something he had not considered. "So you have a beef with America?"

"Doesn't everybody?"

"No. Actually we get along pretty well with most people." As Rapp's eyes adjusted to the change in light he could see that Gazich was sweating. "Would you like another shot of morphine?"

Gazich hesitated. He was not stupid. He had a fairly good idea how this game was played. "Not very sporting of you, the way you sneaked up behind me."

"Back in Cyprus?"

"You hid behind that doorframe like a woman. The same way your pilots like to drop bombs from the sky."

Rapp laughed. "Yeah, you Bosnians are famous for fighting fair. Is that what you were doing when you rounded up all those innocent Muslim women and children and slaughtered them?"

"I have no idea what you are talking about."

"So you're not a Bosnian?" Rapp asked in a sarcastic voice.

"I am Greek."

Rapp shook his head. "You're a liar. And a bad one at that, but I'll play along with you for a while. What were those Russians doing in your office last night?"

"I don't know. I have never seen them before."

"So the guy on the street. The one sitting in the front seat of the parked car . . . you just shot him for no reason."

"I do not know what you are talking about."

For the first time Rapp was starting to think that Gazich might not be very smart. "I watched you walk down the street, stroll up to the open window, and shoot the man twice in the heart. And then you stood there and talked to him for a while before you took off and did your little dance across the roof tops."

Gazich squirmed under the straps. After a long moment he said, "It was a disagreement."

"So you do know them?"

"No."

"Who was the disagreement between then?"

"A friend of mine and those Russian gangsters."

Rapp eyed Gazich with suspicion. He wondered for a moment if it was possible that the attack in America and the Russians showing up in Cyprus were in fact unrelated. Once he started with the Russian he'd get to the bottom of it. The man would not be hard to break.

"The café owner?"

"Yes."

"That's interesting."

"Why?" Gazich shut his eyes as he was hit with a wave of pain.

"The café owner says those Russians were looking for you."

"He's not all right in the head. He owed them money. They were threatening him, so I stepped in to help him out. We Greeks stick together."

Rapp looked down at him, his patience quickly running out. He squatted down on his haunches and said, "I'm not a particularly patient man, so I'm going to get down to business. I know who you are. I know you're not Greek, I know that those Russians were sent to Cyprus to kill you, and I know you were in Washington two and a half months ago."

"I'm afraid you are confused."

"Confused." Rapp chewed on the word for a moment. "I'm a lot of things, but confused is not one of them. I'll tell you what I am, though. I'm the last man on the planet that you want to piss off any further than you already have. I don't enjoy this shit, but each time you jerk me off with one of your bullshit answers, I lose what little sympathy I have for you."

"You don't strike me as the caring type anyway."

"You'd be surprised."

"Do you care about the truth? About justice? Are you open to the idea that maybe your cocksure American attitude has blinded your judgment? Do you think it's possible that maybe I'm not the man you're looking for?"

Rapp grinned and scratched the black stubble on his chin. "Oh . . . boy. You just don't get it. You're in way over your head."

"I would like to speak to a lawyer."

"Lawyer," Rapp laughed. "That's a good one. Did I forget to show you my badge?" Rapp patted his pockets. "Oh that's right. I forgot. I don't carry one." He leaned in closer. "There aren't going to be any lawyers. No judge. No jury. Just a really painful interrogation, a confession, and then your execution. Based on your attitude so far, I'd say there's about a ninety-five percent chance that's the way things will turn out."

Gazich licked his lips and blinked his eyes. Rapp's words were having very little effect on him due to the fact that he was more focused on the ever-increasing pain that seemed to be shooting from every inch of his body. "And the other five percent?"

"Compared to option A, I think it's a pretty easy choice, but then again you haven't shown yourself to be the most rational person so far."

"What is it?"

"You tell me everything. Who hired you, how it was planned, where the money is. Everything." Rapp could see Gazich weighing his options. "You and I both know," Rapp added, "you're going to tell me either way."

"Then why not torture me? You seem like the type who would enjoy it."

Rapp shook his head. "I'd prefer to do it the civilized way."

"And when you're done with me?"

"We'll stick you in a prison for the rest of your life. Maybe you'll be eligible for parole in thirty years, I don't know." Rapp was making it up as he went. He knew he had to give the man some hope. "Someone higher up than me will be making that decision."

"Doesn't sound like a very good deal."

"Compared to months of torture and an execution, I think it's a pretty great deal."

"You're not the one on the receiving end."

"I'm not the one who set off a car bomb that killed the new president's wife." Rapp watched as Gazich blinked and then looked away. The words had hit home.

"How about a shot of morphine?" Gazich asked in a tight voice. "I'd like to think about your offer."

Rapp reminded himself that time was on his side. "All right. I'll show you how nice we Americans are. I'll give you the shot and then . . ."

The cabin door opened and Brooks stepped into the space. She had a satellite phone in her outstretched hand. "Someone needs to talk to you."

There was something about her tone that told Rapp it was serious.

"All right." Rapp looked back at Gazich and said, "I'll be back in a minute." He stood and started shutting the container doors.

"What about the morphine?" Gazich yelled.

Rapp sealed the doors and Gazich's screams were reduced to a hollow muffle. Rapp walked across the open space and asked, "Who is it?"

"Director Kennedy."

Rapp took the phone from Brooks, held it to his ear and asked, "What's up?" He listened for ten seconds and then said, "Have you people lost your fucking minds?"

# 19

The horse had left the barn. That much Kennedy understood, and there was no getting it back. Attorney General
Stokes and FBI Director Roach were over by the president's desk using two separate secure phones to get their people
moving. The president and president–elect were talking in earnest,
still in the two chairs in front of the fireplace. The news of his wife's
killer's capture had melted the wall between them. Kennedy had
seen Alexander on only two occasions since the election. Both
times the future leader seemed somber and detached, which was
very uncharacteristic for the charismatic forty-five-year-old from
Georgia. The news had reignited a spark in him that had been missing since the tragic death of his wife.

Kennedy watched the president and president-to-be talk one
on one. She couldn't help thinking of the photos Baker had shown
her less than twenty-four hours ago. Based on the way Alexander

had acted over the last few months, Kennedy doubted he knew of his wife's infidelities. But she had seen stranger things. Washington was replete with torrid tales of the rich and powerful and their strange marital arrangements. Her instincts told her Alexander was genuinely bereaved, but she'd been fooled by politicians before. Thomas Stansfield, her mentor, had taught her that the good politicians were better than any actor in Hollywood. They were real stage actors; performing in front of a live audience three or four times a day. And they often did it on the fly.

With Alexander, though, there was something about his pain that seemed very real. Kennedy wondered how much of her assessment was formed by wishful thinking. The alternative made her shudder. The best part of her wanted to believe that he was a good man. A man she could support. That was back on the table now. Kennedy could see clearly now what President Hayes had been up to. What he'd been trying to do for her and for the CIA. With Vice President–Elect Ross in Europe, Hayes saw his opening and used it. Ross and Kennedy did not get along. Alexander had virtually turned over the national security piece of the puzzle to his running mate, the former director of National Intelligence. Alexander was focusing on the domestic and economic teams and Ross the defense and intelligence. Translation: Kennedy would be out of a job shortly after the two were sworn in.

What Hayes was trying to do was show Alexander that Kennedy and her people were really effective at what they did. Not the type of people you simply threw overboard because your running mate doesn't like them. A running mate who happens to have a massive narcissistic complex. While all of these kudos felt good for a change, Kennedy saw a potential problem. The president should have seen it as well, but he probably thought the ends would justify the means. The problem was Mitch Rapp. He'd sooner get a colonoscopy than deal with the Justice Department. Add to that the media firestorm that was sure to follow, and he was sure to be in a foul mood for months to come. She could try to lay it all at the feet of the president, but Rapp would be so upset that an operation was dragged into the public eye he would feel the need to spread his anger around.

Kennedy stood and took a step toward Hayes and Alexander. They stopped talking and looked up.

"I'd better inform Mitch of the change in plans. If you'll excuse me I'm going to go down to the Situation Room and call him."

"We'll come with you," announced Hayes. "I'd love to congratulate him."

"And I'd like to thank him," Alexander added.

Kennedy winced ever so slightly and said, "I don't think that's a good idea. At least not at the moment."

Alexander looked confused and asked, "Why?"

President Hayes laughed. "Mitch does not like the limelight. He's going to hate all of this."

"You're right, sir."

Hayes seemed to take great joy in the fact that all this would bug Rapp. Alexander was frowning like he didn't get it.

Hayes looked at him and said, "He's not like us. We hang all of our awards on the wall for everybody to see. His medals and commendations are kept in a safe out at Langley, and I'll bet not once has he ever gone to look at them. Am I right?" he asked Kennedy.

"Yes, sir. You are."

"Have you met him?" Hayes asked Alexander.

"No. I've heard a lot about him, though."

"Don't believe everything you hear. Especially if it comes from your vice president's mouth."

Kennedy decided this would be a good time to exit. "As soon as I'm done I'll come back and give you an update."

She turned and left the room, cutting through the secretary's outer office and then down the stairs and past the White House Mess. She stopped outside the secure door of the Situation Room and grabbed her bar-coded and laminated badge that was clipped to the lapel of her jacket. She stuck it under the scanner next to the door and listened to the click. A small camera above the door monitored her every move. When the door clicked she entered and was greeted by a fresh-faced man in civilian clothing with an obvious military bearing.

"Major Hansen, I presume."

"Yes, Ma'am."

*Another marine,* she thought. They were always throwing around Ma'am instead of Ms. She didn't take the use of the antiquated phrase personally. It was a byproduct of being yelled at by their drill instructors for three straight months while they tried to make it through Boot Camp or Officer's Candidate School.

"Would you please contact the Global Ops Center and have them get Mr. Rapp on the line for me. I'll take it in the conference room."

"Yes, Ma'am. Anything else, Ma'am?"

She considered telling him to stop calling her Ma'am, but figured the call was more important. "Just the call, please."

Kennedy went into the conference room and set her purse down on the table. While she waited for the call to be connected she tried to guess on a scale of one to ten just how upset Rapp would be. She considered the possibility that this might be one of those rare occasions where she would need to bite back. It wasn't her style, and it could be a dangerous proposition when dealing with Rapp. Often the best way to manage him was to let him blow his lid and get it out of his system. If it wasn't something that was her direct fault she could often ride it out in silence and then make him feel bad for losing his cool. She hoped that would be the case this morning.

The large, white, secure phone rang once. Kennedy grabbed the handset and identified herself. The voice on the other end asked her to hold and then a moment later a woman came on the line. It was Agent Brooks. Kennedy asked for Rapp and then waited.

About thirty seconds later a tired, gruff voice came on the line and asked, "What's up?"

"You're not going to like this," Kennedy started, "so I'm going to get right to the point. The president just told the president-elect that you found Gazich and are on your way back to the States." Kennedy paused knowing it was the next part that would upset him. In a voice lacking conviction she said, "Alexander wants the man put on trial. When you land you'll be met by the FBI and they will take custody of the prisoner." There was a five second pause before Kennedy got her reply.

"Have you people lost your fucking minds?"

Kennedy took a deep breath and said, "No."

"This guy is a terrorist. A hired assassin. A foreigner with I don't know how many passports and aliases. I kidnapped him, for Christ sake."

"And?"

"And," Rapp screamed, "think big picture. Think tactics and techniques. I don't want the FBI asking me a bunch of questions about how I run my operations."

"We'll be able to limit that."

"Bullshit! You know you won't. If they put him on trial that means the piece of crap gets a lawyer, and that means I get to spend a week in some conference room getting deposed by a bunch of socialists who do pro bono work for fucking Amnesty International."

"Mitch, you know I won't let that happen."

"You can't promise that. A year from now, when this all goes down, you're not going to be in a position to protect me. You're gonna be writing a memoir and giving speeches for a hundred grand a pop."

Kennedy was expecting him to be upset, but not this upset. "Mitch, I don't see the problem. You said you were a hundred per-cent sure this is the guy. You must have some pretty good evidence against him."

"Not the kind of evidence you use in court!"

Kennedy detected something in his voice. "Did you torture a confession out of him?"

"No," Rapp muttered.

"That didn't sound convincing."

"I did not torture a confession out of him."

"Then what's the problem?"

Rapp muttered something again, swore, and then said, "I shot him."

"We can deal with that. I'm sure you had cause."

"I shot him four times."

"And he's alive," Kennedy snapped.

"I wasn't trying to kill him."

Kennedy placed her hand over her forehead. "Oh god! Please don't tell me you kneecapped him. Please don't tell me you've been torturing him."

"No!"

"Then why in the hell did you shoot him four times?" she barked. "You're supposed to be an expert marksmen."

"Oh . . . fuck. You're killing me. If I have to listen to another desk jockey question what I do in the field I'm going to go postal."

"I'm killing *you?* Are you kidding me? Mitch, you need to help me. You need to explain to me why you shot the prisoner four times, because when you land the FBI is going to take this guy into custody, and they sure as hell are going to ask."

"Trust me, you wouldn't understand."

"Try me."

"You work behind a desk and I work in the field."

"Mitchell!" she snapped.

"He was armed, I was in his backyard, there were other people involved, and I was operating without backup."

"Where were the others?"

"They got delayed at the airport."

"And you couldn't wait for them?"

"No."

"Or was it that you didn't want to wait for them?"

"Yeah, Irene. I wanted to be the lone cowboy so I could get all the credit. I'll tell you what. Maybe I'll have the pilot drop us down to five thousand feet, I'll open the cargo door and kick this piece of crap into the ocean and you can all kiss my ass."

"Mitch, I'm not saying you did any of this to try and get credit, what I'm doing is . . ."

"Second-guessing me from thousands of miles away."

"I'm not second-guessing you. I'm trying to find out what happened so we can figure out what to say to the FBI."

"It was like I said; it was his home turf, he'd already killed two people and I didn't have time to wait around for backup so I moved in and took care of the situation."

"Why did you have to shoot him four times?"

"This guy's good. I was flying solo, so I needed to put him out of commission fast."

"What do you mean put him out of commission?"

"I needed to cripple him."

Kennedy thought about what that meant for a moment.

Filling the dead air, Rapp said, "This isn't the type of guy who surrenders when you shout, *freeze.*"

"So you shot first and asked questions later."

"Basically."

"Where did you shoot him?"

"Once in each knee."

"That's only twice. You said you shot him four times."

"And then in each hand."

"So you crucified him."

"No. If I'd shot him in the feet I would have crucified him."

Kennedy was starting to figure out how bad this would look. "Don't you think you might have gone a bit overboard?"

"Irene, I'm going to say this one more time. I'm the one out here risking my ass to hunt this guy down. I'd just seen him kill two men in the span of about ten minutes and neither of them had a chance. This guy is good. I was the one on-site. I was the one who had to make the decision, and anyone who wants to second-guess me can go fuck themselves."

"Including me?"

"Yes, including you, and President Hayes and President–Elect Alexander and anyone else who wants to armchair quarterback me. In fact, I'll tell you what. The next time this shit happens you can all get off your bureaucratic asses, pick up a gun, and head out into the real world and see how you fare. You try taking a guy like Gazich, and he'll put a bullet in your head before you finish uttering *freeze.*"

Kennedy clutched the phone in one hand and had the other one on her hip. She was staring straight ahead at the wood paneled wall and asked, "Are you done?"

"Yeah . . . I'm done. In fact as soon as I land, I'm on the next plane out."

"What do you mean the next plane out?"

"The next plane out. The first plane I can get on that will get me as far away from Washington as possible."

"You can't do that, Mitch. You need to be debriefed by us, and then the FBI is going to want to talk to you."

"Well, tough shit. I did the hard part. The rest of you can figure out how you're going to run your circus because I'm not going to be a part of it."

"You can't do . . ." The line clicked and then went dead. Kennedy stared at the white handset for a second and shook her head. In all her years she had never known anyone who could so thoroughly annoy her as Mitch Rapp.

The main door to the conference room opened and the president entered with Alexander.

Hayes saw Kennedy holding the phone and asked, "Is that Mitch? Let me talk to him. I'd like to pass along my thanks, and I'm sure Josh would as well."

Kennedy shook her head. "We're having some technical problems."

"Well let's get them fixed. These guys down here are whizzes when it comes to that."

"Maybe we should wait awhile. It sounded like he had his hands full."

Hayes looked at Alexander and then back to Kennedy. "Fine. Maybe Mitch can stop by this week, and we can thank him personally."

Kennedy looked the president in the eye, and uttered a polite but untruthful reply. "I'm sure he'd appreciate that, sir."

# 20

Rapp was leaning forward, both hands placed flat against the bulkhead as if he was trying to push the plane through the air. His eyes were shut. His head down. Coleman and Stroble were up, standing in their stocking feet in the galley. They had been awakened by Rapp's heated conversation with Kennedy. With sleep still in their eyes they looked at Rapp tentatively, unsure of what had him so pissed off. Brooks was standing in the aisle next to her seat, a look of deep concern on her face.

Coleman looked at Brooks for a clue. She shrugged and shook her head.

"Mitch," Coleman asked, "what happened?"

Rapp didn't bother to open his eyes or raise his head. "The politicians are involved."

"How bad?"

"Bad. The FBI is going to meet us when we land and take our guy into custody."

"Didn't we pretty much always know that was a possibility?" Brooks asked.

Coleman looked at her and quickly shook his head from side to side.

Rapp dropped one arm and looked at Brooks with a withering stare. "Yes, it was a possibility," he said with an edge, "but considering how things went down in Cyprus, I would have advised against handing him over to the FBI, or at a bare minimum I would have made sure we had a week with him to make sure we interrogated him properly."

Brooks nodded sheepishly and then looked at the ground.

"They're going to meet us at the airport?" a surprised Coleman asked.

"Yes."

"How in the hell did the FBI find out so fast?"

"Hayes told Alexander that we caught the guy who killed his wife. Alexander wants him put on trial. He wants the whole world to see that we caught the guy."

"But we don't have any hard evidence against this guy."

"I know. They jumped the gun."

"So they're going to meet us at the airport?" Coleman asked again. "When we land." He looked at his watch. "In less than two hours."

"That's right."

"What about media?"

"Who the fuck knows?"

"This isn't going to work," Coleman said with real concern.

"Why?" Brooks asked. "What do we have to be ashamed of? We did their job for them."

"You're not thinking of the big picture. News like this is huge. I'd bet my left nut that the phone lines in Washington are burning up right now. Everybody is going to try and get in on the act and either take part of the credit or act like they were in the know."

"I still don't see the problem. This is a huge success for us. For the Agency."

Coleman laughed. "I don't work for the Agency, and I sure as hell don't need any publicity."

"Well the Agency does."

"That's debatable," Rapp said.

"Come on, Mitch. We're the redheaded stepchild. I've heard you say it a dozen times over the past month. We need some good press."

"You're assuming the press is going to treat us well."

"Well, why wouldn't they?"

"Every news story has its cycle. And when it's about the Agency, no matter how good it looks at the beginning, it eventually gets ugly."

"Come again?" Brooks said in a skeptical tone.

"It all comes down to our methods. They're vegetarians. We're meat eaters. We'll never see eye to eye. This plane, our tactics, the way we deploy, the way we put a black bag over someone's head in the middle of the night, sneak them out of a country without anyone knowing . . . it will all come under scrutiny."

"I think you're being a bit paranoid."

"I think you're naïve." Rapp looked at his watch. "We don't have a lot of time, so here's what we're going to do. Our Russian friend here." Rapp pointed over his shoulder at the slumbering oaf in the corner. "Have any of you told anyone else that he exists?"

Coleman, Stroble, and Brooks all shook their heads.

"Good. He doesn't exist."

"What are you going to do with him?" Brooks asked.

Rapp's patience was wearing thin. "This would be a good time for you to watch and learn."

"Are you going to kill him?"

"Brooks, look me in the eye, so there's no doubt between any of us that you understand what I'm about to tell you."

Brooks guardedly folded her arms across her chest and looked at him with her greener than brown hazel eyes.

"Stop asking questions. This isn't a fucking debate club. It's a benevolent dictatorship, and I'm not feeling very benevolent right now, so unless you want to find your ass transferred out of the Clandestine Service and into some secretarial pool at one of the offsite locations, you're going to do everything I tell you to do for the next two hours. Can you do that?"

She took a moment to decide and then reluctantly said, "Yes."

# 21

app yanked open the light aluminum door and looked down at Gazich. It was obvious by the prisoner's pasty skin that the morphine had worn off. His forehead and upper lip were covered with beads of sweat, and his entire body quivered beneath the drab gray blanket. Rapp knew from firsthand experience that simply going from darkness to light in such an agonizing state could be painful. He watched the Bosnian shut his eyes and winced with understanding. Rapp did not like Gazich, but he took no joy in his discomfort.

Rapp had just spent the last five minutes on the phone with Marcus Dumond learning more about Gazich. There were passports, financial information, a key to a safety deposit box, cash, weapons, computers, backup disks, and hard files all found by Hacket and Wicker at Gazich's office and home. All of it was scanned or photographed and sent to Dumond back in DC. At first glance the information gave them a pretty good idea of what Alexander Deckas had been up to for the past seven years. Dumond had already taken to referring to the prisoner as two separate people. Gavrilo Gazich was the man wanted by The Hague for war crimes in Bosnia, and Alexander Deckas was a seemingly legitimate businessman who had run a company called Aid Logistics Inc based out of Limassol, Cyprus.

Hacket and Wicker had taken the hard drives from both the office and home computers of Gazich and uploaded them via satellite to Dumond. So far the encryption programs had frustrated the MIT genius, but he expected to have them decrypted by later in the day. Rapp told him to make sure no one at Langley knew what he was up to, including DCI Kennedy. Dumond was used to working on a need-to-know basis, but DCI Kennedy was pretty much always in the need-to-know loop. Rapp told Dumond he was short on time and would explain everything when he saw him later today. The more pressing issue at the moment was to get Gazich to talk before he had to turn him over to the FBI.

Moving one step to his left, Rapp managed to block out the light that was hitting Gazich in his face. The CIA operative held out a syringe and said, "Here's how we play this game. I'm going to ask you a series of questions. If you answer them truthfully, you get your shot of morphine. If you lie to me, just once, no shot."

Gazich nodded eagerly.

"I want to be really clear about this . . . I know more about you than you can possibly imagine. I've talked to the big Russian," Rapp lied. "The one whose face you were in process of carving up. He had some very interesting things to say about you."

"Russians are professional liars," Gazich growled.

Rapp help up a cautionary finger. "We've gone through your office and your house and have run your photo through our facial recognition system. We have you on tape buying coffee at the Starbucks on Wisconsin Avenue the morning that the bomb went off. If you lie, even once, I shut the door and we start over again in thirty minutes."

"I'll tell you whatever you want. Hurry up and give me the shot."

"Oh no." Rapp laughed. "We talk first, and then you get the shot."

"Then hurry up with your questions."

Rapp had a theory, and he was going to test it after he started with a few easy questions. "Who hired you?"

"I don't know," Gazich moaned in frustration.

"Fine." Rapp took a step back and started closing the door.

"I swear!" Gazich yelled in a panic. "Everything was handled over the Internet."

Rapp stood there with the door half closed. This was the answer he expected. If Gazich had given him a name he would have been suspicious. Big money contracts like these were rarely handled face to face.

"You didn't know them, but they knew you?" Rapp asked.

"By reputation only."

"Then how did they track you down?"

"I don't know," he snarled. "I was in the process of finding that out when you burst into my office and shot me."

"How did you get into the U.S.?" Rapp watched Gazich hesitate before answering. So far the man had denied any involvement in the attack on the motorcade. "Be careful. Take your time to think this one through. You wouldn't want to lie to me."

Gazich squirmed under the strain of the straps and said, "I flew into New York the day before."

"Which airport?"

"JFK."

"The explosives?"

"They were waiting for me."

"Where?"

"Pennsylvania."

"The state?"

"Yes, the state. Now give me my shot."

"Not quite yet. You're doing a good job, though. So you pick up the van, drive it down to Washington . . . when, on Friday?"

"No," Gazich snapped. "I told you I arrived in New York on Friday."

It was possible to fly into JFK, stop in Pennsylvania, and get to Washington in one day, but Rapp wasn't going to argue with him. Not yet. The fact that his fuse was so short was a good sign. He wanted the morphine big-time.

"So you stayed in Pennsylvania on Friday night?"

"Yes . . . Yes! The van was waiting for me and I drove it down to Washington early on Saturday morning. I found my spot, I parked it, I waited, and then when the time was right I blew it up. End of story. There you go. Now give me my shot."

Rapp squatted down and pulled back the blanket to reveal Gazich's hand. A port was taped to the back of his right hand. Stroble had put it in earlier so he could give Gazich a bag of plasma and his first two shots of morphine. Rapp popped the cap off the premeasured dose and was about to insert the needle when he thought of one more question.

"Where were you standing when you detonated the bomb?"

Gazich's eyes were focused on the needle with such intensity that he didn't understand the question. "What?"

"When the bomb went off . . . where were you standing?"

"The fucking tree!" Gazich yelled. "I was standing behind a tree a half block away! Now give me the shot."

Rapp nodded. Agent Rivera had been right. He slid the needle into the white port and pressed the plunger. The dose was just enough to keep him comfortable for thirty to forty-five minutes, and then the pain would come back with a vengeance. Rapp watched as Gazich began to relax almost immediately. His body went from rigid to relaxed, and his breathing settled into a normal pattern as the alkaloid drug eased his pain.

"So they tried to back out of paying you the rest of the money after the job." Rapp said this casually. Like one professional talking to another.

"The second part?" Gazich scoffed. "They wanted their deposit back."

"Not very professional," Rapp said with a disappointed look on his face. "So you waited a few seconds too long and you only got one limo instead of both."

The drug was working fast. Gazich looked up at Rapp with dilated eyes and slurred his first few words. "I did exactly as I was told. I fulfilled my part of the deal. They were the ones who screwed up."

"How so?"

"They told me to hit the second limo."

Rapp's brow furrowed with surprise. Tactically this made no sense. The van had enough power to take out both limos. Picking just one from the outset cut your odds of success in half. "Why not take out both?"

"I don't know. I'm not paid to question my employers."

"So when did they tell you to hit the second limo?" Rapp was thinking maybe he'd received the order when he'd picked up the van.

"Twenty to thirty seconds, before it all went down."

"Before the blast?" asked a surprised Rapp.

"Yes."

They must have had a spotter that morning watching the candidates get in their vehicles. Rapp wondered if Agent Rivera shuffled the limousines as they left the compound. It was a fairly common Secret Service tactic. That would explain why they blew up the wrong limo.

"The phone you received the call on . . . where did you get it?"

"It was waiting for me in the van."

"Was it also used to remote detonate the bomb?"

"Yes."

"I don't suppose you hung on to it?"

"No."

"Okay." Rapp was trying to wrap his mind around the entire operation. It wasn't how he would have done it, but then again the enemy had proven in the past that they weren't always logistical geniuses. He stood and looked down at Gazich. "One more question. I read your file. You obviously hate Muslims. Why work for them?"

Gazich smiled for the first time. "My enemy's enemy is my ally."

"That and the fact that they probably paid you a shitload of money."

"The money was fine, but I wanted to strike a blow for my country."

Rapp would have gladly debated him on the issue, but it would have been a waste of crucial time. Guys like Gazich didn't simply change their mind after a brief conversation. Rapp began closing the cargo door and said, "We'll be landing in an hour."

# 22

The big plane touched down softly at 10:47 a.m. Eastern Standard Time. Rapp and Coleman joined the pilots in the cockpit as they taxied to the cargo portion of the airport. They half expected to be greeted by a welcoming committee of police cars, FBI sedans, and a gaggle of news vans. Fortunately, it appeared their cover story had held. It looked cold outside, which was a good thing. Customs officers were humans too. The cold weather would keep them huddled inside rather than out on the tarmac nosing around. Rapp took one final look out the window and then turned to Coleman who was now wearing the same uniform as the pilot and copilot: black pants, white shirt with black and silver epaulets, and a black tie. He was listed as Tom Jones, the plane's navigator on the official manifest. He had a full set of worn credentials to match. Coleman would clear customs with the two pilots and be off the airport property in thirty minutes or less.

Rapp stuck out his hand. "I'll see you in a few hours."

"Good luck with the handoff," Coleman replied.

"You sure you don't want to come along?"

"Yeah . . . right after I get my barium enema."

Rapp laughed at him and left the cockpit. He passed Stroble who was now wearing a soiled BWI ground crew uniform. "Don't drop the container."

"I won't, boss."

"And stop calling me boss."

"Sure thing, boss."

Brooks was waiting by the cargo door with her two bags.

"Are you all set?" Rapp asked.

"Yes."

"Good. Let's go."

The two of them proceeded into the storage area with Stroble following them. The big Russian had already been transferred into the container and placed bound and gagged on the floor next to Gazich. Like Gazich, he was also drugged. There was just enough room for Rapp and Brooks to sit at each end of the container. Once Rapp and Brooks were situated, Stroble closed and locked the doors.

The plane was guided to its spot on the tarmac, and the engines were shut down. Ten minutes later two trucks pulled up, one with a set of stairs, the other with an extending cargo box. The two pilots and Coleman came down the stairs, their black trench coats flapping in the wind. They held their hats with one hand and dragged their carry-on bags behind them as they made their way to the cargo terminal. The forward port cargo door opened from the inside, and the aluminum cargo container was pushed into the back of the truck's extended cargo area and secured. Stroble shut both the truck's and plane's cargo doors and walked back through the plane and down the stairs. When he hit the tarmac, two more trucks manned with BWI ground personnel pulled up and went to work emptying the cargo in the lower holds.

Stroble gave the guys a wave and a nod as he jumped in the front passenger seat of the truck he had just loaded. The man sitting behind the wheel was someone he had never met and didn't care to know. Someone who worked for Rapp at the CIA handled this end of the operation. The truck headed straight for the customs checkpoint. A customs officer left the warmth of his booth just long enough to grab the paperwork from the driver and then he retreated inside. Stroble assumed this guy was also on the payroll. Thirty seconds later the guy came back out with the paperwork and gave it back to the driver. They rolled through the gate and stopped at a truck yard no more than a quarter mile away. A truck of similar size, but without the ability to lift the cargo box vertically, was waiting with its rear door open. Stroble jumped out, opened the cargo door, and climbed in. The truck from the airport backed up until the two cargo areas were aligned with just a six-inch gap in between. The cargo container had ball bearings on the bottom so it could be easily maneuvered in tight spaces. Stroble unhooked two straps that had kept the container in place and then pushed the aluminum box from one truck into the back of the new one.

Once the truck from the airport left, Stroble jumped behind the wheel of the new vehicle and began driving toward an industrial park on the Patapsco River. Only four miles away, he took the quickest route, just like Rapp had told him. Five minutes later, he pulled into an old brick warehouse and closed the door. The entire trip took just under thirty minutes.

Two white vans were waiting side by side. Other than that the place was empty. Stroble let Rapp and Brooks out of the cargo container and they transferred Gazich into one van and the Russian into the other. Rapp put his bags and Brooks's bags in the van with the Russian and then walked Brooks over to the other van.

"Do you know where you're going?"

She nodded. "What if they won't let me in?" She held up a passport. "This isn't even real."

"I told you I'd call and make sure you're on the list. Candice Jones . . . just give them the passport, and they'll tell you where to go."

Brooks shook her head and frowned.

"What?" Rapp asked.

"They're going to be expecting you."

"Yes they are. But I'm not going."

"Why do I have to do this?"

"Because you're the one who thinks this will be good P.R. for the Agency."

"I do, but I don't see why you're dumping it all on me."

"Cindy, listen to me. I promise you this will not hurt your career. In fact, it will probably help it. Just hand Gazich over and leave. Don't hang around and let them start peppering you with questions. There's going to be an agent there who I know pretty well. He's a big guy. Late fifties. His name is Skip McMahon. Just tell him I'll call him."

"When?"

"Today . . . tomorrow . . . I don't know. You'd better tell him today. But whatever you do don't tell him how we got into the country. Are we clear on that?"

"Yes."

"Good. Follow us to the interstate and then once we hit the exit for Andrews you're on your own. Give them Gazich and get out of there. I'll call you in an hour. All right?"

"Yeah . . . I got it."

"Good. Let's roll."

Brooks climbed behind the wheel of the one van and Rapp got into the passenger seat of the other. Stroble pulled down on the gearshift and put the van in drive. They pulled out of the garage and headed toward Interstate 95.

Stroble looked over at Rapp and said, "They're going to shit their pants when they figure out you're not there."

"I know they are."

"So what's your master plan?"

"Sandbag them."

"Huh?"

"Sooner or later the media and the Clark Kents at the FBI and Justice are going to turn the spotlight on me and make this about my tactics."

"Yeah."

"I'm just making sure they do it sooner rather than later."

"And why is that a good idea?"

"I'm going to give them enough rope to hang themselves, and then I'm going to kick the chair out from under their legs."

"I'm still not sure I follow."

Rapp held up his Treo phone and played back the recording he'd made of the session he'd had with Gazich. "Don't worry," he said to Stroble. "By tomorrow evening they're all going to be diving for cover."

# 23

---

Ross had flown commercial with his Secret Service detail even though a private jet had been offered to him by one of the billionaire attendees at the conference. The offer was tempting, but Ross knew the media, the vicious bloggers, and the crazy talk radio folks would light him up. Taking a private jet home from a conservation summit smacked of elitism and hypocrisy. He could wait one more week until *Air Force Two* was at his disposal.

Besides, the Air France flight wasn't bad. The stewardesses up in first class were extremely attractive and spared no effort in fawning over him. His fellow passengers wanted their photo taken with him. Ross was a man of the people. His not-so-pleasant conversation with Green in the wine cellar the night before had driven him to drink more wine than he should have, and he had boarded the plane with a head-splitting hangover. Everything after midnight was a slight blur. He remembered being in the kitchen with Speyer, and the lanky blond talking, though about what, he could not remember for the life of him. Music was playing, the blond started dancing, and the next thing Ross knew, he was pinned against the refrigerator; her ass pressed firmly against his groin. He had a glass of wine in his left hand; she had his right hand wrapped around her body and placed dangerously close to her left breast.

Ross would have had her right there in the kitchen if it hadn't been for Speyer and the lascivious look in his eye. The president of one of the world's most private banks, Speyer didn't so much keep secrets as he did collect and trade in them. A prince of Europe's unofficial gay mafia, the banker would have loved nothing more than to be able to hold such a salacious bit of information over Ross's head. The vice president–elect had managed to extricate himself from the situation by playfully chastising Speyer and giving the leggy blond a kiss and a promise that he'd put her on his dance card for next year's conference.

The Secret Service had arranged to get Ross off the plane first and expedite him through customs. They'd also arranged to have his skis and bag picked up and delivered to his house. Ross walked through the terminal with a real sense of purpose and optimism. He'd miraculously banished from his mind all thought of Cy Green and the debt he owed him. His detail of agents were spread out around him, three in front, one on each side, and two more behind. The formation looked like a kickoff, which in turn reminded Ross that his New England Patriots had a playoff game this afternoon. Ross was born and raised outside Wilmington, Delaware, and had cheered for the Colts growing up. After graduating from Princeton, he worked at the CIA for a few years before getting a law degree from Yale and then moving on to Wall Street where he'd made his fortune. By thirty-five he and his wife had moved to the ultra-rich enclave of Greenwich, Connecticut, where they raised a boy and a girl, and where Ross eventually decided to jump on the Patriots' bandwagon.

Ross's son was out in Seattle trying to find himself. This bothered the politician more than he cared to admit, but he was too busy to obsess over the fact that his twenty-five-year-old son had gone to the nation's best schools and still couldn't figure out what the hell he wanted to do with his life. His daughter was a new mother and living in New York City. They were for the most part good kids. They burned through money at an alarming rate, but at least they stayed out of trouble. Their mother had done a relatively good job. Ross hadn't been around all that much. He was too busy making money and having fun. And it had all paid off. He was now only six days and one heartbeat away from the most powerful job in the world.

Just on the other side of the security checkpoint Ross saw his chief of staff, Jonathan Gordon, waiting for him. Ross smiled and gave him a little wave. Gordon was a good man. Very loyal. The Secret Service agents all knew Gordon and made just enough room for him to enter the inner protective circle. The scrum kept moving toward the exit without missing a stride.

"Jonathan, nice of you to come all the way out here on your day off."

"In this business there are no days off."

"Not even the Sabbath?" Ross was joking, knowing full well Gordon's agnostic views.

"Especially not the Sabbath." The group passed through the large sliding doors and out into the cold January day. "I assume you haven't bothered to turn your phone on?"

"No." Ross smiled and patted the left breast pocket of his jacket. "I forgot all about the damn thing."

"Well, I've left you a few messages, and I'm sure I'm not the only one."

"What's wrong?"

"Nothing's wrong. It's just a bit of breaking news."

They were midway between the door and the waiting limousine when a car came flying around the corner to their left; tires squealing and engine revving. Ross and Gordon looked toward the noise and slowed their step.

Agent Brown, who had stayed consistently one step behind Ross from the Jetway to the curb, placed his large hand in the middle of Ross's back and grabbed a handful of fabric. He did not slow for a second. He picked up his pace, driving Ross forward, leaving Gordon behind. The scrum picked up speed, coats were thrown open, hands reached for guns, some eyes turned toward the possible threat, others turned away to make sure it wasn't a diversion of some sort, and then it was over before it began.

The car, a black Lincoln Town Car, skidded to a halt at the end of the motorcade and the rear passenger door flew open. Agent Brown was one step away from tossing his protectee headfirst into the back of the limo, when he saw Stu Garret emerge from the back of the Town Car. Brown released Ross and straightened out his jacket before turning to find the agent who was in charge of the ground detail. The access to the upper ramp was supposed to be shut down until they had Ross out the door, buttoned up, and on his way.

Garret marched along the sidewalk, moving agents out of his way like a bowling ball through pins. He had on a puffy down jacket with a floppy fur-lined hood.

"Mark," Garret yelled.

Even Ross was a bit miffed. The speeding car and the way the agents had reacted had caused his heart to race. "Yes, Stu?"

"I need to talk to you."

It was classic Garret. No greetings. No niceties. No small talk, formality, or informality. The campaign manager, and head of the transition team, was forever in a rush.

"Great to see you too," Ross quipped. "Did you get a new jacket?"

"I'm fucking freezing my ass off. If there wasn't so much to do I'd get on a plane right now and fly back to California."

Ross looked at the sky. It was a gray overcast afternoon with little wind. The temperature was probably somewhere in the high thirties. Not really that bad.

"You need to toughen up."

Garret entered the inner circle and growled, "You need to pull your head out of your ass and turn on your damn cell phone."

The smile on Ross's face disappeared. "Excuse me?"

"Get in the limo." Garret grabbed Ross by the elbow and pointed at the open door. "Let's go."

Jonathan Gordon tried to follow, but Garret put out a hand and said, "Ride in one of the other cars. I need him alone."

Gordon was eye to eye with Garret. He had grown to detest this foul little man. Gordon had been with Ross since the beginning of his political career. It had been his job to temper Ross's narcissistic tendencies without crushing his fragile ego. He had been fiercely loyal, even during the campaign when Garret had been brought in to shake things up.

"Jonathan," Ross called out from inside the limo. "It's all right. We'll talk when we get to the house."

Garret climbed in closing the door behind him. He sat in the seat opposite Ross and craned his neck around to make sure the privacy screen was up. It was. Garret spun back around, threw open his coat, and rattled off a series of expletives.

Ross kicked out his feet and said, "I see the holidays haven't improved your mood."

"Holidays . . . that's a good one. Almost as good as you flying commercial."

The limo started moving. Ross looked out the window and said, "Considering the fact that I was at an environmental conference, I think it was a rather good idea."

"How was the conference?"

"It was nice. The skiing was great. The foot soldiers really appreciated me showing up."

Garret leaned forward placing his hands on his knees. "He was right. You're drunk on power."

"What are you talking about?" Ross asked with a frown.

"Do you think I give a shit about the skiing, or how impressed the tree huggers were that you showed up?" Garret shook his head in disbelief. "I'm not kidding . . . you need to pull your head out of your ass."

Ross's face flushed with anger. "Stu, you need to watch your mouth."

"My mouth is the least of your problems. Fuck." He sat back and frowned. "I was on the phone with our friend for nearly thirty minutes this morning."

"Who?"

"Our friend." Garret tilted his head and looked at Ross to see if he was putting two and two together. "The one you had wine with last night."

"Oh . . . that friend."

"Yeah . . . that friend. He's pissed. He says you're delusional. You've somehow managed to rationalize this whole thing and wash your hands of it."

"I've done no such thing."

"He sounded pretty convinced."

"He's not exactly the most stable person I've ever met."

"Do you have any idea how fucking serious he is?"

"There's only so much I can do."

"I get the feeling your idea of what you can do and his are miles apart."

"I told him," Ross pointed his finger at Garret, "that I would do everything I could to help him, but in the end it would be up to you know who."

"No, I don't know who."

"The president."

"Current or future?"

"Current."

"I seem to remember you also telling him if Hayes balked you would get Josh to do it once he took the oath."

"I did not."

"You sure as hell did. I heard you. You said that between you and his father-in-law you would get him his pardon."

"Shhhh . . ." Ross held his finger to his lips.

Garret glanced over his shoulder at the two agents in the front seat and then looked back at Ross. "You fucking think they have us bugged? You really are out of your mind."

"In this town you never know."

"Fuck . . . you're paranoid."

"And you're a rude little bastard, Stu."

"Yeah well guess what? We're not in high school anymore. I'm not trying to win any popularity contests. My job was to get you elected. And I did that."

"You weren't the only one working on the campaign."

Garret shook his head and said, "Our friend told me that you actually said you thought you were making up ground in the polls and that you had momentum on your side. He told me you said we may have won the thing all on our own. You didn't really say that, did you?"

Ross looked out the window yet again. "Stu, elections are a strange business."

"Mark, elections are my business. I've been running them and rigging them for over thirty years and I'm going to tell you right now you guys were dead in the water. You had about as much of a chance to win that thing as a Republican does the mayoral race in San Francisco . . . which is to say none."

"You don't know that."

"Yes, I do, Mark, and you'd better fucking snap out of it, because I'm telling you right now our friend over in Europe is not the type of man you want to fuck with."

Ross had heard just about enough. "Next Saturday, I'm going to be sworn in as the vice president of the United States of America. I think our friend should start thinking about who *he* wants to fuck with."

"Yeah, well . . . he's not your only problem, Mr. Vice President." Garret looked out the window and said something under his breath.

"What?"

"The FBI, Department of Justice, and CIA have scheduled a joint press conference for tomorrow morning at ten."

"Why?"

"The word on the street is that they caught the guy who was behind the attack on the motorcade."

"The guy behind the attack," Ross repeated with eyes as big as saucers. "You mean the guy who carried out the attack?"

"Or one of his associates. There are a lot of rumors flying around right now. I don't know for sure who they have."

"Does the media have the story?"

"Yeah, they're all running it on the crawler, but they don't have any specifics yet."

"Shit," Ross swore. "He told me he was going to take care of this. He told me last night when I talked to him."

"When I spoke with him this morning, the news hadn't broke yet, and I don't think he knew or he would have said something."

"Can this be traced back to us?"

"I've been thinking about that." Garret hesitated and then shook his head. "I don't think so."

"You don't think so . . . Your lack of certainty isn't exactly comforting me."

"What do you want me to tell you? The only way we can be linked to this is through Cy, and he's a very careful guy."

"He'd sell us down the river in a heartbeat."

"For sure, but if I know Cy, he covered his tracks."

"Have you talked to Marty?" Ross was referring to the attorney general.

"I tried, but he's not taking calls."

"Well, he'll take mine." Ross retrieved his mobile phone and turned it on. While he stared at the small screen waiting for it to come to life a contingency plan occurred to him. He was about to float the idea with Garret and then decided at the last second that it was best to keep it to himself. He would have to first find out what the attorney general knew.

# 24

R app stood in front of the TV in his towel and brushed his teeth. The perky duo on the screen told him a warm front was moving into the Potomac River Valley. The forecast for Monday morning was clear skies and an afternoon high of fifty degrees. By tomorrow they expected the mercury to hit sixty. The morning TV anchors were doubly excited about this in light of the ice storm that had hit the city the previous Friday. Rapp cared about the weather only to the extent that he needed to know how he should dress. Other than that he tended not to get excited one way or the other. It was what it was, and there was nothing he could do about it. What he really wanted to know was how much play the upcoming joint press conference was getting.

The apartment didn't have cable. It didn't have much, in fact, other than the essentials. This was Rapp's crash pad. His bolt-hole that he kept in Washington. His brother Steven was the only other person who knew about it. He'd shown it to his wife on one occasion. He brought her late at night so no one would see them, and he showed her how to enter from the back fire escape. The building was an eight-unit brownstone that his father had bought as an investment a few years before his death. Rapp was just eight years old but he remembered riding with him to the apartment on the weekends to clean the hallways and the laundry room.

The brownstone was located approximately a mile north of the White House in the Columbia Heights neighborhood only a few blocks away from the upscale Adams Morgan neighborhood. Columbia Heights was one of the many neighborhoods in the city that had fallen to urban decay in the sixties and seventies. Rapp's father, a real estate attorney, had bought the place for next to nothing. It was four units up, four units down, sturdy as all hell, and full of character. Rapp's mother almost sold the place twice after his father had passed away of a massive heart attack, but Steven had been adamant that they keep it. Steven, just a year and half younger than Mitch, could spot trends even back then. They weren't losing money on the brownstone, but it was a real pain. It was a rental property in a bad neighborhood; drugs, prostitution—there'd even been a murder right in front of the building. There were lots of complaints by the tenants, late rent checks, and more evictions than they could count. Not the type of hassle a single mother of two from the suburbs needed in her life.

Steven persisted, though. He insisted that their father had said the building was a gold mine. As soon as the neighborhood turned around they'd make a small fortune. Steven even went so far as to put an ad in the paper for a new building supervisor. He dragged his mother down there on a Saturday morning and helped her pick a nice old man whose apartment building was scheduled to be torn down by the city to make room for a section eight housing development. The man worked for free rent. He stabilized things and got good long-term tenants to move in. The neighborhood started to turn in the late eighties, and then the super passed away in 1991 and they decided to sell each unit as a condominium. Their father had been right. Over a three-year period they sold all eight units and made a small fortune. One of those units was bought by an LLC out of the Bahamas.

The CIA had taught Rapp to be a careful man. He'd operated for years without an official cover in some very hostile places. He'd been ordered to do things by his superiors that he knew were illegal. The fact that this apartment was illegal in the eyes of the CIA didn't bother him for a second. He'd been trained to live a lie. To deceive. To do whatever it took to survive and complete the mission without being caught. This apartment was a natural extension of what they had taught him.

Rapp walked into the bedroom. Sparsely furnished like the rest of the place, it contained a queen-size bed with a wooden headboard that matched the nightstands and dresser. Rapp threw the towel on the end of the bed and grabbed a pair of boxers, white T-shirt, and black socks from the dresser. He put them on and opened the closet. There were half a dozen shirts and two suits all wrapped in plastic. Rapp put on a light blue shirt and the blue suit. He found a silver and light blue tie and held it up to the mirror on the back of the closet door. It worked. He knotted the tie and walked over to the dresser.

On top sat a metallic Rolex submariner, his Maryland driver's license, a wad of hundred-dollar bills, a sleek Kahr 9mm pistol, a small conceal-to-carry holster, an SIM card, and a new cell phone that was partially dismantled. Rapp put the gun in the holster and placed it inside his waistband at the small of his back. He put the new cell phone in his left breast pocket and the battery and battery cover in the right breast pocket of the suit coat. He walked back out into the living room, turned off the TV, and looked out the window. It was 6:38 a.m. on Monday. The press conference was a little more than three hours away. Rapp grinned and wondered if they were still going to go through with it. They really had no choice. They had a person in custody. Someone they could blame for the attack. If they canceled the press conference they would look like fools, so Rapp was willing to bet that it would go off as scheduled at 10:00 a.m. Between now and then he had a few calls to make, but he didn't dare do it from the apartment. He would leave the neighborhood and then make his calls.

# 25

Brooks had never set foot on the seventh floor before, let alone the director's suite. She sat nervously in the small reception area with two very large men staring at her and one very small woman ignoring her. The men were ex-military for sure. They had short hair, and broad forward-slouching shoulders that were caused by too many bench presses and curls and not enough back exercises. They wore the telltale signs of a bodyguard on each hip. Gun most likely on the right hip and a radio and extra magazines on the left.

She'd gone through twenty-four years of life never noticing such things, and then she went down to the Farm, where the CIA trained their new Clandestine Service recruits. The Farm changed her forever. It was like someone lifted the curtain and showed her another dimension to life. There was nothing magical about it. They simply taught you that your survival one day would likely depend on how aware you were of your surroundings. Brooks thought back to the months she'd spent at the Farm and tried to remember what they'd said about insubordination and being threatened with obstruction of Justice.

Brooks looked up to see Special Agent Skip McMahon enter the small reception area. He was a big man with an even larger presence. He looked Brooks over from head to toe, frowned, shook his head, and then looked at the director's gatekeeper.

The diminutive woman sitting behind the desk said, "Good morning, Skip. Go right in. She's expecting you."

McMahon mumbled something unintelligible and entered Kennedy's office closing the heavy door behind him with a thud.

Brooks looked down at the floor and wondered how she had let Rapp put her in this situation. Here was a man she'd been ready to strangle with her bare hands less than forty-eight hours before, and now he had talked her into putting her entire career on the line. He was Mitch Rapp, though. An honest-to-god, living, breathing legend. He had Kennedy's ear, he had saved the president's life, and it was said that Hayes would do anything for him. She'd worked with him in the field, one of the few covert operatives at Langley who could make such a claim. Even if it was more like watching him than working with him, the experience was invaluable. Rapp promised her that while things might be uncomfortable for a day or two, in the end she would want to be on his side. They'd found the man responsible for the attack on the motorcade, and they were going to go public with it. The CIA was actually going to get some credit for a change.

With her entire career ahead of her, Brooks thought this sounded like a pretty good deal. She would forever be linked to an important manhunt even if all she did was act like arm candy for Rapp. At least she thought it all sounded like a pretty good deal.

Now she was starting to wonder. Special Agent McMahon had been predictably upset when Brooks had delivered the prisoner to him at Andrews Air Force Base. He'd been expecting Rapp, and he'd been expecting more than a shot-up, drugged man on a stretcher. McMahon must have asked her ten times where Mitch was, and every time she told him she didn't know. And the truth was she didn't. Brooks had left Andrews and returned to her apartment in Alexandria for the first time in almost a month. She turned off her phones, just as Rapp had told her to do and laid down for a nap. He'd told her all the action and lack of sleep would catch up to her and she would sleep like a baby. He was right again. She took a six-hour nap. When she woke up it was dark and her message light on the home line was blinking. She turned on her Agency-issued mobile phone, the one that she had been told in training to never turn off. There were thirteen messages. Each one was progressively worse. It started with her supervisor, then his boss, and then her boss and Jose Juarez, the deputy director of the Clandestine Service. He stated very clearly that he expected to see Brooks in Director Kennedy's office at 7:00 a.m. on Monday or her relationship with the CIA would be terminated.

Brooks found the use of the word *terminate* very unsettling. Especially when uttered by the head of the Clandestine Service. Interestingly enough, though, Rapp had predicted all of this. Even the 7:00 a.m. meeting. Brooks was turning all of this over in her mind when Jose Juarez came marching into the reception area.

Juarez was six feet tall with thick black hair and an even thicker black mustache. Born in Honduras, his parents immigrated to America when he was nine. Juarez graduated from high school in Miami and joined the Marine Corps. After four years of exceptional performance he was accepted into Officer Candidate School. Shortly after he had accepted his commission, the CIA discovered him and borrowed him for a little conflict they had in Central America in the mid-eighties. Juarez had performed so well the CIA offered him a permanent position.

Brooks had never served in the military but she jumped to her feet upon seeing the spy boss. Juarez's jacket was already off, his top button of his white button-down shirt was already undone, and his sleeves were rolled halfway up his arms. He marched straight for Brooks and stopped two feet away, his thick black eyebrows scrunched into a frown.

"What in the hell is your problem?"

"I'm sorry, sir. I don't . . ."

"I don't want to hear you're sorry. I asked you what your problem is."

"Sir, if I may. Rapp told me . . ."

"Is Mitch Rapp your boss?" Juarez barked.

"No."

"I didn't think so. Sit your butt back down." Juarez pointed at the chair. "If the director wants to see you, I'll let you know. My advice is that she fire your ass and ask the FBI to investigate you." Juarez turned around and went back to the reception desk. He stuck out his hand and said, "Sheila, pad of paper and pen please." When the receptionist had given him what he wanted Juarez marched back to Brooks and said, "You may want to update your résumé." He dropped the pad and pen in her lap and then entered Kennedy's office.

Brooks looked down at the yellow legal pad and then up at the two stone-faced sentries. The receptionist finally acknowledged her presence by saying, "That Mitch Rapp is a real charmer, isn't he?"

Brooks looked at the woman. She was approximately fifty. A little overdone. Hair a bit too red, and makeup a bit too heavy.

"Excuse me?"

"Didn't you spend a month in Europe with him?"

"It was hardly a vacation."

The woman smiled and said, "I'll bet."

Brooks looked down at the blank piece of paper, her mind struggling to reconcile the severity of the situation with this older woman's lustful fantasy. Brooks was way out of her league, without any sign of this thing turning out well for her. Sure, Rapp would be fine. He was Mitch Rapp. He had a career of successes he could point to, but she was just some little peon who would be labeled an insubordinate malcontent for the rest of her career. How could Rapp have possibly expected her to withstand this kind of pressure?

# 26

Stu Garret exited the Willard lobby onto Pennsylvania Avenue and turned immediately to his left. It was five to seven in the morning. He was tired and crabby. A night owl even as he approached sixty, Garret didn't like to get out of bed before 9:00 or 10:00 if at all possible. But this morning he couldn't sleep. There was simply too much on his mind. He needed to make a call. A gust of wind hit him square in the face and he swore out loud as he clutched for the fur-lined hood of his puffy down jacket.

"Six more days and I'm done with this shit hole," he grumbled to himself.

Garret pulled the hood over his head and zipped the jacket all the way up under his double chin. Born in Detroit, he left when he was eighteen and never returned. He hated the weather, and the people. Detroit was for losers, and Garret wasn't afraid to tell that to people. Especially his clients. The place was a shining example of how unions and special interest groups could come together to suck a city dry by driving off its tax base.

Southern California was the place to be. San Diego in particular, where Democrats were liberal on social issues only. Fiscally, they were as conservative as any northeastern Republican. The people who flocked to San Diego sunk their money into real estate. Very expensive real estate. They had worked too hard for their money to watch property values plummet due to the governance of a few bleeding-heart liberals. Abortion, gun control, and the environment were all hot-button issues across America, but in San Diego real estate was the big overarching issue. People's entire life savings were tied up in their homes, and after living in sunny San Diego, retiring to Arizona or Florida made no sense. Garret couldn't wait to get back to San Diego and his toys.

Garret took quick strides and kept his head down. His retainer for the campaign had been a million dollars. That was just for him. He was a one-man gun for hire. Stu Garret, the political savant. By the time the campaign was over he'd burned through the retainer plus another million. On top of that his contract called for a million-dollar bonus if they won. Garret was flush with cash. He'd now managed two separate presidential campaigns and won both. Candidates across the country were reaching out for his advice. He'd even received a few calls from abroad. He was at the top of the heap. People were lining up to hand him large retainers. For the first time in his career he considered bringing someone else on board.

Garret tried to tell himself it wasn't about money. His home was paid for, his wife was as frugal as he was, and their only child, a daughter, had married an SOB of a trial lawyer who made gobs of money. The two of them, and their two children, lived up in L.A. with all the beautiful people. There was one area where Garret really spent money, though. He loved to collect vintage muscle cars and rare motorcycles. Beyond that he was pretty much addicted to golf, and then there was the big forty-two-foot cruiser he kept down at the marina. The boat and golf membership were for entertaining clients. Golf was a must. It was an intricate part of his business. He'd sealed more deals on the golf course than in an office by a landslide. The cars and the motorcycles, those were purely for his own gratification. He supposed they brought him back to his youth and his own father who had worked on the assembly line for General Motors. Back when they made great cars. Garret only collected American vehicles made before 1970. Everything made after that was shit. Although, Detroit had begun to turn out some decent vehicles lately. Ford had a new Mustang Shelby that was supposed to be out of this world, and Chevy was coming out with a new Camaro. If he caught another big fish this week he could buy one in every color.

That was part of the reason Garret had given into hanging around town. It was only Monday, but already the party's big-money people were arriving for Saturday's inauguration. He had meetings set up all week. Those running for the U.S. Senate or a state governorship were the only two he'd touch. He was done with congressional races no matter how much money they were willing to pay. He already had his eye on the next presidential campaign. No campaign manager had ever won three presidential elections.

Garret cleared the Treasury Department and was hit with another blast of wind. He turned left, put his head down, and reminded himself to avoid taking on any new clients from northern states. He continued east, passing the White House and picking up Pennsylvania Avenue at 17th Street. From there he angled northwest for two blocks to the building that housed what was left of the campaign offices. At the height of the campaign they'd leased two full floors. After their victory, ninety percent of the space was converted into transition offices for the new administration. The personnel and furniture all pretty much stayed the same. The only real difference was who paid the bills. During the race, the campaign wrote the checks. Now it was the federal government. To the victor go the spoils, or something like that.

The lobby was enclosed in glass. The floor was covered in white marble with a green border around the edges. In the middle was a black elevated desk that looked like it belonged on a sci-fi movie set. There was a black woman sitting behind the desk and beyond her were three elevator banks. Garret pushed his way through the main door and started for the elevator bank on the far right. Still chilled, he didn't bother to take his hood off. He walked straight past the toy cop and the stupid little sign-in sheet.

"Excuse me, sir," the security guard called from behind her desk. "I'm going to need you to sign in."

Garret didn't break stride. He pulled his office badge out of his left pocket and went straight for the elevator. He took it up to the fifth floor and stepped into an empty reception area. Red, white, and blue campaign signs hung from the wall like vintage artwork. The big banner right behind the reception desk was filled with signatures and a few drawings. It had been Ross's idea to motivate the troops. They were going to present it to Alexander after he was sworn in on Saturday. Garret supposed it would be hanging in the man's presidential library someday. Garret looked to his left and then his right. The floor was covered with dark gray carpeting and the walls were covered with light gray wallpaper. The place was bland, but more importantly, empty.

Garret pictured all the young volunteers still sleeping in the their hotel rooms. They were no longer volunteers of course. They were now on the government payroll. With the pressures of the campaign behind them, they were partying even harder than they had during the election, which one would think impossible. It was standard operating procedure on campaigns to provide volunteers with four things: coffee, food, liquor, and a place to sleep. The booze, the fact that the bulk of the volunteers were in their twenties, and the fact that they all pretty much stayed at the same hotel, created an interesting environment. If the general public had any idea how much fornicating happened on these campaigns, they'd be shocked.

To his right were some of the transition offices and to his left, four actual offices and another dozen workstations for the campaign staff. Garret's office was in the far corner. He hesitated for a moment and then decided it would be better if he made this call from someone else's desk. He started toward the transition offices. He passed a few rooms, all empty. Looking out across the sea of cubicles he listened for a sign that some loser who didn't get laid was in early to impress his boss. There was nothing but the hum of the overhead lights.

Garret walked into the next office, left the light off, and shut the door. He retrieved a piece of paper from his pocket. It was from the Willard, with just a phone number with an international dialing prefix on it. No name. Garret picked up the handset and entered the number. This was the real reason he was still in town. It helped to meet some of these fat cats in person, but he could have traveled to see them or they could have visited him in San Diego. The negotiating always went well after a round of golf and a few cocktails on the boat. He would have definitely gone back to warm sunny California if it hadn't been for this last piece of business.

After a few rings a woman answered, and Garret said, "I need to speak with Joseph."

"May I ask who is calling?"

"No. Just get him on the phone."

Garret looked around the office. There were no personal photos. Nothing that could tell him whose office it was. On the wall
next to the door was one of those stupid motivational posters. It
showed a men's crew team rowing on a river. In large letters across
the top were the words, "Team Work." Garret shook his head. Any
jackass who needed to find motivation, inspiration, or anything else
in some mass-produced trite piece of junk wasn't going to get far in
this business.

Joseph Speyer finally came on the line and in a cautious voice
said, "Hello?"

"We've got a problem," Garret blurted out.

"Oh . . . hello, Stu. My assistant told me there was a rude American on the line. Which is fairly redundant, don't you think? But
nonetheless, I should have guessed it was you."

"Very funny."

"Why did you not come to my party? Your boss came."

"He isn't my boss."

"Oh Stu . . . such a big chip on your shoulder. It must be difficult going through life so angry all the time."

"Yeah," Garret laughed gruffly. "But probably not as bad as taking it up the ass, like you do."

"Stu," Speyer said with mock surprise. "You are a Democrat.
You are supposed to support my people."

"You might want to drop using my name every other line, and
I do support your people. Go ahead, get married. What the fuck do
I care? It's just not my bag . . . what you guys do between the
sheets."

"Maybe you should try it some time."

"No thanks." Garret looked out the window and watched a cab
pass by on the street below. "Back to the point. We've got a major
fucking problem!"

There was a sigh and then Speyer said, "How could we possibly have a problem? Everything turned out exactly as you wanted."

"Your buddy promised that he was going to button things up on his end."

"And as far as I know he did."

"You don't know shit. The FBI is going to hold a press conference in a few hours."

"Why?"

"They've arrested someone."

There was a long pause before Speyer responded. "Do you know who?"

"I don't have a name, but I've heard it's the guy."

"Impossible. I just spoke with your boss on Saturday. He said the FBI's investigation was dead in the water. He was being briefed daily."

"It wasn't the FBI who found him."

"Who was it?"

"The CIA."

"That is wonderful news," Speyer said with feigned enthusiasm.

"Just fucking great."

"I will make sure to pass it along to our friend."

"Yeah . . . you do that, and on an entirely different matter, tell him I want scorched earth. Do you follow me?"

"I think so."

"Good."

"You know this man the CIA grabbed . . . it's too bad that it's probably as far as they'll get. I've seen how these people operate. They rarely know who hired them."

"So I've heard."

"I will call you back after I speak with our friend."

"Don't bother," Garret said. "Just tell him if he doesn't handle this problem immediately I have no intention of following through on our end of the bargain."

"He will not be happy to hear that."

"I don't give a fuck what makes him happy or not. He needs to do what he said he would do and he needs to do it today." Garret slammed the phone back into its cradle and walked out of the office.

# 27

Kennedy sat behind her desk and watched and listened as McMahon and Juarez worked themselves into a frenzy. She knew both of them extremely well. It was not abnormal to see either of them get this upset. They were very passionate about their jobs. The unusual part was seeing them upset at the same time. Well, that wasn't exactly right either. The abnormality lay in them being upset over the same thing. Their jobs dictated that they approach situations from different angles. Angles that didn't always intersect. What Juarez deemed to be best for America did not always jibe with the FBI's vision. In essence, McMahon's job was to enforce the law and investigate and arrest those who broke it. Juarez's job was to send men and women to foreign countries to recruit spies, gather information, conduct covert operations, and pretty much break laws on a weekly if not daily basis. There was an undeniable conflict between the two missions.

Mitch Rapp had somehow managed to get both men on the same page, which was another red flag to Kennedy. Mitch was a disrespectful, almost always unmanageable asset. He was akin to a company's top sales rep, who was often the same guy who thumbed his nose at the sales manager, showed up late to meetings, or didn't show at all and in general did whatever in the hell he wanted, just so long as he kept hitting his numbers. Pretty much every successful company had a rep that fit that bill. Men and women who were at their best when management stayed out of their way. Smart bosses knew it was wise to turn them loose and look in the other direction. In a sense Rapp had been the CIA's top rep for ten-plus years and counting, and Juarez was his de facto sales manager. Juarez did not resent Rapp. He'd been on the messy end of black ops himself and the two men shared that unique bond, which was no small thing in a bureaucracy where ninety-nine percent of the employees had a desk job. Juarez respected Rapp, even revered him and depended on him in situations just like this to get results where others had failed. The problem, Kennedy knew, lay in the fact that Rapp had corrupted one of Juarez's precious recruits. Rapp had gotten Brooks involved in what could quickly become a criminal investigation. If this went south it would be a big blow to the Clandestine Service. Juarez might even lose his job over the deal.

"The videotape," McMahon said, "from the Starbucks . . . is not enough evidence to convict this guy. The attorney general is losing his mind over this. You told us he was the guy."

"He is," Kennedy said calmly. She'd had almost a day now to consider the situation, and she was slightly embarrassed that she had allowed her own emotions to cloud her judgment. First off, getting upset with Rapp served no purpose. She should have known that after all these years. He was going to do what he thought best regardless of orders from HQ.

"Can you back that up?"

"Not at the moment."

"Shit." McMahon had his dark blue pinstripe suit jacket open and a hand on each hip. A bulky pistol sat on his right hip and his badge was clipped to his belt above his left front pocket. As a general rule he didn't carry his passport sized FBI credentials. Some people acted funny around guns, so he kept his badge displayed.

"You're going to have to do better than that," the agent continued. "The press conference is in less than three hours, and I need some real evidence. All I've got at the moment is a shot-up Greek guy who keeps claiming he was kidnapped and tortured. This could get really embarrassing."

Kennedy wondered if that was what Rapp was up to. Punishing everyone for going public with this.

"Let's get Brooks in here," Juarez said. "She knows what the hell is going on."

"Are you sure about that?" Kennedy asked.

"Hell yes. She told me herself that Mitch told her to say nothing. He said he would show up in a few days and take care of everything, and in the meantime she was to keep her mouth shut."

"I know that's what he told her, but that doesn't mean she knows what he's up to."

"How about simply telling us what in the hell really happened in Cyprus?" Juarez asked.

"How about telling me anything?" McMahon jumped in. "She shows up at Andrews yesterday in a white rental van, from where, we have no idea. We were expecting them to land on a plane. My people ran down the plates on the van. It was rented by some LLC out of Baltimore that exists on paper only. We checked the gate logs at the base. She showed up five minutes before the handoff. We called Customs and Immigration. They show no record of Brooks or Rapp entering the country yesterday. I don't suppose either of you would like to tell me what aliases they were traveling under?"

Kennedy and Juarez didn't bother looking at each other. They both shook their heads in response to the agent's question.

McMahon looked down at the ground and grabbed the back of his neck with his right hand. After a moment he said, "Now I might not care how in the hell they got this guy from Cyprus to the States without clearing him through customs, but I know a whole lot of other people who *are* going to care. People at Justice are already asking questions, and I'm sure when this guy gets a lawyer he is going to want to review the chain of custody. Add to that the press and you guys are going to get a whole lot of unwanted attention. My office tells me they're already receiving calls. They're going to be all over you by this afternoon."

*That was it,* Kennedy thought to herself. This was exactly what Mitch was worried about. Their tactics and methods being exposed. So the question she had for herself was, *What was Rapp really up to? Was he destroying evidence or collecting evidence? Or both?*

"I say we get her in here." Juarez said in an impatient voice.

"Brooks," Kennedy replied.

"Yes."

"I think you two are being a bit hard on her."

Juarez's eyes practically popped out of his head. "Hard on her? I've had the kid gloves on until now. I'm half tempted to get the Office of Security in here. Have them turn on the hot lights and polygraph her ass."

Kennedy placed her glasses on top of a leather briefing folder. She used both hands to square them up perfectly in the center of the smooth, brown surface. Kennedy had thought Juarez would threaten to do this, but she wondered how much of it was bluster. The move carried with it certain risks. The Office of Security would start a paper trail that just might get the Inspector General's Office involved, and then they were only one step away from the Department of Justice and the FBI.

"I think she's been put in a very difficult position."

"What's so difficult about being debriefed by your boss?"

"I think everyone needs to take a step back and look at this from a different angle."

"What angle could that possibly be?" Juarez asked sarcastically.

Kennedy shot him a look and said, "Mitch's angle."

"Irene," Juarez's jaw was clenched, "I have a lot of respect for Mitch, and he has pulled some pretty goofy shit over the years, but this one takes the prize."

"You were as upset as I've ever seen you yesterday," McMahon said. "Why the hell are you all of a sudden defending him?"

Kennedy leaned back in her chair and glanced out the window before answering. "I was distracted yesterday. I think I made a mistake."

"What mistake?"

"I did not advise the president as closely as I should have on this."

"How so?"

"Going public . . ." Kennedy shook her head, "this fast . . . bad idea."

"Mitch told you this was the guy. One hundred percent. The smart thing for you to do was turn him over."

"We could have waited . . . should have waited a week or two, or maybe we should have just let Mitch take care of the problem for us."

"I didn't hear that," McMahon said as he shut his eyes tightly.

"What's done is done," Juarez added. "What I want are answers. I'm willing to give Brooks one more chance. Let's bring her in here, lay out her options, and get to the bottom of this. I want to know what in the hell Mitch is trying to hide."

Kennedy studied Juarez for a moment and then looked to McMahon.

"Would it help," McMahon asked, "if I left?"

"Probably," Juarez answered.

"I don't think it's going to matter."

"Why?" asked Juarez.

"I don't think she's going to talk, but we'll give it a shot." Kennedy leaned forward and hit the intercom button on her phone. "Sheila, would you please send Ms. Brooks in?"

Kennedy stood and pointed to the couch and chairs opposite her desk. She read the look of disapproval on Juarez's face. "We're going to try this the civilized way first."

"Fine," Juarez grumbled. "You go ahead and play the good cop. Skip can play the bad cop. I'll just play the boss from hell. In my current mood it won't require much acting."

# 28

The cyber café was one of those coffee shops that you could find in virtually every hip counterculture neighborhood across America. Each one, a stand-alone sole proprietorship or maybe an LLC with ownership of a half dozen shops at the most. They were all different, yet the same. United in their hatred of Starbucks, these shops were a blind chain with an unintended common theme. They were adorned with rickety, second-hand furniture, old laminate countertops, and a wait staff who tended to be open to body piercings, tattoos, and bad hairdos. The shops provided free Internet connection, service with an attitude, and a refuge from America's shallow thirst for comfort through the similarity of franchise hell.

This particular place was called Café Wired. A big hand-painted brown and white sign hung above the large glass window that fronted the sidewalk. The name was bracketed on one side by a steaming cup of coffee and the other by a laptop. There were now three of the shops in the city. One in Bethesda, another by American University, and this one a few blocks away from Howard University, not far from Rapp's condo.

Rapp was a silent investor in the cafés. He and his brother Steven had put up the money, and Marcus Dumond ran the places. Rapp had worked with the cyber genius going on five years now. Dumond had attended MIT with Rapp's brother. While earning his master's degree in computer science at MIT, Dumond had managed to get into some pretty big trouble with the feds. To win a bet with some of his fellow geniuses, he hacked into one of New York's largest banks and then moved over a million dollars into several overseas accounts. He wasn't caught because he left a trail. He was caught because he and his friends got drunk one night and began bragging about how easy it had been. A fellow student got wind of it and turned him in to the authorities. Dumond was facing serious jail time. That was until Steven Rapp called his brother to see if he could intervene.

The CIA doesn't like to advertise the fact that they employ some of the world's best computer hackers. These men and women spend their days and nights trying to sneak undetected into the networks of America's adversaries. More often than not they are successful, and they are one of the country's best-kept secrets. Dumond's skills in this arena were unsurpassed. He split time between the cyber unit and the Counterterrorism Center.

Rapp circled the café twice before entering. He checked all the windows, the cars, and the people on the corner waiting for the bus. It was more out of habit than any real fear of being followed. He opened the door to the coffee shop and walked straight to the back, past the line of customers waiting for their morning fuel. The women's room was on the left. The men's on the right. Directly ahead was a door with a security camera and call box mounted to the side. Rapp pressed the button and put his hand on the door- knob. A second later a buzzing noise announced that the door was open.

Rapp went down the narrow stairs to the basement and past two open office doors to a third heavy steel door with rusted rivets ringing the perimeter. This one also had a call box next to it. Before Rapp could push the button he heard the buzzing release of the lock. He leaned into the heavy door, twisted the handle, and en- tered.

The first thing that Rapp noticed was that the room was a good ten degrees warmer than the rest of the basement. He'd been down here before. Dumond kept an apartment on the second floor, but for security reasons he kept his nerve center locked up in the basement. Rapp was not a detail guy. At least not when it came to computers. To him, they were like cars. Corvette, Ferrari, Mustang GT, Mercedez—when you got to the high end how much did a tenth of a second really matter in a zero to sixty challenge? He knew it mattered to the purists, just like he knew processor speed really mattered to Dumond, but in Rapp's case—who really cared? One look at a red Ferrari and you'd have to be an idiot to not in- stinctively know it was fast. No need to look under the hood. Same with Dumond's setup. All you had to do was look at the four flat-screen monitors that sat atop the half-circle desk, and you knew whatever was under the desk had to be the best that money could buy.

"How are things going?" Rapp asked as he took off his trench coat.

"Fine," Dumond answered as he took a final drag off a cigarette and stabbed it out in a large glass ashtray. The twenty-nine-year-old African American exhaled a cloud of smoke and said, "The blogosphere is on fire with news that the FBI is going to announce the arrest of the primary suspect in the motorcade attack."

"Did you leak the name?"

Dumond nodded. "Drudge just ran with it. It'll be on the wire within the hour."

"What about the Greek embassy?" Rapp laid his trench coat over the back of a chair.

"I already made the call."

"You disguised your voice . . . right?" Rapp approached the desk.

"No," Dumond said in a sarcastic voice. "I gave them my name and phone number in case they needed to get a hold of me." He snatched his pack of cigarettes from the desk and fished out a stick.

"You're a brave man this morning."

"What the fuck do you expect from me?" Dumond stuck the cigarette between his lips and started searching for his lighter. The desk was covered with keyboards, mice, disks, memory sticks, card readers, speakers, and other odds and ends. "I've been up all night working on this shit, and you won't even tell me what's going on." He found his lighter under a pile of disks in clear jewel cases and lit his cigarette.

"I told you what's going on. It's classic disinformation. We're going to get them leaning in one direction and once they're committed we're going to deliver a knockout punch."

"You and your sports analogies." Dumond frowned at Rapp and then went to work on one of the keyboards.

"Man, you are one crabby cuss this morning."

"Whereas you are just a breath of fresh air."

Rapp smiled. He truly liked Dumond. "Thank you for working on this. I owe you."

"You're damn right you do. I've been up all night and I have to be at work in an hour and a half."

"All right," Rapp put his hands up in surrender. "I owe you big-time. The next time you get arrested, I'll bail you out." The comment was a reference to the fact that if it weren't for Rapp, Dumond would be sitting in a federal prison.

"How long are you going to hold that over my head?"

"I'm not. Now give me the full update."

"I posted twenty-six blogs last night, under ten separate pseudonyms. I started out responding to other bloggers who were reporting that the assassin was caught. You could tell by most of them that the leaks were coming out of the White House. Traffic was pretty hot on the subject. At five this morning I started putting it out there that there were major problems with the case against this guy . . . signs of torture, no real evidence, the fact that he was grabbed without alerting the Greek authorities."

"Who did you say your sources were?"

"All anonymous. State Department, Justice, FBI, CIA. I spread it around."

"Did you float my name?" Rapp asked.

"Not yet. I thought you wanted me to hold off on that."

"I did. When we finish up with this next thing, go ahead and leak it."

Dumond studied him for a second. "I have no idea what you are up to."

"You'll see soon enough. When was the last time you spoke with Hacket and Wicker?"

"About thirty minutes ago."

"And?"

"They dumped the bodies at Gazich's house and left the gun there. They're outside the bank right now waiting for you to call."

They had found a safety deposit box key along with a file of financial documents at Gazich's office. One of the banks listed in the file was the Hellenic Bank of Cyprus. Dumond penetrated the bank's network and found out that they had a safety deposit box registered under the name of Alexander Deckas. While he was inside the network he also collected some additional information.

Dumond handed Rapp a file. "The president of the bank is Manos Kapodistras. He has a little more than three hundred thousand dollars in cash deposits at the bank. In addition to that it looks like his ownership is about fifteen percent."

"Foreign deposits?"

"A lot of Saudi money."

"Anyone we know?"

"About a fifth of the royal family."

Rapp glanced at the file and then asked, "Anything unusual?"

"Doesn't appear to be, but these bankers can be pretty sneaky with their money."

"Your advice?"

Dumond took a drag and said, "Play it straight up. Tell him in his line of work his reputation is everything. We can either do this in a very private manner or a very public one."

Rapp nodded and then closed the file. "All right . . . let's call him."

Dumond waved him behind the desk. "The screen on the left is a mirror image of the banker's. That is exactly what he's looking at right now."

"Do you know if he opened your e-mail?"

"Yes."

"Has he replied to it?"

"No."

"Did he check the name *Deckas* against the bank records?"

"No."

"Okay. Connect me to his direct line."

Dumond went to work on his keyboard and donned a headset. Using a sophisticated telecommunications program he bounced the call around so it would be untraceable. When it started to ring he picked up the handset and gave it to Rapp. After the third ring a man answered in Greek.

*"Yeea sas."*

"Mr. Kapodistras, I need your assistance in a very important matter."

There was a long pause and then the banker asked, "Who am I speaking with, and how did you get this number?"

"Neither is important at the moment. What is important is that I am in a position to help you avoid a potentially embarrassing situation."

"Are you an American?"

"Yes. Did you get the e-mail I sent you about a press conference the FBI is going to hold today?"

"I did."

"Did the name Alexander Deckas mean anything to you?"

"No." There was hesitation in the voice. "Should it?"

"That depends how involved you are with your clients."

Dumond pointed to the monitor that was mirroring Kapodistras's screen. The banker was searching his database looking for a match. After a few seconds the client profile for Deckas popped up on the screen.

"It is the stated policy of our bank to not discuss our clients under any circumstances."

"Mr. Kapodistras, I see that you were a vice president at the bank back in two thousand and one. Do you remember what it was like in your business when it was discovered that Osama bin Laden had been using Cyprus banks to hide his al-Qaeda funds?"

Rapp had seen the official report. Greek regulators and U.S. federal agents had descended on the Mediterranean island, and the banking business had been thrown on its ear. Decades of the Cyprus banking industry marketing itself as the Switzerland of the Mediterranean was destroyed overnight by the actions of a militant few. People banked on Cyprus because it gave them the same thing the Swiss did: absolute privacy with exceptional service. And they did it in many cases for half the fee. The reduced fees were nice, but the privacy was paramount. Clients fled in droves. Clients who had nothing to do with terrorism, but nonetheless did not want any government knowing how much money they had, or worse, how they had obtained it.

"It was a difficult time to be in my business, but in difficult times comes great opportunity."

Kapodistras sounded like a man who might be willing to deal. "Well, I have an opportunity for you today."

"What kind of opportunity?"

"An opportunity to spare your bank."

"From?"

"Scrutiny that you do not need. An army of regulators from Athens, and an even bigger army of U.S. federal agents going through your bank file by file . . . line by line. Media parked out in front of your bank for a week driving your customers away. It won't be pretty."

There was an extremely long pause before Kapodistras replied. "Whom do you work for?"

"The American government."

"And why are you paying me this courtesy?"

"I am an impatient man and I believe the two of us can get what we both want without turning this into a public spectacle."

"You are interested in this Alexander Deckas?"

"Yes."

"May I ask why?"

"Yes. Do you remember the attack on President–elect Alexander's motorcade this past November?"

"The one that killed his wife?"

"Yes."

"What about it?"

"Your client was the man who detonated the bomb."

There was no uncomfortable laugh. No denial. Just silence for at least ten seconds and then, "What proof do you have?"

"More than you could imagine, including a confession, but for the sake of brevity I'm going to cut to the heart of the matter. In two and a half hours the FBI is going to announce that they have arrested Mr. Deckas. The evidence against him is overwhelming. A team of FBI agents is en route to your island right now. They should be landing in a few hours. I am offering you two choices. The easy way, or the hard way."

"I'm listening."

Rapp placed his hand over the mouthpiece and whispered to Dumond, "Tell Wicker and Hacket to go to his office." Rapp removed his hand and spoke into the phone. "On Saturday night my people took Mr. Deckas into custody and transported him back to America. We went through his office and home in Limassol and are in possession of his banking records as well as a key for a safety deposit box in your bank."

"And you would like to see what is in that box."

"That's correct."

"And if I say no?"

Rapp sighed. "If you say no, I will turn everything over to the FBI. They will probably show up at your home tonight with the Greek authorities and drag you down to the bank and force you to open the box. The FBI being the thorough, distrustful gents that they are will want to go through all of your records to make sure none of your other clients are connected with Deckas. The Greek authorities will allow this because they will want to look like good allies . . . and after all, the man killed the future president's wife. People will start to talk, and you will become known as the bank of choice for terrorists and assassins. Your legitimate customers will leave out of fear of association and your unsavory customers will do the same for the exact same reason. By the end of the week I would imagine your deposits will be cut in half and your fifteen percent stake in the bank will be worth considerably less. Who knows . . . you might even be forced out."

"Whom do you work for? The CIA?"

"I can neither confirm nor deny that, Mr. Kapodistras."

"How can I trust you?"

Rapp detected the tension in the man's voice. He was being faced with a very tough but ultimately easy decision. "As far as I can tell, sir, you have brought none of this on yourself. Your job is to protect your bank, your depositors, and your investors. The best way to do that is to give me what is in that box. If my instincts are correct, the sooner you distance yourself from the contents of that box the better off you and your bank will be."

"What will prevent you from turning any evidence over to the FBI?"

"I'm not looking to put anyone in jail."

After a long pause the banker said, "I need some time to think about this."

"I'll give you one minute."

The banker laughed thinking Rapp was joking.

"I'm serious. Two of my men are probably talking to your secretary as we speak. They expect you to come out of your office and take them down to the safety deposit room. If you do not, they will call me and I will turn everything I have over to the FBI. I will also tell them that we have spoken and that you were extremely unhelpful. In addition to that there are some other very nasty things I could employ, but we don't want to get into that over the phone. I'll send someone to talk to you about it in person."

"But there are procedures: signature cards, passwords, the key."

"We have the key, and one of my men can forge the client's signature. All you have to do is provide the password."

"I will need to inventory the contents of the box."

"Go right ahead. In fact . . . I'm sure there's some cash in there. Keep half of it for your troubles. The rest of it, though, my men are taking with them. Do we have a deal?"

"Yes," the banker said without any hesitation. "We have a deal."

"Good. Now go straight out to your reception area and greet my men. Act like you have met them before. The big one you may call Kevin and the shorter one Charlie. Take them straight downstairs and do whatever they ask of you. If all goes well, they will be out of your way in ten minutes or less. Any questions?"

"No."

"Good. Thank you for being so cooperative." Rapp placed the handset back in the cradle and said to Dumond, "Continue to monitor all of his calls and e-mails. If he doesn't do exactly as we asked, crash his entire system and tell Wicker and Hacket to get out of there."

Rapp walked over and grabbed his jacket.

"Where are you going?" Dumond asked.

"I need to run down a lead."

"What do you want me to tell them at Langley if they start asking about you?"

"You never saw me."

"You got it."

"And find out who the Russian is."

"I'm working on it."

# 29

Brooks heard the director's voice on the intercom and her heart began to race. This was it. Her whole career would be decided in the next ten minutes. Sheila, with the overdone makeup and the infatuation with Mitch Rapp, told her she could go in. Brooks stood. Her blond hair was in a tight ponytail, and she was wearing a black pantsuit. She'd seen Kennedy on TV before wearing virtually the same outfit. Brooks had intentionally decided to wear it today. She was looking for any advantage she could get. She tugged on the front of her white blouse, adjusted the collar, and grabbed the door handle. Brooks took one last deep breath and opened the door.

The door swung in and the first thing Brooks saw were two stone-faced men sitting on a couch directly across the room. It was Juarez and McMahon. Director Kennedy stepped into view and extended her hand.

"Cindy."

"Director Kennedy." Brooks took her hand. "It's a real honor to meet you. I just wish it was under better circumstances."

Kennedy smiled warmly. "Don't worry, we'll get this mess straightened out. Please," she gestured toward one of the armchairs opposite the couch, "take a seat."

Brooks took the chair on the right and glanced nervously at her boss and the agent from the FBI. Neither man looked away. Between the two of them they had to have had sixty plus years of hard experience. McMahon was the Special Agent in Charge of the investigation into the motorcade attack. The FBI wouldn't give that job to just any agent. They would bring in their best.

"Can I get you anything to drink?" Kennedy asked as she took a seat in the chair next to Brooks.

"No, thank you." Brooks crossed her legs and clasped her hands over her right knee.

"Gentlemen?"

Juarez and McMahon didn't take their eyes off Brooks. They simply shook their heads.

"Well," Kennedy said as she withdrew her hand from the coffeepot in front of her, "it appears we have a bit of a problem." She turned sideways so she was facing Brooks. "I've known these two men here for some time. I've seen them both in various states of anger, but you, young lady, have somehow managed to really get them riled up." Kennedy tilted her head and smiled.

Brooks, not knowing how else to react, laughed nervously.

"Why do you think that is?"

Brooks regained her composure. "For starters I would like to apologize. Mitch Rapp ordered me not to discuss this operation with anyone until he cleared me to do so."

"Really." Juarez ran his thumb and forefinger down his mustache and then leaned forward. "Would you like to show me the org chart where it says that Mitch Rapp is anywhere in your chain of command?"

"Sir, I . . ." Brooks struggled for a response.

"There is no such chart!" Juarez snapped. "The director and I outrank Mr. Rapp. We are your bosses. He isn't, and if you don't get that through your thick head, you are going to find yourself in a whole shitload of trouble."

Kennedy looked at Juarez, her eyes telling him to back off. She looked back to Brooks. "Cindy, here is the situation. The FBI has in custody a man who is alleged to have been behind the attack on President—elect Alexander's motorcade. You delivered that man to Andrews Air Force Base yesterday afternoon. Correct?"

"Correct."

"Do you believe this man is in fact the person we have been looking for?"

"Yes."

"Why?"

"Why?" asked Brooks.

"What evidence do you have?"

"I know this isn't what you want to hear, Director Kennedy, but I gave my word to Mitch that I would not talk about this with anyone until he cleared it."

Kennedy tried not to take offense. She knew Rapp was the real issue here, not this young rookie. "I understand that Mitch asked you not to talk about what happened on Cyprus, but I'm asking you as the director of the Central Intelligence Agency," Kennedy put her arms out and looked around the spacious office, "the person who is responsible for this organization, to tell me what happened."

Brooks looked down and clasped her hands tightly together. She was really in a bind. She couldn't help but think that even if

Rapp did make good on his promise, she would forever be stained by this complete lack of respect. Rapp had told her on the flight home not to worry. Just hang in there for twenty-four to thirty-six hours tops and everything would be fine. She remembered him making her look him in the eye. Those beautiful, yet intimidating, almost black eyes, and he asked her if she trusted him. At the end of it all that was what it came down to. She trusted him.

Brooks looked up at Kennedy and in a very polite voice said, "Director Kennedy, may I ask you one question?"

"Sure," Kennedy replied after a slight pause.

"Do you trust Mitch?"

At first Kennedy felt blindsided by the question. Almost tricked. But she could tell by the look on Brooks's face that she was sincere. The debate strategy would have been to throw the question back at Brooks or ask her a different one, but Kennedy didn't want to. This young operative had just put the discussion into a very interesting light. She smiled at Brooks and said, "Yes, I do. I trust him completely."

Brooks nodded and brushed an errant strand of blond hair back behind her ear. "Personally, I don't particularly care for him."

"Really?"

"He's not the easiest person to work with."

"You think so?" Juarez asked sarcastically.

Kennedy ignored him. "Lone wolf."

"Very much so."

"I'm afraid a great deal of that is due to his training. When we recruited him, he was very much a team player. Very social. We had to teach him how to operate as an individual . . . a lone wolf."

"That's only part of it. He's not well."

"How so?"

"The mere mention of his wife sends him into a tirade. At one point I actually thought he was going to hit me."

Kennedy searched the young operative's eyes for a hint of dishonesty or a possible self-aggrandizing agenda, but she didn't see a sign of either. She was simply giving a dispassionate summary. "He's been through a lot."

"Yes, I know, but that doesn't excuse the fact that he hasn't been referred for counseling." Brooks watched Kennedy look away from her and then check her watch. She had hit a nerve. "It is not a criticism of management," Brooks added quickly. "He's not ready for help. You'd have to institutionalize him."

"Commit him to a psychiatric institution?" Kennedy asked with a look of real shock on her face.

"Yes. For his own good."

"Your graduate degree is in psychology?" Kennedy asked.

"Yes."

Kennedy glanced over at Juarez who was shaking his head. Turning to Brooks she said, "That was tried once before. Years ago."

"Before his wife?"

"Years before."

"How did it go?" Brooks asked.

Kennedy looked to Juarez who said, "He killed the man who had him committed."

"Killed?" Brooks said with surprise.

"Killed," Juarez repeated himself. "Snapped his neck with his bare hands."

Brooks looked at Special Agent McMahon with a mix of shock and horror on her face.

"Don't look at me." McMahon put his hands up. "I turned my hearing aid off five minutes ago."

"Relax," Juarez said. "It turned out the treasonous bastard had it coming, but that's a whole other story. One that you're not cleared for."

"The point is," said Kennedy, "You don't simply commit someone like Mitch. People would get hurt."

"I think people might get hurt if he doesn't get help."

Kennedy considered that possibility for a moment.

"This is bullshit," Juarez said. "We're completely off the subject
here. This meeting isn't about Mitch. I'll deal with him when he
comes in. He's pulled this shit before. Just never quite so brazenly.
This is about you," Juarez leaned forward and pointed at Brooks,
"young lady. It's about you doing your job and telling me and the
director here, just what in the hell Mitch is up to. You either do that,
or your career is over. It's that simple."

Brooks looked to Kennedy. The director looked at her without
an expression.

"And by the way your career isn't simply over. I own your
ass right now. You have no rights. You signed them away your first
day on the job. If you don't tell me what I want to know, I'm
going to march you down to the basement and have the boys from
the Office of Security run you through the ringer. Hot lights and
lots of difficult questions all while you're hooked up to a lie detector."

Brooks was seriously considering telling them everything when
an intercom buzzer sounded from atop Kennedy's desk.

"Director?"

Kennedy turned toward her desk and in a louder than normal
voice asked, "Yes, Sheila."

"I have Mitch for you on your direct line."

Kennedy stood quickly. "Did you start a trace?"

"He told me if I tried to trace the call he'd never speak to me
again."

"For god sakes, Sheila! Does anyone work for *me* anymore? Put
a trace on the call." Kennedy grabbed her handset and pressed line
one. "Mitch, we were just talking about you."

"Only nice things, I'm sure."

"Of course. Where are you?"

"Across the street from the Hoover Building. I'm thinking about turning myself in."

"Why in the world would you do that? You haven't done anything wrong."

"You didn't sound so sure of that when we spoke yesterday."

"I've had some time to reconsider. I think it was a mistake to go public with this so quickly."

"You think so?" Rapp asked, his voice full of sarcasm.

"I'm trying to be magnanimous."

"Easy with the big words, boss. Remember I'm not Ivy League."

"I'm serious."

"No you aren't. You're just trying to keep me on the line so you can trace this call, which we both know is a waste of time and resources. As soon as we're done, this phone is history."

Kennedy turned her back to the others and sat on the edge of her desk. "Would you like to tell me what you're up to?"

"I'd love to, boss, but I think it's best if I kept you out of the loop for another twenty-four hours. How is Brooks holding up?"

"Fairly well considering you've put her entire career in jeopardy."

"Jose being pretty tough on her?"

"He's just getting started."

"Tell him to take it easy on her and tell him I'm one hundred percent sure this is the guy."

"I'll tell you what, why don't you come in and we'll talk about it?"

"I can't. Not yet. There are a few more things I need to run down. Just tell him to hold firm, no matter what he hears. This guy is guilty as shit, and I've got the goods."

Kennedy looked at the credenza behind her desk. Inside it was a safe and inside the safe were the photos Baker had given her on Saturday. In a much softer voice she said, "I have something I need to show you."

"What?"

"I can't talk about it right now. When are you coming in?"

"Tomorrow . . . I hope."

"All right, I'll give you until tomorrow and then we need to sit down. Am I clear?"

"Crystal."

"Good."

"Tell Jose I'll call him in fifteen minutes, and tell Skip that no matter what he hears, this is the guy."

"I will."

"Thanks. I'll talk to you tomorrow."

The line went dead and Kennedy slowly put the handset back in the cradle. She turned around and relayed Rapp's message to both Juarez and McMahon. And then she looked at the two men and said, "Now, if you'll excuse me, I'd like to have some time alone with Ms. Brooks."

# 30

WASHINGTON, DC

Rapp got off the metro at the Farragut West stop and took the escalator up to the sidewalk. It was before eight and traffic was still light. The wind had picked up a bit, but it wasn't bad. Nothing wrong with a little frigid gust of wind slapping you in the face to let you know you were alive. There was the inevitable Starbucks directly across the street. There was also one half a block down on his right and another one around the corner to his left and to the south a few storefronts. Rapp figured there were over a hundred of them in the downtown area.

Rapp had been trained to avoid routines. Routines led to predictable behavior and identifiable tendencies. Things that could be used to an adversary's advantage. Effective people developed routines and efficiencies in their day-to-day lives. Those routines almost always manifested as extremely predictable behavior. Rapp knew because he'd used it to his advantage many times.

People woke at the same time every day, or at least Monday through Friday; they ate at the same three or four restaurants, worked out at the same club, typically at a set time, and got their coffee at the same one or two Starbucks every day. Usually the one closest to their home and the one closest to their office. There were of course exceptions. There was Caribou and Seattle's Best and a few others, plus the independents, but in sheer number of stores, none of them could compare to Starbucks. America was a caffeine nation and Washington being its capital was no exception.

Rapp wasn't sure if the person he was looking for was a coffee drinker or not. There was probably a twenty percent chance that she was one of those yoga bending, new age health nuts. She took care of herself. That much was obvious. Rapp had visited her shortly after the attack on the motorcade to get her version of the events. He was helping put together a kind of postmortem report for the CIA. Something that would not be shared with the other agencies. The FBI was running the official investigation, and the Secret Service had already done their own internal investigation. Rapp had not seen that report, and he'd wondered how rough it had been.

Rapp looked west down I Street and then east before crossing. He entered the Starbucks and walked up to the clean, organized counter where he was met by a nice young black woman who greeted him warmly and asked him what she could get for him and said it like she meant it. Good service minus the attitude. Rapp grinned and ordered a medium dark roast. She asked him if he wanted room for cream and he said no. While she poured the coffee he checked out the other two employees behind the counter. Not one of them had a visible tattoo, pierced body part, or bad hairdo.

When the woman returned with his piping hot coffee, Rapp gave her three dollars and told her to keep the change. She told him to have a nice day, and then added that he should stop back in. Rapp smiled and thanked her. He didn't feel like telling her he doubted he would be. With a napkin in hand he took his coffee over to the ledge by the window, set it down, took the cap off, and placed it on the tan recycled napkin. It would be too hot to drink for at least a few minutes. Rapp had already noted the faces and general demeanor of the other five patrons in the place. They all looked harmless enough. Probably accountants and admin types.

Rapp set his phone on the counter face down and inserted the SIM card and the battery. After he'd turned it on he opened his address book and hit W. The first name that came up was Jack Warch, former Special Agent in Charge of President Hayes's Secret Service detail and recently promoted deputy director of the United States Secret Service. Rapp hit the send button and brought the phone up to his ear.

After a few rings a voice answered saying, "Warch here."

Rapp brought his free hand up to partially cover his mouth. He whispered into the phone, "I have a bomb."

There was a long pause and then Warch said, "Excuse me?"

Rapp muttered a quick sura in Arabic and then repeated his assertion. "I have a bomb."

"You have a bomb?" the concerned voice on the phone asked.

"Yes."

"What are you going to do with it?"

"I'm going to shove it up your ass." Rapp started to laugh.

There was a pause and then Warch said, "Is that you, Mitch? You jerk."

"Come on," Rapp said while still laughing, "I'm just trying to liven up your day now that you're full-time management."

"Very funny."

"I'm sorry. I won't do it again."

"Yes, you will."

"I know, and I'm not sorry."

"Where the hell are you?"

Rapp looked out the window. The Secret Service headquarters was only a few blocks away. "I'm in town."

"I hear people are looking for you."

"Yeah . . . so what's new?"

"Some people are saying you fucked up, Mitch."

"Nothing I'm not used to."

"Is this really the guy?"

"Absolutely."

"You're a hundred percent sure?"

"One hundred percent."

"Is that your gut or your brain talking?"

"Both."

"My guy who's working with Justice on this says they don't share your conviction."

Rapp smiled. That was exactly what he wanted to hear. "I doubt they would approve of my methods, but let me tell you something, Jack. This guy is absolutely, one hundred percent the guy who detonated the bomb."

"Evidence?"

"More than enough to send him to the gas chamber."

"We don't use those anymore."

"Well for this guy we should. Maybe you could get them to resurrect Old Sparky?"

"The electric chair . . . considering the fact that he killed the next president's wife, I'd say it might actually happen. Are you going to give the Justice Department the evidence, or is this the type of stuff you don't want dragged into open court?"

"They'll get it all in a day or two, but don't tell anyone I told you that. I want them to sweat it a little longer."

"Is it true?"

"What?"

"You shot the guy four times."

"I have no idea what you're talking about. I read the man his rights, handcuffed him, and handed him over to the FBI. The last I saw of the guy he was in perfect physical health."

"So if he was shot, it was the FBI."

"Absolutely."

Warch laughed. "I'll have to tell the president that. He'll get a real kick out of it."

"Listen," Rapp said getting serious, "I need to talk to one of your people."

"Who?"

"Agent Rivera."

Warch was quiet for a moment. "Why?"

"Don't worry, Jack. I'm not going to get her in trouble. I just have a few questions about how things went down back in October."

"I'm not sure how talkative she's going to be."

"Why?"

"The preliminary internal report was released to the top brass yesterday."

"And?"

"She got pretty beat-up."

"Don't tell me you fuckers blamed the whole thing on her."

"I had nothing to do with it, but you know how it works. We're like the Navy . . . something goes wrong on your command and it doesn't matter if it was your fault or not. You go down with the ship either way."

Rapp was tempted to argue with him about their tactics, but he hadn't seen the report and it wasn't why he called. "Do you have a number where I can reach her?"

"Yeah . . . hold on a minute."

"So is she going to lose her job?"

"I don't think they'll fire her. They'll stick her in a boring job pending the completion of the official investigation and then they'll stick her in an even more boring job." Warch found the number and gave it to Rapp.

"When is she usually in?"

"Nine. She works out at some karate studio over on thirteenth and L. I guess she's a real badass."

"Yeah, right?"

"I'm serious."

"So am I."

"Mitch, I'm not kidding. There isn't a guy at the Service who will spar with her. That's why she goes over to this other place. Word is she's been taking her frustration out on them."

"Thirteenth and L."

"Yep."

"Thanks." Rapp put the white lid on his coffee cup. "Do me a favor."

"We never talked."

"You got it." Rapp smiled. Warch was a solid guy.

"Mitch, one other thing . . . Thanks."

"For?"

"Catching this guy. The Service really appreciates it, and I mean that. You ever need anything . . . all you have to do is ask."

"Jack, it was my pleasure." Rapp pressed the end button and considered calling Rivera on her mobile. He decided against it and pulled the battery and SIM card out of the phone. He took his first sip of the hot coffee and then headed out the door. He figured it would take him about five minutes to walk to the studio. It was better to surprise her and get an honest, unprepared reaction.

# 31

Rapp knew enough to finish his coffee before entering the dojo. It would be a sign of disrespect to bring any food or beverage inside. The karate training hall fronted 13th Street. In the typical American fashion, pedestrians could stand on the sidewalk and watch the class. The place had two large picture windows with a door to the left. The reasons for the windows were twofold. First, it helped demystify the martial art to the average person, which would encourage more walk-ins, and secondly it provided an additional distraction that the students needed to get used to. Rapp stood at the window for several minutes watching the sensei run the class through their routines. They were currently sparring. Eight students paired up, practicing their sanbon kumite, or three-step moves. Their sensei walked between them either complimenting or correcting. Everything was done low key. No yelling or badgering.

Rapp picked Rivera out right away. It was hard to miss her black ponytail flying around as she twirled and kicked. Just as Warch had told him, she was a black belt. The man she was sparring with looked to be a few inches taller and a good forty pounds heavier. He was the only other black belt in the class, and she was kicking the shit out of him. Rapp took his last few sips of coffee and smiled as she delivered a blistering combination that left her opponent dazed and on his back. The sensei stepped in, giving Rivera a disapproving look. Rapp was surprised to see Rivera begin talking back to her sensei, a move that was frowned upon. The instructor's face flushed, and then in a further sign of disrespect Rivera turned her back on the man.

Rapp had been in a fair number of street fights as a kid, but it wasn't until he went to work for the CIA that he really learned how to fight. They'd started him out with karate and then judo. He had little difficulty learning both, and while the fundamentals were sound and the discipline was needed, he instinctively knew that in the real world, fighting was far more frantic. Judo and karate had too many rules. Too many constraints. It was on a trip to Fort Bragg for some additional training that he sat in on a jujitsu class. From the first minutes he knew this was a form that was more suited for real world combat. While karate used mostly feet and hand strikes, and judo used mostly holds and throws, jujitsu combined both and then added knees, elbows, head butts, choke holds, submission holds, and even a few more. Rapp began training in earnest, eventually spending several months in Brazil learning Gracie Jujitsu from the grand master himself, Helio Gracie. Over the years he added some Thai boxing to his regimen, but for the most part he focused on Gracie Jujitsu, eventually earning a third-degree black belt.

Rapp looked through the glass at the red-faced sensei and wondered if he would make an example of her. All instructors were not created equal. Some looked good in their white robes and black belts, and could hold their own when practicing one- and three-step moves. Jiyu kumite, or freestyle sparring, was a whole other matter. Worse, put them in a no-holds-barred situation where any form of fighting could be used and they were in serious trouble with their narrow, disciplined approach. Outside their particular area of martial arts, their ability to predict their opponents' moves was all but gone.

This sensei appeared to be in his fifties and looked as if he'd been in a few scrapes. His nose was flattened out a bit, which meant it had been broken on more than one occasion, and he had scar tissue built up around his eyes. Rivera turned around to face him and put her hands stiffly at her sides. Rapp couldn't tell what the sensei was saying to her, but after ten seconds Rivera bowed and walked away. Rapp laughed to himself and decided to go in. He dropped his coffee cup in the garbage by the door and entered the small foyer. It had benches on both sides and hooks on the wall. Shoes were lined up under the bench. Rapp looked through the glass into the training room and caught Rivera's eye. He gestured for her to join him. She shook her head and motioned for him to come into the training room. Rapp hesitated for a second and then figured what the hell. He took off his shoes and placed them under the bench and then hung his trench coat on a hook. With his gun at the small of his back he kept his suit coat on.

Rapp stepped into the training room. The floor was covered with a wall-to-wall blue mat. Looking across the room at the sensei, Rapp bowed, showing his respect, and then looked at Rivera and said, "May I please have a word with you?"

She put one foot in front of the other and rested a hand on each hip. "Why don't you go back to the locker room and put on a gi. We can talk while we spar."

Rapp smiled and said, "I don't think so."

"Really." Rivera walked across the mat and stopped just a few feet short of him. "Come on, tough guy. Are you afraid?"

"No." Rapp shook his head. "I have more important . . ."

Suddenly, Rapp was jerked off his feet. He realized what was happening a split second too late. He recognized the hold. It wasn't karate, it was judo. A double-handed shoulder throw. Midway through the air Rapp heard a tearing noise and knew instantly it was his suit coat. He was so caught off guard by Rivera's lack of discipline that he never saw it coming. His only choice was to go with it and lessen the fall as much as possible. When he hit the ground, the gun that he was carrying at the small of his back dug into his spine. Rapp's entire body arched with pain. Rivera held onto his arm and put her bent right knee against his side. The white-hot pain at the base of his back was excruciating. Above it all, though, he heard the voice of the sensei ordering Rivera to stand down.

The man's face appeared above Rapp. "Are you all right?"

Rapp took a shallow breath and then another. The sensei offered a hand and Rapp took it. When he got to his feet he only had one thing on his mind. He looked at the sensei and said, "Gi, please."

The sensei looked at Rivera with extreme disappointment and then ordered one of the students to go fetch one of the white uniforms and a belt. Rapp walked over to the corner and took off his suit coat. Reaching around he grabbed his gun and its holster and unclipped them from his waistband. Rapp held up the gun and showed Rivera what he had landed on. She looked slightly embarrassed, but her intensity didn't wane a bit.

By the time the student came back with a uniform, Rapp had

his tie and dress shirt off. Not caring a bit what the class thought, he peeled off his white T-shirt to reveal his scarred upper torso. Three pucker marks from bullet holes and a big half-moon scar on his back from a surgery he'd had to remove a lodged bullet and repair some vital organs. Rapp stripped down to his boxers and put the gi on. He paused momentarily as he looked at the brown belt. It occurred to him that he had never worn one. His original karate and judo training was done in secret and he'd worn only white belts. His training had been more about teaching him how to kill and disable than passing exams. It wasn't until he showed up at the Gracie school that he was run through the wringer. After a solid month of training and fighting, where he had beat all comers except the Gracie boys themselves, he was presented with a black belt. At the time he'd had no idea how unusual this was, but the Gracies made their own rules and they prized the ability to beat an opponent over all else.

Rapp tied the belt the way he'd been taught almost eighteen years ago and looked up at Rivera, who was now in the middle of the room bouncing around rolling her head one way and then the other like a prizefighter.

She held up a clear mouth guard and said, "Freestyle."

Rapp looked to the sensei and said, "Jiyu kumite."

The sensei nodded and looked to his pupils, who without having to be told lined up along the far wall and dropped to their knees. Rapp walked to the middle of the room, his guard up this time. He had no idea what her problem was, or whether it was with him directly, men in general, or the entire world. At the moment, he couldn't have cared less. Karate was as much a discipline as a sport and what Rivera deserved right now was to be taught a lesson. The only question for Rapp was how long to make the lesson. He didn't give a shit how many black belts she may have racked up, she didn't have a chance. If you could last a minute on the mat with one of the Gracie boys, who were basically bred to fight, there wasn't a woman on the planet who could take you.

Rapp gave the ceremonial bow and Rivera did the same, although she had a smile on her face. She had no idea what she was in for. Rapp took two steps back and was just settling into a relaxed back stance when she came charging forward. Rivera unleashed a series of combination kicks and strikes, spinning and lashing out, up and down. The only problem was she never came within a foot of hitting her target.

Rapp's hands stayed clasped at the small of his back. He countered her every move by stepping back to either his left or right and twisting his body clear of her hands and feet. Rivera chased him in a counterclockwise circle around the mat, unleashing five separate combinations of three moves or more, screeching a loud kiai, or shout, with each move.

She stopped after the last move, which happened to be her best. It was a spinning back kick that she'd used to knock out countless opponents. She'd assumed Rapp was good, but she beat men all the time. There wasn't an agent at the Secret Service anymore who would step onto the mat with her. The first four moves usually had her opponent so confused and bewildered that they left themselves wide open for the spinning back kick. A little love tap to the chin and it was over before it really got started. Rapp was left standing, however, and his hands were still clasped behind his back. Rivera couldn't believe it. He was taunting her. She paused to catch her breath and assess the situation for a second before redoubling her attack.

Rapp reversed his retreat, having identified the fact that like most fighters she preferred to mount her attack from right to left so she could get her strong side, which appeared to be her right side, into the fight with more velocity. She was coming at him even faster now, with more abandon, leaving herself open to counterattack. She came within inches of landing a rising elbow strike and left herself so wide open that Rapp couldn't resist taking a shot. He was already dropping his weight to miss her elbow, so he simply continued the downward move and began to spin 180 degrees until his back was to her. His left leg shot out so fast Rivera never saw it. His heel struck the center of her solar plexus with about half the force he could have delivered.

Rapp pulled out of the move and stepped back rather than press the attack. Rivera brought her forearms down and her elbows in to protect her midsection. She paused for a beat, angry that he had got the better of her.

Blocking out the pain, Rivera said, "Is that all you can put behind a kick?"

Rapp shook his head. "Not even close."

He didn't know if he should admire her or send her to the hospital. He decided to change styles and give her something else to worry about. Rapp rose up out of his relaxed back stance and moved forward a half step to his left. His arms and fists came up like a boxer, but higher. His entire body bobbed one way and then the other. Suddenly, he hopped forward, landing on his right foot. His hands were up near his face, reaching out for Rivera. He performed the move so quickly that she was left with only one choice and that was to stay in a defensive position. As Rapp's hands came down on her shoulders his left knee came up. He leaned back slightly and thrust his rear hip forward, bringing his knee up and into her stomach.

Rivera partially blocked the blow with her right forearm, but it didn't matter much. It landed with such force that her whole body came off the mat and she let loose a low guttural groan. Rivera tried to clutch his leg before he wound up for another shot, but he simply backed away.

Rapp could have finished her off. One more knee strike followed up with a downward elbow strike to her back and it would have been over, but he wanted to see what she was really made of. It was one thing to attack someone who you thought was an inferior opponent; it was another thing to attack someone when you knew you were outmatched.

Rivera staggered to the side and backed far enough away so she could stand up and take in a deep breath. As she did so, she felt a stabbing pain in her side and realized she might have a broken rib. She vanquished the thought and stared across the mat at Rapp. There was a split second of doubt, but she suppressed it. He was standing tall, which opened him up to a leg sweep. If she could get him on the ground maybe she could put him into a submission hold. Rivera pulled in her core and pushed away the pain. In that slight pause in the fight she saw her strategy. She would deliver a flying kick, which she would pull at the last second and then land and sweep his legs out from underneath him.

Rapp saw the look in her eye. He'd intentionally baited her by staying tall like a Thai boxer rather than dropping back into a karate stance. He saw her eyes quickly check his feet and then he watched as she gathered herself up for the attack. She backed up a few steps getting the bounce back in her step and then sprang forward. Rapp waited until the last possible second. He didn't want her to abort the move. As soon as she brought her right leg up for the expected flying kick Rapp stepped forward and to the right, closing the distance and occupying the space Rivera planned on using to unleash her leg sweep. Rapp deflected the leg kick with his left hand and continued past her.

Rivera landed off balance, and before she could recover, Rapp had hold of her. One arm slipped around her throat and the other came up under her left armpit. He pulled her back off her feet and allowed his full weight to collapse her to the mat. Rapp sat her down on her ass, dropping to his own knees and tightening the rear stranglehold on her throat.

Rivera had been in this hold only once before, and it hadn't ended well. She drew her legs in and tried to stand, but he leaned on her even harder and tightened the hold around her neck. She grasped for a finger to snap, but couldn't get a hold of one. Spots started to enter her vision from the sides. She was winded from fighting and needed air. She knew all she had to do was raise her fight hand and submit, but she couldn't allow herself to do that. With one final effort she dug her nails into his forearm and then started scratching for his eyes.

Rapp didn't bother to ask her to submit. She knew how this game was played. It was hers to ask for and his to grant. He also knew it was unlikely that she would. In a final attempt to break free she reached up to gouge his eyes. Something that was perfectly expected in a street fight, but here in the dojo it was strictly forbidden. He turned his head away and she gave him a good scratch on his cheek. Rapp held the hold firmly and a few seconds later Rivera went limp.

# 32

Rapp hadn't worked up a sweat, so he got dressed and waited outside for Rivera. She came out ten minutes later, her hair wet and pulled back in a ponytail.

"So, I suppose you hung around to gloat." Rivera threw open the right side of her black trench coat and placed her hand on the hilt of her service pistol.

"No, but from your tone it sounds like you could use another ass kicking."

"What do you want with me?" She sounded irritated.

"We need to talk. Have you had breakfast?"

She looked at her watch. "No time. I can't be late for work. I'm under double secret probation."

"Is that the reason for your attitude?"

"If you really care to know, yes it is. Three months ago I was a rising star and now I'm an embarrassment."

"Come on." Rapp grabbed her by the elbow. "I spotted a breakfast place around the corner. We need to talk about a few things."

"I told you I can't. They're looking for an excuse to fire me. I need to get to work."

"Fuck 'em. You didn't do anything they didn't train you to do. Come on, let's go."

She dug in her heels. "What is that supposed to mean?"

"You followed Secret Service procedure. Plain and simple."

"And what is wrong with our procedures?" she said defensively.

"Oh, you're a pain in the ass. Just drop the feminist, bull dyke bravado for thirty minutes, alright? I'm buying. Let's go."

Rivera's eyes squinted. "Did you just call me a bull dyke?"

"No . . . I said drop the bull dyke attitude. You know . . . the whole female cop that has to prove she's tougher than any man."

"You think I'm a lesbian?"

"I don't care if you're gay, straight, bi, or whatever the hell floats your boat. All I'm telling you is that I don't need your *fucking* attitude. I showed up here this morning, because I have something important to talk to you about, and you pull that classless, cheap shot, bullshit move, thinking you're all tough." Rapp got in her face. "My *fucking* back is killing me. You dropped me on my *fucking* gun . . . You're lucky I didn't break your jaw."

"Yeah . . . well if it makes you happy, I think you broke one of my ribs." Rivera slid a hand under her jacket and winced as she touched her side.

"Good." Rapp looked around and then said, "Can we go have breakfast now?"

"I'm not kidding. They're building a file on me. Any excuse to get rid of me."

It occurred to Rapp that she was so outside the loop that she had no idea he'd captured the man responsible for the motor-cade attack. "Did you read the paper or turn on the TV this morning?"

"No. I got up and ran five miles and then came here."

"Five miles and then you came here?"

"Yeah . . . that's probably why you beat me. Next time I'm going to make sure I'm ready."

"Are you delusional?"

"No . . . just realistic."

Rapp shook his head and started walking. "Come on. I need something to eat."

"I'm serious. I have to go. Maybe we could meet for lunch?"

Without breaking stride, Rapp yelled over his shoulder, "Did I mention that I found the man in the red hat?"

Rivera hesitated for a second and then called back, "What?"

"You heard me." Three seconds later the Secret Service agent was at his side.

"Are you jerking me around? Because if you are, I swear . . ."

"Easy, killer. You really need to calm down."

"You should talk."

"I'm a guy."

"There you go with the sexist stuff again."

Rapp glanced at her sideways and decided to ignore the comment. "I found the guy on Cyprus, dragged him back here yesterday, and handed him over to the FBI. They're going to announce the whole thing at ten o'clock this morning."

"Does the Secret Service know?"

"I talked to Jack Warch this morning. He knew."

"Bastards. You think they would have called me."

"Relax. There's a chance they only found out this morning."

Rivera shook her head. "You don't understand. I don't exist to them anymore. All I am is a reminder of one of the Service's greatest failures."

Rapp supposed she was right. They came up on a small diner, and Rapp grabbed the door and held it for her. They went to a booth near the back, and Rapp practically had to fight Rivera for the side that faced the door. Rapp took off his trench coat and when he sat down he lifted his right arm and checked out the torn seam on his suit coat.

"I'm going to pay for that," Rivera said.

Rapp ignored her. "So I have a few questions for you."

"I'm serious about paying for it. Don't ignore me."

"Are you always this confrontational, or is this all related to work?"

"I think I used to be a pretty positive person." She got reflective for a moment. "I was happy with my job. My life was good, although, things were a little barren in the love department, but when we're in campaign mode there's no time for anything, and then the damn bomb went off and it's been pretty shitty ever since then."

Rapp studied her, slightly surprised by her honesty. Rivera was an extremely attractive woman. She could use a little softening around the edges, but the beauty was undeniable, and it was all natural. She didn't have to work at a thing. Without any makeup or real sense of style she was an effortless eight. At a place like the Secret Service that would make her a ten, and like all law enforcement agencies the Secret Service had no shortage of puss hounds. If he remembered her file right she was in her mid-thirties. Any woman who was this attractive, and still single at this point in her life, must have some issues.

"You ever wish you had died in the attack?" Rapp knew it was a common reaction from survivors. Especially, survivors whose job it was to protect those who died.

Rivera studied Rapp for a moment and then said, "I think *wish* might be a little strong, but yeah, I've thought about it."

The waitress pulled up to the table and killed the conversation. They both ordered coffee and water, and Rivera ordered the heart-healthy omelet while Rapp asked for the corned beef and hash. When the waitress was gone, Rivera began peppering him with questions about the man in the red hat. Rapp gave her the vanilla version only, maybe just a little more than what the FBI already knew and then he took control of the conversation.

"I haven't read the report in sometime, so I can't remember, did you use electronic jammers that morning?"

Rivera shook her head. "That was one of the things I've been criticized for."

"They were available to you and you didn't use them?" Rap asked a bit surprised.

"That's what they say, but there wasn't a person on the detail who knew that, and no one back at headquarters ever told us directly that they were available. They dug up some bullshit, cover your ass, interoffice memo that they claim was sent to us. The only problem is, during the campaign, we're on the fly nonstop. We don't have time to read a forty-page memo on our BlackBerry."

"So no jammers."

"Correct."

Rapp grabbed the salt-and-pepper shakers and lined them up one in front of the other and then switched them. "But you shuffled the cars, right?"

Rivera shook her head.

Her answer shocked Rapp, but he hid his surprise. "All right, walk me through the last five minutes, please. How were you deployed? When did you begin to roll . . . the whole routine." While Rivera began to talk, Rapp started to consider the possibility that

Gazich had lied to him about the phone call telling him it was the second limo. If he'd lied to him about that, what else had he lied to him about? Rapp only half listened to Rivera as she relayed the details of the tragic afternoon. He was already trying to figure out how he could get his hands on Gazich for a more in-depth interrogation.

# 33

The idyllic town of Geneva was perhaps the most conflicted city on the planet. As the bedrock of puritanical Calvinism the city was as buttoned up and straitlaced as any in a country that prided itself on cleanliness, good manners, and lots of rules. That was by day. The cars, most of them BMWs, Mercedes, or Audis, were spotless. The men, most of them bankers, financiers, accountants, or lawyers, wore expensive handmade suits that never went out of style. By some estimates as much as a quarter of the world's private wealth was deposited in the vaults of Geneva's banks, which meant that a town with only a quarter million people held more private assets than New York, London, Paris, Hong Kong, or Tokyo. It hardly seemed possible, but it was.

The Genevese, like the long line of religious hypocrites who had gone before them, had somehow managed to reconcile their Calvinist beliefs with an absolute lust for money. How could a quarter of the world's private wealth end up in a relatively small city, you might ask. The answer was pretty straightforward. The Swiss maintained absolute secrecy when it came to their banking records. Many of their clients were legitimate business people and members of European royalty who simply wanted to keep their finances their own business. A disproportionate number, though, were reprobates and sociopaths. People who had lied, cheated, and even killed to amass their wealth.

If these bad eggs had simply deposited their ill-gotten gains in the high-polished banks of Geneva, the story of the city by the lake would have been fairly boring. There was a byproduct of this secret banking relationship, however, that the community's modern-day leaders had never predicted. Geneva had become a magnet for wealthy scoundrels and criminals from every continent. Because many of them obtained their wealth by breaking the law, they were wanted by their home countries for prosecution and in some cases the gallows.

This influx of sociopaths and megalomaniacs had created an extremely interesting social experiment. At least Joseph Speyer found it interesting. The fifty-six-year-old banker had grown up in Geneva, and like many gay men of his generation was forced to hide his sexuality until well into his thirties. His family was strict Protestant Reformation. Lots of rules and not a lot of fun. They were not unique in this regard, but all this repression ended up breeding a lot of closet gays, masochists, and perverts in general. Add to that the influx of extremely wealthy people suffering from a vast array of antisocial personality disorders and you had the perfect recipe for a city with a depraved counterculture.

Speyer was on his way to find one of Geneva's chief reprobates. It was Monday evening. Mondays were the one day of the week that the city's hot nightclubs were closed, nightclubs that when you stripped away the thirty-dollar drinks and fancy décor were nothing more than whorehouses. Prostitution was legal in Switzerland. That had been a big dilemma for the lawmakers. The fathers of the Reformation would have never approved of making the flesh trade legal, but it was argued that the banking business needed it to stay competitive. The influx of wealthy Arab princes and other international players who began flocking to the city in the seventies liked their women and they didn't mind paying exorbitant sums of money for them. After several decades of lying to themselves, and looking the other way, the ordered society came to grips with the problem, legalized it, and began collecting taxes.

Speyer took perverse joy in all of this. He was a voyeur at heart, and few things excited him more than meeting the needs of his sexually depraved clients. Cy Green was one such client. The man had a thirst for sex that to some might seem like an addiction, but comparing it to a few other people he knew, Speyer saw it as simply a healthy appetite. Green wanted sex every night. He had confided in Speyer that he thought it was all part of the alpha male persona. Monogamous sex was out of the question. Green preferred two women and foreplay that almost always involved him watching. Speyer knew because he'd been forced to sit through it.

Speyer wedged his BMW sedan into a spot a block away from Green's apartment and walked along the narrow sidewalk. He stepped into the relatively small foyer and approached the bulletproof glass to speak to the doorman. Geneva had become a city of bulletproof glass and bodyguards. Far too many of its wealthy immigrants were wanted by their former governments and business rivals. At least once a year, if not more, there was a salacious murder.

The man behind the glass recognized Speyer and greeted him in French before picking up the phone to call the penthouse. Green owned the top floor of the building. Six thousand square feet, which might not be obscene by normal wealthy standards, but was huge for downtown Geneva. After a moment the doorman buzzed Speyer through. When the banker reached the elevator, the door was already open. He stepped in, pressed the button for the top floor, and took off his leather driving gloves. The trip to the fourth floor was quick. When the door opened, Speyer found two men waiting for him. The older of the two was Green's personal valet and butler. He was dressed in a black waistcoat, black vest, white shirt, and black bowtie. Speyer handed him his gloves and turned around so he could take his coat for him. As soon as the valet had the gray cashmere overcoat off, the bodyguard stepped in with a handheld metal detector and ran it around the periphery of Speyer's body. It was the same routine every time; Speyer never complained and Green never apologized.

When they were finished, Speyer was escorted into the living room and asked if he cared for anything to drink. He told the manservant he was fine and checked his watch. He hoped Green wouldn't make him wait too long. It had been a long day and it was sure to be a long week. Some very big promises had been made and the time left to deliver on them was waning.

Six minutes later Green appeared in a blue silk robe with white piping and matching house slippers. His dark hair was slicked back and slightly messed up in back. The eternally tan billionaire strode across the room pulling on the robe's belt.

He looked at Speyer with a devilish grin and said, "You've come to watch, haven't you?"

"No." Speyer took off his black-framed glasses and placed them in his suit pocket. "I'm afraid I'm simply playing the role of messenger."

Green considered this for a moment and with a shake of his head said, "Follow me."

Speyer sighed and said, "I'm afraid I'm short on time."

Green kept walking. "Nonsense. We have important things to discuss. Plus I do not want to miss the show." He disappeared down the hallway and then a few seconds later his head popped back around the corner. "By the way, I just opened a bottle of ninety-two Screaming Eagle. Even a French wine snob like you can't say no to that."

A smile formed at the corners of Speyer's mouth and then his feet started to move. Green was right. Screaming Eagle was very rare and very hard to resist. He followed him down the hall to the master bedroom suite.

"Close the door behind you," Green commanded.

They walked through a wood-paneled library with a big screen TV and a sitting area. The heavy beat of Euro techno music could be heard beyond the double doors that led to the actual bedroom. Green thrust open the doors. Straight ahead was a turned-down king-size bed with black silk sheets. Speyer looked to his right knowing full well that was where the action would be. The large window that looked out over Lake Geneva was obscured by heavy black drapes that acted as a backdrop to the sex show that was taking place in the alcove of the window. Green had designed the small stage himself. The alcove was ten feet wide by four feet deep. On both sides were narrow doors that when opened revealed a series of hooks, chains, and ropes. Standing in the middle of the stage was a young blond wearing pigtails, clogs, and a short summer dress. Behind her stood a tall dominatrix covered, literally, in black latex from head to her spike heeled boots. The only openings were for her mouth, eyes, breasts, and crotch. The woman had a riding crop in one hand and an impossibly large dildo in the other.

"Sit," Green ordered.

Two chairs were already set up. Green brought over the bottle of wine and poured a second glass. Speyer, even though he was gay, had been titillated the first time he'd attended one of these private shows. Green mistook his excitement as proof that he was actually bisexual. Speyer had experimented with a lot of things over the years, but he was simply gay. Nothing really too complicated about it. He'd figured it out when he was eleven and then spent the next ten years or so trying to repress it. He knew now that the aspect of the sex show that had originally excited him was the corruption of youth. The fall from grace of a young heterosexual woman. After that one show, though, Speyer couldn't get past the fact that the women were simply Russian prostitutes whose fall from grace had taken place long before. Woo a duchess or other high society type, or even a straitlaced colleague over to the forbidden side, and that would be worth watching. These were just two hungry young women trying to earn some money by exciting a perverted billionaire.

"What do you think?" Green asked without taking his eyes off the women.

"Don't tell anyone."

"Since when did you get shy about this type of stuff?"

"I mean the wine." Speyer took a sip, savoring the California wine.

"It's good, isn't it?"

"Very, but I'm serious. You must not tell anyone."

"Relax." Green grinned. "Now, what is the message you've been sent to deliver?"

"I received a call this afternoon from Mr. Garret."

"Don't tell me that little fucker is trying to wiggle out of the deal?"

"It's interesting you should put it that way, because if I didn't know better, I would say that is exactly what he is trying to do."

Green's tanned face slowly turned toward Speyer. His eyes narrowed and he asked, "What in the hell did he say? I want to hear it word for word."

"Supposedly, the person who was hired to do the job has been captured."

"What?"

"The man who Vasili hired was caught. The Americans have him in custody. There was a press conference this afternoon." Speyer knew that Green was hearing this for the first time. The man never watched TV and left the Internet up to his assistants.

"How is that possible? Vasili told me himself that it was being taken care of."

"Obviously he was premature in his promise."

Green stood and began waving his hands. "Stop . . . stop. Girls, take a break. I'll be back in a few minutes." He grabbed the bottle of wine and said to Speyer, "Follow me."

They went out into the library and closed the double doors. Green set the bottle of Screaming Eagle on the fireplace mantle next to the pool table. A large portrait of none other than Green himself dominated the wall above the mantel.

Speyer stood on the other side of the pool table and looked at Green next to his portrait. The double image spoke volumes of the man and his ego. "As I'm sure you can imagine, Mr. Garret was extremely upset."

"When isn't that little fucker upset? Have you ever met a more irritating person in all your life?"

Speyer decided it was better to not answer the question. "He has a point this time."

"I'm beginning to question your wisdom. You were the one who advised me to do this. That's what I pay you to do. You said it would be a good return on my investment."

It was almost impossible for his clients to surprise him. He'd seen it all. Their selective memory, their ability to rationalize or simply forget every bad decision or deed they'd ever committed, was endless, while their capacity to fixate or create blame elsewhere was eternal. "Cy, before we go any further, I want to make it very clear that you brought this proposal to my attention. You expressed your desire to proceed from the very beginning and you never vacillated. You wanted to do this. I merely supported you."

Green stared at him for a moment and decided to change the subject. "I'll tell you what pisses me off. I've already spent millions of dollars on this. I've leveraged some of my most important contacts, I've risked a lot . . . and what have they done?"

Speyer shrugged.

"They haven't done shit. Where's my fucking pardon?"

"They always said it wouldn't happen until the last minute."

"What are they waiting for? There isn't much time left."

"I've told you it would likely take place this Saturday."

Green began pacing in front of the fireplace. "Are we sure the Americans have the right guy?"

"I have no way of knowing. Plus I have no idea who the right guy is."

"Yeah," Green said as if he had figured something out. "Vasili is the only one who knows. Have you called Vasili?"

"No." Speyer did not like dealing with the Russian mobster directly. Not if he could avoid it.

"I'll call him and find out what's going on, and in the meantime you call that little prick Garret and tell him I said I want my pardon."

Speyer nodded, took a large gulp of wine, and questioned once again the wisdom of working with men like Green and Garret.

# 34

The Justice Department sat directly across Pennsylvania Avenue from FBI headquarters. Ross's motorcade pulled up to the building unannounced at 9:30 on Tuesday morning. Stu Garret, Jonathon Gordon, and Ross emerged from the back of the armored limousine and proceeded across the wide sidewalk surrounded by a phalanx of Secret Service agents. A single agent ran into the building ahead of everyone so he could alert security that the vice president–elect was coming in to see the attorney general. Much of the hassle could have been avoided if they'd called ahead, but Ross liked to make surprise visits. The vice president to be told the agent in charge of his detail that it was a way of getting a better sense of how things actually ran. The agent suspected it had more to do with Ross liking to keep people off balance.

Ross, his chief of staff, and his campaign manager skirted the security lines and crowded into an elevator with four tall agents. They went to the top floor and down the hall to the attorney general's suite. During Ross's short stint as the director of National Intelligence he spent many mornings attending security briefings at the Department of Justice. They passed several administrative assistants in the hallway. Ross, always the politician, smiled and greeted them.

The attorney general had a good-sized outer office where three secretaries sat behind large desks. Ross was about to say good morning when the door to Stokes's conference room flew open. A six-foot-tall blond appeared in the doorway with her back to the reception area. She was wearing a brown, long-sleeved, formfitting dress, belted at the waist, and a pair of leather boots.

"You guys are out of your minds," she yelled. "You can find someone else. I'm not going anywhere near this thing."

"Peggy, please come back in here and sit down."

Ross and his entourage stood motionless and silent on the threshold between the hallway and the reception area. Ross knew this woman, and although he couldn't see Attorney General Stokes, he knew his voice well enough to know it was he who had asked her to come back in and sit down.

"Marty," the tall blond said, "you more than any other person in this building should know he is the wrong guy to mess with."

"Just close the door, and sit down. I'm in no mood for the theatrics this morning."

"Theatrics," she yelled. "You want to see some real theatrics, keep doing what you're doing. He gets wind of this and he'll eat you for lunch."

Ross grinned. It appeared they had stepped in to the middle of a disagreement. The three secretaries were looking back and forth between the next vice president of the United States of America and the leggy blond deputy attorney general in the doorway. The leggy blond was Peggy Stealey. Ross knew her by reputation more than anything else. She was an intense lawyer who did not suffer fools lightly.

"Peggy, I'm serious," Stokes said raising his voice. "Get back in here. We need to finish discussing this."

"Marty, did I somehow give you the impression that I wasn't taking this seriously? Because if I did, I would like to set the record straight. Where Mitch Rapp is concerned, I take things very seriously." She folded her arms across her chest. "If you want to continue down this path, which I am advising against, that's your prerogative. Just go find someone else, because I'm telling you I want nothing to do with it."

"You're the deputy assistant attorney general in charge of counterterrorism. This case is yours whether you like it or not."

"I never said I wouldn't handle the case. I'm just not going to investigate Mitch Rapp, and that's final."

Stealey turned to leave but after a step she noticed the group of men standing in the doorway and she stopped dead in her tracks. Before she could speak the attorney general yelled from the conference room, "Times are changing, Peggy. Rapp and his boss have made a lot of enemies in this town, and this mess he created isn't going to win him any friends."

Ross looked at the blue-eyed woman standing before him. With her high cheekbones and strong jaw, she looked decidedly Scandinavian. Ross extended his hand. "Ms. Stealey."

Stealey hesitated for a second, unsure of which title to use. "Mr. Vice President."

Ross clasped her right hand firmly, took a step closer and then placed his left hand on her shoulder. Smiling warmly he whispered, "He's right, you know."

"Excuse me?" Stealey was taken slightly aback.

"Times, they are a-changing."

"That tends to happen around here every four years or so."

Ross studied her. She was nearing forty and her skin was still flawless. Ross leaned forward placing his mouth within inches of Stealey's right ear. "Don't worry about Mitch Rapp. You won't recognize the CIA a year from now."

Stealey's blue eyes narrowed into an analytical stare. "I don't make mistakes very often, but when I do, I learn from them."

Ross nodded and smiled. He thought of something Stokes had once told him about Peggy Stealey. He had compared her to a thunderstorm. The anticipation of her arrival was made up of equal amounts of fear and excitement over the awesome spectacle that was about to commence. If she blew through quickly it made for a rather enjoyable watching. But if she hovered or stalled, she could cause serious damage.

"And what am I supposed to glean from that comment?" Ross asked.

Stealey pulled Ross closer and in a soft voice said, "Don't fuck with Mitch Rapp." And with that she was gone.

Ross stood motionless for a few seconds, his perma-smile plastered across his face. Slowly he turned and watched his entourage move out of the way for Stealey. Ross kept smiling even though, inside, his temper was raging. Stokes may have found the woman's outspokenness refreshing, but Ross found it downright disrespectful.

Garret came forward and in a quiet voice asked, "What did she say?"

Ross, smiling like a ventriloquist's dummy, said, "I'll tell you later." He turned and walked into the conference room, finding the attorney general and two of his deputies sitting at the far end of a massive conference table. Stokes and the other two men quickly got to their feet when they saw Ross.

"No . . . no," said Ross after they were well out of their chairs. "Don't bother getting up." He gestured in a downward motion with his hands. "I just wanted to drop in and congratulate you on your victory. President–elect Alexander asked me to personally thank you for catching the man responsible for his wife's death."

Attorney General Stokes looked awkwardly to his left and then his right. The three men all shared an uncomfortable look.

"The case might not be as strong as we were originally led to believe."

Ross swore rumors spread quicker in Washington, DC, than any other city in the world. There were so many reporters, so many po-litical hacks on both sides of the aisle and far too many people who strived to prove their self-worth by acting like they were in the know. The news of the arrest sent shock waves through DC. The story was simply too big to keep a lid on. President Hayes made it clear that he wanted Langley to finally get some credit. The DOJ and FBI could ride the CIA's coattails, but Langley deserved the lion's share. People at the three agencies began leaking almost im-mediately. By the time the press conference took place on Monday morning half the town knew what was going on. It all sounded like a major victory for the CIA.

By mid–afternoon, though, the rumor mill began churning out a different story. It started as a whisper. There were some problems with the case. By evening the whisper had grown into a murmur. Suddenly, the three agencies were tight-lipped again, which was al-ways a sign that something was wrong. Now this morning, the press was on the offensive, burning up the phones trying to get sources to confirm the worst-case scenario, which was that the CIA had grabbed the wrong guy. Garret, never one to miss an opportunity, went into full spin mode. He quickly drafted a battle plan, but cau-tioned Ross that they needed to go over to Justice and find out

272 / VINCE FLYNN

what was fact and what was fiction before they took a hard position.

So Ross found himself playing dumb and looking to an old colleague from the Senate for confirmation. "What's wrong?"

"Ah . . ." Stokes sighed, "I'm not even sure I know where to begin."

"I'm a little miffed here, Martin. Last I heard, this thing was a slam dunk."

"That's what I was told as well, but now some problems have popped up. Some potentially embarrassing problems."

"Such as?"

"Such as . . . the man we have in custody might not be the right guy."

"Excuse me?" Ross's eyes got wide and he thrust his chin out.

"The man in question is a Greek citizen. He has proclaimed his innocence since the moment he was handed over to the FBI on Sunday afternoon."

"This wouldn't be the first time a criminal claimed he was innocent."

"Tell me about it. If it was just that I wouldn't give it a second thought, but there's more, or should I say less." Stokes shared an uncomfortable look with his two deputies. "For starters the Greek ambassador is filing an official letter of protest that I'm told will be delivered to the State Department this afternoon."

"Why?"

"They are claiming that the CIA kidnapped this man."

"Who really cares?" Ross had thought this one through. "If this is the man who attacked the motorcade, the Greeks can file all the damn letters of protest they want."

"The problem is, we're not sure this is the right guy."

"What do you mean, you're not sure?"

"We were told this is the guy. We were told there was hard evidence against him."

"And?"

"We've seen nothing."

"What do you mean, you've seen nothing?"

Stokes let out a frustrated sigh. "On Sunday afternoon we received a prisoner. The prisoner was wounded. He'd been shot four times. Once in each knee and once in each hand."

"Tortured?" Ross asked.

"I'd say so." Stokes looked to his deputies for a consensus and both men nodded.

"Has the man admitted to anything?"

"Not to us, but the CIA claims he confessed during transit from Cyprus back to the States."

"While he was being tortured," Ross said with his best, you've got to be kidding me look.

"That is what he's claiming."

"The suspect?"

"Yes."

"Shit. Do you have a tape of the confession?"

"No."

"Why not?"

"We've been asking the CIA for over a day, and have gotten nowhere."

Ross cocked his head to the side. "Excuse me?"

"I assume you've heard it was Rapp who found this guy."

"I have heard that rumor."

"Well, it's true. The problem is no one knows where he is. This was his op. He was the one who found him."

"So what's the problem?"

"We don't have a single shred of evidence in our possession that can connect this guy to the crime. The prisoner has submitted to and passed a lie detector test, and the Greek government has no record of him leaving Cyprus during the time of the attack. The suspect claims to have witnesses that will swear to the fact he was at home, on Cyprus the day of the attack."

Ross turned to look at Garret who in his typical unvarnished manner blurted out, "It sounds like Rapp grabbed the wrong guy."

The three men from the Justice Department all shared uncomfortable looks and then Stokes said, "No one is willing to say it yet, but that's our worst fear."

"For Christ's sake," Ross swore. "Have you told the president any of this?"

"I'm heading over to the White House for lunch. I'll break it to him then."

"What about Josh?"

Stokes shook his head. "Maybe you could break the news to him."

Ross acted like he didn't want to, but he did. It was an opportunity to prove to his running mate how well connected he was. "I'm having lunch with him today. I'll tell him then. In the meantime, you'd better find Rapp. We don't want our new administration to start out under the cloud of scandal."

Ross had intentionally used the first person plural possessive *our.* Stokes was a useful man in that he was both politically hungry and well liked. For months they'd been dangling the possibility of carrying him over into the next administration. They'd even hinted that there might be something bigger on his horizon.

# 35

The warehouse was old. Built during the early days of WWII, it housed crucial supplies for Britain. It was all part of the Lend-Lease program that FDR had fought so hard for. Once the United States entered the war, the brick building doubled in size and became a beehive of activity until the Nazis surrendered. After the war U.S. Steel moved in and the Marshall Plan kept things busy as the U.S. continued to ship supplies to help rebuild Western Europe. Business remained good for U.S. Steel until the mid-seventies, and then things really slowed down. The entire area fell into a long cycle of neglect and disrepair.

When Scott Coleman first looked at the place, there wasn't a window that wasn't broken, the roof leaked, and a series of bad tenants had come and gone without bothering to take their junk with them. For most people the smell of urine and years of neglect was hard to get past, but Coleman, who had traveled the world with the

U.S. Navy, was used to such things. Where others saw nothing but neglect, Coleman saw an opportunity. As a friend in the Navy used to say, "They aren't building oceanfront property anymore."

The place was out on Sparrows Point, just south of Baltimore on the Patapsco River. The SEAL Demolition and Salvage Corporation was Coleman's brainchild. He'd seen too many of his fellow special forces operators leave the military and grow miserable living the civilian life. Coleman himself used to have nightmares that one day he'd be forced to take a job as a greeter at Wal-Mart. During long deployments, he began to flush out the idea for his own company. Going to work for someone else didn't seem very appealing. Not after taking orders from others for so long. He asked himself one simple question. What skills had the navy taught him? There were many, but some of the more unique ones were diving, shooting, and blowing things up. Legally speaking, the first and last skills were more transferable than one might think. Ports and shipyards all over the world were in need of expert divers who knew how to get rid of debris.

SEAL Demolition and Salvage Corporation started with that express purpose, and their very first job illustrated the need for such special talents. British Petroleum had a problem brewing that needed to be solved before it became an international issue. They had quietly contracted to have one of their abandoned oil rigs in the North Atlantic demolished. Somehow, word had leaked out, and Greenpeace was mobilizing a group of protesters to occupy the rig and prevent the demolition. They wanted BP to dismantle the rig girder by girder. To the executives at BP the decision was simple: demolish the rig at a cost of two hundred thousand dollars or dismantle it piece by piece at an estimated cost of five million.

BP scrambled to get its people together and blow the rig before Greenpeace could mobilize. BP's best estimate was that they could have all of the charges in place and ready to go within forty-eight hours. They found out that a boat loaded with Greenpeace activists was docked in Reykjavik, Iceland, and set to leave port the following morning. The activists would arrive at the rig by noon the next day and storm the platform, creating an international media event that would bring public and political pressure on BP to dismantle it piece by piece. BP needed to slow the protesters down so that the company would have enough time to blow the rig.

The vice president of operations at BP was told to find a way to stop the activists from reaching the rig, and to make sure BP was insulated from any fallout. The executive made several calls to his contacts in America and Britain and found out that there was a new upstart company in Maryland that might be perfect for the job. The man called Coleman and explained the situation to him. He had twenty hours to get to Reykjavik and stop the boat from leaving the harbor. He didn't care how it was done, just so long as no one was hurt.

Coleman had a rough idea of how much it would cost BP if they had to dismantle the rig, so he said he'd do the job for $300,000. The BP exec agreed, and Coleman, Stroble, and Hacket were on the next flight out of Dulles with their diving gear. They landed in Reykjavik just before sundown and were down at the pier by 11:00 that evening. Thanks to years of training by the United States Navy, they knew exactly what to do. During their tenure as SEALs, they had spent countless hours swimming around dirty harbors attaching explosives to hulls and disabling propellers and rudders.

The only difficult aspect of this specific mission was the water temperature. Even with their cold-water gear they could stay in the water for no more than fifteen minutes at a time. They took turns swimming over to the ship from a berth about two hundred feet away. Using an acetylene torch, they cut away at the U-joints where the drive shafts met the propellers. The boat would be able to maintain steerage and prop speed up to maybe ten knots for a limited period of time. Anything more than that and the laws of physics would take effect. The increased torque on the propellers would cause the sabotaged joints to snap and the boat would be dead in the water.

They sat at a café the next morning and wagered as to whether or not the ship would make it out of the harbor. Coleman didn't feel guilty about the job. He'd been around the ocean his whole life and had a deep respect and healthy fear of it. Sending a couple thousand tons of steel to the ocean floor wouldn't harm it a bit. As they drank coffee and waited for their 8:00 a.m. flight back to Washington, a tug moved in and towed the ship out to the main channel. The lines were released and the ship was under way. A white froth churned up behind the stern of the boat as it headed for the open sea. It had just cleared the seawall when the frothy wake subsided and the ship stalled, turning sideways in the middle of the channel. An hour later Coleman, Stroble, and Hacket were on their way back to Washington.

That little company that Coleman had started before the terrorist attacks of 9/11 now had annual revenues of over twenty-five million dollars a year, and had grown to over 20 full-time employees with another 100-plus independent contractors under employment. Those 100-plus employees were all former special forces operators, men who used to make $30,000 to $40,000 a year who were now making a quarter of a million dollars and up.

Coleman moved the growing company to new digs in a more business friendly area midway between DC and Baltimore, but hung on to the old warehouse. Through an off shore company he had an attorney approach the owner and acquire the building. The place was simply too private to part ways with, and in Coleman's line of work privacy was paramount.

Two large cargo doors and one service door faced the street. There was no signage, only a street address painted in white above the service door and the faded remnants of the U.S. Steel logo. Inside the warehouse, the old cracked and chipped floor had been acid washed, patched, and painted. Along the left side was a mix of storage lockers, racks, and large metal tables. Lined up on the right side were two motorcycles and a car, all three under gray tarps, and a twenty-eight-foot Boston Whaler with two Merc 150 HP outboards. A black Chevy pickup and a big Ford Excursion were both backed in and parked in the middle. At the back of the building were the offices, bathroom, and workout area. A metal staircase led to the second floor. There were two offices and a conference room, all with large glass windows that looked out onto the floor.

Coleman was in the right corner office sitting behind a large gray metal desk. It was military surplus. Sturdy, cheap, and functional. He was working on clearing his e-mails. He received on average a hundred per day, and they came at all hours. He had men in Iraq, Afghanistan, Kazakhstan, Jordan, Qatar, Kuwait, and Indonesia, and those were only the places he could admit to. A beeping noise caused him to turn around. He ran a hand through his sandy blond hair and looked at the two twenty-eight-inch flat-screen monitors. The one on the left showed a man lying on a bed in a cement-walled room. The room was the building's WWII bomb shelter that they had converted into a cell several years before. The man on the cot was the mystery Russian whom they had brought with them from Cyprus. The screen on the right was split into four separate pictures. One of the stairs leading down to the bomb shelter, the back door to the warehouse, the front door, and the fourth and final frame rotated between shots of the roof and the sides of the building.

Two cars were lined up in front of the main cargo door waiting
to be let in. One was a silver Audi A8, and the other was a blue
Toyota Land Cruiser. Coleman knew both vehicles, and he was expecting them. He turned back to his computer, grabbed the mouse
with his right hand, and clicked on a security icon at the bottom of
the screen. A menu popped up listing the building's doors and their
status. Coleman maneuvered the mouse's arrow to the main cargo
door and clicked on the Open tab. Coleman watched the vehicles
roll in and then closed the big door. He pushed himself away from
his desk and walked out onto the catwalk. Coleman put both hands
on the top railing and watched Rapp climb out of the Audi and
Dumond the Toyota.

"Irene wants you to call her," Coleman said to Rapp.

Rapp looked up at Coleman. "Yeah, I know. Everyone's looking for me. I'm sure I'll be threatened with arrest if I don't turn myself in."

Coleman started down the stairs. "How much longer are you
going to keep this up?"

"This afternoon maybe. Tomorrow morning at the latest."

"And why are you doing this again?" Coleman reached the bottom and turned left into a hallway instead of heading the other way
to meet Rapp.

"You don't want to know." Rapp followed Coleman, and Dumond followed Rapp.

"You'd better not push them so far that they actually end up
trying to arrest you. I don't need the FBI poking around here looking for you." Coleman entered a small break room with a table for
four, a coffee machine, a microwave, and a refrigerator. Someone
had hung a Marine Corps recruiting poster on the wall and written
some not-so-flattering comments on the Semper Fi slogan. Coleman poured two cups of black coffee, handing one to Rapp and
keeping the other for himself.

"Marcus, what can I get you?"

"You got any Coke?"

"In the fridge."

"So what did the boys find in the safety deposit box?" Rapp asked.

"Two guns. One Makarov and a Beretta. Silencers for each and a few extra clips of ammo."

"Serial numbers?"

"Removed."

"What else?"

"Six hundred thousand dollars in cash," Coleman said with a grin.

"You're kidding me?"

"Nope."

Rapp looked at the far wall and thought of the agreement he'd made with the banker. "Kapodistras must have shit himself."

"Who?"

"Kapodistras, the banker."

"Wicker said he was a nervous wreck the whole time, but as soon as he saw how much cash was in the box, he stopped complaining. Did you have any idea there would be that much cash?"

"No," Rapp shook his head. "What else was in there?"

"Passports, credit cards . . . the standard stuff. He also had one of those new memory sticks that mirrors your hard drive."

Rapp looked to Dumond.

"When are they due in?" Dumond asked Coleman.

"They left Paris this morning and should be landing just before noon."

"What did they do with all the cash?" Rapp asked.

"They gave it all to the banker and instructed him to wire half of it to our account in the Bahamas."

"The guns?"

"Left them in the box with the fake passports and credit cards."

"Nice touch."

"There was one other thing of interest in the box. Two index cards. One with a series of apparently random numbers. The other with dates and dollar amounts."

"They sent me photos of the cards," Dumond announced as he held up his PDA for Rapp to see. "The first card is a series of codes, probably for other accounts he has. The second card," Dumond pressed a button and the tiny screen showed the second photo, "looks like a list of deposits."

"Maybe." Rapp studied the tiny image for a moment and then said, "Or they might be something else."

"Like what?"

"Jobs."

"Jobs?" Dumond wasn't following.

"They're notches on his belt. My guess is each one coincides with a hit he made and how much he was paid."

Dumond looked at the small screen. "Some of them don't have a dollar amount."

"Kills he didn't get paid for," Rapp answered.

"Sick fucker," Coleman added. "You keep track of your kills?" he asked Rapp.

"No."

"The only guys I ever knew who did were the twisted ones."

Dumond's phone rang and he walked out into the hallway to take it. Rapp looked at Coleman and said, "Gazich lied to me on the plane."

"About?"

"How things went down."

"And that surprises you? This guy has a black heart. I wouldn't trust anything that comes out of his mouth."

Rapp frowned. "I believed him. You know how you get a feel for these things after you've been through enough of them?"

"Yeah."

"Well, he had no incentive to lie. He's a one-man operation. Whoever hired him was in the process of trying to kill him when we showed up."

"What did he lie about?"

"He told me he received a call right before the attack that told him the target was the second limo."

"Yeah," Coleman said.

"I talked to Rivera yesterday, and she told me they didn't shuffle the limos."

"What does that matter? He was trying to take both of them out, wasn't he?"

"No." Rapp shook his head. "He claims he was only trying to hit the second limo."

Coleman leaned against the Formica countertop. "So he was probably trying to hit both cars."

"Which means he lied about the phone call."

"Well, don't get yourself too worked up. Skip called me this morning. He'd also like you to give him a call."

"He'll have to take a number."

"He says he's under a lot of pressure. Gazich volunteered for and passed a lie detector test. Skip said they had the Bureau's best guy running the machine, and this fucker beat it."

Rapp smiled. "This is just too perfect."

"Yeah. Skip says Justice is freaking out, State is freaking out, and even some of the boys at the Bureau are starting to waiver."

"He say anything about the media?"

"He said the phone is ringing off the hook. The press is digging hard."

"Good."

Dumond came back in the break room with a big grin on his face.

"What's got you so excited?" Rapp asked.

"I just found out who our guest is." Dumond pointed at the floor.

"The Russian?" Coleman asked.

"Yep, except he's not Russian."

# 36

---

No one spoke. Not in the elevator. Not in the lobby. Ross wanted to speak, wanted desperately to speak, but didn't dare until he was away from the Secret Service agents and Gordon. They were halfway between the main door and the waiting limousine when Garret reached out and grabbed Ross's elbow. The two men stopped and then Gordon stopped and then all six agents stopped. Only one agent looked at the protectee. The other five adjusted their positions to shield Ross as much as possible. The men did not look comfortable. They'd been trained to move people from one secure area to the next. No loitering in between. Forty feet away was a brand-new armored limousine engineered to handle twice the explosion that had torn apart the older model limousine that fateful day back in October. All six Secret Service agents fought the instinct to literally grab Ross by the collar and throw him headfirst into the limo.

Special Agent Brown approached Ross and Garret. "Excuse me, sir. It's not good to stop in the open like this. Could you please get in the limo?"

Garret ignored the agent, while Ross shot him a withering look. "This was an unscheduled stop. No one knows I'm here. Relax and back off. I want some privacy."

Brown concealed the anger he felt toward Ross. It had been building up ever since he took over for Rivera, and it had peaked in Switzerland the previous weekend. The guy was a power-hungry son of a bitch. What did it matter to him if they talked in the back of the limo or here on the street? Brown backed away, stayed calm, signaled for his men to spread out, and made a mental note to add the incident to the file. The hell if he was going to take a fall like Rivera's.

Gordon was checking e-mail on his BlackBerry and began drifting back toward his boss and Garret. Garret put out his hand and said, "Why don't you go make a few phone calls?"

Gordon stopped and looked up at Garret. He was yet again the odd man out. Saturday couldn't come soon enough. Gordon thought he might even offer to drive Garret to the airport himself.

As soon as Gordon was out of earshot, Garret moved within a half foot of Ross and in a hushed voice said, "This is too good to be true."

"I know. Now I can go out there and really clean house."

"I don't give a shit about the CIA. I'm talking about the fact that they got the wrong guy."

"We don't know that for sure."

"Give me one good reason why Rapp would refuse to come in. He knows he fucked up. He's not going to come back here and face scrutiny. He's gonna run, or who knows he might even try to frame this guy to save his own ass."

"So what do we do?"

"Pour gas on this thing."

"Huh?"

"We light the match and fan the flames. We get you out in front of this thing."

"Are you sure?"

"Absolutely. Even if this is the guy, and that's looking pretty iffy at the moment, Speyer told me there is absolutely no way he can be traced back to us. You're a statesman now. You come out hard on this thing. Very law-and-order. What Rapp did was wrong. Excessive force. The U.S. doesn't condone torture and will not tolerate it. Then you make some statement demanding an inquiry."

Ross shook his head. "Too strong right now. I think we'd be better off taking a position off the record."

"With Tom Rich from the *Times.*"

"Yep. That way we drive the story and then when the other shoe drops we ask for Rapp's and Kennedy's head."

"I like it." Garret glanced over each shoulder. "These damn agents make me nervous. You go on without me. I need to make a few calls. I'll see you back at the hotel for lunch."

Ross watched Garret leave and then started for the limo. Gordon was standing next to the open rear door replying to an e-mail with both thumbs. Ross could see that he was unhappy with being excluded and a thought occurred to him. It was something he'd been thinking about since Garret had arrived at the airport on Sunday. The vice president–elect climbed into the back seat and waited for Gordon to settle in.

"Jonathan, have you noticed any strange behavior from Stu lately?"

The expression on Gordon's face seemed to say, "Are you kidding me?" He put his BlackBerry away and took off his reading glasses. "I've always found Stu to be a bit strange."

Ross smiled. "I know. The man is a real pain in the ass, but he's extremely good at what he does. He's short-term. You're long-term. Long-term friend and confidant. Please don't ever forget that."

"I won't. Thank you, sir."

"You're welcome." Ross smiled. The vehicle started to move. He glanced out the window and said, "So back to Stu. Any odd behavior lately?"

"Sir, to put it bluntly the man is an asshole. And I mean twenty-four-seven, so it's hard to judge, but I at least expected him to relax this week."

"Me too."

"This is our time to celebrate. People are lining up to hand him retainers. Hell, I have people calling me to see if I can set up meetings for them."

"The victory was very good for his business."

"And I have no problem with that. I'd think, though, that the guy would let his hair down a little bit, but instead he has been an even bigger jerk than usual this week."

"I agree. It's almost like he's preoccupied with something else."

"How do you mean?"

"I don't know." A practiced perplexed expression fell across Ross's face. "I don't know how to put my finger on it, but something is bothering him. It seems like he's worried about something."

Gordon looked with concern at his boss. "Do you want me to do some checking?"

Ross hesitated like he was thinking long and hard about the question, and then shook his head. "No. I'm sure it's nothing. We've put up with him this long. What's five more days?"

# 37

Facial recognition software was not a precise science. The programs could be tricked, people's appearances often changed over time, many people shared the same facial features, and in the end the programs were often limited by the quality of the photograph itself. Beyond that you had to actually have a photograph on file that you could compare to the new image. The search for the identity of the mystery man in the converted bomb shelter of Coleman's warehouse had been complicated by three facts. The first was that the man had easily gained over a hundred pounds since his last official photo, the second was that he had many of the common features associated with the Slavic peoples of Eastern Europe, which dumped him into a large pool of candidates, and the third was that he was not Russian.

Rapp read the dossier thoroughly, as did Coleman and Dumond. An analyst at Langley had made the discovery after talking to his contacts at French intelligence and Interpol. The analyst factored in the weight gain and broadened his search to include intelligence officers in Ukraine, Belarus, Poland, Bulgaria, Latvia, Lithuania, Estonia, and Romania. The man, it turned out, was Belarusian. He had never worked for the KGB, but he had worked for the Belarusian KGB or BKGB as it was known among intel types. The BKGB was KGB's little brother. Where many of the former Soviet Republics had gone on to establish real independence Belarus by far maintained the closest relationship with Mother Russia. The man had worked for the state security service for nearly a decade. During that time it was suspected that he also worked on the side for a former high-ranking communist official who was waging a violent war to become the mob boss in Minsk.

His real name was Yuri Milinkavich. French intelligence had started a file on him back in 1996 when he was running a counterintelligence team in Minsk. Three French business executives had traveled to the Belarusian capital to bid on a contract to build a hydroelectric dam. The bids were to be presented in person over a two-day period. The French executives were arrested on the way to present their bid and detained under suspicion of espionage for three full days and then let go with no explanation. French intelligence suspected, but could not prove, that the German company that won the contract had paid to have the French team taken out of the picture. During his tenure with the Belarusian Security Service four more similar complaints were filed. One more by the French, two by the Italians, and one by the Japanese. Interpol eventually started a file on Milinkavich and they now suspected that he was now working for the Belarusian mafia.

Rapp considered all of this carefully. The information fit, which was a big hurdle to get past. Rapp believed without a shadow of doubt that the man in the bomb shelter was in fact Yuri

Milinkavich. Now the question was, why in the hell had he been trying to kill Gazich? Rapp ordered Dumond to begin pulling everything they had on the Belarusian mafia. Russia and its former states were far from Rapp's area of expertise. His was Europe, and more specifically, the Middle East and Southwest Asia. Rapp had followed Russia's demise nonetheless. With the collapse of the centralized government, former regional party officials became crime bosses overnight, stepping in to fill the power vacuum. The ensuing battles that erupted between vying interests made Chicago's infamous mob wars of the 1920s look like a schoolyard fight.

Rapp struggled to put it all into context. How brutal was Milinkavich? To some this might seem ancillary at the moment, but for Rapp it was a crucial question. There was no ticking bomb to be dealt with. No lives to be saved by pulling answers out of the large man. The need for torture was not pressing. For the moment Rapp decided he would limit the interrogation to a simple Q&A. Give Milinkavich a chance to tell the truth and explain why he was trying to kill Gazich. He had already proven himself a liar by claiming to have worked for the KGB, but the Russians and the other Slavic people were funny when it came to the truth. Absolutes were a rare thing. There were more often than not degrees of honesty. In Milinkavich's mind, saying he worked for the KGB might not be a lie. He was more likely to see it as a partial admission. He had worked for the BKGB, but not its better-known big brother. But the bigger distinction was that he claimed he still worked for them. Gazich had been right back in his office when he laughed at Milinkavich's claim that he worked for the KGB. Gazich had known back then that Milinkavich worked for the mob. That was after spending only a few minutes with him. That meant the two possibly knew each other from a previous job.

The task as Rapp saw it was to give Milinkavich a chance to

come clean. To explain what he really did for a living, and then they could move onto the bigger question. Just what in the hell was the Belarusian mafia doing working with Arab terrorists, and who in particular had paid for this operation?

Rapp descended the stairs to the bunker with a general outline in his head of the questions he would ask, and how he would handle things if Milinkavich continued to lie. At the bottom was a small six-by-four-foot landing with a rusty floor drain in the middle. Above the heavy metal door to the right was a small TV. On the screen Rapp could see Milinkavich reclined on the cot. He was a big man. Rapp guessed six foot three and pushing three bills. Rapp, at six foot and a hundred eighty pounds, just might provide a tempting target for the big man and part of Rapp was hoping for just that. As much as Rapp did not like torture, he also wasn't a patient man. There were too many things to do, and he wasn't about to waste a week trying to get inside this guy's head.

There was no handle on the door. Just a bolt. Rapp extracted a key from his pocket and slid it into the bottom of the large padlock. He hung the padlock on a hook next to the door, checked the TV one more time, and then opened the door. Milinkavich instantly sat up on his elbows. Rapp took one step into the room and closed the door behind him, leaving it cracked just slightly. Rapp watched Milinkavich's eyes register the fact that the door was not locked. Other than the bed, there was a small port-a-potty in the corner, which smelled of disinfectant. A single light fixture was bolted to the ceiling and encased in a protective steel cage. There was no blanket or pillow on the bed. No sheet. Just a thin mattress. Milinkavich would have made a queen-size bed look small. The twin looked ridiculous under his girth.

Rapp moved over to the side of the door, leaned against the wall, and folded his arms across his chest. He'd taken off his suit coat and tie and left his gun in Coleman's office. His dark eyes studied Milinkavich for a second. They'd stitched up his nose and ear and although they hadn't taken X-rays, they were pretty sure his jaw was broken.

Rapp pointed to a book on the floor and asked, "Have you found time to read?" Rapp had left a copy of George Orwell's *1984* in the cell in hopes that the prisoner might read some of the torture scenes.

Milinkavich glanced down at the book and shook his head. "I do not need to read this book. I lived it."

Rapp smiled. "Unfortunately, you were on the wrong team."

"What do you mean?"

"You told me you worked for the KGB." There was a doubtful tone in Rapp's voice. "If you worked for the KGB, you were on the wrong team."

"Not every person who worked for the KGB was a bad person."

*A true enough statement,* Rapp supposed.

"We are not so different, you and I." The big man placed one foot on the floor and sat up.

Rapp noted that he moved with difficulty. The combination of stress, confinement, and his sheer size would have left his muscles stiff. They had taken his shoes away as well. If he tried to make a move with his socks on he would find it difficult to get traction on the smooth cement floor.

"You know who I am?" Rapp asked with an amused expression.

"American . . . probably CIA. Maybe Defense Intelligence Agency. Definitely special forces training."

Rapp was happy to hear that Milinkavich only had a generic guess as to who he was. He was tempted to tell him he worked for the Israelis. It was an old ploy that often put the fear of god into godless communists. Especially Belarusians, who had been cruel to the Jews.

"Maybe . . . maybe not."

Milinkavich looked around the room. "Where are we?"

Interrogation 101: Confuse and disorient the subject. Rapp had tried to put himself inside Milinkavich's head. He'd been drugged for most of the transport from Cyprus to Baltimore. There was a chance he sensed that they had landed midway in between, but there were no windows for him to look out. The most obvious conclusion he would draw was that they were back in America, but he would also think there was a chance that they had taken him from Cyprus to an Eastern Bloc country for interrogation, possibly even Belarus. It was no secret that the U.S. government outsourced some of the less gentile aspects of the war on terror to the former Soviet satellites.

"We are someplace very private. Someplace my own government knows nothing about. Just the two of us. I would prefer, as I'm sure you would, to solve this problem in a very unofficial way."

Rapp watched as Milinkavich's eyes darted to the unlocked door and then quickly away. He would be weighing his chances of escape.

"I did not know we had a problem," Milinkavich said in an upbeat voice. "Our two countries are no longer enemies."

Rapp seized his opening. "I'm sorry. I forgot. Which country did you say you are from?"

"Russia."

"And you used to work for the KGB?"

"Yes."

"And you are sure about that?"

"Yes. Absolutely."

"And you want to be my friend?"

"Yes. Absolutely."

"And you seek to win my friendship by lying to me," Rapp said casually.

"I am not lying to you," Milinkavich said with great conviction.

"I want you to think long and hard about this, because I've got a lot of questions for you. You tell me you worked for the KGB, which means you know how this works. There is an easy way to do this and the hard way. If you want to do it the easy way you need to be absolutely honest with me. If you want to keep lying to me we'll do it the hard way. Which means I'm going to have to string you up by your ankles and play baseball with your nuts."

The Russian brought his hands together, clapped them, and said, "No problem. I only speak the truth to you."

Rapp cocked his head to the side and his left eyebrow shot up. "I'm going to say it one last time. This is not a game and I'm not amused by your reassurances. You have two choices. You either tell me the absolute truth, or I will make things extremely painful for you."

"Absolutely. I speak only the truth."

Rapp wondered if maybe he hadn't broken the man's jaw. He was speaking without too much difficulty. "Where were you born?"

"Moscow."

*Probably a lie,* Rapp thought, *but not absolutely provable at the moment.* "Where did you grow up?"

"Moscow."

*Most likely a lie.* "And you work for the KGB?"

"Yes," the big man said as he slid his other foot off the bed. "I have already told you that."

Rapp watched him shift his weight and inch toward the edge of the bed. "I guess we're going to have to do this the hard way." Rapp turned over his left shoulder and pressed a white button on a gray intercom box. "Bring down the car starter and the alligator clips."

Milinkavich sat up a little straighter. "What do you mean, car starter?"

"It looks like we're going to have to run some electricity through your brain and see if it helps jog your memory."

"No." The man stood, waving his hands as he took a step toward Rapp.

"Sit back down," Rapp said in a firm but calm voice.

"I speak only the truth." He took another step.

Rapp pushed himself away from the wall and got ready. The only question left was whether Milinkavich would go straight for the door or try to take Rapp out first. Rapp was betting that the man would be misled by his size advantage.

"Sit back down right now, or you're going to get hurt."

Milinkavich, only six feet away, made his move. He charged straight at Rapp, his left arm out in front of him, reaching to grab hold of something, and his right arm cocked and ready to deliver a forceful blow. Time slowed down for Rapp. Everything so far was expected. Big men always attacked this way. They came in high thinking they could smother their opponent. The only problem was they left their legs and midsection open. Milinkavich had a hell of a tire around his waist. Rapp had noted this and knew that in these tight quarters it would be difficult to get enough force behind a blow to have much effect. That left two knees and two testicles. Rapp decided on the right knee.

The big man's right arm came in straight like a battering ram. Rapp stepped quickly to his left and swept his right arm up and around in a clockwise motion grabbing Milinkavich's right elbow. Using the man's own momentum Rapp pulled him closer and turned him away at the same time. He brought his right leg up and then sent his foot crashing down on the completely exposed outside of Milinkavich's right knee. There was hideous crunching noise as ligaments snapped and the knee collapsed inward. Milinkavich hopped once on his left leg and then fell to the floor screaming in agony.

Rapp stood over him, ready to strike another blow, his jaw clenched in anger. He was pissed that this idiot had forced them to go down this road. "Where were you born?" Rapp yelled.

"Minsk. I was born in Minsk."

"And who do you work for?"

"The KGB."

Rapp kicked him in the bad knee and the Belarusian howled in pain. "You mean the BKGB."

"We are one and the same."

"The hell you are." Rapp kicked him in the knee again. "I'm done fucking around with you, Yuri." Rapp bent down and looked him in the eye, noted the shocked expression on his face. "That's right, you dumb fucker. I know your name. I know all about you. I know you're not Russian. I know you never worked for the KGB, and I know you were one corrupt motherfucker when you worked for the BKGB. My friends at the KGB told me you got fat working for the Minsk mob." Rapp mixed facts with suppositions to build his case and chip away at Milinkavich's confidence.

"I need a doctor," the man wailed in pain.

"You aren't going to get shit until you start answering my questions." Rapp stomped on the bent knee, and shouted over Milinkavich's cries, "Who do you work for?"

"The Minsk mob!"

"And who do you answer to?" Rapp brought his foot up and held it in the air.

298 / VINCE FLYNN

"Aleksandr Gordievsky."

Before this morning Rapp would not have recognized the name, but he'd just read it in the file Langley had sent over. Aleksandr Gordievsky was none other that the former communist party chairman of Belarus and the current mob boss of the entire country.

"And why were you on Cyprus?"

"To kill the man."

"Which man?"

"Deckas. The Greek."

"Why?" Rapp yelled.

"I don't know."

Rapp lifted his foot.

"I swear." Milinkavich put his hands up. "I do not know."

Rapp's foot came crashing down. "Bullshit!"

Milinkavich screamed in agony and tears began spilling from his eyes.

"You want me to kick you again?"

"No!"

"Then tell me why you were sent to kill him."

"All I know," the big man gasped for air, "is he was hired to do something and he fucked up."

"He was hired to kill someone," Rapp wanted to be clear on this.

"Yes."

"Who?"

"I do not know."

"You want me to kick you again?"

"No!" he screamed. "No, please I have no idea."

"When did your boss start doing business with the Arabs?"

A look of real shock fell across Milinkavich's face. "Arabs?"

"Arabs . . . Islamic Radical Fundamentalist . . . terrorists."

"Mr. Gordievsky would never work with such people."

The look on his face was believable, but the words weren't. "Bullshit." Rapp stomped on his knee again.

Milinkavich screamed and then began sobbing. "I am serious. He is Eastern Orthodox. Very involved in the church. He thinks Islam is the invention of Satan. He would never do business with them."

All Rapp's senses told him Milinkavich was telling the truth, but it didn't add up with what he already knew. Rapp needed to be careful. If he began asking blind questions, he could end up weakening his position. The better thing to do at the moment was to leave and try to confirm what he'd just been told. Then if he found out the man was lying to him, he would come back and the interrogation would begin with renewed vigor.

"I'm going to call my friends in the KGB and find out if you're telling the truth. And you'd better hope they corroborate your story, or I'm going to come back in here and things are going to get real ugly. In fact when I come back, you are going to tell me from start to finish everything you know about Deckas. And I mean everything. When you first heard of him. How many jobs he's done for you. Everything. You do that, and I'll get you set up with painkillers. You decide to lie to me some more and I'll snap your other knee."

Rapp stepped over Milinkavich and closed and locked the heavy door. He climbed the steps up to the main floor and then walked past the break room and up to Coleman's office. When he entered Coleman was on the phone signaling for Rapp to stay quiet.

"Irene," Coleman said, "I have no idea where he is." He listened for a bit and said, "I'll have him call you as soon as I hear from him. I have to go now."

"What did she want?" asked Rapp. "She all pissed off about Gazich?"

"No. I asked her that. She said she's not worried. She knows he's the guy."

"Then what's the problem?"

"She says she has something she needs to show you."

"What?"

"She wouldn't say. All she said was it was very important that she see you as soon as possible."

"She didn't even tell you what it was about?" Rapp asked.

"All she said was that it might cause you to look at something in a different way."

Rapp took a second to guess what that might be.

"What are you going to do?" Coleman asked.

"I'll call her back."

"When? She was pretty adamant."

Rap looked at his watch. It was almost noon. "This afternoon. I need to call an old contact at the KGB, and then I want to see just how full of shit this Milinkavich is."

"What about Dr. Hornig?"

Rapp had already thought about getting her involved. She was a shrink the CIA used to interrogate high-value prisoners.

"This guy might be a pathological liar, Mitch."

"Yeah, I know." Pathological liars were the most difficult people to interrogate. Plus Rapp didn't have the stomach to keep kicking the crap out of the guy. "I'll talk to Irene about it this afternoon, and then I'll let you know."

# 38

Mark Ross strolled down Peacock Alley, where Washingtonians and visitors went to see and be seen. The Willard Hotel had been a Washington landmark since before the Civil War. Ross basked in the recognition of the dozens of people who were enjoying afternoon tea. It was a walk that had been done by the likes of U.S. Grant, Mark Twain, and many other famous and infamous figures. Digital cameras snapped, people reached out just to touch him, and a few of the really brazen stopped him for a photo. The prize for sheer audacity, though, went to a woman in a blue dress with a ridiculous red hat topped with a white feather plume. She stepped in front of Ross, blocking his path and waving her cell phone. Her daughter was on the phone, and she was a huge fan of the soon-to-be vice president. Ross disguised his irritation and played along. His Secret Service detail looked on disapprovingly from fifteen feet away. Ross had been forced to give them another lecture after having already snapped at them earlier in the day. They needed to give him some freedom. No one was looking to assassinate a vice president–elect.

The party's faithful were taking over the town. Planeloads, trainloads, and busloads were arriving by the hour. The first official function was tonight and then it was a whirlwind of breakfasts, lunches, and balls. The big affairs were reserved for Saturday night: eleven separate black-tie balls. There wasn't a hotel room in town that wasn't booked. It was really going to happen. He was going to be vice president of the United States of America. Ross could hardly believe it. He couldn't remember the first time he'd dreamt of rising to such political heights but he'd been young. Usually the dream focused on the top job, but he did remember a time when he was away at boarding school and he read a book about Teddy Roosevelt. There was a man of destiny. T.R. was one of the greats. He remembered a fellow democrat criticizing the old Bull Moose president for being a bully. Ross responded by telling him, "Bully or not, his face is on Mount Rushmore."

History favored the decisive. Those who weren't afraid to grab power and use it. Ross had decided long ago that he would create his own opportunities and when the time came he would seize the reins of power without hesitation. Like the great Teddy Roosevelt he would leave little to chance. He would use the press to shape his image and dispose of his enemies, and just maybe he'd get lucky like T.R. and get promoted early. Josh Alexander was young and healthy, but stranger things had happened.

The possibility brought a smile to Ross's face. He shook a few more hands and stopped briefly at the entrance to the Round Robin Bar, waving to the faithful who were well into happy hour. The crowd around the circular bar began whooping and hollering. Ross thought it would be fun to join them for a drink, but he needed to get upstairs for a meeting. He smiled and pumped his fist to the crowd and then retreated. Four agents joined him in the elevator. He'd cut Gordon loose to grab some downtime. It wasn't that he didn't trust him; it was simply that he didn't want the right hand to know what the left hand was doing.

An agent was posted outside the door to the Oval Suite. The party had secured the room for him to do interviews, hold meetings, and stay there if he wanted, although Ross owned a 4,200-square-foot condo that overlooked the Potomac. Alexander was in the opulent Abraham Lincoln Suite and his father-in-law was in the spacious Capitol Suite. Without being consulted Ross had been forced to settle for the hotel's third nicest suite. He was mildly irritated by the oversight, but there were more pressing issues at the moment.

Ross entered the suite and found Stu Garret sitting in the oval shaped living room with Tom Rich of the *New York Times*. Just like the real Oval Office, two couches faced each other with a small table in between. Rich was of average height and slender with the exception of a small pouch around his midsection. He had a youthful head of brown hair that he liked to show off by avoiding regular visits to the barber. He looked close to forty but in truth he was actually fifty-one. National security was his beat and he had a reputation for being very critical of the CIA and the way they waged the war on terror.

Rich stood. Garret didn't. Ross extended his hand. "Tom, thank you for coming to see me."

"My pleasure, sir."

"Please, call me Mark when we're in an informal setting like this."

Rich nodded but kept his game face on. He was wearing a blue, button-down oxford, a gray and black tweed sport coat, a pair of jeans, and brown Timberland boots. He looked at Ross in his expensive blue suit and tie. "I apologize for my appearance. I was at home working on a story when Stu called. He told me to get down here right away. He said he had something that couldn't be discussed on the phone."

Ross nodded. "Yes, I'm afraid he's right. Before we get started, may I get you something to drink?"

"No, thank you."

"Well, have a seat." Ross unbuttoned his suit coat and sat on the couch across from Garret and Rich. "I assume you've been following the story about the arrest that was made in connection to the motorcade attack."

Rich nodded enthusiastically while reaching in to his sport coat and retrieving a notebook and pen. "I've got a piece running in the morning."

"What's your angle?"

"Angle?" Rich looked either surprised or offended.

"What's your story about?" Garret asked in his typical no-nonsense way.

Rich hesitated and then said, "I'm hearing rumors. Grumblings . . . really."

"About?" Ross asked.

"That the case against this guy isn't as strong as the FBI claims."

Ross and Garret shared a knowing look and then Ross said, "Off the record."

"Of course." Rich wrote the word *Off* across the top of the page.

"What have you heard so far?"

"Basically that this guy was dumped in the FBI's lap with some very weak evidence."

Ross nodded. "Continue."

"There are some major problems with the case. The FBI and Justice are fighting, and neither of them is happy with the CIA. The Greek government is going to file an official complaint with the UN in the morning and supposedly no one knows where to find Mitch Rapp, who my sources tell me ran the team that grabbed this guy."

"You've got the broad brushstrokes down, but there's a lot more. Rapp not only ran the team, he was the one who identified, grabbed, and tortured the suspect."

"Did you say torture?" Rich looked up with wary eyes.

"What would you call shooting a man once in each knee and then in both hands?"

"He kneecapped him?"

"And shot him in both hands."

Rich kept his eyes on Ross while his right hand flew across the page. "Let me guess . . . he tortured a confession out of the guy?"

"No one knows."

"What does Rapp say?"

"No one knows because Rapp has been AWOL for three days now."

"AWOL?"

"Absent without leave. Rapp had his team bring this guy back from Cyprus and he has yet to report in. We literally have nothing on this guy other than Rapp's word. The Greek government is furious. The State Department is outraged. The Justice Department says they have no case against this guy and then here's the kicker. The guy volunteered to be polygraphed."

"And?"

"He passed with flying colors."

"So this might really be the wrong guy?"

"That's a distinct possibility, and even if he is the guy, Rapp screwed things up so bad by torturing him that I don't think there's any chance of convicting him."

Rich wrote frantically. This was going to be a huge scoop. The type of story that could win him his second Pulitzer. After a moment he gained control of his escalating euphoria and remembered that he was a journalist. He looked up at Ross and asked, "Why are you telling me this?"

Ross was prepared for this question. "When I was director of National Intelligence, I warned President Hayes that Mitch Rapp was a malcontent. I told him, 'Sir, sooner or later he's going to do something that will permanently damage America's international standing.'" Ross sat back and crossed his legs. "And now, here we are. President Hayes is on his way out, and we're on our way in. Well, I'm not going to allow this administration to pay for his poor leadership."

"I assume you mean President Hayes."

"Yes. And, Tom, I can't stress it enough. This is off the record. Way off the record."

"I know," Rich said, as he scribbled frantically. "So this is Hayes's fault?"

"I'm not willing to go that far on or off the record. You'll have to draw your own conclusions."

"So who do you blame besides Rapp?"

"His boss, for starters."

"Irene Kennedy?"

"Yes."

"Are you going to ask for an investigation?"

"I'm going to leave that up to the attorney general and my former colleagues on the Hill."

"Is it safe to say that your administration will be looking for a new person to run the CIA?"

Ross liked the ring of "your administration." He could get used to that. He looked at Rich with a very serious expression and said, "Director Kennedy and Mitch Rapp should make sure their résumés are up to date."

Rich smiled as he wrote down the exact quote. When he was done he pulled out his mobile phone and checked the time. It was 4:51 in the afternoon. Looking at Ross he said, "Excuse me for a second. I need to call my editor and tell her to hold a spot on the front page."

Ross nodded and kept his delight in check. The article would cause a feeding frenzy. He only wished that he could be there to see the expression on Kennedy's face when she read it.

# 39

Rapp was cruising down Georgetown Pike in a rented white van at five miles an hour over the posted speed. It was almost 7:00 in the evening, which meant he was late for his meeting with Kennedy. He wasn't crazy about getting together in her office, but she'd insisted. What she had to show him could not leave the building. That bit of information got Rapp's imagination working overtime. It also helped him make up his mind that he would transfer Milinkavich to Dr. Hornig.

After a long afternoon of Milinkavich changing his story over and over and sobbing like a child, Rapp decided that he didn't have it in him to interrogate the man properly. Coleman couldn't stand being in the presence of Hornig, so Rapp rented another van and drove the Belarusian himself. The drive from Baltimore to an off-budget CIA facility in Northern Virginia took longer than expected, and then Hornig wanted to talk. She wanted to know every intricate detail of the subject. Rapp told her what he had discovered and handed over audiotapes of the interrogations he'd already conducted, and left as quickly as he could.

He turned off the Pike and approached the main gate of the CIA. Normally a rental car would cause problems, but the security officers recognized Rapp and after a speedy check of the cargo area, he was waved through. Rapp parked in the visitors' lot near the main door and hustled up the steps and into the lobby. Straight ahead to the right were the security desk, metal detectors, and turnstiles. Rapp hung his badge around his neck and stayed to his left, walking past the undersized statue of Wild Bill Donovan, who was more or less the patron saint of the CIA. Just past the statue Rapp turned left into a small vestibule and then to his right up a couple steps to a small landing. Directly in front of him was the director's private elevator. Rapp grabbed his badge and held it in front of the scanner. A moment later the door opened and he was on his way to the seventh floor.

The outer office was empty of all support staff. Even Kennedy's bodyguards were nowhere to be seen. Rapp knocked on the heavy office door twice and then entered. Kennedy was behind her desk with the phone to her left ear and twirling her reading glasses in her right hand.

Kennedy gave Rapp a slight smile and said to the person on the other end of the line, "I have no idea what you're talking about. He's standing right in front of me."

Rapp mouthed the words, *Who is it?*

Kennedy let her chair spring forward. "Hold for a moment please." She hit the hold button on the black phone and looked up at Rapp. "It's Tom Rich from the *Times.*"

"Little fucking traitor. What does he want?"

"The *Times* is running a story on us tomorrow. He'd like to give us a chance to comment."

Rapp checked his watch. It was 7:04 in the evening. They'd be putting their East Coast Edition to bed pretty quickly. "What's the story about?"

"Basically that you grabbed the wrong guy on Cyprus. Justice, the FBI, State, the Greek government, they're all mad at us and you and I are out of a job next week and may be facing formal charges."

"What did you tell him?"

"No comment."

"Good."

"He also said he heard you were AWOL. Possibly had fled the country to avoid prosecution."

"He's making shit up." Rapp pointed at the phone. "Put him on speaker."

Kennedy hit the blinking button and said, "Tom, I have Mitch Rapp here in my office. Anything you'd like to ask him?"

"So you've come in from the cold?" The reporter's voice sounded amused.

Rapp had met Rich once before at a social function. Rapp's deceased wife had introduced them. She was NBC's White House correspondent and the two ran in the same circles from time to time. "What a surprise. I would have never guessed a big lefty like you to be a Le Carré fan."

"He's my favorite. *The Spy Who Came in from the Cold* . . . it doesn't get any better than that, and besides you know I'm independent. Like all good reporters, I know how to keep politics out of the story."

"Yeah, right." Rapp noted the levity in Rich's voice. Like all egocentric reporters he was probably already working on his Pulitzer Prize acceptance speech.

"Listen, I'm kind of short on time, but I was wondering if you would like to comment on a story that I'm working on for tomorrow's paper?"

"I see you've given yourself a lot of time to get the other side of the story."

"Deadlines are a bitch. What can I tell you? So would you like to comment on the fact that you tortured a bogus confession from a Greek national named Alexander Deckas?"

"Are you recording this conversation, Tom?"

"Of course," he said in a patronizing tone.

"Thanks for the heads-up."

"Come on, Mitch. You know how the game is played."

"Sure do, Tom." Rapp smiled at Kennedy and then asked, "Just wondering . . . you're Jewish, right?"

Rich didn't answer right away, and then when he did the levity was gone. "I don't see what that has to do with anything."

"Well, I know how you reporters pride yourselves on being neutral, but I was wondering how proud you're going to be of that Pulitzer of yours after some crazy Islamic fascist nukes Israel off the face of the map." Rapp paused to look at Kennedy, who was giving him a wary look. Rapp smiled and hovered over the speakerphone. "At least you'll be comforted by the fact that you stayed neutral on the issue."

When Rich spoke again, he was all business. "I take it you're not going to comment on the accusation that you apprehended the wrong man and tortured him."

"I'd love to comment on the accusation right after you tell me who your source is."

"Sources," Rich stressed the plural. "I have more than one, and you know I can't reveal them."

"I don't suppose you'd consider delaying the story for a day or two?"

"Let me think about that for a second," Rich paused one second and said, "I don't think so."

"Well, fuck you very much and thank you for wasting my time." Rapp reached down and disconnected the call before plopping down in the winged back chair in front of Kennedy's desk.

"I don't think that was very professional." Kennedy looked disapprovingly at Rapp.

"That guy thinks he's going to string me up by my balls tomorrow." Rapp shook his head. "He has no idea how big a mistake he's about to make."

Kennedy studied Rapp with suspicion. "Would you mind telling me what you've been up to?"

Rapp pulled a memory stick from his jacket and handed it across the desk. "This is going to be fun."

Kennedy held the stick in front of her and asked, "What's this for?"

"Your press conference."

"What press conference?"

"The one you're going to hold at the White House tomorrow in response to the grossly inaccurate front page story that the *Times* is going to run in the morning. I took the liberty of putting everything into a Power Point presentation for you."

Kennedy smiled. "What's on here?"

"The video from the Starbucks on the morning of the attack. Agent Rivera's official statement of what she saw seconds before the explosion. Customs and Immigration surveillance footage of Deckas at JFK the day before the attack. He entered the country using a fake passport, of course."

"What else?"

"His complete confession."

"Which the media will say was coerced."

"Not after they hear it. It was very convincing. He admits to flying into JFK the day before the attack, spending Friday night in Pennsylvania, where he picked up the van, and then driving down to DC Saturday morning. He even admits to standing behind the same tree that Rivera saw him behind. All of it without provocation."

Kennedy shook her head. "They'll say you rehearsed the story with him."

"Let them say what they want, because there's more. The guy isn't even Greek."

"Excuse me?"

"He's Bosnian. His real name is Gavrilo Gazich, and here's the best part." Rapp grinned and added, "He's wanted by the War Crimes Tribunal in The Hague for atrocities committed against civilians during the civil war."

"You're sure?"

"One hundred percent."

Now it was Kennedy's turn to smile. "Anything else?"

"A list of people he is suspected of killing. Most of them in Africa over the past five years or so. One U.N. official, a couple of relief workers, and a bunch of politicians, warlords, and generals."

"All of it's ironclad?"

"As solid as it gets. The FBI is going to have a field day. The U.N. might even thank us."

The director of the CIA turned the gray stick over in her fingers and thought of the photos that Cap Baker had given her. "Any idea who hired him to take out the candidates?"

"No, but I know who tried to kill him after he screwed up."

"Excuse me?"

Rapp folded his hands across his lap and explained to her what had happened on Cyprus. How he had spotted the other team keeping an eye on Gazich's office. How Rapp watched Gazich casually stroll down the street, shoot the one lookout in the car and then lure the other two up to his office, where he killed one and began torturing the other. Having watched Gazich operate, Rapp explained that he'd decided the man was too dangerous to do anything other than cripple him. Telling a man like that to drop his gun and lie down on the ground would have ended with one or both of them dead.

"Who were these people trying to kill him?" Kennedy asked.

"At first I thought they were Russians. One of them maintained that he was KGB."

Kennedy gave him a you've-got-to-be-kidding-me look and said, "You're not serious?"

"As it turns out they were Belarusian, and at least one of them was former BKGB. I brought the leader of the group back."

Kennedy was surprised yet again. "On Sunday?"

"Yes."

"And why am I hearing about it now for the first time?"

"I needed to check some things out."

"Where is this man?"

"I handed him over to Dr. Hornig this evening."

"You were having a hard time getting him to talk?"

"No. He talked all right. We just couldn't separate the truth from all of his bullshit."

"So what does the Belarusian mafia have to do with all of this?"

"That's a good question. The guy we have in custody, his name is Milinkavich. He claims he was sent to Cyprus to kill Gazich for screwing up some contract he'd been hired for. I asked him if they did a lot of work with the Saudis and I got an interesting reaction out of him."

"What was that?"

"He says his boss, Aleksandr Gordievsky, who runs the Belarusian mafia, hates Muslims. Says the man is Eastern Orthodox and, I quote, 'thinks Islam is the creation of Satan.' He claims they would never work for the Saudis."

Kennedy's thoughts returned to the photos. "Anything else?"

"There's some stuff that's not adding up."

"Such as?"

"Gazich, not that you can trust the guy, claims that he did exactly as he was told. That he didn't screw anything up. It was the people on the other end of the operation who gave him bad intel."

"How so?"

"Gazich says a half a minute or so before the explosion he received a phone call that told him the target was the second limo. So I figure that the Secret Service must have shuffled the limos after they left the conference. Someone is standing on the street, they watch the candidates get in the second limo and they make the call to Gazich. Then the motorcade starts to roll, and a block later the Secret Service has the second limo move up to the lead position. They do that stuff all the time. You can easily see where the terrorists screwed up."

"It sounds like it all adds up, though."

Rapp shook his head. "I talked to Rivera. She says they didn't shuffle the limos."

"They didn't shuffle the limos?" Kennedy repeated, her surprise obvious.

"Nope, which leads me to believe that Gazich is lying."

The sick feeling in Kennedy's stomach grew. After a moment she said, "Or he's telling the truth."

"Why would you say that?"

Kennedy looked across the room, out the window and into the darkness, and sighed. "I think it's time I showed you something."

# 40

ennedy opened her safe, retrieved the oversized envelope, and walked over to the sitting area across from her desk. Rapp followed and came to a stop at her left as she laid out the photos in a slow, deliberate manner. At first Rapp had no idea what he was looking at, other than the fact that they were surveillance photographs of two people, who if he had to guess probably weren't married. There was something vaguely familiar about the woman. Rapp ignored her naked body and focused on the face. She was rather animated in the first six shots but in the seventh, the camera had caught her with her mouth closed, her face relaxed, and her eyes looking off in the distance. She had a detached vacant look on her face that was definitely familiar. Rapp finished looking at all the photos and then went back to the seventh one. He almost picked it up for closer examination, but his professional instincts stopped him. No sense leaving his fingerprints on something that obviously had Kennedy spooked.

Again, Rapp focused on the face, and ignored the beautiful body. The high cheekbones, the thin nose, the long, wavy, chestnut hair tangled and partially obscuring the right side of her face. There was something definitely familiar about the woman. Rapp blocked out every feature except the eyes, nose, and mouth. Suddenly everything clicked. He pictured the woman with her hair up in a kind of loose ponytail, dressed stylishly yet conservative, playing the role of a candidate's wife. It was Jillian Rautbort. The president-elect's wife. Rapp's focus intensified as he remembered the sorrow he'd felt for the political couple after the attack. Jillian Rautbort wasn't much older than Anna had been when an explosion had taken her life. Rapp felt Alexander's pain. He'd seen some of the footage of the funeral and the public statements Alexander had made in the immediate aftermath. He'd watched the man on election night when his opponent had conceded the race. Even in victory the man seemed irreparably wounded. It appeared that the greatest achievement of his career was tempered by a loss that could never be repaired.

These photos now forced Rapp to call those painful memories into question. Was it an act? Rapp had a hard time believing it. His job depended on being able to judge people in a split second. Picking friend from foe in a foreign land where the wrong decision could mean his life. Alexander's pain seemed so genuine. If he'd been faking it, the man was an absolute monster.

Rapp's eye settled on the man in the photos for the first time. The collage started with the two standing and then with Jillian riding the man on a lounge chair next to the pool. The guy was big. Jillian Rautbort looked tiny on top of him. Where Jillian was completely naked, the man still had on most of his clothes. His pants were pulled down to mid-thigh. There was something oddly familiar about him as well. Rapp noticed something coiling from the man's left ear. His eyes opened a bit wider and he began searching the other photos for the same coil. He found it in two other photos.

"Jesus Christ," Rapp said softly.

He looked at the photos where the man was on his back. Specifically the right side of his belt line. He expected to find either a radio or a gun. The photo wasn't clear enough, but something was there.

Without taking his eyes off the photo Rapp said, "Please tell me this guy is not a United States Secret Service agent."

"Unfortunately he is."

"You have got to be fucking kidding me."

"I wish I was."

"Who is it?"

"Special Agent Matt Cash."

Rapp looked at the photos again, from left to right. "When were these taken?"

"Labor Day weekend at her parents' Palm Beach estate."

"How did they come into your possession?"

"Cap Baker. He bought them from an unknown individual for what was probably a large sum of money."

"Can you believe him?"

"I think so. He claims he had no intention of using them. His candidates were ahead in the polls."

"Then why did he buy them?" Rapp asked a bit skeptically.

"He says the campaign was flush with cash and he thought the best move would be to take them out of circulation. He thought there was a slight chance they could be released and might cause sympathy for Alexander."

Rapp laughed. "Yeah, right. When did he buy them?"

"Mid-September, I think."

"A lot could've happened between then and the first Tuesday in

November. His candidate could have fucked up in one of the debates and overnight his lead would have vanished. These photos were his insurance policy."

"I agree."

"So why did he decide to give them to you?"

Kennedy sighed. "This is where things get interesting. Apparently there's some bad blood between Baker and Stu Garret."

"Alexander's campaign manager?"

"Yes. They despise each other. In early October, Baker decided to give Garret something to really sweat over, so he took three of the photos, wrote, 'You'll Never Win,' on the back, and had them delivered to Garret's hotel room in Dallas."

"Did Garret know they came from Baker?"

Kennedy shrugged. "If he did, it was a guess."

Rapp put his hands on hips, looked down at the photos, and then shook his head. "Did Special Agent Cash happen to be in the second limo on the day of the attack?"

"Yes."

"Wonderful."

Kennedy walked back to her desk and grabbed a two-inch file in a red folder. She returned to Rapp's side and said, "I want you to take a fresh look at the case from top to bottom." She handed the file to Rapp. "This is the Secret Service's preliminary report. Read through it and talk to Special Agent Rivera. I want to know if she knew one of her people was screwing the boss's wife."

Rapp nodded. "So you're thinking Gazich might be telling the truth."

"That the second limo was the target . . . I think that a lot of people rushed into this thing assuming certain facts. Read the report. Especially the investigator's notes. The entire investigation was conducted through the prism that the attack was perpetrated by terrorists. Give it a fresh look and we'll talk about it in the morning."

Rapp lifted the file up and looked at it for a second. "Anything else?"

"Yes." Kennedy hesitated briefly and then said, "Have Marcus do a thorough check on Stu Garret."

"Stu Garret," Rapp said with obvious surprise. "That little pud. You think he's capable of pulling something like this off?"

"There are some things you don't know about Mr. Garret, and I'm not going to get into them right now, but trust me when I say the man is capable of almost anything."

"Okay. I'll have Marcus start right away."

"Have him focus on the month before the attack."

"You got it. Anything else?"

"No. Just be careful and move fast. We don't have much time."

# 41

Wednesday morning arrived with a bit of a hangover for Mark Ross. He had actually tried to leave the hotel at one point, but the festive atmosphere continued to build until well after midnight. After the meeting with Tom Rich from the *Times,* Ross had gone up to see Alexander, who was in a black mood. There'd been times over the past month when Ross had wanted to grab Alexander by the shoulders, shake him violently, and tell him the harsh truth about his deceased wife. The woman was a slut. She deserved to be the First Lady of the United States about as much as a street hooker from New Orleans did. What Ross wanted to do and what was prudent, though, were miles apart. Besides, Alexander had proved very malleable in his grief. He'd basically let Ross run the transition team, which enabled him to stack the administration with people who were loyal to him. There were a lot of people from Georgia, to be sure, but Ross made sure they got jobs at Transportation, HUD, Education, Veterans' Affairs, and the like. Defense, State, and Justice, the crown jewels of any administration, were loaded with his people.

After meeting with Alexander in the Abraham Lincoln Suite, Ross headed down to the Round Robin Bar for a much-needed drink. That was shortly before six. Four hours later he found himself more than a little cockeyed, drinking a glass of cognac and smoking a big fat Dominican cigar with two big Hollywood producers. Party big-hitters from across the country kept showing up, and with Alexander sulking in his suite, it fell on Ross's shoulders to thank them for their hard work and support. At midnight he finally tore himself away from the party. One of his aides convinced him to stay at the hotel and offered to fetch him a change of clothes before morning. Less than stable on his feet, Ross took the young man up on his offer.

He awoke a few minutes before 7:00 a.m. and ordered room service before jumping into the shower. The food arrived while he was shaving and he asked the young man to set it up in front of the TV. He finished shaving and then sat down in his hotel robe and dug into his eggs, toast, and bacon. He used the bacon and toast to poke at the rich yellow yolks. He chased it with some grapefruit juice and then started in with the coffee. Within minutes he was feeling better. Then there was a knock on the door.

Ross cocked his head in the direction of the sound and considered ignoring it. It was rare these days that he got to spend time alone. There was more knocking. This time it was much louder. The door shook. Ross threw his napkin on the table and walked across the suite. He yanked open the door to find Stu Garret standing there with a huge grin on his face.

Garret pushed his way past Ross and said, "I heard you tied one on last night."

Ross closed the door and followed him, saying, "I was merely trying to be a good host."

Garret went straight for the room service cart and snatched a piece of bacon from Ross's plate.

"Don't touch my food, Stu." Ross was dead serious.

"Relax," said Garret as he grabbed a newspaper from under his arm and presented it to Ross. "Isn't this beautiful?"

In large black type across the top of the paper was the headline, "CIA Tortures Wrong Man." Ross snatched the paper from Garret's clutches and began reading in earnest. The grin on his face was even bigger than the one Garret had when he'd answered the door. "This really *is* beautiful. He mentions both Kennedy and Rapp in the first paragraph." He kept reading and a few moments later added, "I'm not going to have to lift a finger. The press is going to tear them apart for me."

"Like hyenas descending on a wounded rhino. It's already started." Garret picked up the remote for the TV and turned on CNN. "It was picked up by all the wire services and amplified on the cable news stations, AM radio, the Internet. You name it. The blogosphere is going nuts. They might not make it to Saturday."

Ross laughed and shook his fist in the air. "Stu, this has to be one of your better calls."

Garret nodded in agreement. "Pretty well played, if I do say so myself."

A former CIA employee was on screen laying into Director Kennedy for not keeping Mitch Rapp on a tighter leash. He claimed that he had been warning people for years that the man was out of control.

"Do you think there's a chance he could go to jail?" Ross asked.

"Who knows? It's typically against the law to kidnap people and shoot them." Garret found his comment amusing and started laughing.

"We should probably think about coming out with a statement."

"Not yet. Too early. Let everyone else do your dirty work. Maybe tomorrow or Friday you could release something. For now I'd just sit back and enjoy the implosion of Kennedy's career."

The advice sounded good to Ross. He wondered how Kennedy was taking the news. Morale out at Langley would not be good this morning. The thought of all the long faces gave Ross a delicious idea. He clapped his hands together loudly, and then rubbing them together, started for the bedroom.

"Where are you going?" Garret asked.

"To get dressed. I've got a busy morning and I need to squeeze in an unscheduled stop."

# 42

K ennedy was late for the senior staff meeting, which was very unlike her. Even more unusual was the fact that she'd slept in. She needed to catch up after a long, restless night. She had gone to bed watching Letterman and worrying about the possibility that this thing could go all the way to Josh Alexander. She fell asleep before the first guest, woke up some time around 3:00 in the morning, and then tossed and turned for two plus hours trying to figure out just how damaging the entire thing could be. If the second limousine was the target, and it was done to both eliminate a problem for the candidates and drum up sympathy, an election had not simply been stolen. It had been manipulated, which added another layer of concern to an already horrible problem.

Innocent lives had been taken, but Kennedy was being paid to worry about an even bigger picture. Chiefly, the safeguarding of the country and its institutions from foreign attack and subversion.

What worried her the most was the possibility that the Belarusian mafia may have had a hand in the affair. Russia and Belarus were very close. The communication between their intelligence agencies was good. It didn't always flow both ways, but in the end Mother Russia got what it wanted. The separation between their intelligence services and organized crime was at times nonexistent. If the Belarusian mafia helped plan the attack on the motorcade, it was an almost certainty that the KGB knew about it. With that type of information in their possession the KGB would be in a perfect position to subvert the next administration.

She'd fallen back asleep sometime around five and was woken up by her son at 8:15. He was late for school and she was late for work. Normally this would have created a panic, but when Kennedy took a look at the front page of the *New York Times,* she decided she'd take her time. Langley would be rife with recrimination this morning. Longtime coworkers, some of them friends, would be weighing their options. Many of them would come to the conclusion that it was time to distance themselves from Kennedy. Her tardiness would only add to the rumors and unease, but that couldn't be helped.

After dropping Tommy off at school, she unfolded her copy of the *Times* and read the article while her driver brought her straight to Langley. She read it twice and both times she smiled. Rapp had been right about two things. The first was that Rich definitely thought he was going to win a Pulitzer for the story, and the second was that this was going to be fun.

When she stepped off the elevator just outside her office, her administrative assistants were both on the phone. Pink call messages as thick as a deck of playing cards were waiting for her. Sheila, with the overdone makeup and the red hair, gave her a look that said *Help.* Kennedy smiled, said good morning, and walked into her office. Three men were waiting for her at the far end of the room. They were seated at the conference table. Kennedy set her briefcase behind her desk, closed the office door, and then hung her black cashmere overcoat in her closet. She tugged on the sleeves of her white blouse and unbuttoned the jacket of her blue pinstriped pantsuit. She'd picked the outfit with the press conference in mind.

Sitting at the table were Deputy Director of Intelligence Charles Workman, Deputy Director of Operations Jose Juarez, and Deputy Director Roger Billings. All three men sat in silence with their hands resting on the polished wood surface of the long table. They were obviously waiting for her to speak first. Kennedy walked to the far end where a singed American flag was framed. It had been pulled from the rubble of the Word Trade Center.

Kennedy pulled a chair out and said, "Sorry for being late this morning." She was about to sit when she noticed a copy of the *Times* underneath her briefing folder. Kennedy slid her leather bound briefing book to the side and said, "May I get any of you something to drink before we get started?"

All three men declined by shaking their heads. Kennedy eased into her chair and set her reading glasses atop the leather briefing folder. "So what do you have for me this morning?"

Juarez was sitting on her left. The dark circles under his eyes were more pronounced this morning. She was sure Tom Rich had probably called him for a comment last night, and she was also certain he had said nothing. As for the two men on her right, Kennedy couldn't be sure. They were good men, but they did not have the screw-you attitude of a Clandestine Service officer. Juarez had survived some very nasty stuff in the field. He would not be spooked by an investigation and the possibility of a new director. Workman and Billings, though, were desk jockeys. They'd spent the vast ma-

jority of their careers right here in Washington. They were en-
sconced in their nice suburban homes, Workman with three kids
and Billings with four. The older ones were in college, which added
financial pressure, and the younger ones were thinking about college, which added even more. They were both nearing fifty, and
they were both in a position to succeed Kennedy if she got the
boot. Which, from their vantage point this morning, looked like a
certainty. Juarez, on the other hand, knew he would never get the
top job. He was more spit than polish and had the irritating habit of
speaking truth to power.

To become the director of the CIA you needed to be nomi-
nated by the president and confirmed by the Senate. There'd been
many presidents in tune to the fact that they needed people like
Juarez around to balance out all the ass kissers who were so enam-
ored of the office. The Senate was a different story, though. Especially the older senators who'd been around for three terms or
more. They had a sense of entitlement, and often perceived disagreement as a sign of disrespect. Juarez did not get along with these
men, and he made no effort to disguise his dislike of them. Workman and Billings, on the other hand, worked very hard to curry
favor from this crucial block of senators.

Billings was Kennedy's number two. He'd grown up in Vermont
and attended Dartmouth. He was as steady as they came, and he did
not like change. A worrier, it showed in his wispy brown hair that
he parted to the side from left to right.

Billings gave Kennedy an uneasy look and asked, "Have you
read the *Times* this morning?"

Kennedy looked at the newspaper in front of her, her name in
large letters underneath the banner. It meant nothing to her. She'd
gotten over seeing her name in print years ago. She hadn't put a lot
of thought into how she would handle this. She had a 10:30 meet-

ing with the president, and until then she wanted to keep the information on Gazich as quiet as possible.

"I have read the article."

"And?" Billings asked.

She studied the two men on her right, and saw two worried civil servants who had devoted their entire adult lives to what they thought was an honorable and worthy cause. They did not want to see their Agency embroiled in another scandal.

"It's interesting."

"Interesting," Billings repeated. He did not attempt to hide his disbelief. "You're about to be burned at the stake, and *interesting* is all you have to say."

The right corner of Kennedy's mouth turned upwards showing the slightest hint of a smile. "I don't think anyone is going to be burned at the stake over this."

"Four senators have already called me this morning," Billings said.

"And I've talked to two," added Workman.

Kennedy looked to Juarez.

"I stopped counting."

"And what have you told them?" Kennedy asked all three. None of them decided to answer. Kennedy turned her gaze on Workman who was usually the most vocal. "Chuck, what did you tell them?"

He fidgeted in his chair and said, "I told them the truth."

"The truth, I've found, can be very subjective around here."

"Not on this one, Irene."

"Then let's hear it. Tell me what I need to know."

"I know you and Mitch are close, but I've been warning you for I don't know how long that sooner or later he's going to get us all into a lot of hot water."

Juarez leaned back in his chair and scowled at his counterpart from the intel side of the business. "I'm sure you'll find some way to save your own ass, Chuck."

"Don't defend him, Jose. Do you know how many times I've sat here and heard you complain about him?"

"There's a big difference between keeping our disagreements within the family and shooting your mouth off to some reporter."

"What in the hell is that supposed to mean?"

"You run the intel side, Chuck. You don't need some knuckle dragger like me to explain things to you."

"Are you implying that I spoke with this reporter from the *Times*?"

Jose grabbed his copy of the *Times* and read, "According to an anonymous senior CIA official, Mitch Rapp's methods and lack of control have been a growing concern for some time." Juarez slammed the paper on the table and said, "It sounds like you wrote it yourself."

Workman's pale complexion turned bright red and he snapped, "How dare you accuse me of having anything to do with this."

Kennedy watched with a critical eye as Juarez and Workman bandied back and forth. She had also wondered who the senior CIA official might be. She was about to intercede and end the argument when her office door opened unexpectedly. Juarez and Workman continued shouting across the table, completely oblivious that an interloper had just entered the Agency's inner sanctum. Kennedy's face revealed nothing, but inside she was fuming that this man had yet again barged in on her office without so much as a phone call or a knock.

Vice President—elect Ross strode across the room and stopped at the far end of the conference table. He was in a charcoal gray wool suit with a white shirt and a silver-and-blue tie. In his manicured right hand he held a copy of the *Times*. He threw it down on the conference table, unbuttoned his suit coat, and placed a hand on each hip.

"I have great appreciation for how difficult this business is, but this can't continue. I'm trying to save your jobs right now." Ross pointed to each of the four. "I've explained to Josh that we have a good team at Langley. I don't agree with everything you do, but I've told him you are competent people. Now, this morning I wake up to this, and I've got the next president of the United States asking me if I've lost my mind."

Ross paused. He looked at Kennedy. There she sat at the head of the table with her damn unreadable expression. "I explained to him that this is a business where batting a thousand is not possible. Even if these accusations are true, they need to be tempered against Rapp's past successes. His response was that if even half of what was printed in the article is true he wants me to come out here and clean house." Ross waved his hand above them as if in one fell swoop they could all be dispatched. He leaned over and stabbed his index finger on top of the newspaper. "You know what really boils my blood about this article? This quote in here from a senior CIA official. You people think this is Hollywood, where you settle your disputes by calling up a reporter and stabbing one of your colleagues in the back?"

No one answered. In fact Kennedy was the only one who looked at him.

Ross's fiery eyes settled on her. "I'm under direct orders from President–Elect Alexander to get to the bottom of this and put it behind us as quickly as possible. Please tell me this reporter has got it all wrong. That there is a simple explanation for why Mitch Rapp shot this man four times."

Kennedy's antennae were up. There was spying, there was sub-

terfuge, and then there was espionage. Real old-fashioned espionage where it wasn't enough to simply steal the enemies' secrets,
one had to launch double, triple, and quadruple feints and get them
to turn on themselves. Misdirection layered upon misdirection until
the enemy couldn't trust their best friend. During the Cold War the
Russians had been masterful at sowing distrust among CIA officers.
They even went so far as to send real intelligence assets over as defectors. These men and women were so good they were impossible
to tell from the real defectors. The damage they did was incalcu-
lable.

Kennedy couldn't help getting the feeling that Ross was up to
something. The man did not like her. He did not care for the greater
good of the Agency. He cared for himself first and last. Kennedy had
guessed some time ago that he was a borderline obsessive compul-
sive with narcissistic tendencies. In everyday parlance that meant he
was a backstabbing control freak. Just simply winning for these
types wasn't enough. It was boring. They needed the thrill, the
drama of the fight. Winning through subterfuge was nirvana. It
helped validate the narcissistic ego. It proved that they were smarter
than everyone else.

Kennedy could have easily taken the memory stick from her
safe and showed Ross the mountain of evidence that they had
against the man Rapp had arrested, but she decided to keep it from
him. There was still too much to learn, and her instincts told her
Ross could not be trusted.

"Sir," Kennedy said, "the entire matter is under investigation,
and I think it would be a disservice to comment on it before all the
facts are in."

"That sounds like damn lawyer speak," Ross snarled.

Kennedy remained calm. "If you had called, sir, and informed
me that you were coming, I might have been able to put together a

preliminary report, but I'm not sure what you expect out of me on such short notice?"

Ross's nostrils flared in anger. He hesitated for a split second before answering and then said, "I expect you to do your job, and I expect you to follow the law. Get this mess sorted out and do it fast, or you're all going to be looking for new jobs. And that comes straight from Alexander himself." Ross turned and marched out of the office.

Kennedy had studied his every move. The man could have been a stage actor. The way he turned his emotions on and off at a moment's notice. She'd made the calculated decision to push his button and find out if he would drop the savior act and he had. He had displayed genuine anger that she had dared to defy him.

Kennedy pushed her chair away from the table and stood. "That's all for this morning."

"We're done?" a surprised Billings asked.

"Yes. We'll reconvene right here at one."

All three men grabbed their stuff and got up to leave. Kennedy looked at Juarez bringing up the rear and said, "Jose, I'm leaving for the White House in twenty minutes. I want you to come with me."

"Do I need to bring anything?"

"No." Kennedy followed the men across the room and closed the door behind them. Once behind her desk, she picked up her secure phone and punched in a local number. Rapp answered on the second ring.

"Are you going to meet Rivera?"

"Yes."

"Expand your search to Ross. See if she can get you the Secret Service logs from his detail, and ask Marcus if he thinks he can do a workup on him without raising too much suspicion."

"I'll take care of it. When is your press conference?"

"I'm leaving to see the president shortly. I'll call you and let you know how it goes." Kennedy put the handset back in the cradle and considered the enemy she was about to make. She had never trusted Ross completely, even during his brief tenure as director of National Intelligence, but she had never let on. Once she held the press conference with President Hayes, Ross would know she had withheld information from him and any pretext of a cordial working relationship would be gone. Kennedy looked out the large picture window at the brightening day. She felt a sense of relief that she had chosen her course.

# 43

Special Agent Rivera sat at her desk and flipped through the Yellow Pages. She found *Karate,* and underneath it said *see Martial Arts.* She flipped through the pages to the M's and found it. There were six full pages of listings in the DC area. She shook her head and began searching for one between the office and her apartment. When she'd arrived at the dojo this morning, she found the contents of her locker waiting for her in a brown grocery bag by the front door. Her sensei was in the middle of teaching a class, and he didn't bother to come out and talk to her, or for that matter make eye contact. She was being thrown out after only five weeks, and she didn't need to ask why.

Rivera stopped reading the listings and closed her eyes. *What in the hell am I doing?* she asked herself. She felt as if her whole life was falling apart around her. For three straight months she'd been in denial. She knew her career was over, but she was hanging on in hopes that they would give her a second chance. One of her bosses had actually told her yesterday that he was recommending grief counseling. *The bastard,* she thought.

She'd asked him if he thought she needed the counseling to deal with the loss of her fellow agents who had died in the attack or for her career which was now dead. He looked at her stone-faced and told her no one blamed her for what had gone wrong. He was probably right about that, but it didn't change the fact that no one wanted her around. She was a living, breathing reminder of one of the Service's worst days since Dallas in 1963. Another colleague told her to get out of Washington. Take an assignment in Miami or L.A. Work counterfeit and fraud. It was challenging and gratifying work, and if she didn't want to do that, she could at least apply for the Joint Counterterrorism Center. Do anything just so long as it didn't involve working Personal Protection.

Rivera closed the Yellow Pages and dropped the book on the floor. Why was she bothering looking for a new dojo? Her days in DC were numbered. Everyone knew it. She just needed to come to grips with it. Life was cruel, she decided. She'd been so close to the top. The one job that every agent covets. The SAC of a Presidential Detail. She was on track, and it would have been hers.

Tears welled and she fought them back. The hell if she was going to break down in front of them. That was what they were waiting for. They'd ship her off for another round of evaluation, and she wasn't going to do that. She had more than a month of vacation and personal time banked. It was time to take it. Head out west again and hit the slopes. Maybe she'd stop by and see her family. They'd been worried about her when she'd gone home for Christmas, but after two days she couldn't take the nagging and left early to go meet some friends in Tahoe. She'd hit the bumps hard for three straight days until her back hurt so bad she couldn't take it anymore.

Rivera grabbed a tissue and wiped the corners of her eyes. She threw it in the garbage and decided she'd put in for vacation. She was about to send her boss an e-mail when her phone rang. She didn't recognize the number on the screen but answered it nonetheless.

"Special Agent Rivera speaking."

"Meet me on the street."

"Who is this?"

"Your sparring partner. Get your ass downstairs. We need to talk."

"Oh . . . it's you. Nice article in the *Times*. Sounds like you really made a mess of it."

Rapp laughed. "You should know better than most not to believe what you read in the paper."

Rivera looked over the top of her cube and said, "Based on my current situation, I'm not sure it's a good idea for me to be seen with you."

"Listen . . . I'm a busy guy. I have something you are going to want to see. Trust me. I'm parked at the curb. Silver Audi A8."

The line went dead. Rivera held the handset for a second and then slowly put it back in the cradle. She looked around her empty desk for a moment and considered her empty career and quickly came to the conclusion that she had nothing to lose. She grabbed her purse and started for the elevator. Two and a half minutes later she was climbing into the front passenger seat of Rapp's car.

"This better be good." She put her sunglasses on and looked over at Rapp.

Rapp grabbed the gear shift and pulled it back into drive. "Put on your seatbelt." He hit the gas and darted out into traffic.

"Where are we going?" Rivera fumbled with her seatbelt.

"Nowhere."

She gestured with her right hand at the passing scenery. "We're obviously going somewhere."

"Nowhere in particular. I didn't want to sit in front of your building."

"Fine. What did you want to show me?"

"I have a few questions for you first." Rapp hit his blinker and turned onto 19th Street and headed south toward the National Mall.

"I don't like games. I'm not in the mood today. Just show me what you have."

Rapp lowered his sunglasses a bit and looked over the top at his passenger. "You don't like games? What in the hell would you call what you did to me in your dojo the other morning?"

She ignored the question and said, "I don't know if you've noticed, or if you care, but my career is basically over. Thirteen years right down the toilet."

Rapp stopped for a red light and said, "I haven't noticed, and no, I don't care. I want answers, and I need them fast."

She shook her head and looked out her window.

"At least I'm honest."

"Good for you. An honest spy. You must be real unique."

Rapp wasn't a spy, but he wasn't about to waste his time trying to correct her. "The day of the attack you said you didn't shuffle the limos."

"What are you talking about?"

"When you left the conference, right before the explosion, you told me everyone loaded up. You got in the first limo with Ross and Alexander and Alexander's wife got in the second limo."

"That's right."

The light turned green and Rapp took his foot off the brake. "And the limos were never shuffled. They stayed in that order until the explosion?"

"Yeah. I already told you this."

"I'm just trying to make sure. Who decides who rides in which limo?"

Rivera frowned. Her thin dark eyebrows arching above her sunglasses. "I was the SAC. Typically, I do, but a lot of the times we work on the fly with the protectees and their staff."

"I read in the preliminary report last night that Alexander and his wife arrived in the same limousine, but left in separate vehicles."

"You have a copy of the preliminary report?" Rivera asked, her surprise obvious.

"Yes, and don't worry. You come out of it unscathed." Rapp wasn't being entirely honest, but he didn't need her getting all worked up. "Now is that right? Alexander and his wife arrived in the same car and left in separate cars?"

"Yes."

"And in the report it says you assigned Special Agent Cash to ride with Alexander's wife in the second limo?"

"Yes." Rivera grew a bit tentative. "Where are you going with all of this?"

"Bear with me for a little bit longer, and I'll tell you. The decision to put Alexander's wife in the second limo, was that a staff decision, or was it your decision?" Rapp took a left onto Constitution Avenue, the Washington Monument looming large up ahead on the right.

"By staff I assume you mean campaign."

"Yes. Was it you, or the campaign?"

"It was the campaign."

Rapp's fingers flexed on the leather steering wheel and then gripped it tight. He was homing in on the truth and he could feel it. "When were you informed of the change?"

"Probably fifteen minutes or so before we were going to leave for the vice president's residence. Don't hold me to that, though.

Changes like this happen all the time. Even more so during a campaign."

Rapp nodded. "I won't. I assume if the campaign wants to make a change they need to inform you personally."

"Usually, but I'm not always on."

"When you're on."

"Usually, but not always. Sometimes they'll grab the closest agent and have them tell me, but I made it clear that I wanted all changes to go through me directly."

Rapp nodded as he drove. So far so good. It was how he had envisioned it. "So on the day of the attack, who informed you there was going to be a change in terms of who would be riding in which car?"

"Stu Garret."

Rapp felt his chest tighten a bit as he began to experience a spike in adrenalin. "Stu Garret." Rapp turned his head to the right, cracking his neck.

"Do you know him?"

"Only by reputation."

"He's extremely rude, to put it kindly."

"So I've heard." Rapp got in the right lane and prepared to turn onto 14th Street. "Was Agent Cash already assigned to the second limo or was that a last-minute change?"

"What is your interest in Agent Cash?"

Rapp took a right turn and sighed. "Nothing in particular. Just some inconsistencies we've found."

"I don't know if this will help, but we got in a fight that afternoon when I told him he needed to take Jillian back to her hotel."

"So that was a last-minute change?"

"Yes."

"And why did you decide to pick him over all the other agents?"

"I didn't. She requested him."

Rapp looked surprised. "You're sure about that? Did she tell you personally, or did one of her aides tell you."

Rivera thought about it for a moment and then said, "Actually, it was Garret who told me she'd requested him."

Rapp took a hard left turn onto Jefferson Drive. "You're sure?"

"Yes, I'm sure."

"And this was normal."

"Yes. He was the campaign manager. He was always running around barking at people making last minute changes."

"Was it normal for Jillian to request Agent Cash?"

"Actually it was. We used to tease him about it." Rivera smiled as she remembered her friend. "Some of the agents even joked that she had a thing for him."

Rapp laughed uncomfortably. They drove another block in silence and then Rapp pulled over in front of the National Air and Space Museum. He had to make a decision. Kennedy wouldn't like it, but he was going to go with his instincts. He put the car in park and turned toward Rivera. "I need you to do something for me."

Rivera was caught off guard by both his sincerity and intensity. She looked at him warily and asked, "What?"

"You know Jack Warch?"

"Of course."

"In about an hour and a half I'm going to have the president call him. The president is going to tell Jack that he wants you to look through all of the logs the Secret Service has on Ross and Alexander going back to this past September. I especially want you to look at the two weeks prior to the attack. I want to know if they had any foreign visitors, and I want you to keep an eye out for any mention of Stu Garret."

Rivera took off her sunglasses and studied Rapp's rugged features. "Why did you laugh like that when I told you some of the agents used to tease Cash that Jillian had a thing for him?"

"Laugh like what?"

"Like they were probably right and they didn't even know it."

Rapp looked out the front window and said, "Did you really not know that they were having an affair?"

"Excuse me?" Rivera answered more than a bit shocked.

"You truly didn't know?" Rapp asked in a disbelieving tone.

"I knew Matt Cash for a long time. He was a good father and a devoted husband. There is no way he was cheating on his family."

"Really." Rapp reached in his pocket and pulled out a color copy of one of the shots taken down in Palm Beach. Rapp tossed the photo onto Rivera's lap and said, "If that's not Agent Cash having sex with Jillian Rautbort then would you mind telling me who it is?"

Rivera stared at the photo in shock, unable to speak.

# 44

The lobby at the Willard was coming to life. It was 11:28 a.m. and no one was checking out. There were only arrivals and guests moving about to find food and shop. Garret was actually trying to get work done, and if one more person came up and congratulated him, he swore he was going to bash them over the head with his BlackBerry. Garret sat in an oversized mohair chair facing the door. He assumed the man he was meeting for lunch knew what he looked like because he hadn't the faintest idea what the guy looked like.

Garret focused on the small screen of his BlackBerry with the aid of a pair of bifocals. His thumb spun the black wheel on the side of the device and clicked on the weather icon. The five-day forecast popped up after a few seconds. For months he'd been dreading the inauguration. Every time he thought about it he imagined himself sitting on the West Capitol steps freezing his ass off. A warm front was moving in. The afternoon's high was supposed to be fifty-two degrees and they were forecasting a balmy fifty-eight for the big event on Saturday. Garret smiled. *Fucking weather idiots,* he thought to himself. *They had no idea what they were doing.* Only two days ago they'd been forecasting low thirties for the weekend.

Satisfied with the current forecast he spun the wheel and clicked on one of his saved Web sites. It was an online auction site that specialized in old motorcycles. Garret had a couple of bids he needed to check. One of them was going to shut down the bidding at 10:00 p.m. this evening. As he was looking at the most recent bid the BlackBerry beeped and then a number one appeared in his in-box. Suddenly, three more messages appeared. Garret opened the in-box and saw that the first message was a news alert from the Drudge Report. The other three were from other news services. Something was brewing. Garret clicked on the link and a moment later was staring at the bare bones home page of the Drudge Report. The headline across the top read, "President to Hold Noon Press Conference. CIA Director Expected to Step Down."

Garret pumped his fist up and down and hit the speed dial button for Mark Ross.

Ross answered on the second ring. "Yes?"

"How did it go at Langley?"

"She's dead and she doesn't even know it."

"I think she does now."

"What's going on?"

"Drudge is reporting that the president is going to hold a noon press conference."

"About?"

"He says Kennedy is going to resign."

"You're kidding!" Ross's voice was filled with excitement.

"Nope. Can you believe it? It took less than a day and you barely had to lift a finger."

"Where are you?"

"At the hotel. I'm meeting some clown from Indiana who thinks he's going to be their next governor."

"Keep it short. I'll meet you in the bar at noon. We'll watch it together. I can't wait to see the dejected look on Kennedy's face."

"See you there." Garret hung up just as his 11:30 came strolling into the lobby. The guy had to be six foot six. That was the first thing he noticed. The second was that he had the most pronounced Adam's apple he'd ever seen. Unless the people of Indiana wanted a governor who looked like a stork, this guy didn't stand a chance.

# 45

President Hayes was as relieved as Kennedy had ever seen him. After she'd finished the PowerPoint presentation, he admitted that he'd feared the worst when he'd read the piece in the *Times*. For obvious reasons he did not want his administration to end with a scandal. Instead, he was going to leave on a high note. Gazich was guilty. There was no doubt about it. The Greek government had just this morning filed their official protest at the U.N. They'd jumped the gun and were about to find that out in a very public manner and, best of all, his critics and foes were going to have to eat crow.

Rapp's idea to hold a press conference had been an easy sell for Kennedy. The president couldn't wait to turn the tables on *The New York Times*. Not only was he going out on a high note, he was going to be able to do what few presidents got the chance to do, and that was rub the press's face in their own mistake. Rapp had been right when he'd told Kennedy that this was going to be fun. Her amusement, however, had been brief. Kennedy was filled with dread over how far-reaching the scandal might be, and she'd decided to share none of her deeper suspicions with the president. It wasn't that she didn't trust him, it was that she needed some proof. So far all she had were some very embarrassing photos, a theory, a deep distrust of Mark Ross and the fear that Josh Alexander was so power hungry he'd had his own wife killed to win the election.

Kennedy stood in the small hallway just outside the White House Press Room with Juarez at her side. She wanted him there so she could give the Clandestine Service some much deserved positive publicity. For Kennedy there was no time to celebrate. She was worried about the larger picture. Worried about the truth that Rapp might discover. A truth that would destroy a nation's confidence in its elected officials and damage for decades to come America's international standing. Kennedy needed to be absolutely sure of what had happened and she needed to find out before Alexander and Ross took their oaths.

Kennedy's phone rang. She looked at the caller ID and saw it was Rapp. She pressed the talk button and asked, "How did it go?"

"She had no idea they were having an affair."

"You believe her?"

"Yes."

"Did she confirm that she was the one who ordered him to ride in the second car?"

"Yes."

"Hmmm." Kennedy wondered if they'd just hit their first stumbling block. Part of her wanted it to end right here and now, but another part of her wanted to prove that her instincts were right.

"But, get this," Rapp said. "Garret was the one who told her to make sure Cash and the wife went in the second limo. She said Garret told her the wife had specifically requested Cash."

"And there's no way of proving if she did or didn't."

"There is one way."

"How?"

"I'll grab that little piece of shit Garret and threaten to pluck his eyeballs out with my bare hands."

"Mitch, we can't go around doing stuff like that." Kennedy glanced to her right and then left. "At least not without some more proof."

"Fine. But do me a favor. The president is going to have you say a few words, right?"

"Yes."

"Make sure you really play up the fact that we found certain records in Gazich's office that have given us a good idea as to who may have hired him. Keep it real vague, but sound confident."

Kennedy looked up and saw President Hayes coming down the hall with his press secretary. "I have to go. I'll call you when I'm done." Kennedy silenced her ringer and stuffed it in her purse.

"Are you ready?" the president asked with a confident smile.

"I'm ready if you are, sir."

"Good, let's go." Hayes took Kennedy by the arm and led her into the cramped and hot White House Press Room.

# 46

The first thing Garret did was separate the stork from his staff. The five people seemed put off, but Garret didn't give it a second thought. He walked the wannabe politician over to the far corner of the lobby, grabbed two chairs, and got down to business. The stork was a Baptist who attended church every Sunday, which in a state like Indiana was very important. Even more so for a Democrat. The family was loaded. Grandpa started out buying radio stations in the '30s, Daddy added TV stations in the '60s, and then further solidified the family's fortune with a cable monopoly in the '80s. In the '90s, the stork, who'd graduated from Purdue with an engineering degree, saw the future and convinced Daddy to get into the satellite business. The company now had three communications satellites in orbit, and the family's net worth was estimated to be somewhere in the five-billion-dollar range.

The stork claimed to be happily married and faithful to his wife of thirteen years. He had three kids, no history of drug abuse, and no perverse habits that he would admit to. Garret told the man that before he would commit, he wanted to run some preliminary polls to see what the people of Indiana thought of him. The stork said they already had polling data, but Garret was adamant that he would need to do a poll of his own. The aspiring candidate would of course have to foot the bill. Garret would also hire a private eye to check for dirty laundry. It was a steadfast rule of his to have all potential clients investigated. He didn't like surprises. He'd been burned one too many times by candidates with an over inflated sense of importance and a selective memory.

Garret saw a Secret Service agent enter the main door. He vaguely recognized him as one of the agents assigned to Ross's detail. The man stopped, swept the room from right to left with a robotic gaze, and then brought his left hand up to his mouth and spoke into a small microphone. Garret knew Ross would be coming through the door shortly, so he apologized for such a brief meeting and promised to call the stork early next week. Even if he didn't need to meet Ross, he would have kept it short. He wasn't about to dither with a potential client.

Garret saw two more Secret Service agents come through the door. One stopped to survey the guests while the other continued on to the elevator bank. A second later Ross entered the lobby. The murmurs started almost immediately. Those who saw him first whispered to the others and all heads turned to watch the party's second most important person. One of the guests shouted something that Garret didn't quite catch. Ross smiled and pumped his fist and then the other guests broke into applause.

Garret set out on a course to intercept Ross midway between the door and the elevators. The stork called out his name, but Garret didn't bother to turn around. The guy probably wanted to meet Ross, but Garret had no time for introductions or pleasantries. He wanted to get up to Ross's suite and turn on CNN. Garret fell into step with the vice president—elect and his bodyguards and marched straight for a waiting elevator. No words were exchanged.

Ross, Garret, and four agents stepped onto the elevator. When the doors closed, Garret looked over at Ross and asked, "How did things go out at Langley?"

Ross kept his eyes on the floor numbers above the elevator door. Out of the side of his mouth he gave a one word answer. "Interesting."

*Interesting,* Garret thought. *Interesting* meant he had something to say, but he didn't want to talk about it in front of the agents. They passed the rest of the short ride in silence. When the doors opened, another Secret Service agent was waiting for them. They walked down the hall to Ross's suite where yet another sentinel was posted. The agent slid a card key into the reader and opened the door for Ross and Garret. They entered the suite where the smell of breakfast still hung in the air.

As soon as the door clicked shut, Ross pulled off his suit coat and said, "I can't wait to see the look on that bitch's face when she's forced to resign."

Garret already had the remote control in his hand and was working the buttons.

Ross draped his coat over the back of a chair and added, "Maybe we should get the Justice Department to launch an investigation. If we're lucky, she'll end up in jail."

Garret frowned and made another attempt at entering the channel for CNN. "Be happy with your victory and leave it at that. The last thing we want is more investigations."

"You should have seen her this morning." Ross placed his hands on the back of the chair and looked at the TV. "She was so smug. She sat there in her office with her damn expressionless face and told me she didn't think it was appropriate to comment on the article. When I was her boss, she used to pull the same shit."

"What did you expect her to say?" Garret extended the remote, turned up the volume, and in a falsetto voice said, "I screwed up. I'm sorry." Garret shook his head. "People like Kennedy . . . they always think they're the smartest person in the room. No way she's ever going to admit she blew it."

The image of the White House Press Room came on the screen. It was just the podium and the blue backdrop with the cutout of the White House. Next to the White House logo a large flat-panel monitor hung from the ceiling. The crawler at the bottom of the screen said the president was expected to make an important announcement. The CNN White House correspondent was reporting the speculation that CIA Director Kennedy was expected to announce her resignation.

"No shit." Garret laughed. "Isn't this great?"

"Yes, it is." Ross flashed a proud smile. "This is real power. Being able to manipulate world events."

"Look," Garret said, "here comes bobble head."

Ross snickered. Garret could be brutally funny some times. After President Hayes had rebuffed the campaign for the umpteenth time and made it clear that he would not be campaigning on behalf of Ross and Alexander, Garret had taken to calling him bobble head. It was a crude reference to the way the president's Parkinson's made him shake.

"He must have taken his medicine this morning. He's not shaking too bad."

"Turn it up," Ross commanded.

A series of escalating green bars appeared at the bottom of the screen while the president arranged his notes behind the podium. The expression on his face was very serious. Finally, Hayes cleared his throat and then grabbed the small mike pulling it a bit closer.

"I'm going to make a brief statement," he said, "and then I'm going to turn things over to Director Kennedy." Hayes paused for a second to look down at his notes. "I have been blessed in my life to work with some extremely talented people. At the top of that list I would put the woman to my right." The president stopped and looked at Kennedy with a paternal smile.

Garret said, "He's going to build her up before he drops the ax."

"Director Kennedy has been one of my closest advisors over the past four years, and she and her team at the CIA are some of the finest folks in public service today. Many of her successes you will never know about because they are classified. Her failures, unfortunately, often end up on the front pages of newspapers across the country and beyond." The president stopped, his eyes floating over the press corps with an expression that was somewhere between anger and disappointment. "I would like to say to the country today that there is no one I have depended on more over these past four years than Irene Kennedy. I owe her a deep debt of gratitude. The *country* owes her a deep debt of gratitude." Hayes stayed at the microphone, but turned to look at Kennedy. "I am a very lucky man to have worked with someone so talented and loyal."

The president stepped away from the podium and opened his arms for Kennedy.

Garret shook his head in disgust and said, "You see! That's what happens when you're done running for office. You don't give a shit who you hug. If he was up for reelection, there's no way he'd be doing this. I'd bet he wouldn't even be caught in the same room as her."

Kennedy stood behind the podium with empty hands. She

looked decidedly smaller than the president, but she exuded a quiet confidence. Her straight brown hair was tucked behind her ears, and she was wearing a pair of diminutive black-rimmed glasses. A strand of small white pearls hung around her neck. She looked smart, classy, and in control.

She looked straight at the press corps and said, "Since the terrorist attack here in Washington this past October, the CIA has been actively trying to identify the person or persons behind the assault on the motorcade. This past weekend a team of CIA operatives, after nearly a month in the field, apprehended a man on the Greek island of Cyprus. This man has been identified by *The New York Times* as Alexander Deckas, a Greek national. Just this morning the Greek government filed an official protest at the United Nations accusing the United States of kidnapping one of their citizens. The Greek government is demanding Mr. Deckas be returned immediately."

Kennedy looked to her right and gave a nod to someone off-screen. A second later the flat-panel monitor that was perched over her right shoulder flickered to life. Kennedy moved around to the far side of the podium, raised her right arm, and pointed it at the screen. A black-and-white image appeared on the screen.

"This surveillance footage was taken at a Starbucks on Wisconsin Avenue only a few blocks away from the explosion that took place this past October. Based on the testimony of a Secret Service agent who was in the motorcade that day, we believe the man standing at the counter wearing the baseball hat is the person who detonated the bomb."

Kennedy raised her hand, pressed the remote and the screen split in two. The left half showed the Starbucks footage, and the right half showed a new surveillance image. "The picture on the right was taken at JFK the day before the attack. Using facial recognition software, these two photos were analyzed. Experts in the field concur that there is an eighty-plus percent chance that these two men are one and the same."

Ross's eyes narrowed and he asked, "What in the hell is she up to?"

"The man on the right entered the U.S. using a Greek passport and was traveling under the name of Nicholas Panagos." Kennedy hit the remote again and the screen was now split into thirds. "This new picture on the far right is of Alexander Deckas, the man we apprehended in Cyprus this past weekend. Using facial recognition software our experts concur that there is a ninety-nine percent match between the photo in the middle and the one of Mr. Deckas on the right." Kennedy paused and looked out at the reporters assembled before her.

A hand shot up and then a man stood blocking a good portion of the camera angle. The image on the TV quickly switched to show the reporter from the front. As he began to speak his name appeared at the bottom of the screen along with the newspaper he worked for. It was Sam Cohen, the White House correspondent for *The New York Times*.

"Director Kennedy, are you denying reports that the CIA kidnapped Mr. Deckas from his home on Cyprus?"

The camera angle switched back around to Kennedy. "I would use the word *apprehended.*"

"So you're not denying it?"

Kennedy pursed her lips for a moment and then said, "No."

Cohen wrote while he talked. "Are you denying reports that Mitch Rapp shot this man four times, once in each knee and then again in both hands?"

Once again Kennedy paused and then gave her one word response. "No."

Cohen had a look of surprised amusement on his face. "Were these injuries inflicted while Agent Rapp was torturing Mr. Deckas?"

"They occurred during the apprehension of the suspect, but I think you're getting a bit ahead of the story here, Sam."

"With all due respect, Director Kennedy, I think the torturing of a fellow human in any situation is an outrage. Our courts have repeatedly said the same thing. The torturing of someone whose guilt or innocence has yet to be proved is an utter travesty."

"If the man was indeed *innocent,* and he had in fact been tortured, I would agree with you."

"You have shown us nothing that comes close to proving that this Deckas fellow was the one who attacked the motorcade and I can't conceive of a scenario where an individual gets shot in both knees and both hands while being arrested."

Kennedy's calm neutral demeanor melted into a playful smile. "That's because you interrupted me, Sam. It appears to be a habit of *The New York Times* to jump to conclusions before gathering all the facts."

The smile was what gave Ross reason to pause. It was the same smile one would give during a chess match when an opponent had stepped into your trap. Something was wrong. Her expression was not what he expected from someone who was about to be gang-raped by the media. Ross watched as she turned back to the screen and pressed the remote. The photo of Deckas stayed on the screen and was joined by a second, younger photo of him.

"Mr. Deckas is in fact not a Greek citizen. His real name is Gavrilo Gazich, and he is wanted by The Hague for war crimes committed in the former republic of Yugoslavia. Mr. Gazich is a person of Bosnian heritage who is charged with killing over three dozen men, women, and children during the war. Five years ago he moved to Cyprus and set up a fake identity and a company that specialized in bringing aid to the impoverished nations of Africa. Based on information we found at his office and home, we are now looking into the fact that he may have been involved in as many as sixteen assassinations over the past decade. His targets included a United Nations official, relief workers, politicians, warlords, generals, and at least one reporter."

Garret tore his eyes away from the TV and said, "What the fuck is this?"

Before Ross could answer Kennedy continued. "Mr. Gazich has admitted his role in the attack here in Washington this past October."

"Was that confession made before or after he'd been shot in both knees?" The voice was that of Sam Cohen of the *Times*. He stayed in his seat this time.

Kennedy did not bother to look at the screen. She kept her eyes on Cohen while she hit the remote, bringing up two new photos. The screen was filled with two ashen-faced dead men. "While observing Mr. Gazich's movements on the island of Cyprus, the CIA team watched him kill these two men. We do not know who they are, but we have reason to believe they are Russian. We also think they were sent to kill Mr. Gazich so he would no longer be a liability to whoever it was who hired him to attack President–Elect Alexander's motorcade.

"Here is a brief excerpt of Gazich's confession. I can't play all of it for you because he told us some things that we are still investigating." Kennedy pressed a button again and a typed transcript appeared on the screen of the audio. A second later, voices could be heard.

*"How did you get into the U.S.? Be careful. Take your time to think this one through. You wouldn't want to lie to me."*

*"I flew into New York the day before."*

*"Which airport?"*

*"JFK."*

*"The explosives?"*

*"They were waiting for me."*

*"Where?"*

*"Pennsylvania."*

*"The state?"*

*"Yes, the state. Now give me my shot."*

*"Not quite yet. You're doing a good job, though. So you pick up the van, drive it down to Washington . . . when, on Friday?"*

*"No, I told you I arrived in New York on Friday."*

*"So you stayed in Pennsylvania on Friday night?"*

*"Yes . . . Yes! The van was waiting for me and I drove it down to Washington early on Saturday morning. I found my spot, I parked it, I waited, and then when the time was right I blew it up. End of story."*

Garret stood abruptly. "This is all bullshit . . . right? I mean she's making this shit up. Isn't she?"

Ross had his arms folded across his chest, his fist balled up and under his chin. Without bothering to look at Garret he snapped, "Shut up, so I can hear what she's saying."

"Director Kennedy," it was Cohen again, "was that tape made before or after the suspect had been shot?"

"What's your point, Sam?"

"When someone has been shot in both knees and both hands and then interrogated, it's reasonable to assume that they would say anything to avoid further pain. That's called coercion. And if Mitch Rapp shot this man before questioning him there's not a judge in the land who is going to allow this confession into evidence."

"I don't know if you've been paying attention, Sam, but this is a pretty nasty business. You don't send a Boy Scout out to capture a monster like Gavrilo Gazich. You need to send someone like Mitch Rapp. You don't yell *freeze,* you don't flash a badge, you disable the man, so you don't end up like these two guys." Kennedy pointed the remote at the screen and returned to the photo of the two dead men. "As for your question as to whether or not the confession was coerced, I'll let the totality of the evidence speak for itself."

Kennedy put a photograph of Gazich up on the screen. "This is the man who remote-detonated the bomb that killed nineteen Americans this past October. In addition to his confession, we have discovered some key evidence in his home and office that we think will lead us to the people who hired him. I thank you for your time this morning, and I'd be more than happy to take a few questions."

The room burst into a free-for-all as more than a dozen reporters burst to their feet and began shouting questions.

Ross quietly swore to himself while Garret let loose a string of profanity.

"What the fuck are we going to do?" Garret asked. "Those assholes said they were going to take care of this."

Ross stood motionless, with his arms folded and his fist looking like he might drive it through his own chin. Slowly but surely he began to tremble and his face turned crimson.

Garret paced back and forth before him. Ranting and raving. "Did you hear what that bitch said?" He stopped and pointed at the TV, as if Ross might think he was talking about someone else. "She said they have information. Information that is going to lead them to the people who hired Gazich! Did you fucking hear her?"

"Yes, I fucking heard her!" Ross snapped and then clenched both fists in front of him like he wanted to pound the hell out of someone. He stepped toward Garret and lowered his voice. "I tell you what you're going to do, Stu. You are going to get on a plane this afternoon, and you are going to fly over there, and you are going to tell those *idiots* that I don't care who they have to kill to put a lid on this thing. I want anyone outside the immediate circle dealt with, and I mean *anyone*. And don't take any shit from them. They promised this guy would be dealt with and they blew it, so I don't want to hear another word about a pardon until they have erased all possible connections between them and this Gazich guy. Have I made myself clear?"

Garret did not feel like getting on a plane to go anywhere other than California, but he knew Ross was right. They were too close to let this thing fall apart and Green and his associates couldn't be trusted.

"Yes, you have. I'll go."

# 47

Kennedy finished loading the dishwasher and dried her hands on a towel hanging from the refrigerator door handle. The clock on the microwave read 10:29. Her son was in bed, and a pot of coffee was ready to go. They would want coffee, even at this late hour. Kennedy walked through the dining room to the formal living room. She looked out the window to see if they'd arrived. A man was out walking his golden retriever. Kennedy recognized the dog before the owner. It was Rookie and Mr. Soucheray, her neighbor.

Even though Kennedy loved her neighborhood, she had considered moving. Potomac Palisades was, in her biased opinion, the nicest area in Washington, DC. It wasn't the most expensive, or the most exclusive, but that was part of what made it one of the nicest. It was old. Good-sized homes with bigger than normal city yards. Yards that people mowed themselves. Kennedy didn't mow her own lawn, but instead of hiring a service she had one of the neighborhood boys handle the chore. In another year or two Tommy would be able to take over. Potomac Palisades was not a bedroom community. People knew each other.

Her mother lived less than a mile away in the Foxhall Village neighborhood. Kennedy had tried to get her to live with them, but the woman wanted her independence, and Kennedy respected that. The Palisades ran along the eastern edge of the Potomac river. With its rolling terrain and luscious growth it felt like a sanctuary far from the nation's center of power. In truth it was a straight three-mile shot from the White House. Four if you wound your way down the Potomac. The only reason she considered moving was out of respect for the quiet neighborhood and the nice people who lived there. The CIA made a lot of people nervous. In Washington the institution tended to be less polarizing. Pretty much everybody knew somebody who worked for the CIA or had worked for the CIA. When you saw those people pulling up to a soccer game or the grocery store in their minivan it took a lot of the mystique out of the job.

Being the director of the CIA was a slightly different matter, though. Shortly after she took over the top job, Langley replaced all the windows in her house with bulletproof glass and installed steel doors and door frames with overlaid wood veneer. They wanted to do even more, like installing a ten-foot privacy fence in back. She put her foot down and told them no. Instead, they landscaped, putting in pressure pads and laser and microwave sensors. A panic room had been built in the basement and the home was swept twice a week for listening devices. A bomb tech and his German shepherd checked her car every morning before she left for work. Next to the panic room in the basement they'd also built a security shack that was the nerve center for the extremely expensive security system. The house was as secure as they could make it without tearing it down and starting over.

After all the security precautions were implemented, another group at the CIA took it upon themselves to do a threat assessment on Kennedy. At the top of their list was the suggestion that she move to a location with a long driveway. The current house was a scant forty feet from the street. Any terrorist with a couple thousand dollars and a rudimentary understanding of chemistry could simply drive down her street and level her house. Welcome to the post-9/11 world. She was a high-value target and her neighbors were understandably uneasy that their peaceful neighborhood might become ground zero.

Kennedy's response was to shelve the threat assessment. She thought of the risks her father and stepmother had taken. Her dad had also worked for the CIA. He'd been the station chief in Beirut back in 1983 when a car bomb leveled the place. Her stepmother worked for the State Department. Kennedy's parents divorced when she six. Her mother, it turned out, wasn't cut out for the world of international espionage. Kennedy spent a significant portion of her teens and early twenties overseas. She'd lived in Cairo, Damascus, Baghdad, and Beirut before everything fell apart. Having walked the streets of Beirut with machine-gun fire in the distance and mortars going off only blocks away it seemed ludicrous to think that such violence could come to the tranquil streets of Potomac Palisades.

When President Hayes decided not to seek reelection, Kennedy put the decision to move on hold. When Alexander and Ross won the race, she banished any thought of moving. Kennedy was an exceedingly civil person. Always polite and rarely confrontational. She was a woman in a man's world, and she knew her mere presence could be threatening to the insatiable egos of the men who were drawn to work in Washington. Thomas Stansfield, her mentor, had warned her often about the perils of working for men who needed to constantly prove that they were right. Kennedy avoided most of the frays by staying respectful, but firm. She also avoided gossip and politics. She had tried to do the same with Ross, but there had always been signs that there was an agenda lurking beneath the surface. Nothing big, just little things, but the little things often spoke volumes about people.

For example, Ross was habitually late for every meeting. Kennedy remembered Stansfield telling her once that when someone is constantly late, they fall into three categories. The first, he called *idiot savant*. The type of person who is so smart in his or her field of expertise that their mind is literally elsewhere. In layman's terms he explained that these people were smart in school and dumb on the bus. The second category was made up of perfectionists, people who were incapable of letting go of one task and moving on to another. These people were always playing catch-up, rarely rose to any real position of power, and needed to be managed properly. The third category, and the one to be most wary of, were the egomaniacs. These were the people who not only felt that their time was more important than anyone else's, but who needed to prove it by constantly making others wait for them.

Kennedy was worried. She looked out the window and checked for headlights. Rapp and Dumond had said they'd found some interesting stuff and they were on their way over. In the past she had always tried to keep her personal feelings separate from her job, especially when dealing with those who'd been elected to office. Ross was making that difficult. It was as if she'd seen him for who he really was, for the first time, this morning. The man had yet to take his oath of office. If he'd called and questioned her about the article, she would have understood. If he'd called for an appointment, she would have thought he'd had more important things to do, but would have accommodated him nonetheless. But showing up unannounced was peculiar. It was as if he needed to see her beaten down.

A pair of bluish white xenon headlights appeared at the far end of the block. A few seconds later a silver Audi came to an abrupt halt at the curb. Kennedy watched as Dumond and Rapp got out of the car and started up the walk. The younger man, Dumond, moved with a carefree gait, his attention focused on some small device he was carrying in his left hand. Rapp moved with an athletic grace. There was nothing herky-jerky or rushed about his movements. His head swiveled from left to right and then back, like a radar searching for potential threats. She remembered seeing that awareness when she'd recruited him all those years ago at Syracuse. Kennedy strode through the living room to the foyer and punched a code into the security panel on the wall. Somewhere behind the wall she heard the faint whirl of an electronic motor as it retracted three steel pins from the door.

Kennedy opened the door and immediately noticed a puzzled look on Dumond's face. "What's wrong?"

"I'm not sure. I'll know more in a minute." He stepped into the foyer and kept tapping the keys of a very small laptop.

Rapp closed the door and kissed Kennedy on the cheek. "Tommy in bed?"

"Yes. He has school in the morning."

Rapp took off his coat and handed it to Kennedy. Dumond was too focused on his computer to bother removing his jacket and continued down the hall toward the smell of coffee. Rapp and Kennedy followed him.

"Would anyone like coffee?" Kennedy asked.

"Please." Rapp backed up against the black soapstone counter and placed his hands on the edge. He looked at Dumond, who hadn't answered Kennedy, and said, "Hey, dip shit?"

Dumond tore his eyes away from the small screen and said, "Huh?"

"Coffee?"

"Sure."

"How about 'please'?" Rapp prodded.

"Please," Dumond said without taking his eyes off the screen. "With cream and sugar."

Kennedy poured two cups and took the cream from the fridge. She handed one cup to Rapp. "So what have you learned?" She placed the other cup on the table next to the cream and slid the sugar bowl over.

"So far," Rapp said, "nothing concrete, but we have a few interesting tidbits. Back in early October, Garret flew to Switzerland for a day."

"Another October surprise." Kennedy was referencing a conspiracy theory which held that the Reagan camp had met secretly with members of the Iranian government and conspired to delay the release of American hostages until after they beat Carter in the 1980 presidential election.

"All we have are the dates of his departure and return. We have no idea who he met with. He did call a bank in Geneva several times before and after the trip, but again we have no idea who he spoke with."

"E-mails?" Kennedy asked.

"We're still trying to track all those down. The guy has at least six different addresses and he must receive and send easily a hundred a day."

"What about Ross?"

"He was in Switzerland last weekend for an environmental

summit." Rapp held his white coffee cup by the handle. "Rivera got me the list of the people he met with while he was over there. We cross-referenced it against some of the other data and one name got kicked out: Joseph Speyer."

"Should I know him?" Kennedy asked with a furrowed brow.

"No, but he happens to be the president of the bank in Geneva that Garret called back in October."

"What do we know about the bank?"

Rapp pointed at Dumond. "Marcus is working on that. Apparently it's one of Geneva's oldest and most secretive institutions."

"And by far the most difficult one to hack into," Dumond added without looking up.

"Is that what you're working on?" Kennedy asked.

"No. Something else." Dumond hadn't touched his coffee. His two index fingers were busy tapping keys.

Kennedy's stoic gaze shifted to Rapp. "What about our Belarusian friend?"

"Nothing yet. Hornig says she needs a little more time to soften him up."

"When?" Kennedy asked impatiently.

"She thought maybe she could start in the morning." Rapp could sense her frustration. "I didn't think we were operating under any time constraints."

"In two days we're going to have a new president and vice president who might be guilty of murder and treason and god knows what else. Based on how Ross has been acting, I don't think he's going to waste any time getting rid of me. We need to get to the bottom of this while we still have the power to."

"Yes," Dumond said triumphantly. He looked up smiling. "That little bastard took me longer than I expected."

"What little bastard?" Rapp asked.

"T-Mobile's firewall. They must have brought in some new hot shot. It normally takes me a minute or less. This time it took me a full ten minutes."

"What are you looking for?"

"Garret has two phones. One is a BlackBerry that he has with Verizon, and then he has a Motorola that he has through T-Mobile." Dumond spun the small computer ninety degrees so Rapp and Kennedy could see the screen. "Here's all of his calls."

Kennedy looked nervous. "Marcus, I assume there's no way this can be traced back to you."

"Huh," Dumond laughed. "Anyone with half a brain can hack into a system. When I do it, there's no trace I was ever there."

"Anything to Switzerland?" Rapp asked as he bent over to look at the screen. All it showed were the numbers that he had called or had called him. No names. There appeared to be no international calls. "Can you get us a reverse directory on these phone numbers?"

"No problem." Dumond spun the computer, made a few keystrokes, and then spun it back. "Here's the names associated with numbers he dialed and the time and date."

Rapp leaned in close so he could read the tiny print. The calls were listed in descending order with the most recent one at the top of the screen. Rapp scanned the column, and halfway down the first page a name jumped out at him. "Why, I'll be damned."

"What?" Kennedy asked. She didn't have her reading glasses with her.

"Our little buddy Tom Rich from the *Times* called Garret right in the middle of your press conference this afternoon."

"That seems like a bit of coincidence," Kennedy replied.

Rapp scrolled down to the previous day's calls. "Look here. Garret called Ross three times yesterday. And Ross called Garret five times. Look here. He called Garret at seven-oh-nine last night. I remember looking at my watch when we were in your office. It was seven-oh-four. He got off the phone with us and must have called Garret right away."

Rapp grabbed his phone, opened it, hit talk, scrolled down to the number he wanted, and hit talk again. A few rings later Agent Rivera was on the phone. "How are the logs coming?"

"Slowly."

"Have yesterday's logs been filed?"

"Yes, but I don't have them in front of me."

"Can you get them?"

"Yes. I can pull them up on the computer."

Rapp backed away from the kitchen table and waited.

"I've got them up on the screen. What are you looking for?"

"Who did Ross meet with yesterday?"

Rivera started reading a long list. Within fifteen seconds, Rapp lost his patience and asked, "Did he meet with Tom Rich?"

"The reporter?"

"Yes."

"Mitch," she said uncomfortably, "I'm not sure I should be giving you that kind of information."

"I don't have time for this right now, Maria. Trust me when I tell you it's important."

There was a long moment of silence, and then Rivera said, "They met yesterday evening in Ross's suite at the Willard."

"Thanks. I'll call you later." Rapp closed his phone and pointed at Dumond's computer screen. "These calls match up perfectly. Garret set up the interview and Ross was the high-level source who fed Rich the story. Look."

Kennedy bent forward and squinted, but before she could begin reading a new screen popped up and covered the T-Mobile page. Some type of ominous law enforcement shield sat in the middle of the screen. "Whoa," Kennedy said, fearing their unlawful intrusion had been discovered. "Marcus, you'd better take a look at this," she said as she backed away.

Dumond quickly set his coffee down and grabbed the computer. He spun it around, studied the screen for a split second, and then began hitting keys.

"What is it?" Rapp asked with no real worry in his voice. Dumond was the master of his own little universe. He would never initiate an incursion that could be traced back to him.

"Customs and Immigration web site. When I was in their database earlier today I put a flag on Garret's passport."

"A flag?" Kennedy said in a slightly alarmed voice.

"Not the normal kind of flag. I set it up so I would receive an alert if he tried to leave the country. I also tapped into the airline's reservation system while I was checking his travel." Dumond typed in several commands. The screen changed as quickly as his fingers flew. "Well, I'll be damned." Dumond stopped typing and stared at the screen.

"What?" Rapp asked.

"Garret just checked in for an Air France flight from Dulles to Geneva."

Rapp and Kennedy looked at each other, their thoughts passing without words.

"When does his flight leave?" Kennedy asked.

"Twelve twenty."

"I'll call Jose and have him put his best people on it," Kennedy said.

Rapp checked his watch. "There's a chance I can get there first. Besides, I don't think we want to use embassy people for this. Tell him I want NOCs only."

"You're probably right." Kennedy watched Rapp punch numbers into his mobile phone. NOC stood for Non Official Cover. They were Langley's most coveted operatives. "Are you sure you should go?"

"You have any better ideas?"

"Not at the moment."

Rapp could tell she still wasn't sold on the idea. "Like you said, Irene. We have less than two days. If these guys were involved in any way in that attack, I'm willing to bet the answers are in Switzerland." Rapp looked away from Kennedy and spoke into his phone. "Scramble the boys. We need to be in the air by midnight." Rapp listened for a second and said, "Across the pond. Mostly surveillance, but you never know. I'll see you in thirty." Rapp closed the phone and looked at Kennedy. Her expression radiated concern. "Don't worry. I'll be fine."

Kennedy frowned and said, "I'm not worried about you."

"Then who in the hell are you worried about?"

"Stu Garret." Kennedy shook her head. "I know how you think, Mitch. I don't want you slapping him around."

"Irene . . . come on," Rapp said as if he was complaining.

"Well . . . at least not until he gives you a reason."

# 48

Garret was in a supremely foul mood. He'd boarded his flight convinced he would sleep his way across the Atlantic. He had it all planned out. He'd have a vodka on the rocks before takeoff and two or three glasses of red wine with his meal, and then he'd kick off his shoes, recline his seat, put on the little mask they handed out, and he'd snooze until the sun was gleaming off the snow-capped Alps. Unfortunately, he didn't account for his enlarged prostate. An hour into his slumber he awoke to make his first of three trips to the head. When he landed in Geneva, he was tired, grumpy, and more than a bit out of whack. He was at least happy, though, to be out of Washington. No one bugging him for photographs and advice.

A driver was waiting for him at the airport. The man took him to his hotel and on the way showed him where he would be meeting Mr. Speyer for dinner at 8:00. Garret was immediately put off that they were going to make him wait for six and a half hours to discuss business, but there wasn't much he could do about it. Speyer wasn't answering his phone, and he wasn't about to call Green.

He checked in to his hotel a little before 2:00 in the afternoon and asked for a 7:00 p.m. wakeup call just to be safe. When he got up to his room the jet lag hit him hard. He turned off both mobile phones and hit the Do Not Disturb button on the hotel phone. He must have been dehydrated from the flight because he slept straight through to his 7:00 p.m. wakeup call without disturbance from his prostate. Garret showered and shaved and put on a blue sport coat, white dress shirt, and dark gray slacks.

When he arrived downstairs a car was waiting for him. Garret walked outside with his puffy down coat and stopped for a moment on the sidewalk. Across the street was Lake Geneva. The city lights flickered on the surface. As a political consultant, Garret had a keen sense of awareness when it came to people. He liked Geneva. It was a city of scoundrels, many of whom tried to portray themselves as aristocracy. It was a voyeuristic heaven. You got to watch the charade of social pretense that masked insatiable appetites for food, drugs, drinking, gambling, and sex. It could be a very fun place to visit.

Garret stuffed his hands in his jacket and climbed into the back of his waiting Mercedes sedan. The driver said hello in French, and Garret nodded to his reflection in the rearview mirror. The car eased out into traffic and rolled down Quai du Mont-Blanc, toward the finest restaurant in all of Geneva. Garret was looking forward to the meal, but he was not looking forward to the company. He decided he would have to order the most expensive thing on the menu. He didn't have to worry about the wine. Speyer would take great care to make sure something extremely expensive was selected.

# 49

Mitch Rapp sat in the backseat of the car and studied Garret through the opaque glass of the backseat side window. The fingers on Rapp's right hand clamped down on the cuff of his black leather jacket. The entire team was carrying miniaturized encrypted radios with wireless earpieces. Rapp pressed the Transmit button sewn into his cuff and said, "He's on his way."

He released the button and looked at Hacket who was behind the wheel. "You know the routine, Kevin. Hang back for a second and make sure no one else is following him."

The black Mercedes sedan began to roll. The flight from DC had taken six hours and eleven minutes. They were wheels up at 11:47 p.m., and with the time change they were on the ground in Geneva a few minutes before noon; a full hour before Garret's plane was due to land. No one slept on the way over. There was too much work to be done. Dumond went online and hacked into the networks of seven different hotels before he found out where Garret was staying. He was booked at the Beau-Rivage on Quai du Mont-Blanc overlooking the lake. If he had business at Speyer's bank, the hotel made sense. It was a short walk.

After analyzing the Rivage's reservation system, the best they were able to do was get a room on the same floor as Garret two doors down. There was no adjacent hotel with a direct line of sight to Garret's room so they would have to bug his room instead. After they cleared customs, they found two identical black Mercedes sedans with heavily tinted windows and a white Volkswagen cargo van waiting for them. In the trunk of each sedan they found a full complement of silenced weapons, and in the back of the van a surveillance kit. Everyone was dressed in business attire, except Coleman and Stroble, who were wearing pilot's uniforms. Coleman and Stroble took one of the sedans and parked out in front of the Air France terminal. Rapp, Dumond, and Hacket took the white van and followed Brooks and Wicker, who were in the other Mercedes, to the Rivage. Brooks and Wicker checked into the room at the Rivage while the rest of the team went to the D'Angleterre a few blocks away. Rapp and the other two waited outside until the newlyweds finished bugging Garret's room.

Dumond in the meantime managed to insert Garret's mobile phone numbers into the National Security Agency's Echelon system. The CIA worked closely with the NSA on overseas matters. Neither wanted to be embarrassed over the discovery that they were intentionally targeting U.S. citizens abroad, so they'd developed a system where numbers could be monitored for a brief period, a day or two, and then they would be purged from the system as if they'd never been looked at in the first place. Garret's e-mail addresses were also added to the list. So far the hardest part of the op had been getting a reservation for Brooks and Wicker at Le Bearn. Wicker slid the concierge at the Rivage a hundred-dollar bill and the guy barely batted an eye. It took two more C-notes before the guy could guarantee a table.

A laptop was sitting on the seat next to Rapp. The screen was divided into four pictures. Wicker and Brooks had already arrived at Le Bearn and had planted several miniaturized cameras and listening devices in the bar, restaurant, and bathroom. Dumond was monitoring everything from the back of the van which was parked a half block away from the restaurant. The screen currently showed a picture of the street outside the restaurant, the front door of the restaurant from the inside, and two more interior shots of the dining area. Dumond was recording everything.

# 50

Garret stepped through the front door a few minutes early and was immediately cut off by three men wearing tuxedos. Le Bearn wouldn't let you into the bar if you didn't have a reservation for dinner. The shorter of the three men greeted Garret in French. He was polite but unyielding. Garret ignored the greeting and told the man he was meeting Joseph Speyer for dinner. Their attitudes changed immediately. One man grabbed his coat, the third disappeared, and the other began singing the praises of one of Geneva's most well-respected bankers.

The man himself showed up just moments later. Next to Garret, with his frumpy demeanor and ill-fitting clothes, Speyer looked as if he'd just stepped out of a *GQ* ad. His two-button, blue-gray flannel suit had a faint light gray pinstripe. The fabric hung from his thin frame perfectly, the pants breaking at the perfect spot above a pair of handmade light brown Italian shoes that matched the frame of his glasses. Speyer's thinning light brown hair was cropped short and styled slightly forward.

They had just made it to the bar when four men came through the door. Two of them were huge. Standing well over six feet tall and weighing upwards of three hundred pounds, everything about them screamed *bodyguard*. The two older men sandwiched in between them were Cy Green and Aleksandr Gordievsky. They were opposites of sorts. Green had a relaxed air of confidence about him. His permatan, slicked-back hair, open-collared shirt, gold necklace and watch, and double-breasted blue sport coat was the uniform of the ultra-wealthy. Compared to Green, Gordievsky looked a bit pasty. His brown hair was mostly gone, except around the sides and in back, where he grew it a bit too long. His suit was a bit too shiny, and the mock turtleneck sweater that he wore under the jacket screamed Eurotrash.

Handshakes and greetings were exchanged, and the restaurant staff made a great production out of taking care of the group. They were escorted to their corner table where Green and Gordievsky insisted on sitting with their backs to the wall. The two hulking bodyguards were given the table next to them. Water and bread were left, and drink orders were taken. A special wine list was brought to the table and offered to Green, who quickly declined and gestured for it to be given to Speyer.

While Speyer perused the list Green looked across the table and flashed Garret a devilish look. "You have picked a good time to visit. Tonight is going to be great fun. When we are done with this exquisite meal we are going to hit some fabulous clubs and then we will head back to my place for some truly unique late-night entertainment."

Garret hadn't flown all the way from DC to party. He wanted to get the nasty stuff out of the way, so he said, "We have a problem."

"May we at least eat before we talk business?" Green said.

"I'd rather get it out of the way. You guys promised me that you were going to tie up all the loose ends over here."

"And we have," Green smiled at a passing woman.

"Didn't you see the president's press conference yesterday?"

Green dismissed Garret's worries with an unconcerned look. "I'm not worried."

"They found *the* guy."

"There is no way they can trace the Bosnian back to any of us," Green assured him.

"How can you be so sure?"

"Tell him, Joseph."

Speyer did not bother to take his eyes off the wine list. "Everything was done with cash. We never met him."

"How did he get the money?"

"We put it in two separate duffelbags and flew it into Cyprus on a private plane. The assassin gave us some coordinates. The bags were left behind a stone wall in the middle of the night on a deserted stretch of road outside Limassol."

"So no one ever met him face-to-face?"

"Nope," Green said.

"And there's no financial records anywhere, or e-mails that could be traced back to you?"

"None."

"So the CIA is lying," Garret smiled.

"Or the Bosnian is lying," Green added.

"Who the fuck knows with the damn CIA?" Garret said. "They have got to be the most incompetent idiots on the planet." He sat back and took a drink of water.

Green folded his perfectly manicured fingers in front of his face and asked, "So how is my pardon coming along?"

Garret squirmed in his chair for second then looked Green in the eye and said, "It's coming along just fine."

"I think you are lying to me," Green said flatly.

"Cy," Garret moaned, "we've come this far. I'm not going to screw you on our deal."

"I want my pardon," Green said in a slightly threatening tone.

"And you're going to fucking get it," Garret snapped.

"If I don't get my pardon, you are a dead man."

Garret's throat suddenly felt dry. His life had just been threatened by a man who he knew was capable of following through. "I told you from the very beginning that we were probably going to have to wait until the last minute." Garret spoke in an even tone. "If the press finds out they could kill this thing. The eleventh hour . . . Saturday morning . . . that's when it will be signed."

Green ran his palms along the sides of his slicked back hair and accepted Garret's answer with a nod. Then his face grew serious and he said, "That is fine, but just remember, if it doesn't get signed, you and your boss are going to pay."

Garret was not used to being threatened like this. He was usually the one doing the bullying. Feeling as if his back was against the wall, he decided to go on the attack. "For the last time he's not my boss, and as long as we're throwing around threats, why don't you chew on this one. What do you think your old business partner, Pinky, would do if he found out you killed his daughter?"

"Shhh . . ." Speyer hissed.

Garret lowered his voice a notch and said, "You think just maybe he might call a couple of his old Mossad buddies and have them pay you a visit?"

Green flashed a thin smile at the political huckster sitting across the table. "Pinky should have given that little slut a lobotomy like Joe Kennedy did to his daughter. Trust me," Green said trying to further undermine Garret's threat, "she was a constant headache for him. He's not as upset about her death as it might seem."

Garret looked at the billionaire through squinted eyes. "Well, how about Josh, then? How do you think the soon to be president of the U.S. of A. would react if he found out you killed his beloved wife, just so you could keep some of your ill-gotten billions?" Garret leaned back, certain the thrust had hit home. "He might send a Tomahawk missile right up your ass. Or maybe he'll have one of his aircraft carriers accidentally ram that yacht of yours when you're out in the middle of the Med some night." Garret picked up a piece of bread. "I sure wouldn't want to piss off the commander in chief of the world's lone superpower."

Green's face turned crimson with rage. "You ungrateful little shit. This wasn't my idea."

"The hell it wasn't," hissed Garret.

"You and your boss came whining to me about your problems."

"He's not my boss!"

"Excuse me," said Green. "Your soon-to-be vice president."

"Our . . . remember. You're the one who wants American citizenship back so fucking bad."

Speyer couldn't take any more. The restaurant was loud, but even so, a few patrons had glanced their way. "Gentlemen, I think you have both made your point. You have made a deal. Cy has completed his end of the transaction and now it is your turn, Stu. May I suggest a toast?" Speyer raised his glass. "To Cy's pardon, which I'm sure will be signed on Saturday."

They all clinked glasses, and Green smiled, saying, "It had better be."

Garret returned the smile and said, "Don't worry, it will be. Now, if you'll excuse me I need to take a piss."

When Garret was gone, Speyer looked at Green and said, "I

have never trusted that man. I told you this was a terrible idea. What is so bad about the life you have here? Why do you need to go back to America?"

"You'd never understand. You weren't born there." Green looked across the room. There was a pretty blond sitting at the bar. He held up his glass and gave her a smile. Looking back to Speyer he asked, "Are you going to join us later? It should be a wonderful show."

Speyer wished everyone would leave him alone so he could pick a selection of wines. "I'm not sure. I'm supposed to meet some colleagues later."

Green smiled his big Cheshire cat smile. "Where . . . Le Pretexte for a little male bonding?"

Green was right. Speyer planned on meeting a few friends at Geneva's premier gay nightclub. "What is that American saying you like?"

"Different strokes for different folks." Green held up his glass. "Find a friend and bring him with. I will have them send a couple of well-endowed boys along with the girls. We will show Mr. Garret how we entertain in Geneva."

# 51

Rapp had watched Garret enter the restaurant via the feed on his computer. By the time Speyer arrived he was in a position to see him pull up to the curb and valet his car. When a big black Hummer pulled up to the curb Rapp had a feeling he was about to get a look at the final two members of the four-person dinner reservation. His expectations increased when a man the size of an NFL lineman got out of the vehicle and went into the restaurant for a quick look before coming back out. Another mountain of a man climbed out of the truck, while a third stayed behind the wheel. Then came the two men whom they were protecting.

Rapp recognized Gordievsky immediately. He'd studied his file on the flight over. There was something familiar about the second man, but Rapp couldn't place it. As they entered the restaurant, he turned his attention back to his screen and picked up a small ear bud that was plugged into the laptop's audio port. The sounds from inside the restaurant instantly filled his ear. Rapp and Dumond were the only two who were monitoring the audio feed from inside the restaurant. Rapp sat back and got comfortable. He fully expected it to be a long evening of watching, listening, and waiting.

Less than a minute later he was on the edge of his seat, struggling to hear every word as Garret and the man named Cy argued about their arrangement. When Garret got up to go to the bathroom, Rapp pressed the transmit button for his radio and asked, "Did you get all that?"

Dumond's voice crackled back, "Yeah."

Rapp took the ear bud out that was streaming audio from inside the restaurant and asked, "Can you clean it up a bit? Get rid of the background noise?"

"I'm already on it."

"How long?"

"Maybe a minute."

"Good. As soon as it's ready, encrypt it and send it off to Irene."

"Roger."

Rapp glanced at the computer screen and the three men at the table. Speyer had his back to the camera. The bald man was Aleksandr Gordievsky; Rapp was certain of that. He'd read Langley's file on him the day before. The third man, the one Garret called Cy, Rapp felt there was something familiar about, but no matter how hard he tried to make the connection it remained just beyond his grasp. His thoughts returned to the conversation. So they had kept it from Josh Alexander. Rapp thought for a moment about how they would break the truth to the man and he quickly concluded that it might be better to let him go on thinking she'd been killed at the hands of terrorists.

"Mitch," Dumond's voice crackled through Rapp's earpiece. "Garret is making a call on his mobile phone."

"Where is he?" Rapp grabbed the ear bud and put it back in his left ear.

"The bathroom."

"I don't fucking care." It was Garret's voice but it sounded tinny. "This guy is crazy. Get a hold of Stokes and tell him State is all his if he can make this happen." There were a few moments of silence while Garret listened to whoever it was he was talking to. "Tell the prosecutor in New York she can have any job she wants. Hell . . . I'll make her the next senator from wherever the hell it is that she's from." There was more silence while Garret listened to the other person. "I don't care what you have to do, Mark. Just get your ass over to the White House first thing in the morning with Stokes and get Hayes to sign this damn pardon, or I'm telling you, Cy Green will make our lives miserable."

The name and the face connected in Rapp's mind and it all came back. Cy Green was a sleazy expatriate who had fled New York under indictment for selling arms to Iraq after the first Gulf War and Libya before they decided to play nice. There was also some other problem involving the purchase of cheap tin and copper at a heavy discount from corrupt Russian oligarchs and cash kickbacks for their favorable pricing. The millions he'd made off that deal weren't enough so he shorted the market, betting that the prices would go down, and then unloaded all his underpriced commodities which then collapsed the world tin and copper markets. Rapp seemed to remember that a few years back Langley had looked into grabbing Green but had been overruled by the State Department. It made him think of the old adage that sometimes it's easier to ask for forgiveness than permission. This time around Rapp would be asking for neither.

Rapp looked at the screen and watched as Garret rejoined his fellow traitor at the table. He picked up the secure satellite phone sitting on the seat next to him and pressed the transmit button in his sleeve. "Did you send it off to Irene?"

"Yeah."

"What about the last little bit? Are you going to be able to pull the whole conversation off Echelon?"

"I'm working on it right now. It's near real time, not absolute neat time, so I need a few minutes."

"All right. Let me know as soon as you have it." Rapp punched Kennedy's direct line into the phone and looked at his watch. It was 8:24 in Geneva, which meant it was 2:24 in DC.

Kennedy answered by saying, "I was just going to call you."

"What's up?"

"I just got off the phone with Dr. Hornig. She tells me your friend is very talkative."

"Yeah, but is he saying anything worthwhile?"

"Apparently he took a little trip to the States back in October of last year."

Rapp looked up slowly and stared out the front window of the car. "He was the one who delivered the van to Gazich."

"You're quick."

"That's how they found him." Rapp imagined Milinkavich photographing Gazich as he picked up the van.

"What?"

"Never mind. It's not important right now. Do you have the e-mail?"

"Yes. It just landed in my in-box."

"Open it and hit the play button on the audio clip. And make sure you're sitting down."

Rapp could hear the clip start. He couldn't make out every

word, but since he'd already heard it, it was easy to follow. When the clip was over, Kennedy cleared her throat and said, "So Ross was involved."

"Yes. You're going to get a second clip in shortly. Garret made a phone call from the bathroom. I'm pretty sure he was talking to Ross."

"I assume this Cy I heard talking was Cy Green?"

"How did you know?" Rapp asked, a bit surprised.

"He and Pinkus Rautbort were business partners. A lot of real estate in New York and a few oil deals. They parted ways when Green got indicted. Very messy. Justice stepped in and seized a bunch of their joint real estate holdings in New York."

"Didn't we look into snatching him a few years ago?"

"Yes. Someone on the National Security Council tipped off the State Department and they went nuts."

"Well, if there's any silver lining here it's that Alexander wasn't involved."

"I would agree."

"I don't think we should tell him," Rapp said.

"Why not?"

"It'll tear the guy apart."

"So you think ignorance is bliss?"

"I wouldn't call losing your wife blissful. No matter what their marital situation was, it seems like he really cared for her."

"I think you're right."

"Then tell me how telling him the truth will make him a better president?"

"As the president, he needs to know the truth."

"In most cases I would agree, but not this time. If you tell him what really happened, all you're going to do is turn him into a miserable, bitter, paranoid man."

After a long pause Kennedy said, "You're probably right."

"Just let me clean things up on this end."

"Slow down a minute. I want some time to think about this."

"Don't bother."

"Mitch?" Kennedy said, her voice filled with caution.

"I'm going to do what someone should have done a long time ago."

"Can we at least think it through?"

Rapp laughed. "I don't need to. The wheels are already spinning."

"Don't touch Garret."

"Are you out of your mind?"

"No. We have a bigger fish to fry. Too many coincidences will cause way too much scrutiny. Just let him go and take care of the others. And do me a favor. Ask Marcus if he can get Ross's medical files from Bethesda for me."

"Anything else?"

"No."

"I'll see you tomorrow." Rapp hit end and held the phone in his lap for a second.

"Marcus," he said as he pressed the transmit button for the secure radio, "find out where Green and Gordievsky live." He paused and then added, "And see what you can find out about this Le Pretexte place they were talking about."

# 52

The nightclub Speyer was going to was not far from the restaurant, but then again nothing was far in Geneva. Green and Gordievsky were taking Garret to a different club farther away. The place was filled with young Belarusian girls who worked for Gordievsky. The going rate was a thousand dollars for a romp in the sheets. Gordievsky bragged during dinner that he pocketed ninety percent of the fee. Garret had tried to get out of it, but Green had insisted. One stop at a club and then they would take him back to his hotel. Speyer agreed to meet them back at Green's penthouse for the midnight show.

Rapp's plan was falling into place. It was 10:41 in the evening when the four of them came out of the restaurant. At the moment, Rapp was only worried about Speyer. He was going to be the key. Rapp had detected something in his voice during dinner. A certain regret that he was associated with the others. Speyer handed the valet his ticket, and the man took off at a trot. Speyer waved good-bye as the others piled into the Hummer.

"Kevin," Rapp said to the guy in the front seat. "You think those bodyguards are wearing vests?"

Hacket shook his head. "I don't think they make 'em that big."

Rapp nodded. He was sure somebody did, but these guys were probably already uncomfortable enough from their extra girth. He doubted they would put on a stiff, hot bulletproof vest. "Here comes the valet. When he pulls in to give Speyer the car, pull out and get in front of him. We'll have him follow us to Le Pretexte."

The valet jumped out of Speyer's BMW and held the door for the banker. Hacket put the car in drive and pulled out onto the Quai de la Poste and headed east. Speyer fell into line behind them. Their destination was just a half mile away. Speyer stayed a polite distance back the entire way. Rapp and Hacket had already checked the place out while Speyer and his guests were eating their main course. Rapp wanted to see the exact layout. He spotted the club from a block away. It was hard to miss with its huge neon sign looming above the street. Even with the temperature hovering in the mid-forties, patrons were lined up halfway down the block.

"Remember, slow down," Rapp said. "Let me out right here." Rapp was ready to go. Before the car came to a complete stop he had the door opened and he was out. He slammed the door closed behind him and darted between two parked cars and up onto the sidewalk. Rapp was wearing a black leather jacket with the collar turned up, a pair of dark jeans, and heavy-soled black lace-up shoes. Turning left, he started down the sidewalk toward the front door of the club. Rapp watched Hacket drive off with the BMW right behind him. The patrons were now lined up against the building on his right. He was going to have to adjust his pace to time it perfectly.

Hacket approached the intersection and turned right, stopping immediately.

The BMW pulled up to the valet and Speyer got out. He took the ticket and walked around the trunk just as Rapp expected. Rapp sped up. There was no way a guy like Speyer was going to wait in line with the others. Again Rapp was right. Speyer stepped onto the curb and was heading straight for the door. His attention was on his valet ticket, which he was trying to slide into his wallet.

Rapp met him midway between the curb and door. He reached out with his left hand, grabbing the banker by the right elbow. "Joseph," Rapp said loud enough for the bouncers to hear. "It has been a long time." Rapp kept moving, taking a startled Speyer with him. In a much quieter voice Rapp said, "You're lucky my boss wants you alive, because I'd just as soon kill you right here, right now."

Speyer looked at the strange man with shock in his eyes. He tried to pull away but the man's grip was simply too tight. "What?" His words were cut short by a stabbing sensation in his side.

"Don't put up a fight and don't raise your voice. Look at my right hand." Rapp held his knife out in front of him so the banker could see it. The tip of it was crimson with blood. "If you don't do exactly as I say I'll slit your throat and leave you to die right here. I know what you and Cy Green have been up to." Rapp saw a flicker of worry in the man's eyes. "That's right, I'm an American. If you cooperate, you'll make it through this fine, which is more than I can say for your friend Green. Let's go." Rapp started toward the waiting Mercedes.

"Who are you?"

Rapp kept walking. "I'm the guy who's going to solve all your problems."

They reached the Mercedes and Rapp opened the rear passenger door. Instead of getting in, Speyer's eyes darted back in the direction of the club. Rapp smiled and said, "Tell me you don't regret getting into business with Green, and I'll let you go. I'll go kill the fucking piece of shit myself, and then I'll tell President Alexander that you helped facilitate the murder of his wife and eighteen other Americans." Rapp looked past the glasses, into the banker's eyes. He could see the man running the numbers. Asking himself which was the path that would save his hide. In a more reasonable voice Rapp added, "Either that or you can get in the car and you can help me."

"What do I get out of it?"

Rapp smiled and said, "You get to live."

# 53

Rapp sat sideways with his left leg up on the seat. He'd already frisked the banker. All he found was a wallet and phone. He took both and dropped them onto the front passenger seat. He'd switched the knife from his right hand to his left and pointed the tip at Speyer's face.

"Why should I believe a word that comes out of your mouth?"

The banker gave him an analytical look and said, "You shouldn't."

"That's right."

"But you were correct when you noted that my life would be much easier if Cy Green were out of it."

Rapp had picked up on Speyer's tone during dinner. It was obvious that he did not enjoy the company of men like Green and Gordievsky. That didn't make him any less guilty at this point, just slightly more likable. Rapp saw potential in Speyer. It wasn't every day that the CIA had the opportunity to own the president of one of Geneva's most influential banks. The information they could get from Speyer would be extremely valuable.

"So tell me again about the security." Rapp turned and looked down the block at Green's building.

"I already told you three times."

"Tell me again." Rapp wanted to make sure Speyer wasn't leaving anything out.

"The lobby has bulletproof glass. The doorman is not on at this hour, so we call the penthouse, they buzz us in and send the elevator down."

"And once we get to the fourth floor?"

"The door opens and one of the bodyguards is waiting for us. Sometimes two."

"And they run a metal detector over you?"

"Yes."

"What about the butler?"

"Sometimes he's there. Sometimes he isn't. It usually depends how late it is."

Rapp didn't like the idea of killing the butler. "I thought you said he lives there."

"I mean there when you get off the elevator."

"Even at midnight?"

"Working for Cy Green is a twenty-four-hour job." Speyer pushed his glasses up on his nose.

Through Rapp's earpiece he heard Coleman say, "They just dropped Garret off at his hotel and are en route."

Rapp passed the information onto Speyer, who began wringing his hands nervously. "That's not going to work."

"What?"

"You getting all nervous. You need to stay calm."

"How can you honestly expect me to stay calm?"

"Just relax and think about how nice your life is going to be without Green and this Belarusian pig in it."

"Yes, but how do I know you won't shoot me in the back?"

Rapp smiled and checked his watch. It was 11:56. At least these guys were punctual. Speyer had given them the name of Green's favorite escort service. Rapp called the service and told them Mr. Green wanted to let them know he was running an hour late. The person at the service said she would change the arrival time to 1:00 a.m.

"Joseph, I know a good opportunity when I see one."

"What do you mean?"

"If you go in there and do exactly as I say, I'm not going to shoot you. You're going to get up in the morning and go to work. You'll get to keep your house in the mountains and your flat in Paris. The only thing that's going to change is that you'll be rid of these two assholes."

"I don't get it. What are you going to get out of this?"

Rapp smiled. "You are going to start spying for the CIA."

"I can't!" The look on Speyer's face was one of shocked indignation.

"Yes, you can, and you will, or I'll have that little talk with President Alexander about your role in the death of his wife and then the bank, the mountain house, the flat in Paris . . . they all go away. And then he'll send me back over here to kill you." Rapp shook his head. "Trust me. Take option A. The other way will be no fun at all."

Speyer tilted his head back and took in a nervous breath. "I can do this."

"You're damn right you can," Rapp said, happy that Speyer was finally seeing things his way. "All you have to do is stay calm and let me take care of the rest."

The Hummer came rolling down the narrow street, towering over the smaller European-made cars. It stopped in front of Green's building, and one sumo-sized bodyguard got out. Rapp smiled to himself. The big ones were great for show and good for deterrence, but they moved too slowly to be effective against a well-trained attacker. Green and Gordievsky got out next and then another of the giants stepped down from the truck. All four men continued into the building and the truck drove away to find a parking space, Rapp presumed. Coleman would follow the man and take him out when the time was right. Rapp looked down at his watch just as it struck midnight.

Looking at Speyer he said, "Let's go."

Both men got out of the car. Rapp slid his knife into the right outside pocket of his leather jacket and transferred his silenced Glock to the left pocket. He walked around the front of the car and joined Speyer as they crossed the street. They continued down the sidewalk to the front door of the building. Speyer adjusted his glasses and reached out for the buzzer.

"Remember . . . smile," Rapp whispered. "We're supposed to be having fun."

Speyer grinned awkwardly and pressed the buzzer. A few seconds later Green's voice came out of the tiny box. "Joseph, you came, and you brought a friend. How good of you. Come straight up."

A clicking noise sounded the release of the lock. Rapp leaned into the door with his shoulder, not wanting to touch the glass with his hand. He pushed it open and gestured for Speyer to go in first. They walked across the relatively small lobby to the elevator. The white lights above it told them the lift was descending from the fourth floor. Rapp flexed his knees several times and cracked his neck from side to side.

Speyer looked at him sideways. "What are you doing?"

"Loosening up. Bend your knees . . . relax."

The banker tried it.

"Now take a few deep breaths, and just think about how happy you're going to be when this is over."

The elevator doors opened and they entered. Speyer turned around and leaned against the back wall. Rapp did the same and slid close to him so their shoulders were touching. He wanted it to actually look like they liked each other. The doors closed and the elevator began to move.

Rapp smiled and asked, "So how long have you been in the banking business?"

"Please don't shoot me."

Rapp got the feeling positive reinforcement didn't work well with Speyer. He put his mouth up to Speyer's ear and said, "If you fucking bring it up one more time . . . I might." He then moved away and smiled. "All you have to do is stand still and stick your arms out. I'll take care of the rest."

A tense moment later the elevator doors opened slowly. As they did Rapp turned to face Speyer and gripped his pistol. There was just enough play in his jacket that he could fire from the hip if he needed to. The bodyguard was standing in the middle of the foyer with a handheld metal detector. The second bodyguard had already taken up a not-so-alert position in a chair against the wall to his left. No butler. Rapp casually checked out the entire room from right to left as Speyer stepped off the elevator. He did a quick inventory of both bodyguards; hands, feet, and eyes. The feet were flat and the hands so puffy Rapp bet he could count to five before they were able to wrestle their guns from their holsters. Their eyes were bloodshot and dull. There was a good chance they'd been drinking.

Speyer stuck his hands out like a scarecrow so the big guy could

give him the once-over with the metal detector. Rapp stayed behind him, turning a touch to his left as he drew his pistol, concealing it against the black leather jacket. The guy did a sloppy job
checking Speyer. Rapp began circling around to his left and acting
like he was interested in the artwork. As soon as Speyer put his
hands down, Rapp pulled his knife out of his pocket with his right
hand and held it up above his head.

"I suppose you guys will want to take this from me." Rapp's eyes
darted back and forth between the two men. Both of them were
frozen by the sight of the knife. Neither saw the pistol. Rapp fired
from the hip. Two shots in under one second. The man in the chair
was hit in the exact middle of his forehead. The man standing was
hit just under his right eyebrow. He took one step forward and
started to fall. Rapp moved quickly to try to break his fall. With the
knife still in his right hand he reached out and tried to slow the man
just enough to keep him from hitting the floor too hard. The guy
thudded to his knees and then fell onto his left side. Rapp put one
more in each guy's head and stuffed the knife back in his pocket.

"Let's go." Rapp grabbed the back of Speyer's coat and pro-
pelled him down the hall.

They made it to the big living room and turned left. Everything
was exactly as Speyer said it would be. The double doors to the
library and billiard room were straight ahead. Rapp could see shadows and hear voices. He drove Speyer forward, keeping him where
he could see him. They reached the doorway. The room ran to the
right. Rapp turned Speyer that way and then continued straight so
he could gain a full field of fire. He was more exposed than he
would have liked, but he didn't want Speyer making some unpre-
dictable move that might screw up a shot.

Gordievsky was at the far end of the table getting ready to
break, his bald head shining from the overhead light. His mouth

started to form a word, but the sound never made it out. The bullet hit him in the top of his forehead, forming a red dot the size of a dime. Gordievsky's knees gave way, and his chin slid down and bounced off the end of the table. Just like that he was gone. Green stood on the far side of the table, both hands gripping his cue, the tip in front of his chin. All his weight was back and his posture slouched. Here was a man who paid others to do his dirty work.

Green looked at Rapp and without blinking said, "Whatever they're paying you, I'll double it."

Rapp laughed and said, "I'm not for sale. This is courtesy of the U.S. government, you piece of shit." Rapp squeezed off a round. It struck Green right between his eyes and the billionaire fell over with pool cue in hand. Rapp walked over to him and put three more rounds into the right center of his chest.

Rapp pressed the transmit button and said, "Everything is secure up here. I'll send the elevator down. Remember, we want all the garbage packed up and out of here within an hour."

The banker's face was white and he was shaking uncontrollably. Rapp walked over to him and said, "Let this be a lesson, Joseph. As long as you're honest with me, and you don't do anything to harm me or my country, this will never happen to you. But so help me god, if you fuck me over just once, you'll end up just like these greedy assholes."

# 54

Kennedy clutched her purse in one hand and the President's Daily Brief in the other. She'd lost count how many times she'd delivered the PDB to President Hayes, but it probably averaged out to four days a week for the past two years. The PDB was essentially a highly classified newspaper that was prepared by the CIA's Office of Current Production and Analytical Support. President Hayes read the document every morning, as well as several newspapers.

Kennedy stopped outside the president's private dining room and smiled at the Secret Service agent standing post. The director of the CIA had not slept well, and it had absolutely nothing to do with Rapp. By the time she went to bed, he was at the airport preparing to take off. Green's penthouse had been scrubbed clean and the bodies disposed of. She had other things on her mind. Everything had to work perfectly or she could make an already pathetic situation worse. The hardest part had been placing her trust in several in-dividuals. Individuals who carried badges and had sworn an oath to uphold the law and protect and defend the constitution. What she had to offer them was justice. There was no doubt about it. The al-ternative was to go public and watch America descend into suspi-cion and chaos.

Kennedy knocked on the door once and entered. President Hayes was sitting at his private dining table. He was in a white dress shirt and tie, reading glasses perched on the end of his nose. As al-ways he had his four newspapers: *The New York Times, The Washington Post, The Washington Times,* and *USA Today.* Each paper was folded in quarters, two on the left and two on the right. Carl, the president's Navy steward, arranged them just so, every morning.

"Irene," the president said, rising slowly, "I think this is going to be one of the things I'll miss most about this job."

Irene could hear someone working in the pantry right around the corner. "You mean Carl's cooking?"

The president laughed. "What's so hard about a bowl of blue-berries and half a grapefruit?"

Carl came around the corner with a plate in hand and said, "It is not my fault you have turned into a health nut." He set the plate down in-between the president's perfectly folded newspapers. Then, ignoring the commander in chief, he turned to Kennedy and in a much nicer tone asked, "How are you doing this morning, Director Kennedy?"

"Fine, Carl, and you?"

"Counting the minutes until he is gone." The Filipino steward jerked his head toward Hayes.

"It won't be the same, will it?"

"Yes, very sad. I remember once I had an abscessed tooth pulled. I was equally upset to see it go."

The president laughed. He loved ribbing and being ribbed by Carl.

"What would you like to eat this morning?" Carl asked Kennedy. "And please don't order the other half of his grapefruit."

That was exactly what Kennedy had been about to do, but she didn't want to disappoint Carl. "How about an omelet?"

"The best you have ever had."

Carl disappeared down the hall and into the pantry. Kennedy turned to face the president. She handed him the PDB.

Hayes took it, and held it for a second. Then looking at Kennedy he said, "I've never been one to live life with regrets. Even more so since the Parkinson's."

"It is one of your most admirable qualities, sir."

"Well, as Carl said, the minutes are ticking away, and they've got me running crazy today so I don't want to forget to tell you how much you've meant to me."

"Thank you, sir."

"I mean it, Irene. You have given me nothing but wise and measured council during some very difficult times. I'm going to miss having breakfast with you every morning." Hayes opened his arms and gave Kennedy a big hug.

When they parted she said, "I'll have to visit you in Ohio. Maybe I can bring Carl."

They both laughed while they took their seats at the table. Carl brought Kennedy some tea and refilled the president's coffee. The president skimmed the PDB, but his heart wasn't in it. With a little more than a day left in office there wasn't much he could do. Besides, there was something else on his mind.

"So, you're sure it was Ross and Garret who planted that smear piece with the *Times*?"

"Yes," Kennedy said with absolute confidence.

"He called late yesterday."

"Who?" Kennedy asked even though she knew.

"Ross. He said he'd like to bury the hatchet with me."

"That's good?"

"I don't trust him."

"You should follow your instincts."

Hayes looked out the window with a troubled expression.

"What does he want to talk about?"

"A pardon of some sort." Hayes turned his attention back to Kennedy and said, "And you."

Kennedy feigned surprise. "Me?"

"Yes. He claims he may have been wrong about you."

"That's interesting." Kennedy knew all about the meeting, knew that Ross and Stokes were going to ask for a pardon, but she didn't know that she was going to be dragged into it so directly.

"Yes," Hayes said skeptically. "I think he's up to something."

"Probably. Would you like me to join you?"

Hayes thought about it and nodded. "I don't want any backstabbing on my last day. If he has anything he'd like to say, he can say it with you in the room."

"Good."

Kennedy's omelet arrived browned to perfection. Hayes was a fast eater, and Kennedy was a light eater. Kennedy had made the decision not to tell Hayes what they had learned. It wasn't that she didn't trust him, it was that he had given so much, seen so much, that he deserved to leave office unburdened by what they were about to do.

Kennedy heard footfalls coming from the Oval Office behind her and turned to see Jack Warch, the deputy director of the United States Secret Service, entering the dining room.

"Well, look what the cat dragged in," Hayes said.

"Good morning, Mr. President, Director Kennedy." Warch stopped at the side of the table. "How are you feeling on your last day?"

"I still have tomorrow."

"Last full day?" Warch had served as the special agent in charge of Hayes's detail for the first three years.

"I feel good."

"Fantastic." Warch clapped his hands together. "With your permission, I'd like to accompany you and the First Lady back to your home in Ohio tomorrow."

Hayes looked touched. "You don't have to do that, Jack."

"I know I don't, sir. I want to."

"That would be great. I'd really like that, and I know the First Lady will appreciate it."

"It'll be my pleasure. Now I hate to break up your breakfast, but Lorie asked me to tell you that the attorney general and vice president–elect are ready when you are, though before you meet with them, I need to go over a few things with you."

Kennedy set her napkin on the table. "I'll leave you two alone and ask Lorie to send in the attorney general and V.P. Ross."

"Are you sure?" the president asked.

"Absolutely. We don't want you playing catch-up on your last full day."

"Thank you," Hayes smiled.

Kennedy grabbed her purse and her cup of tea and started down the short hallway from the president's private dining room to the Oval Office. On the left was the pantry. Kennedy stopped and said, "Carl, the omelet was fantastic. Thank you."

"Oh . . . you are always welcome."

"Would you please do me a favor and set up coffee service for two and maybe some water in the Oval?"

"Absolutely."

Kennedy continued down the hallway through the Oval Office and into the outer office where the president's administrative assistants were located.

"Good morning, Lorie."

"Good morning, Director Kennedy."

"Would you please send the attorney general and Vice President-elect Ross in."

Kennedy went back into the Oval Office. The setup was always the same. Two arm chairs were in front of the fireplace and two long sofas stretched out taking up the majority of that side of the room. In between the sofas was a fairly large glass coffee table. There was a pecking order when it came to the seating arrangement in the Oval Office. The president always sat in the chair to the right of the fireplace. The chair to the left was reserved for the vice president, a visiting head of state, or in a less formal setting, anyone the president offered the chair to. Kennedy doubted the president would offer the chair to Ross. He simply didn't like the man well enough. That meant Ross would sit on the couch closest to the president. Stokes would likely sit next to him.

Carl appeared with the coffee service and set it in the middle of the glass table.

"I'll be back with the water in a moment."

"Thank you." Kennedy was wearing a black pant suit. The jacket had three buttons down the front and two small pockets on either side. Kennedy tugged on the bottom of the jacket to straighten it and patted each pocket for a last check.

Ross entered the office first. There was a flash of surprise on his face, but he quickly covered it up with a phony smile.

"Irene," he said as he walked across the room, "what a pleasant surprise." The vice president-elect extended his hand across the coffee table.

Kennedy took it. "Good morning, Mr. Vice President."

"Not for another day." Ross wagged his finger playfully at Kennedy.

"Irene," Attorney General Stokes said.

"Good morning, Martin."

"I didn't expect to see you here this morning," Ross said, his voice void of any obvious malice.

"I was having breakfast with the president. He got hung up with something, so he asked me to keep you two company for a few minutes." Kennedy pointed at the couch behind the two men. "Sit. May I get either of you coffee?" Kennedy had sat through countless meetings with both men and she couldn't remember a time where either had said no.

"Sure," said Ross as he lowered himself into the spot closest to the president's chair.

Stokes set his briefcase on the floor and said, "Please."

Kennedy reached out to grab a cup, her hand hovering over the top of it for a second. Looking across at Ross she said, "Cream and sugar, right?"

"Yes."

Kennedy placed the cup on top of a saucer and filled it three quarters to the top with coffee. She then added cream and a cube of sugar before stirring it thoroughly. She set the spoon on the tray and placed the cup and saucer directly into Ross's hands.

"Thank you." Ross blew on the coffee for a second and then took a sip.

Kennedy poured Stokes a cup and slid it across as Carl returned with a crystal pitcher of water and four glasses. He set them on the table next to the coffee service and left.

Kennedy looked at Stokes and said, "I assume your people are happy with the information we put together on Gazich?" She took an empty glass of water and filled it to the top.

"Are you kidding me? The guy is as good as fried."

"Good."

Ross took another drink of coffee and said, "Any luck running down the financial leads?"

"No." Kennedy frowned. "I'm afraid we ran into a wall there."

"I thought you were pretty confident that you were going to make a connection?" Ross sounded a bit let down.

It took all the composure Kennedy could marshal just to sit in the same room with the man. To have to watch him fake concern was nearly unbearable. "More than anything, we floated that to see if we could spook some potential suspects into making a stupid move." She took another sip of her water and then placed it on the table with both hands.

"That's too bad," Ross said with a disappointed voice. "But great work on tracking that other guy down."

President Hayes entered the room with his suit jacket on. Carl closed the door behind him, and the other door to where the administrative assistants sat was also closed. "Sorry I'm late, gentlemen."

Ross, Stokes, and Kennedy stood. Hayes marched over with his large coffee mug in hand.

"So how is everyone feeling today?" Hayes asked in an upbeat voice.

"Fine, sir," Ross answered.

Kennedy kept her focus on Ross as the president and Stokes exchanged pleasantries. Hayes extended his coffee mug and asked Kennedy to top him off. She picked up the pot and filled his mug.

"Sit," Hayes said. "So what can I help you gentlemen with this morning? Let me guess. Someone wants a pardon."

"You are very astute, Mr. President," Ross said with a big smile.

Kennedy saw perspiration beginning to form on Ross's fore-head.

"Before we get to that, though, I would like to apologize to Irene."

Kennedy wondered where the snake could possibly be going with this.

Ross looked directly across the table at her. "I was wrong to doubt you over an article written by a reporter with an obvious ax to grind."

"Thank you," Kennedy lied in her most congenial tone.

"And I have spoken to Josh, and he has agreed that it would be a good idea for you to stay on as director of the CIA for as long as you'd like."

"That's great news," President Hayes said with genuine relief.

Kennedy watched Ross reach up and tug on his shirt collar. His forehead was really beginning to shine, just as Juarez had told her it would.

"Irene," President Hayes said, "do you have anything you'd like to say?"

Kennedy had a lot she'd like to say, but she didn't want to spoil her very well rehearsed plan. Continuing the charade, she said, "I would be honored to serve your administration, Vice President Ross."

"Good," Ross said as he tugged at his collar. He blinked once and gave his head a quick shake. "Now about this pardon business." He shook his head again and rubbed his eyes. "We have managed to get everybody at Justice who matters to sign off on this thing, which will really help insulate you from any fallout." Ross stopped abruptly and took in a deep breath.

"Are you feeling all right?" asked Hayes.

"I'm not sure."

Kennedy seized her opportunity. She reached across the table and handed Ross her glass. "Here, have some water."

Ross eagerly grabbed the glass and took several large gulps.

Kennedy watched with a kind of analytical detachment. Juarez had explained how it would work. The drug that she had dropped into his coffee was designed to increase heart rate and bring on nausea, but more importantly it was designed to mask the second drug. The one that she had slipped into her own water glass after taking several sips. Unknown to all but a few, the Secret Service had a tiny camera in the ceiling of the Oval Office. It was for security reasons. Everything was taped unless the president specifically asked for the system to be turned off. This morning Kennedy wanted it on.

Ross took a few more sips of water and then looked at the president. His breathing seemed labored. "I think it's my heart. I have a bad heart." Suddenly he seemed to wilt. The water glass dropped from his hands, tumbling to the carpeted floor and spilling.

The president was out of his chair, coming to Ross's aid. He grabbed him by the shoulders.

Ross looked across at Kennedy. His breathing was really shallow. "No one knows. I have a bad heart."

*I do,* Kennedy thought to herself without an ounce of guilt. She stood and moved quickly to the door, fully aware that she must keep up the proper appearance. She yanked it open and yelled, "We have a medical emergency! Get the doctor up here and grab the defibrillator!"

Kennedy hustled back to the sitting area. Ross was slumped forward in Hayes's arms. "Let's get him on the floor," Kennedy yelled as she grabbed the end of the coffee table and dragged it from between the two couches.

Hayes and Stokes grabbed Ross and laid him on the floor. Kennedy picked up the fallen water glass and stood over the vice president—elect for a moment until she was forced to back away as the first agents arrived. The room was filling up with people fast. Kennedy looked over and saw Carl standing in the doorway that led to the president's private dining room. Special Agent Warch appeared at his side just as they had planned. He pointed at the coffee table and said something to Carl. The fastidious Navy steward hurried over to the table and began clearing the dishes as more and more bodies piled into the room. With a steady hand Kennedy set the water glass on Carl's tray and walked around the couch on the left to retrieve her purse. The doctor arrived a half minute later and yelled for everyone to clear the room. Kennedy took one last look at Ross's pale face and left the Oval Office.

# 55

Rapp stood in front of Kennedy's desk. He was wearing the same clothes that he'd had on in Geneva. He was exhausted and in desperate need of sleep, but he was even more desperate to find out just how in the hell Mark Ross ended up dead in the Oval Office. They'd landed shortly after 10:00 a.m., when one of the mechanics at the hangar told them about Ross. Rapp tried for close to an hour to get ahold of Kennedy but she wouldn't pick up. Finally, one of her secretaries told him she was on her way back to Langley. Rapp made a beeline for CIA headquarters and found Kennedy sitting alone in her office, writing in a file.

"I see you didn't bother to wait for me," Rapp said.

Kennedy finished writing a note and closed the file. "Jose said we needed to handle this one with a deft touch."

"What in the hell is that supposed to mean?"

Kennedy didn't want to argue with him. "An opportunity presented itself."

"I see that. A fucking heart attack in the Oval Office. Whoever pulled that one off has got a gigantic set of balls."

Kennedy took off her reading glasses and leaned back in her chair.

"What did you guys do, poison him?"

She nodded.

"Jose likes that sneaky stuff. I heard on the radio that he had some heart problem that ran in the family."

"Yes. A reporter uncovered it during the campaign, but I already knew about it."

"How?"

"When he applied here after college he wanted Operations."

"Doesn't everyone."

"He failed his physical. They discovered that he had mitral valve prolapse."

"What in the hell is that?"

"Basically a heart murmur."

"So who the hell poisoned him? Jose?"

Kennedy looked at Rapp for a long moment and calmly said, "I did."

Rapp couldn't speak at first. He stood there dumbfounded. Eventually he whispered, "*You* poisoned him?"

"Yes."

"Are you all right?"

She nodded. "I'm fine."

Rapp studied her. "Are you sure?"

"Yes, I'm sure. You should also know that I had to bring Jack Warch, Maria Rivera, and Skip in on it."

Rapp thought about it for a second and said, "You needed their help."

"Yes."

"What about an autopsy?"

"With the existing heart condition Skip doesn't think Ross's wife will ask for one. Plus the Secret Service has the whole thing on tape. Warch already looked at it. He says there's nothing suspicious."

"What if the widow wants an autopsy?"

"Rivera planted some Viagra in Ross's shaving kit this morning. One of the poisons was also heavily laced with the drug."

Rapp looked skeptical.

"Politicians' wives know how to keep things quiet. He wasn't sleeping with her, so she's going to assume he was using the Viagra with other women. Trust me, she will not want to open that can of worms."

"What if she does?"

"Jose says even if they do an autopsy, this stuff won't show up on a toxicology report."

Rapp considered how she was handling all of this. Some people could kill and go through life as if nothing had happened. For Rapp it depended on whom he killed. He was happy to get the chance to kill Green and Gordievsky. Proud that they were no longer part of the human race. The two bodyguards he was less excited about. They were foot soldiers who had chosen the wrong side, that was all, and he felt no pride in killing them.

"So you're okay?" Rapp asked.

"I wasn't sure how I'd handle it, but so far so good. The man had to be dealt with, and putting him on trial was not a good option."

"I agree." Rapp looked away from Kennedy, feeling slightly awkward. He would have never guessed that she had it in her.

Almost as if she could read his mind Kennedy said, "You know, Mitch, this morning wasn't that big of a stretch for me."

"What do you mean?"

"All the times I've ordered you to kill. It's really not all that different than slipping some poison in a man's drink."

Rapp saw her point. "You don't get your hands dirty, but you're involved."

"I got them a little dirtier than I would have preferred this morning," she said wryly.

Rapp smiled. "I'm proud of you. You did a good job. You executed a traitor this morning. Ross chose his path. You have any problem sleeping, just think of those nineteen people who were killed last October. Ross got exactly what he deserved."

"That's good advice. Thank you."

Rapp covered his mouth and yawned. "God, I need to get some sleep."

"Why don't you go home? You look tired."

Rapp looked at his watch and shook the sleep from his head. "How long do I have to wait before I kill Garret?"

"I think at least a year."

"Come *on*," Rapp's voice was full of disappointment.

"Mitch."

"A year is a long time."

"Think of it this way. Word will eventually get out that Green and Gordievsky are missing. With Ross's sudden departure Garret is bound to get a little paranoid."

"Probably just the opposite. Knowing Garret, he's halfway to Los Angeles by now, all smug, thinking he's the luckiest man on the planet. I can't wait to be the one to tell him he's not."

"Mitch," Kennedy cautioned, "stay away from him until I say the time is right."

"Fine, but we are going to kill him, aren't we?"

"Yes, we are."